Maude's Score

Book 3
The O-Line Series

Jillian Jacobs

Published by Green Moose Productions
Copyright 2016 by Jillian Jacobs

ISBN: 978-1-942313-10-6

DEDICATION

To those who know the heartbreaking reality of a first crush.

ACKNOWLEDGMENTS

To the sensational six! My beta-girls.
Also thanks to Linda Carroll-Bradd. Best editor ever.
Any mistakes are my own.

1

CHAPTER 1

Jason Stafford slammed his hand against the steering wheel then quickly regretted his actions. "Sorry, girl." Beating against his friend and teammate, Owen Killion's restored '72 Ford Ranchero wasn't a wise choice, because his buddy babied his vehicles. This car was one of many housed inside this six-bay garage with an added workshop and kitchen area. Owen's job might be the center for the Marauders Offensive Line, but his hobby and real love was banging around inside an engine.

In search of a distraction, Jason skimmed through his Twitter feed, replying to his fans and ignoring his haters. His Marauders football fans came from all over the world. Not just this sprawling city in Northern Ohio. Although, he did find his most loyal fans were from Manchester. Monday thru Friday his local supporters were a mish mash of blue and white collar, but, on game day, everybody bled green. His sports agent, Tyrone Speaks would welcome his more positive exchange with his followers, as typically Jason responded with antagonistic comments to those who didn't appreciate his efforts on the football field. His ears still rang from the phone call he'd received from Tyrone just two hours ago. All because, five hours ago, Jason's world had irrevocably changed.

He'd visited Ariel Silvers, a girl he'd been seeing on and off since the beginning of the previous football season. To his utter shock, she'd informed him she was pregnant. After leaving in a bewildered state, he'd gone to Owen's house, but since the hour was so late, he'd settled for sitting in a restored car in his pal's mega-garage.

At the end of their season, Jason's friend on another professional team had experienced the whole pregnancy scare. The girl had claimed to be with child, the guy had claimed no way. In the end, the girl was, in fact, having his baby.

So Tyrone, after chewing his ass out for fifteen straight minutes, advised him not to deny anything, to treat Ariel with kid gloves and wait until the facts were known, because his friend had been raked over the coals by the media.

Broiled, steamed, and baked over scalding hot coals. The situation had gotten ugly fast. The public saw his friend as just another example of a pro-football player mistreating a woman.

Tossing his phone on the dash, Jason rubbed his eyes and sighed. Thing was, he liked Ariel. Nice, hot blonde he'd met through his lawyer, not at a party or bar. She understood, as he always laid out the truth, relationships weren't his thing. For twenty-seven years, he'd lived his life loose and carefree, but now the tether of parenthood had wrapped around his throat and snapped him back to Earth.

Not that Jason didn't like kids, he did…mostly. Hadn't he just spent the past two days with a whole passel of them while shooting a "FIT 365" commercial for the National Board of Health's Get Kid's Active initiative? He and Chewy, the Marauders' quarterback, had even tossed around a football with a few of the tiny creatures during the shooting breaks. Was this his future? What did he know about being a father? A few days of entertaining grade school kids was one thing—a baby was another.

Jason clenched his jaw, fighting the urge to call Ariel and demand she take a pregnancy test right now. Yet, his agent was right, he should play this cool. Lord knew, the press already thought him a partying playboy. True except for the fact that he didn't drink or use drugs. Not after his childhood.

"Jason?" A familiar female voice asked from outside the passenger door. "What are you doing out here?"

"Sweet baby Jesus." Jason, the offensive line's burly right guard, clutched his chest and just might have shrieked like a girl as he spotted Maude Killion, Owen's sister, popping her head through the open passenger window. "What the hell, Maude? You can't just sneak up on a guy like that. I think my heart exploded." He rubbed a hand against his breastbone.

Head tilted, Maude arched a reddish-brown brow. The color was the same as the waves of hair falling against her shoulders. "Why are you sitting out here?"

Not wanting to delve into his issues, Jason shrugged. Though he knew Owen would answer, he hadn't called or taken the twenty or so steps necessary to enter the house. Instead, he'd just sat close to where his friend and his awesome family lived, like a penniless kid at the candy shop window.

Tapping a finger against the steering wheel, he glanced at Maude. "Why are you giving me a hard time at 3:00 a.m.? Shouldn't you be in bed?"

She leaned forward with her elbows resting on the open window. "When I pulled up the drive, I saw a light coming from over here. I thought maybe Owen left it on." She rubbed her red-rimmed eyes. "I was just coming in from a…a date."

Damn, the wind on this chilly Ohio spring night must have blown open the door *and* blown his cover.

He studied her blotched cheeks and her pink-tipped nose while avoiding her initial question. "Was your date with Brady-bunch?"

Sighing, she rolled her eyes. "Is it really necessary to keep calling him that?"

"Is it really necessary to keep dating him?" Jason shot back. Brady Stephens annoyed him on many levels. He'd seen the jackass at the clubs prior to, and during, his "supposed" dating of Owen's little sister and did *not* approve. Fucker always pranced around like he was the shit. Although, if Jason really wanted to be truthful, so did he, but he actually *was* the shit. He inwardly chuckled before bracing against the usual onslaught of whatever-the-hell physical attraction ricocheted through his body when Maude entered his immediate vicinity. Since those feelings were a flagrant foul, he generally resorted to picking on her like a little boy on the playground with a secret crush. "Did Brady ever finish that stupid lion tattoo on his forearm? Does he think he's king of *your* jungle?" He arched a brow. "Does he roar in bed?" Biting back a smile, he mentally patted himself on the back for that snappy comment.

"Leave Brady alone." After rolling her eyes again, Maude opened the door and slid into the front seat beside him. "He finally finished the tattoo a few weeks ago. He wanted me to get one, but..." She shrugged, shoved her phone into her small purse, and then placed it on the floorboard.

Her lavender scent enticed him, as did that damn brown, slightly red hair, her soft brown eyes, and all those curves...and more curves. He couldn't block her innocent beauty. He'd tried—and failed, a lot lately.

Try to at least blink, Stafford.

He shifted in his seat, redirected his gaze to his finger running along the Ranchero's black steering wheel, and blocked all thoughts of turning to run his finger along the strands of Maude's hair. Generally attracted to blondes, something about the gentle waves of Maude's hair enticed him every time. He had enough problems without seducing his best friend's sister.

She sniffed.

"Hey." He nudged her arm. "You been crying?" He tilted her chin and stared into her eyes. "You have. No...don't turn away." Locking his gaze with hers, he gripped her chin between his thumb and forefinger. "What did Brady do? Do you want me to kick his ass? I'm happy to volunteer." Maybe he would, anyway. Jerk had been warned, but perhaps he needed reminding.

Maude shook free of his touch. "I would like to know why you're out here, so how about you tell me why *you're* upset first, and then I'll tell you what happened tonight. Okay?" When he met her gaze, he felt his heart melt a little. This woman was the kindest person he'd ever known, always putting others first. Since meeting him when she was sixteen, she'd had an obvious crush, but during all that time, he'd feigned ignorance. Never teasing her or acting on the chemistry he'd sensed, too. Mostly, because Owen would steamroll his ass. Not only that, Maude deserved someone better.

He waved a hand in her direction. "All right. You go first." He'd let her tell him the reason behind the tears while he concocted a good excuse for sitting in her brother's car like some crazed Marauders fan.

"No. Nope. Nada." Shaking her head, Maude jabbed his shoulder with her index finger. "Not happening. I know you, Jason Stafford. You'll come up with some ridiculous story, and I'll pretend to believe it. But this"—she waved a hand at the dash then back at him—"is too odd. I want the truth, because…you know what?" She grinned, but the sweet smile was absolutely false. "I can make up stories, too. Perhaps I'm suffering from seasonal allergies, and I've been rubbing my itchy eyes."

He groaned. She wouldn't let him get away with anything. She did know him—too well. Six years of playing ball with her brother had them fully acquainted, and they were actually friends, of a sort.

"All right, not like you won't find out eventually, anyway." Jason bit his bottom lip, unsure how this would affect her crush on him—which, to his secret dismay, had died down since Brady-bunch had come into the picture. But still…he didn't ever want to hurt her. Jason shook his head as his stomach churned like he'd digested an acid burger covered with you're-an-idiot cheese. "You won't like this."

"Knowing you, likely not." Maude eased her words with a soft smile. "Let me guess." Head tilted, she tapped a finger against her plump bottom lip. "Your sleepless night involves trouble with a member of your female entourage."

God, he hated when she said stuff like that. Her words made him want to be different. Become a better man—for her. And that was a ludicrous idea. *Ludicrous.* He couldn't ever have her, and now he had to highlight his reckless behavior and potentially lose seeing that admiring glint in her eyes.

Hell, if it were possible, he'd kick his own ass.

He took a deep breath and released it. "The long and short of it is, this woman I'm seeing says…she says she's…pregnant."

Crickets?…or maybe those chirps emanated from the stainless steel refrigerator in the garage's kitchenette. Maude remained silent so long, he stole a glance to be sure she hadn't dozed off.

"Huh." Her word came out more like a grunt than an agreement or denial of his statement.

"Huh?" Jason half-laughed before shoving her shoulder. "In just what context was that huh delivered?" Her reaction mattered…a lot. He really didn't want to see disappointment in her eyes, but what was he searching for? Understanding? Forgiveness?

"I don't really know." Maude almost whispered the words. "The context is shock, I guess." Shrugging, she met his gaze briefly before quickly turning away and studying her nails. "I'm sorry you're going through this. Maybe you should visit the doctor with her, just to…um…to verify things. I guess that would be the right thing to do."

Her tone had gone soft. Damn, maybe he *had* hurt her. However, he quickly changed his mind when she punched his arm. Hard. "You'd better not sleep with her again." Her brow was furrowed, and she jabbed him with a finger right where she'd hit him.

"Ow." He rubbed at the sting on his arm. "Damn, you'll put me on the injured list."

"You need to be," she growled before heaving a put-upon sigh. "I hate to say this, but she could be lying. I know saying that isn't very kind, but these types of accusations make revealing the truth harder for the women who really do get pregnant. Just like that player last fall who said the girl was—"

"Yes, yes, my memory isn't faulty." He waved a hand between them. "I don't need the play-by-play of that news story. Tyrone already made it clear I was not to follow that path." He glanced out the windshield at the workbenches and the walls covered with every kind of tool. All the shiny metal was practically blinding. "Look, I didn't mean to cut you off." He reached over and squeezed her hand. "I've spent the past couple of hours on my phone, looking up articles on how to test a baby's DNA. Plus, if Ariel *is* lying it'll become obvious soon enough."

"Did she say anything about…um…an abortion or anything?" Maude cleared her throat and dropped her gaze to their joined hands.

"She hasn't, but even if she did…I couldn't." He released her hand and gripped the steering wheel again. "Not after losing Jess."

Before Maude could respond, his phone rang with his mom's ringtone. Calls this late were never good, but when his family was involved, not much surprised him.

Jason grabbed his phone off the dash and swiped across the iPhone's screen to answer the call. "Yeah, Ma, what's wrong?" Because why else would she be calling after three a.m.?

"Patrick got arrested for assault."

His mom's coarse voice, thickened from years of smoking, seemed more congested than usual. "And?"

She heaved a sigh. "Your brother was just doing his job, Jason. Some rich kid got his silk boxers in a twist when Patrick tossed his drunken friend from the bar. Then the kid called his daddy and had Patrick arrested."

Jason rubbed his temple. The day's nonstop stressors were building one helluva headache. "Where are you?"

"I'm down at the police station."

"Which one?"

"Manchester on Central Street."

"I'll be there in a minute."

"Oh, but were you sleeping? I can probably handle this. I shouldn't have called."

He tightened his grip on the phone to keep from tossing it out the window. "Ma, don't pull that passive-aggressive shit. Go home. I'll take care of it." After hanging up, he released a few choice curses.

"What's wrong?" Maude placed a hand on his shoulder.

He almost shrieked again, as he'd nearly forgotten Maude was with him. "Same Stafford shit, just a different day."

"Should we wake Owen?" She trailed her hand down his arm then wrapped their fingers together.

Oh, hell. This was why she was hard to resist. Everything about her was real. Nothing was done because he was a star-football player. She truly meant the sincere look in her eye. "No, let Owen sleep." He released her hand, because he couldn't let himself rely on her comfort. Couldn't come to need it…or her.

"My brother gets a little over-eager at work sometimes. In other words, he's a bully." Jason huffed out a laugh and shook his head. "Life is grand, ain't it? Always finding ways to keep you off course, so why bother with the straight and narrow, right?" He glanced at Maude. Lucky girl had an easy life, not a shit-fest like his. "Anyway, I'm sorry, but I have to bail him out, yet again."

"Would you like me to come along?" She squeezed his hand.

Damn it, why did her touch send signals straight to his dick? His current mood had him looking for dangerous ways to remove these dangerous feelings. But, Maude Killion would never be on the receiving end of his tumultuous emotions.

"I can handle Patrick by myself." He shook off her hand and

all the unwelcome feelings she evoked. "Speaking of dickheads, don't think my leaving gets you off the hook. I spilled my story so you'll spill yours." He tweaked her nose with his index finger before opening the door and removing his six-five frame from the car. "Come on. Let's head up to the house."

"I am twenty-two, you know," Maude huffed. "I don't need a chaperone to travel the, what?…twenty steps across the lawn to the back door."

"Let's go, Killion." After coming around to her side and opening the door, he drummed his fingers against the hood. "I got places to be."

"Fine." She eased out of the car and then took his arm. "But if you need me…or, um…if you need Owen, just call, okay?"

"Yeah." But they both knew he wouldn't. Jason led Maude over to the house's attached garage, waited while she punched in the code, and watched as she headed in through the pantry door.

The normalcy of the moment struck square in his gut. He stood, staring up at her window like he was some mooncalf. Dating Maude Killion—wouldn't that be something?

A jagged shard of pain shot through his heart as he considered his own sister, Jessica. She would never date. Never have a boy steal a kiss. Never love. So many nevers.

She'd been so small, yet so tough. Blonde, like him, with the same mischievous sparkle shining in her big blue eyes.

Shuffling his feet through the gravel drive on the way to his hybrid Audi parked along the side of Owen's garage, he glanced up at the stars. Maybe Jess was looking down. Maybe she even watched over her baby brother a little. "Sis, what have I gotten myself into? How am I supposed to take care of a kid, when I couldn't take care of you?"

CHAPTER 2

While pulling into the police department's underground parking garage, Jason considered how much cash he had in his wallet. Would he even have to post bail? The situation his mother described seemed minor. Yet, he never knew what to expect when it came to his big brother.

Five years ago, as the starting center for San Antonio's first pro-football team, Patrick blew out his left knee. Jason's career started about the time his brother's ended, and Patrick had never let him forget. Especially since he played for the Marauders, the team "responsible" for his injury, which made Jason a traitor in Patrick's eyes.

After parking, Jason headed to the elevators and caught sight of his mother's now-bleached blonde hair. A trail of smoke poured from her lips as she sucked on one of her cancer sticks. Too many hard draws had carved deep grooves around her mouth. Ironically, she'd worked her whole life at a pharmacy down the street from his childhood home. Since his recruitment by the Marauders, he'd moved her and his brother into a new place. He'd set up his mom financially so she could quit working. Yet, the stubborn woman got bored and took a part-time job at the same pharmacy. She'd said she missed her coworkers and the customers. At his approach, her blue eyes met his, but hers had lost their shine long ago.

"I thought you quit." Jason waved away the smoke, but the familiar smell still found a way up his nostrils, likely causing additional second-hand smoke damage. His lungs were probably just as black as hers after growing up in a home where both parents smoked.

"I have two boys. Not gonna happen." His mom, Sharon, smiled then coughed. A racking cough that had her doubling over.

"For Pete's sake, Ma, will you quit already?" He rubbed her back, concerned over the depth of this cough.

"What's done is done. Might as well enjoy a few more puffs."

He refrained from dredging up the same old argument, because nothing he said ever made her quit. This display was the very reason he'd studied nutrition and health in college. "I told you to go home."

She shot him a glare before dropping her spent cigarette to the dirty concrete. "Since when did our roles reverse? You're my baby, always will be." She wrapped him in a hug, her arms light and frail as she squeezed him.

He'd inherited his size from his father. Offensive linemen typically tipped the scale over the three hundred mark, so he basically engulfed her as he hugged her back.

"I stayed to tell you to take it easy on your brother. This time, the arrest really wasn't his fault." Her words were slightly muffled against his chest, and she coughed again after speaking.

Frowning, he let her words go without argument, even though he didn't really agree. "Where's your car?" The thought of her traipsing alone through the parking lot at this hour breezed through his mind. Shaking his head, he cupped her elbow and punched the elevator button. "Actually, just come with me, so when I leave, I can follow you home. I have to drop off Patrick, anyway."

At predawn, the lobby was usually quieter. Posters with "Just Say No" and "Don't Drink and Drive" lined the walls. As a child, he'd become familiar with a police station's ebb and flow as his mother had dragged them all down in their pj's to pick up their father after one of his barroom brawls. Jason never understood why they picked him up, since his father just continued the fight once he got home. Lovely childhood memories. All of which were compounded as he breathed in the familiar stench of stale coffee and sweat. Though he'd never suffer through a beating again, he couldn't prevent the shivers of irrational fear slithering down his spine from the memories.

His mother had quit drinking after Jason was born, but his father hadn't, and he'd put them all through hell. And that "hell" still lived the easy life, getting his ass wiped in a nursing home. After being sentenced with aggravated vehicular homicide, and only serving six years before parole, his father lived in a cozy room while his sister, Jess...

Don't go there right now. Jason clenched his jaw against memories of a different night in this same police station. Pregnant girlfriends, Maude being whatever, jailbird brothers, and upcoming training camp already pushed his temper into the red zone. He really didn't need memories of his father intruding into his thoughts. For the most part, he'd erased the man from his life, but that didn't mean he'd ever forget.

Checking in, he was recognized by the receptionist, and she spent fifteen minutes stuttering and even accidentally knocked over her water bottle when she gestured wildly.

He'd been dubbed the All-American male, and refused to lie to himself about his above-average looks. Hell, he even played up his image on his social media accounts with frequent selfies, usually after working out and always shirtless. Had to give those fans what they wanted, right? More fans meant more endorsements, which meant money to bail out his brother, take care of his mom, and anonymously support a few charities—like the one Maude was heavily involved in, which focused on cancer research and helping families who'd lost loved ones to the disease.

After the flustered receptionist handed over the paperwork

for his brother's release, she flushed when he shot a wink and toothy smile her way. He never knew how long the discharge process would take, but he hoped a few extra grins would speed up things. He settled next to his mom, who thumbed through a ragged Reader's Digest. Before writing a single word, he smiled at the young girl, sporting a black eye and holding what looked like a newborn, sitting across from them. "You okay, honey?"

The girl smiled and nodded.

Jason knew she wasn't okay. No one with a shiner that bright was ever okay. "If you're not, then I want you to talk to that receptionist. I bet she might know someone who could help you."

"I'm fine." She frowned and settled her baby against her shoulder.

He dug out his wallet and handed her a couple hundreds he kept for emergencies. If he had to get more out of an ATM, so be it. "Here, take this and get the kid something."

"Why?" She looked at the bills then met his gaze. "That's a lot of money."

"Just take it, honey." His mom moved to sit by her, taking the wad of Jason's cash and tucking it into the girl's hand. She sat with the girl for a while and talked quietly while he filled out the stack of papers.

Once the girl left, his mom returned to his side.

Sighing, he leaned the back of his head against the wall and closed his eyes. "Ma, you realize…my saving Patrick might not always be possible, because at some point, he's really gonna hurt someone. He needs anger management, or therapy, or a serious beat down. I'm about done forgiving him for making a mess of his life. At this point, I'm enabling his behavior. He's got serious issues, and he's pissing me off."

His mom patted his arm. "He's your brother. Family forgives."

She'd repeated that mantra forever. And ever. He'd stopped listening after she'd forgiven his father. Family doesn't *forget* was more accurate. He'd never forgive, or forget, what that man had done to his family.

He heard his mom shuffle to her feet, but he didn't bother opening his eyes until her soft footsteps returned and the smell of coffee wafted across his senses. "Ma." Opening his eyes, he huffed out a sigh. "Where did you get that? That coffee has probably been sitting around all night, and who knows what's in it. Spit, piss, other…liquids." He removed the cup from her chilled hand and stood to dump the contents into a nearly full trashcan by a water cooler.

The carpets in the place had worn down decades ago. A cork poster board hung slightly askew on the wall and was plastered with flyers for bail bondsmen and community counseling centers. The walls seemed to close in and the stifling sensation had him breathing deeply. The whole place was a vile reminder of the darker parts of life. Maybe he should donate supplies to police waiting rooms. He knew how horrid they could be, but perhaps that was the point. He glanced at his mother. "It's ridiculous Patrick called you in the middle of the night."

"I don't mind." She sniffed. "I called you, because I didn't have the cash."

The various reasons she didn't have cash whirled through his mind. He gave her cash. Monthly. So…how much had Patrick "borrowed" this time? "No cash. Really?"

"I'm running short." She shrugged but didn't meet his gaze.

"Don't lie. Just don't." Jason slashed a hand through the air before bracing both hands on his hips. "You have to stop giving Patrick money. He is old enough to take care of himself. His problems are not your problems." He paced before the metal folding chairs and glared at his mom, who stared at her manicured fingers like they held the secrets to the universe. "If you keep giving Patrick money, then I will take over everything—hire someone to pay your bills and to do your grocery shopping." He ticked off each item with a finger. "Patrick has two jobs, so stop giving him cash."

His mother pulled a cigarette from her open pack and fiddled with the coffin nail before placing it, unlit, in her mouth. "He just needed to pay…a guy."

"A guy." Jason nodded with a slight tilt to his head. "You know who those "guys" are, right? He's gambling again. And he's not gambling with your money, he's gambling with mine. And I ain't having it." He roared the words through the tiny room, causing the receptionist to glance up from behind her glass divider. The slight ache from earlier began to pound again in his right temple, banging away, threatening to become a full-blown drum-line. Hopefully, the chick wouldn't take his picture and post his crazy antics on Facebook, because generally anything he did went viral in about five seconds flat.

"I told him to stop." His mom sniffed and finally met his gaze. "But a few weeks ago, a couple guys came by…and, well…they made some threats."

"To you?" He lowered his voice to keep their conversation private and because of the shooting pain firing across his temple. He would murder Patrick, completely kick the stupid bastard's ass for involving their mother this way. Just how much did the stupid idiot owe? And to whom? Talk about charitable donations, looked like he'd be funding the don't-kill-my-brother campaign. "Fuck."

"Jason, they didn't threaten me. They just came by and asked about your brother. I've dealt with bullies before, I wasn't frightened."

"Ma, these aren't bullies, they are murderers." He threw up his hands before raking them through his hair and tugging the strands hard. The slight sting grounded him. Pain generally had that effect, but so would knocking some sense into his brother. "I will kill Patrick myself."

"They already worked him over pretty good."

"What in the hell are you talking about?" Jason stopped pacing and grasped her shoulders.

She waved him off with her unlit cigarette, now settled in its normal place between her nicotine-stained fingers. "When I saw he hadn't left for work, I went over to see what was going on, and found him all banged up."

"Jesus." Jason closed his eyes and counted to ten then did it again. "Ma, you could be in danger. Those kind of people come back and do a whole lot—"

"Oh good, Jay Jay's here," Patrick announced Jason's nickname loudly as he strode into the lobby. "You can spring for breakfast, little bro."

Seeing nothing but red, Jason marched over and punched him square in the jaw.

CHAPTER 3

"What's with the face?" Owen grumbled around a mouthful of cereal while sitting across from Maude in the breakfast nook the next morning.

His kitchen's deep yellow and maroon tones worked well with black appliances and checkered curtains, lending the area a cozy, rustic feel. Since she and her mom, Nancy, and now Ember, Owen's fiancée spent a lot of time gathered here, they felt the warmth of the room was important. Her mom had redesigned the whole room even though she had her own small kitchen in the in-law's quarters of Owen's huge house.

"What face?" Maude kept her eyes focused on the cereal box before her, ignoring her brother's all-too-perceptive gaze.

"You've got a face." Brown eyes narrowed, he pointed with his spoon, which dripped milk all over the table before he sipped from his tall glass of orange juice.

"Don't you have wedding plans to discuss with Ember?" Frowning, Maude yanked a paper towel off its decorative polish pottery holder stationed on the table and wiped up his mess. "Leave me and my face alone."

"I know a fake when I see one. Let's leave the evasive maneuvers to pros like me." He winked. "I *know* there's something behind that face."

"I have no idea what you're saying, and I doubt you do, either." Although they'd frequently sparred in the past, Maude refrained from dumping the entire box of cereal on his head in retaliation. "It's a wonder Ember puts up with *your* face." She chuckled, happy with her comeback even though caffeine hadn't adequately entered her system this morning.

The familiar sound of Ember's fluffy red slippers swishing across the tile floor alerted Maude to her arrival. Her friend ruffled her fingers through Owen's hair. "Ah, Maude, he's got a cute face." Ember's auburn hair, slightly redder than her own, was thoroughly disheveled. Her brown eyes were barely open, and squinting against the light coming in from the windows. Although Ember was a few inches taller, they both had curvy frames, which required hard work and sacrifice to stay trim.

Lately, Ember floated around wearing a big ole smile, especially when she stared at the rock Owen had placed on her finger.

When she watched them together, Maude couldn't help smiling. Nothing like the harmonic perfection of two people deeply in love.

Since their father's death thirteen years earlier from cancer, Owen had assumed many roles in her life. Brother. Friend. Father. She loved him on every level, even if he was a bit officious at times.

He and Ember hadn't had an easy start, but they were stronger now because of the trials they'd experienced. Maybe she and Brady would have to work through their own issues to find happiness. Still, should a relationship be so hard? A few years ago, she'd graduated from college and landed her dream job working for Aceso Pharmaceutical's philanthropy division. Through this job, she'd met Brady Stephens and they'd begun dating. At this point, she wished she'd listened to the warnings of becoming intimately involved with a coworker.

Ember filled the electric teakettle before selecting the correct temperature for the loose-leaf tea she'd measured and dumped into her teapot. "How did your conversation with Brady go, Maude? Did you work things out?"

"Ember, I love you, but did you really have to bring up this subject around him?" She glanced at her brother, who stared with narrowed eyes.

"See?" He proclaimed with a bang of his fist against the table. "I knew you had a face."

"Shut up about my face, will you, please?" Maude rolled her eyes. "There is no face. None."

"That"—Owen drew an imaginary circle around her face with his dripping spoon—is a face."

"Stop with the spoon, before I shove it somewhere unpleasant."

Ember giggled before wadding up a paper towel and tossing it at his head. "Yeah, leave her alone, you big bully." She smiled at Maude. "I'm sorry. We can talk about Brady later."

"You will talk about Brady now." Owen shoved aside his cereal bowl. "What's he done?"

Maude sighed. Early morning inquiries were what she got for still living with her brother. A problem she planned on solving soon. Not that she didn't love her family, but there was love and there was privacy. "All right, fine. Our division is funding the reconstruction of an inner city Rec Center. Since local sports figures have expressed interest in donating, Brady wanted the project. He believes handling this account will benefit his chances when applying to a professional sports team's public relations department." Maude stirred the remaining cereal in her bowl, certain her mother's homemade biscuits and gravy with a side of fried eggs would be much better at soothing her aching heart. She glanced over at Owen and shrugged. "I got the account, and Brady asked me to hand it off to him. I refused. So, if I have a face"—she flashed air quotes with her fingers—"that's why."

While her relationship with Brady was important, so was her

career. Be strong or cave, that was the question. But, Killion women didn't cave. After losing her father, she'd become stronger, going through life with a mission of making proud the man she'd loved and lost. And she *was* proud of her accomplishments. To be chosen to work such an important account meant a lot. Workplace rivalry was not an issue she'd considered when developing a relationship with Brady, but the issue was now an unfortunate consideration in her professional and private life.

Since her brother now leaned back in his chair with both arms braced across his massive chest, Maude decided a distraction from Brady-talk was necessary. "Have you seen my company credit card?"

Lips pursed, Ember shook her head. "No, why?"

Owen merely raised a brow.

He knew her well enough to understand she was evading his lecture. "Friday, I had a big client luncheon, but I couldn't find my company credit card. It wasn't in my purse, so I had to go to my boss, Kathy, and cancel the account. I'm worried someone at the office stole it, because I swear I had the card in the morning."

"Maybe you left it in another purse, or something." Owen tapped his spoon against the table. "Aren't you women always switching purses?"

"You *women?*" Ember raised a brow before throwing a blueberry at his head.

"Hey, quit throwing stuff at my head, lady." Chuckling, he popped the fruit into his mouth. "Now, let's talk about this Rec Center account. Isn't that the charity deal Jason and Chewy are involved with?"

"Yes." Maude nodded, wishing she'd opted for toast in her room, rather than spilling her love life woes to her brother. "Which is a big part of why Brady wants the account. He says he wants to work with *connected* people." She raised her empty teacup. "Ember, can I have some of whatever you're brewing?"

Ember nodded. "Sure, two more minutes of steeping. You looked like you needed a heavy dose of black tea this morning, and that type takes a little longer to brew."

"Connected people?" Owen scratched his chin before glancing at Ember, who merely shrugged.

"You *know* Brady wants a job with the Marauders' public relations team." She glared at her brother because they'd had this discussion before. "After Brady discovered Chewy and Jason were involved with the Rec Center, he believed this would be a perfect opportunity to showcase his job skills to two influential members of the team."

Owen leaned his folded elbows on the table and rested his chin on top of his closed fists. "Brady wants *you* to give up an account, because he thinks this is some magic ticket to *my* team. No go, Maude." He shook his head. "No openings in our PR division and, as I've explained to him before, those jobs usually go to people already in the sports industry, like retired players." After sipping his orange juice, he met her gaze. "Why is this job situation an issue again? I've already told him to drop it."

Maude took a deep breath and remembered her brother loved her and just wanted what was best, but sometimes...

"And you aren't giving in to his bullshit, right? You didn't give him the account?"

"Owen, please, you wanted to know what was wrong, and I've told you. I'd like to handle my relationship with Brady in my own way." Though she never wanted to have this conversation again, she considered Jason's warning last night. He'd likely be worse than her brother, and his recriminations generally hurt a lot more. She shut down those thoughts, because thinking of Jason Stafford only reopened that ache in her heart, and the poor organ was already strained enough with thoughts of ending her relationship with Brady.

Owen reached across the table and gently squeezed her forearm. "I don't like Brady upsetting you and making you feel guilty over doing your job. He shouldn't ask you to change things." Owen, being the center, aka decision maker, for the Manchester Marauders' offensive line figured once he'd declared something wasn't happening, then end of story, don't ask again, game over. Unfortunately, Brady didn't work that way. He wanted to work for a professional sports team in a bad way, like obsessively bad.

"Ember, I don't think I want any tea. Sorry." Maude swirled her spoon in her bowl. "Owen, I really, really don't want to talk about Brady anymore. I appreciate your concern, but I...I don't know." She shook her head. "Maybe I'll talk to Mom." Maude scooted back in her seat then headed for the sink and dumped her soggy cereal.

After flicking on the disposal's switch, she turned on the water and watched everything swirl down the drain. A vicious end for her cereal. Was she ready to face another end? At the beginning of her relationship with Brady, she'd worried his real strategy was using her brother's connections to get close to the team. Based on his current behavior, her fears were correct. He claimed to love her, so why wasn't he proud of her accomplishments? Why did she feel they were more rivals than lovers?

Ember tapped her shoulder. "I think the cereal's all gone." She winked and flicked off the switch before wrapping Maude in a hug and rocking her back and forth. "So, you talked to him last night?"

"Um..." For a moment, Maude worried Ember knew about her garage rendezvous with Jason, but then quickly realized she meant Brady. She pulled back but kept one arm around Ember's waist. "Yeah, he won't budge. He's still mad, even though Kathy gave me the account because I found this place through the cancer-counseling center. One of the girls in my teen group told me about how the Rec Center was all run down."

"Right, I remember. Kids need somewhere safe to play."

Ember should know all about needing someplace safe after enduring her abusive childhood. Maude squeezed her friend once before letting go. "And the kids can get counseling, if necessary. I'm hoping, if we get enough volunteers, we can use funding to hire three or four social workers or a resident psychologist."

"Right." Ember flexed her bicep before striking various bodybuilder poses. "Put me to work."

"You're a dork." Maude laughed at her friend's antics. "I need to take out all my frustrations on the boxing bag. We're still going to class, right?"

"Yep." Ember nodded.

"She got lots of exercise last night." Wearing a ridiculous smirk, Owen rounded the table and headed for the coffee pot.

Keeping her gaze on Owen, Ember flashed a fake smile. "I know whose face I'll envision on the bag."

"You want to hit me, Stems?" Owen spread his arms and walked toward her. "Go ahead. You know I like it rough."

Maude left before things got too pervy for a little sister's eyes, but not before hearing Ember's squeal. Ever since Ember had moved in, Maude had interrupted way too many intimate moments. *Gross.*

As she headed to her room to change into workout clothes, she added 'avoiding seeing my brother's naked butt' to the top of her list of reasons to get her own place. Besides, with her new job, she could afford it, especially since her brother had paid her college tuition. Ever since meeting Ember, and hearing stories of her childhood, she strove to appreciate her family more. "Owen might drive me crazy, but he's never said I told you so about Brady. Small victories, I guess." Maude sighed and thumbed through her dresser drawer, searching for a matching sock.

Considering family issues made her think of Jason...but, well...most things made her think of Jason. She sighed, wishing this girlhood crush would die. Shouldn't she be able to crush a crush? Why call it that, otherwise? She was all too aware of the word's true meaning: the crushing heartache, the crushing knowledge that he'd never reciprocate her feelings, the crushing embarrassment every time he brought another woman to the house. *Crushing, crushing, crushing. All of it.*

Since dating Brady, she thought she'd become less obvious in her misdirected affections. Still, being close to Jason last night was heaven and hell at the same time. As she'd drifted off to sleep, she'd thought of everything that might have happened had she leaned across the seat and comforted him. But, loving Jason Stafford was nothing but that—a dream.

Yet, Jason made her laugh, and he made her smile. She was like an excited puppy every time he entered the room, because he exuded this charm that made everyone feel special. Still, he was crazy, cocky, and…involved with a woman who might be with child. "Perfect, Killion, lusting after a guy who's likely got another woman pregnant and only sees you as Owen's pain-in-the-butt sister." And, as that pain-in-the-butt little sister, she felt texting him was her duty. They *were* friends, after all, and he might need to talk about what happened when he picked up Patrick last night.

Hey, did you get your brother out of the slammer? She tossed her phone onto her bed, not expecting an answer, but then it buzzed. After hurriedly fastening her exercise bra, she grabbed the phone.

Unfortunately, yes. Although he'd look good in orange.

Why her heart palpitated due to a simple text was beyond her. *Orange? No black and white stripes?*

Nope. He's black and blue.

Jason's relationship with Patrick always made her a bit teary, especially when she considered how much she loved Owen. Still, she believed, those you loved could hurt you the most, which was likely the case between Jason and his brother. She sent him a reply. *Black and blue. Courtesy of you?*

Maybe.

Are you black and blue?

A little blue.

And there went the crush doing its crushing. "Ah, poor guy." She pouted. Maybe he could release some stress with her and Ember at boxing class. *Ember and I are going boxing, wanna come?*

I DO wanna cum.

And that was how Jason Stafford handled life when conversations got too serious. *You're gross.*

Yes, yes I am.

I'm leaving now.

So soon?

Yes, as usual you brought the conversation around to sex.

Is Owen going?

He never goes. He tried once and couldn't make it through.

He's a pussy.

Hey, that's my brother you're maligning. So are you, if you don't go.

Oh, challenging my manhood. Nice one, Maudy.

So?

So, no. Besides, someone is calling. Later.

Cya.

Probably the pregnant blonde, Ariel. Though Maude knew her feelings were tinted in ugly shades of green, she really hoped the girl wasn't pregnant. Maude thought she'd met the woman in question…but he'd dated so many. The man was a sex-bot.

At that ridiculous thought, she rolled her eyes and tugged on her pink sweat-wicking T-shirt then shoved on mismatched pink socks. Ariel probably wore designer socks. Probably wore I-don't-shop-at-Target clothes over a perfect I-sweat-at-designer-gyms body. Surely, plastic surgery was involved somewhere in that perfect situation.

Maude shook her head. Why did women do that? Compare themselves? Someone, someday, would recognize her attributes and love her for her. Someday.

Still, when she punched that heavy bag at boxing today, she just might envision that blonde's perfect face.

CHAPTER 4

"So, that's how I did it." Gina finished sharing her tale and took a small sip from her cran-apple martini, the hefty diamond on her left finger sparkling under the bar's lights.

Ariel Silvers nodded, absorbing the story of how this busty brunette bimbo, who she'd always believed had an IQ lower than her cup size, had snared herself a banker. An older rich banker. Gina had manipulated her way into a lucrative marriage deal by using a computer hacker. She'd had him create a nasty portrait of the now ex-wife. The mega-nerd had manipulated the wife's social media pages and her bank account. When her husband saw multiple charges to seedy downtown hotels, along with manipulated pictures of his wife with other men, he'd quickly filed for a divorce. Score one for Gina.

All the accusations were, of course, false. But, when a successful sixty-five year old banker had a hot blonde bank teller ready and willing to replace his wife of forty years, only a few tricks were necessary.

"Is your friend available to take on new projects?" Ariel scanned the mostly empty bar for any socially relevant persons. She and Gina were more acquaintances than friends. Although, they did run in the same social circles. They'd met while working for the same escort service. Tonight, they were enjoying happy hour at Manchester's most exclusive nightclub, Plunder.

Monday night rarely brought in many customers, but Ariel's intention wasn't to be seen. She required the use of someone like Gina's hacker friend, but she knew she couldn't come off too eager. Gina would lap up any desperation like the bitch she was.

"Not that I need assistance on anything right now." Ariel flicked her freshly manicured fingers through the air. "But still…you should share."

"Sure, anything for you." Gina smirked. "Just take a couple pictures of your tits. That's all I did."

They both laughed and then sipped their cocktails. Irreverence being the only emotion they ever allowed to show.

A few men glanced their way. A blond, with a love of tattoos and hair gel, winked.

Ariel rolled her eyes and hoped he wouldn't approach.

"How's your project moving along?" Gina tapped her red nails against the cocktail table.

"Just fine." Ariel plucked the cherry from her drink and popped it into her mouth. No way would she divulge her plans. She wasn't even sure how much Gina knew about her relationship with Jason Stafford. Out of all the women in her social circle, Gina was the most vicious. Not that either would ever do a full frontal assault. Backstabbing and cutting words was how they played the game. "Being pregnant isn't really a project."

Gina barked out a laugh. "You may get other people to buy your lies, Ariel, but not me."

"Who says I'm lying?"

Gina leaned forward, resting her elbows on the table. "Who says you're not?

"You're one to talk about lying, bitch." Ariel sniffed before picking up her phone and reading through her texts. Nothing important. She took another sip of her lemon drop martini. Sweet and sour, just like her. After glancing around again, she heaved a sigh. "No one's here tonight."

"Your little friend, Brady Stephens is over there." Gina waved a hand toward the man.

"As if." Ariel brushed a strand of loose blonde hair behind her ear. "He's drunk already. What time is it anyway? Six?"

Stephens had propositioned her many times before, and had been unreservedly denied. A man only making five figures a year was so not worth her time. Plus, Ariel was pretty sure he had a girlfriend. She'd seen them together a few times.

As she skimmed the inhabitants, Ariel made sure to make eye contact with Patrick, Jason's brother. She caught his eye each time she visited the bar, because he might prove useful someday. An ally in the Stafford family. Or, if necessary, something more…

"So, when should we expect the bundle of joy?" Gina briefly glanced up from skimming her Facebook feed.

"Why? You planning on helping? You're probably used to changing diapers, right?" Ariel tugged her necklace's diamond pendant, a gift from a previous lover, and glanced at Gina. "Shouldn't you head home so you can tuck Grandpa into bed?"

"You're quite humorous, Ariel." Gina fluffed her hair before snapping a selfie. "But, I'm set for life." She tapped out a message on her social media account, sent the photo, and then met her gaze. "A few blowjobs and I've got a killer prenuptial agreement. I'm not trolling bars or hoping some playboy football player will save me."

"I've never needed saved." Ariel narrowed her eyes. "Don't worry about me. You're not the only one capable of scoring big."

"Really? Then why are we meeting tonight? Apparently you're looking for *my* resources to save you."

"Isn't that what friends are for?"

"Friends?" Gina sat back in her chair, folding her fingers over her waist. "Of course, which means you won't forget who helped you."

"As if you'd ever let me."

Gina lifted her glass and tipped it toward Ariel. "So very true, which is why if you want me to talk to El Nerdo, you'll hand over your Manolo's as payment. Those orange sandals you bought to irritate me."

Ah, so the devious bitch wanted more. Didn't she have enough from Daddy Starbucks? Ariel would acquiesce but not before she had a little fun. "They'll make your ankles look fat."

"I'm curvaceous." Gina ran her hands over her enormous breasts. "Don't be such a hater, darling. I'm sorry you've had to pay for your body when mine is au natural."

"An au natural bitch."

"A bitch with killer shoes."

"I seriously hate you." Hearing raised voices, Ariel glanced back at the bar where Brady argued with the bartender, his hands flying all around and a sneer on his lips. Likely bitching over the fact he couldn't get served. *What a loser.* Ariel brought her practiced I-couldn't-care-less gaze back to Gina. "Take my Manolo's. They're out of fashion anyway."

"Oh, I wasn't planning on wearing them." Gina smirked.

"They're pretty delicate. They might not support your weight."

Gina laughed, flicking her hair over her shoulder. "Well done. You win that round, but I win the shoes." She ran her finger around the rim of her drink. "Besides, pregnant women shouldn't walk around in heels. All that baby weight makes you wobbly."

"True."

Gina studied her a moment, head tilted. "The pregnancy card is kind of cliché, don't you think? Couldn't you come up with something more original?"

"Not all of us are as clever as you, *Mrs. Fitzgerald.* And for the record, I do truly care for Jason. He and I are building a family together." Ariel's lips twitched in a fake smile reserved for moments like this. Moments when a smile was more than just a smile. When a smile meant—I'd gladly slam her face in a meat grinder and feed her to the wolves.

Someday very soon, Ariel would lord her six-carat ring and lakeside mansion over Gina and make sure the shoe-stealer regretted ever assuming she needed help.

Jason Stafford was fathering her child. She had him now.

CHAPTER 5

The following Tuesday, Maude wrapped her suit jacket tighter around her body and made a mental note to ask about the Rec Center's furnace. Spring in Northern Ohio was generally cool, and today was no exception. Worries about seeing Brady at work must have overridden her common sense, or else she wouldn't be wearing a thin skirt when the temperature today would only reach mid-forties. Obviously, the heat either wasn't on or wasn't working. She glanced at the others around the meeting table. Their well-dressed appearance in no way matched the chipped walls or rickety six-foot tables. She'd toured the Rec Center a few times before, but the rooms hadn't been this cold. Maybe the furnace issue was recent.

"Thanks for meeting with me today." Maude tapped her papers together on the table. "With your final signatures, we've wrapped up the paperwork. As you can see, the building needed these funds, so thank you. A study of the area's demographics shows a high number of children between the ages of two and sixteen living in downtown Manchester's east side. With your donations, this building can become a positive force in the community."

Jason and Chewy clapped as they sat on either side of their shared lawyer, Tom Taylor.

Maude commended them for taking time out of their busy schedules to tour the facility. Her brother had also donated, but didn't want to make her uncomfortable, so he wouldn't attend.

Throughout the tour, Jason had been his usual vivacious self, despite sporting a black eye—courtesy of his brother, Patrick, no doubt.

Jason's possibly pregnant girlfriend, Ariel Silvers, was in attendance, too, as a paralegal.

Maude fought to disregard the proprietary glances and touches Ariel made toward Jason. Her navy blue suit looked frumpy in comparison to Ariel's custom-fit and pencil-thin black skirt, topped with a light blue blouse that perfectly matched the woman's blue eyes. She and Jason would have a beautiful blonde, blue-eyed baby.

That thought distracted her more than once today as she'd stuck close to the facility coordinator and avoided Jason entirely. Although, Jason Stafford in a suit was a sight to see. He exuded this sure sense of sexuality she'd never sensed in another man.

Raw, hot, uninhibited sex. That's what emanated from his eyes, his cocky smile, and the swagger of his very nice butt. Everything about his muscled body shouted, "Get under me, 'cause I'll make you scream." Ariel had likely screamed. And now she'd cemented a place in Jason's life forever. *Darn it!*

Maude sighed and tuned back in to the conversation around her. The Rec Center's head and the neighboring college psychology professor were working out the possibility of using the facility as a place where students could volunteer and accrue credits.

She listened a while longer before using a lull in the conversation to make her escape. Thanking them both for attending, she shook their hands and waved goodbye.

On her way out, she waved at Chewy, who was speaking to Mr. Taylor, and she dodged Jason, who was making small talk with Ariel off to the side. Small talk. Maybe baby talk. That thought churned the cereal in her stomach, which was a sad state of affairs. Jason would need her support and friendship if Ariel was, in fact, pregnant. He didn't need a jealous little girl.

Still, she'd talk to Jason another time. This was a business meeting not a social hour, plus she needed to get the paperwork back to her office for her boss and board to review.

On the edge of escaping through the front door, she jolted to a stop when Jason grabbed her arm. Of course, it was him. No one else shot that tingling sensation through her body...not even Brady.

"Hey, hold up. We never did finish our conversation."

"What conversation?" Turning to meet his gaze, she frowned and tilted her head. "Our last discussion was when you didn't want to go boxing, remember? You switched over to someone else on the line." Maude flicked a hand toward Ariel Silvers. A name likely made up to go along with all that shiny perfection, but that was petty jealousy talking...maybe. Even now, she could hear her mom scolding her. *Stop being so nasty, Maude Killion. That girl's done nothing to you.*

"No, not that conversation." Jason took her arm and drew her farther down the hall. "Don't try to get out of our deal now, Killion. You were crying. I spilled, now it's your turn."

"Oh." Maude waved him away. "That's old news."

"You crying is *never* old news."

Even with his bruised, blood-shot eye, the man was gorgeous. She couldn't help but caress his face. "Patrick got you good."

"Deflection won't work." He grabbed her hand and settled it back at her side. "Brady. Tears. Why?" Arching a brow, Jason braced both hands on his hips.

Maude bit back a sigh. "Brady was upset he didn't get this job."

"This job?" Jason jabbed a stiff finger toward the floor. "The Rec Center?"

"Yes." She studied a scuff on the tip of her navy blue pumps, unwilling to meet his gaze. What unfair twist of fate had her discussing her boyfriend with her secret crush?

"Explain, Maudy."

"It's personal." Maude shook her head then locked her gaze with his. "Talking about him behind his back is disloyal."

"Okay." Jason nodded, wiping a hand over his chin. "However, talking to a friend, a guy friend especially, and getting a different perspective can be good. Believe me, I've got plenty to say about Brady-bunch."

Maude rolled her eyes. "The big brother routine gets old, sometimes."

"Don't roll those big brown eyes at me." Jason lifted her chin with his index finger. "He doesn't get to make you cry. Period."

Oh, if only Mr. Stafford knew how many times he'd been responsible for the same result. Through no fault of his own, but still…"Brady and I will work it out." She didn't add one way or another, because Jason really didn't need to know things between her and Brady were that bad.

"He'd better be good to you." Jason tweaked a strand of her hair. "Cause I'm not working with him on this here gig. It's just you and me, baby." He wrapped an arm around her shoulders before kissing the side of her head.

She slowly released a breath and endured his warm embrace, because this was Jason's normal touchy-feely behavior. He couldn't know his simple touch created an ache deep in her heart. Still, she leaned into him for a moment, inhaling his unique scent of brown sugar and oranges. His body wash. This she knew, as her stalker-self may have peeked into his shower stall a few years ago when she'd visited his apartment.

"Maude, do you ever wonder—"

The click-click-click of high-dollar heels echoed down the hall, getting louder with each step.

Maude knew who was searching for Jason but refused to

release him until he finished his question. "Do I ever wonder what?" Her heart pounded like she'd just gone twelve rounds with Rocky Balboa. "Jason?"

"Nothing." He released her. "Just, maybe think about finding someone besides Brady, you know?" He rocked back on his heels and patted her cheek. "You deserve better, all right?"

"Yeah, sure. Thanks." Maude fought back a frown. She just knew he'd planned to say something different, or maybe she just hoped that was the case. The click-click-click had stopped. Maude remembered to breathe again, especially after that ridiculous face pat. Who did that? Grandmothers? Great aunts?

Internally growling in frustration over the interruption and everything else that remained horrible in her life, Maude turned to face Ariel.

"Jason, dear," Ariel purred. "A girl could get jealous."

As if Ariel Silvers would have any reason to be jealous. Still, something about the woman made Maude cringe. As if everything about the blonde was off, or faked. No one was *that* perfect all the time. Still, Maude smiled at Ariel, believing in giving others the benefit of the doubt. Maybe this girl *was* pregnant and needed a friend. "Don't mind him, just Jason being Jason."

"I know, Sweetie. He's such a flirt, sometimes." Ariel took his hand before leaning up and kissing his cheek. "If you wouldn't mind, I need to steal him away. I'm hoping I can talk him into lunch." Smiling, she brushed a hand against her mid-section.

Wow, the woman was smooth, making sure she brought attention to her possible pregnancy. Or maybe, a subtle warning?

"Actually, Arial," Jason cut in. "I wasn't finished talking to Maude. I'll meet you out by the car. We need another second."

"Oh." She blinked then glanced at Maude before shifting her gaze back to Jason. "I didn't realize you two had business."

"We do." Jason wrapped his arm around Maude's waist. "Give us a minute."

Flashing pure white teeth, Ariel hesitated a moment before

nodding and clacking back down the hall

Wide-eyed, Maude glared and stepped away from his too-warm and too-familiar hand against her side. "What was that?"

"What?" Jason shrugged.

"We *were* done talking."

He loosened his tie, yanking the knot free. "She shouldn't be interrupting my private conversations and inviting herself to lunch."

"She's having your baby." Maude shoved his shoulder. "I think she can ask for food."

"She's clingy." Rubbing the back of his neck, he wrinkled his nose.

What did he expect when the poor woman walked around with his baby in her belly? Not only that, he'd been with her for more than one date, so…"Jason…you *are* dating her, or seeing her, or…whatever it is you agree to do with women." Maude threw up her hands. "I imagine that, yeah, she'll get a heck of a lot more clingy, not to mention how intensely needy a child is, so get used to it, Stafford."

Jason stared down the hall for a minute then sighed. "Should have dated you, Maudy. No games. No expectations. Just you and me being real."

He wanted real, now? Fine. "You and me? Really? Well, ask me out, then." *Oh, no, what did I just say?*

"I will." He smirked. "When Owen leaves the country."

"That's what I thought." Maude hoped he couldn't hear the return of her thrumming heartbeat. Why would she say such a thing? "Go on." She flicked a hand toward the front doors. "I've got to get back to work. When you want real, you know where I am."

"I've always known where you were."

Jason's quiet response wasn't playful or teasing…and when she met his gaze, he stared right back. "What are you doing?" Maude narrowed her eyes, not in the mood to play his flirtatious games. Or whatever *this* was.

For the longest time, he didn't answer, just turned and stared out the row of small horizontal windows. "I don't know. I think maybe Patrick knocked a screw loose."

"Sure." Maude bit her bottom lip. "I need to get this paperwork back. Take it back to the office, so anyway…I should get back." Flustered by the odd vibe between them, she struggled to make any sort of sense, and since that wasn't working, she walked off, but then turned. "Thanks for asking about Brady. Don't worry, we'll be fine."

Jason scoffed. "It's not him I care about."

She smiled, a genuine smile this time, because she knew he did care about her. Yet, as she made her way to her car, she couldn't keep her smile from faltering, because when it came to Jason Stafford, him simply caring would never be enough.

She heaved a sigh, got into her car, and rested her head against the steering wheel. "Dream on, Dreamweaver. Dream on."

CHAPTER 6

While at a late lunch with Jason, Ariel picked each crouton from her salad and set it on the side of her plate. Bread never crossed her lips, and she certainly wouldn't start today. Jason had followed her to a downtown restaurant just a few blocks away from the office of his lawyer, and her boss. With her future at stake, she had to play this game very carefully.

She glanced across the table at the hefty blond with the striking blue eyes. Last summer, she'd placed herself in Jason's path. Since then, they'd been together intimately on numerous occasions. The man had a very healthy sexual appetite, and she had no trouble appeasing him. In the beginning, he'd made clear he lived in the now, which was fine, up until a point. During the season, he'd slept with other women, but she'd been patient, never saying a word. However, once the season was over, she'd decided to cement her position in his life.

After taking a small sip of water, she cleared her throat. "Jason, listen. I did take a pregnancy test, and the results were positive."

He gave a slight gasp and pushed away his half-eaten salad. He opened his mouth to speak but just shook his head.

"Don't worry. I don't expect you to marry me." In contrast to her words, Ariel had already considered all the designers capable of creating the perfect dress, once she snagged this wealthy man. "I understand a man like you needs his freedom. All I ask is that you are there for our child. We both know how rough a childhood can be without a nurturing father." She reached across the table and placed a hand on his forearm.

"What do you know about my father?" Stiffening, Jason slid away his arm.

Ariel sipped her water again, taking a moment to cover her mistake. She'd researched his family quite thoroughly. "You told me about him, once."

"No." Jason frowned. "I never talk about my father. Ever."

"Yes, dear, you did." Ariel flashed a small, sympathetic smile. "One night, a few months ago. Maybe you don't remember because you were very tired after your game. Anyway, as to *our* child, I'm sure we can devise a plan beneficial for us both. Perhaps, we could even live together…for the sake of the baby, of course." Ariel Silvers never begged. She cajoled, manipulating her way through life with her shapely body and sharp mind, but she'd never again fall to her knees and beg any man.

No longer was she the small-town nobody, Dee Dee Davis. She'd altered everything to become Ariel Silvers, a perfect package created to snare the high-life, paid for by a rich man. Her friends might settle for older sugar daddies, but she refused. Actually, the thought of lying prone again for an old wrinkled bastard made her shiver. Years earlier, she'd fought back the nausea and had done the deed while working for an escort service. Plastic surgery wasn't free, after all.

Originally, she'd set her sights on Charles Hendricks, the Marauders' quarterback, but Jason would certainly do. Plenty of zeroes in his paychecks, especially with all his endorsement deals. Jason was also more of a playboy than Chewy, who seemed to care more about football than his own dick.

Working for Jason's lawyer, she'd learned all about his charitable contributions, which were usually geared toward disadvantaged women and children. Through this information, she'd gleaned his need for family and a strong, independent woman—so she'd given him both.

Jason, who usually ate healthy, broke up the salmon resting on top of his spring greens salad. With his fork, he fiddled with a chunk of the fish before it tumbled off the side of the plate. "All your talk about us co-parenting and moving in together...I think you're moving things along a little fast. You say you took the test, so then the next step is verification by a doctor." He placed his napkin on top of the salad. "You set up an appointment, and I'll go with you."

"Oh, of course." She smiled and took a bite of her salad. Agree with them, smile, and never let them see any break in the artifice. Still, she would only bend so far.

"And I want the baby's DNA tested." Jason met her gaze and raised a brow, as if in challenge.

"I understand why you would want that." Ariel calmly sipped her water, seething inside. How dare he question her when he'd finally been caught? The man shared his dick with any willing participant, but then he had the audacity to question her sex life? Though, he was right to worry. She inwardly smiled. He wasn't the only man in her bed. Still, she had a character to play, so she used the pity card. "People look at me and think, 'She uses her body and beauty to make her way in life.' But I can't help the way I look." Sniffing, she dabbed at the corner of her eye with her napkin.

"Yeah, you can." Jason scoffed before waving a hand by her face. "You've had plastic surgery." He glanced at her breasts then raised that brow again.

She'd love to hold him down and shave it off. Yet, she wouldn't be thrown off course. "I asked you to lunch to discuss how we'll move forward together, not to have my character demeaned. That isn't fair. I'm not overly happy about this turn of events, either. I just started my job last summer, and I hadn't planned to have children for many more years." She released a pained sigh and delved back into her salad, stabbing a tomato with her fork. "We must accept the consequences of our actions." She met his gaze and offered a soft smile. "Plus, I know you'll be a wonderful father."

"No, I probably won't." Jason fiddled with the tiny glass salt dispenser, spinning it between his fingers. "I had a lousy role model." He sat back in his chair. "I know I'm being a dick about this, but I'm always careful about sex. *We* were careful, so I'm having a hard time believing all of this is true. Sorry, but it is what it is." He glanced around the restaurant for a moment.

She followed his gaze and smiled.

A few people pointed at him and tried to stealthily snap his picture.

Ariel hoped they got her in each shot and that the photos went viral. She wanted to be the "Who Jason Stafford is dating" girl, featured in all the magazines. *Maybe I should touch up my lipstick?*

Jason rested both elbows on the table and spoke in a quieter tone. "If we have a kid, fine, we'll take care of him or her, but you and I…we weren't meant to be together." Frowning, he rubbed his temples. "I've explained I don't do long-term. You knew that."

She arched a brow. *Oh, hell no.* If he thought they weren't having sex again, he was sadly mistaken. He'd bent her over every piece of furniture in his apartment, and she'd be there again. Ariel narrowed her eyes. "Regardless of what I know or don't know, I need your support right now." She leaned back in her chair and rubbed her stomach. "As I said, I just started my job. If Mr. Taylor finds out I have to leave in eight months, he might go ahead and fire me now."

"I can talk to Tom." Jason met her gaze. "I doubt he wants to lose both my and Chewy's business."

"Thank you." Ariel nodded before focusing on finishing her salad. The crisp spinach and tangy citrus vinaigrette were inharmonious on her palate. The tinkling of silverware and surrounding conversations were the only sounds breaking the tension, until she sighed loudly. "The man bears none of the responsibility."

Jason shot forward in his seat and spoke through clenched teeth. "I never said I wouldn't bear the responsibility. In fact, that's why I'm having lunch with you, to make that clear." He jabbed a finger against the table, jostling their plates. "But, let me tell you this…if I find out you're lying, then losing your job will be the least of your worries."

"Have we sunk so low as to threats now, Jason?" She lifted her chin and met his gaze, making sure her tone conveyed her dismay. "Can't we at least be friends? We could even be friends with benefits." She winked and drew the tip of her tongue across her lower lip. "Regardless of what you said earlier, I know I pleased you in bed."

Leaning back, he shrugged. "You did, but so have a lot of other women."

"I highly doubt those other women fulfilled your every fantasy, Mr. Stafford." She arched a brow this time. "Finding a lover who is as…I suppose I'll say…versatile, won't be easy. And why search for another when I'm right here?" Ariel reached across the table and took his hand. "I've never asked for more than you can give, and I never will, but I suggest you reconsider our sexual relationship. Don't dismiss what we could have. Give us a chance."

Jason pulled away his hand and rubbed the back of his neck. "I'm sorry, but no."

"Oh, are you interested in someone?" Ariel smoothed the linen napkin resting on her lap before meeting his gaze. "Is it…perhaps, the brunette at the Rec Center? Is she the most recent participant in your bed?"

"What?" Jason's blue eyes went wide, and he raised a hand, palm up. "No, we aren't talking about Maude. She's a friend."

"I'm merely gauging my competition." Ariel knew Maude

was Owen Killion's little sister, so of course she and Jason would be close, but they'd looked pretty cozy when she'd come upon them in the hallway. "I would hope that any new woman in your life would understand I need a support system. I will not go through this pregnancy alone."

"If we discover you're really pregnant, then we'll see about everything else," Jason mumbled then flicked a hand at the passing waiter for the check.

"I *am* pregnant." Ariel snapped back. "I'd never lie about such a thing."

"Listen, I need to go." Jason raked his fingers through his hair. "Text me after you schedule your doctor appointment." He stood and tossed two fifties on the table.

Ariel took a long draw of cool water to calm her fury. How dare he throw down cash, as if paying for some cheap hooker? "Don't you worry, Jason. I'll call." Her Southern accent broke through so she bit her tongue.

Jason turned from the table, but then halted and glanced back. "I'm sorry, Ariel." He rested both hands on his hips. "I just…this is a lot to take in, all right?"

"Of course. It's understandable."

"Look, give me a call if you need anything." After leaning over and kissing her cheek, he took off.

And that was all she needed. A simple kiss.

Well, and the perfect plan, because she would win in the end.

Grabbing her phone, she pulled up her Facebook app and took a photo of her hand over her belly. Due to her work situation, she wouldn't be blatant about the announcement, but she could hint. Plus, none of her coworkers were her friends on the social media site. However, she had to be careful how she released this information.

She typed: *So excited, just learned some great news.*

After hitting Post, she sat back and tapped her knife against the table. All her friends knew about her relationship with Jason, so they'd know who the father was, or they'd ask and she'd just smile.

Most of the girls she socialized with now, she'd met through the escort service or out at bars. A more fierce, backstabbing bunch of bitches she'd never known. Only one woman had ever been her match in the mean-girl department, Nicki Nobles, but Ariel had won that battle. One of the few regrets in her life. Nicki was probably the only person she'd ever loved, but that emotion made her weak, got in the way of her goals, and made her feel. Nicki couldn't give her a diamond-studded future, so she'd had to go.

Ariel shook her head. She wouldn't and couldn't get wrapped up in the past now. Not when she was so close to having everything she wanted. Everything she and Nicki dreamed about when huddled together in a pink sleeping bag under a Virginia moon.

Her phone pinged with Facebook alerts, but she'd wait until she got home after work to respond. Wouldn't do to appear too eager, that response rang of desperation.

And Ariel Silvers didn't do desperate.

CHAPTER 7

The day after her meeting at the Rec Center, Maude inwardly sighed while sitting across the restaurant's table from Brady, her appetite and her patience both no-shows for the evening.

"Maude, you're being unreasonable." Brady brushed a hand through his perfectly-styled blond hair, his tone full of exasperation. "We don't have to break up over this latest disagreement."

Why did he assume he had final say? In the past, he'd always talked his way around her, but not tonight. Tonight, Maude would stand firm in her decision.

Having their private conversation in a fancy downtown steak house, where the wait staff scraped the crumbs off the table and replaced her fork constantly, was not anything Maude wished for, but he'd insisted. "Brady, you basically said I wasn't qualified to do the Rec Center job. I need to be with someone supportive of my career, not a competitor." Maude sipped from her water glass—her never-empty water glass. The water pitcher guy was very enthusiastic about his job, which was nice. Obviously, he was a hard worker, but she was about to float away.

Maude groaned and searched for the restroom sign. Why couldn't Brady dine at someplace simpler? Like a sandwich shop? His attempts at high-dollar living were one more indication they didn't suit. She would've been happy with a can of soup.

"Competition is good for your career." Brady smiled before glancing around the restaurant and nodding at a client sitting at a neighboring table. "It keeps you on your toes. We wouldn't be having this discussion if I could get a job elsewhere." He sighed then sipped his red wine. "I agree, us working together isn't such a good idea. I'll admit I get carried away, sometimes."

"Your competitive nature isn't my fault." Maude wanted a clean break from everything. Brady, her living situation, over-exuberant water boys, everything. She frowned as Brady ignored her comment and checked his phone.

His domineering personality sometimes carried over into the bedroom. Perhaps, he'd find a woman who liked to be tied up or cuffed…or, whatever. Because she'd agreed to bondage once and after being spanked overly hard, she'd been done. He'd even frightened her a little. Reliving those memories had her squirming in her seat and more than ready to finish this awkward dining experience.

"How about we change the subject?" Maude sipped her water before eyeing the water guy to head him off before he pounced.

"Changing the subject won't keep us together." Brady's lips thinned. "I've apologized. Now let that be the end of it."

His tone turned harsh, as it often did when she disagreed. Usually, she rolled over in order to keep the peace, but not tonight. He continued on and on with his usual manipulative spiel. One she'd heard before, but this time, his words meant nothing. She felt nothing. Running a finger through the condensation on her water glass, she realized she'd drawn a J. *Oh, no.* She snapped her hand back and shot a quick glance at Brady.

He tried so hard to be the man-in-charge. Dressing the part in power suits he couldn't really afford, with shoes to match each one. His hair stylist worked downtown at the trendiest salon. His trim build was honed by hours spent with a personal trainer.

Appearances mattered to this man. She'd always wondered why he hadn't dated someone more like Ariel. Now *they* were compatible.

"We've spent months together, building a wonderful relationship. Investing in each other and our future. I won't just throw that away." Brady kept his voice low and didn't meet her gaze, instead he kept glancing around the room.

Likely checking to make sure no one overheard their conversation. For once in her life, Maude wanted to make a scene like in the movies where the girl dumps her water glass over the man's head. She bit her bottom lip to keep from laughing. Placing a hand over her mouth, she met Brady's gaze and nodded. "I'm sorry, what were you saying?"

Finally deigning to meet her gaze, he sighed and shook his head. "I was saying that relationships hit speed bumps, sometimes." He reached across the table to take her hand. "But we're clear of the hurdle, now. Have you—"

The waiter chose that moment to arrive with their meals, cutting off his question.

Sprigs of curled carrots were artfully arranged on the top of her steak, along with some green herb. While she appreciated the chef's presentation, she didn't need all the foo-foo. Didn't need her beef massaged before being tucked into the freezer each night.

Maybe she'd ask water guy for a to-go container and escape before Brady talked her into continuing their broken relationship.

Because part of her considered, why not? Brady was handsome and had a good job. He could be funny, sometimes, though the more she thought about it, his humor was frequently at others' expense. Plus, if she ended their relationship, seeing him at work would be extremely awkward.

Stupid, getting involved with a co-worker. Her brother had warned her, but she hadn't listened. Owen's advice about the men in her life generally was, "He's not good enough," instead of, "Sure give this guy a go." Older brothers. She mentally rolled her eyes at the thought. Still, he'd been right about Brady…and so had

Jason. Not that she'd ever admit that to either of them.

While listening to Brady discuss his work project and office gossip, Maude finished her overpriced six-ounce filet. Deep down, she worried her whole attitude this evening might be a tad selfish and unfair. She and Brady had enjoyed some fun times, and she did love him, in a way…but not a forever kind of love. Which wasn't his fault…or hers, just fact.

Over the past couple days, she'd wished she felt otherwise, that she could just continue the relationship, maybe even try harder, but that was sad and cruel to herself and to Brady. They both deserved more, and finding that more shouldn't be so hard—not if what two people had was right. Sitting here felt wrong and dishonest. Ember and their mutual friend, Rachel, lectured Maude to quit being so nice. She could do this. Had to, or her life would never change.

"Want to share a dessert?" Brady waggled his brows.

She forced a smile. He *could* be cute, at times, which was why her next words were so hard. "Brady, no, I don't want dessert. I didn't even want to eat here, but I did…for you." She shook her head then placed her napkin on her plate. "I cannot be who you want." She ran a finger along the edge of the table, flicking off a breadcrumb. "I'm making changes in my life. And I need some space to figure things out." He started to interrupt, but she lifted a hand to stave him off. "I agree we have worked hard on this relationship, but maybe it shouldn't be so hard. Real love should just flow and exist without having to constantly bend."

Brady took her hand again. "Come home with me and then stay over the weekend. We'll spend all our time in bed. Make-up sex is always the best."

"No, Brady. You aren't listening." Frowning, Maude shook her head and tugged her hand free. "I'm looking at apartments this weekend."

"I'll go with you. Maybe we should take that next step, together."

"Live together?" Interesting. He'd never mentioned this possibility before.

The waiter chose that moment to arrive and drop off the check.

A good thing, as she had time to regroup.

After the waiter left, Brady met her gaze. "Living together is a natural progression. Perhaps, if we are together more often, we can work on your perceived issues."

Throwing her water in his face became even more appealing. Maude poked her tongue in her cheek and inhaled a long breath. Their issues were *not* perceived. One more example of how he could go from kind to manipulative jerk in an instant. "I've already asked Rachel to go along. Being a private investigator, she's good at ferreting out issues. Plus, she knows which neighborhoods to avoid."

"She's become a good friend, hasn't she?" When his phone buzzed on the table, Brady picked it up and responded via text.

Maude cleared her throat to gain his attention. "Yes, Rachel fits in quite well with Bronco, and Owen really likes her, has since she helped with Ember's…um…problems." Speaking of Bronco, he'd likely smack Brady upside the head for staring at his phone instead of really listening. She'd seen him smack the phone out of Jason's hands many times. Bronco's job description suited him well—guard. He'd always been her champion, though he could play the big brother card, too.

"All right." Brady nodded, still glancing at his phone. "I'll escort you to your car once the waiter gets back."

After the bill was settled, they walked down the sidewalk to the crosswalk. The restaurant was right across the street from their downtown office building and the parking garage.

A homeless man huddled with his dog in the doorway of an empty building. Lights from restaurant and bar signs lit up the street. Cars zoomed by, carrying people living their lives. Everyday occurrences. Were they unlucky in love, too? How did a person find the right one in such a sea of people? She thought of Jason's flirtatious behavior the other day. How his arms had felt wrapped around her body. Why couldn't he see her when she stood right before him? Her ongoing feelings for Jason were unfair to Brady, but mostly unfair to her heart.

While walking across the street, she felt a slight breeze sweep through her hair. In northern Ohio, spring temps did tend toward chilly, and even the summers were mild. She glanced up at the stars and wished for warmer weather. Wanting the season to match her own changes. Seeing all the flower buds blooming and the trees filling with green leaves, she, too, wanted to sprout. Grow on her own. Start over.

At her car, Brady bent to kiss her goodbye.

Speaking of mild—no heat or tingling in her toes. Nothing but a wish to break free.

"Maude. Look at me." Standing beside her driver's side door, Brady held her in place with one hand around the back of her neck and the other at her waist. "What we have is forever. I won't let you go." He moved his hand to the front of her neck, lightly squeezed, and used that pressure to lift her chin. "I'll give you space, but I've invested too much time in this relationship to let it fall apart. You are mine, Maude." He narrowed his gaze." Do you understand?"

Wishing to be free of his grip, she jerked back and then rubbed her neck. "I understand what you're saying." Didn't mean she agreed, but the way he held her was slightly intimidating so she refrained from starting an argument.

"Good." He leaned against her, rubbing his hard cock against her hip, before kissing her again.

She turned her head, stomach churning from the scent of cinnamon gum mixed with the coffee he'd drank. "Stop, Brady." She placed a hand against his chest. "I said I needed space."

"Sure, Maude." He nodded, jiggling his keys in his pocket. "I'll see you tomorrow."

After watching him leave, she finally sank into the driver's seat. As she clicked her seatbelt across her waist, she realized her hands were shaking. Apparently, Brady thought he could practice dominance outside of the bedroom. But, that wasn't happening. Anytime. Anywhere.

CHAPTER 8

"Will you stop taking pictures and get back to work?" Owen growled.

In order to alleviate part of the remodeling expenses, Maude scheduled a few clean-up days to prep the Rec Center for the construction crews. All of Jason's Marauders' teammates were on task today. He worked alongside Owen and Bronco while the others did maintenance outside and in other rooms.

Jason captioned the photo he'd just snapped of Owen, Bronco, and him:

Clean-up day at the Rec Center with Thing 1 and Thing 2

They always took photos in the same order they stood on the line of scrimmage, likely just habit.

Jason ignored a couple texts from ex-flings asking if he was partying tonight before sending the picture through his Instagram account, which was connected to all his other sites. With his huge social media presence, he had to keep his fans updated on his status. Plus, he enjoyed the side benefit of annoying Owen. His teammate was all medieval Viking and had likely never even checked his social media accounts. Maybe Owen's agent ran them, or Maude. Speaking of Maude, she'd looked awful cute today with her hair bouncing around her shoulders in a single ponytail and her grubby jeans and faded hunter green Marauder T-shirt—

which sported her brother's number and secretly annoyed him. He'd have to get her a proper Jason Stafford T-shirt. Wanting to mark her as his was highly inappropriate, but he really liked the idea. He glanced at Owen and reconsidered...slightly.

Through playing and wondering about things better left buried, he lifted his chisel and hammer and worked at chipping off old shower tiles in the Rec Center's locker room. A spattering of mold and what seemed like five-hundred layers of soap scum tumbled with each layer he broke through. Breathing behind his white facemask was almost claustrophobic. He scratched at the itchy sweat trickling down his nose.

"Maude's moving out." Behind his own mask, Owen announced those words like they weren't any big deal.

And they shouldn't have been. So, why did Jason feel as if time had stopped and the world was suddenly topsy-turvy? If Maude was moving in with Brady-bunch...he just...he wouldn't...he'd likely do something crazy. Not truly comprehending the reason why, he just knew he would.

This floodgate of Maude-feelings needed to be stemmed with sandbags, a load of concrete, or something, because he had no right to desire his best bud's sister. That shit had been sealed shut for years, so why seep through the cracks now? Ever since his sister's death, Jason had decided to live like he was dying. To revel in life, because he never knew when it would end. In his current job, living that type of lifestyle was easy—women, parties, nothing but good times. Yet, more and more, he craved something else, especially since his two best friends had found the loves of their lives. Seeing their happiness had him reconsidering a whole lot of things. Maude things. But Owen knew everything he'd done. Hell, Jason had done a lot of bragging about his conquests over the years. Women threw themselves at him all the time, and he easily accepted. Owen knew all this. Bronco knew all this. Which didn't make him much of a candidate for whatever he was thinking related to Maude. Plus, he'd just got off the phone with Tyrone, who'd warned him not to do anything stupid until the "Ariel situation" was handled.

"What are you just standing there for, Stafford?" Owen tossed a bit of grout at his head. "Get back to work."

"You may be my boss on the line, Big-O, but not here." Jason pointed the end of his chisel at Owen.

"Rachel was with Maude all morning, checking out apartment complexes." Bronco's deep voice was muffled behind his mask. Jason and Warren "Bronco" Murray had similar features, but his hair was lighter than Bronco's dirty blond and the guy was a bit bigger, though not by much. Jason could still take him—on a good day. He shook his head. Maybe that was stretching the truth. Bronco was a mean-ass fucker. His friend had lived and died football until the little private investigator, Rachel Harris, caught his eye and his heart while helping him solve a family mystery last summer.

Lack of oxygen to his brain due to rebreathing hot air caught in this stupid mask had Jason unreasonably irritated over the two women just up and visiting apartment buildings. Was that even safe? He jabbed both hands on his hips and glared at Owen. "Why in the hell are you letting Maude move out? And if you tell me she's living with that fucker, Brady, I will beat your ass with that rusty shower rod."

Owen arched a brow. "Somebody's a grouchy bitch this morning. I'm not thrilled with Maude leaving, either, but she needs her own space."

"For what? Why does she need space? What is she doing?"

Owen frowned then he started whistling and got back to work.

Dismissing him while he sat on some weird emotional ledge wasn't a smart move. Jason eyed the shower rod in a more serious manner.

Luckily, Owen continued, "Jason, she's twenty-two." He glanced over his shoulder. "Makes sense she wants out from under my thumb." After shrugging, he turned back to work more tiles off the wall. "At least, that's what Ember says. Plus, Bronc' and I discussed our concerns with Rachel before they left this morning. Rachel will make sure the place has good security features and isn't in a bad neighborhood."

"So, that's good enough for you?" Jason lowered his mask. "You're just kicking her out?"

"Dude, what is your problem?" Owen grunted as he jabbed at the tiles. "She wants to leave."

"You didn't answer the question. Is that fucker living with her?"

"No." Owen stopped working and turned to meet his gaze. Quiet for a moment, he frowned and scratched his temple. "At least, I don't think so."

"Great." Jason gripped his hammer tighter before slamming it against the tiles, seeking release from this odd sensation in his chest, his head...and his stupid pounding heart. As he worked quietly for a few more minutes, Jason rejected all the mental pictures of Brady making himself at home in Maude's apartment...and her bed.

"Where the hell is Chewy, anyway?" Bronco dumped a bunch of loose tiles into a wheelbarrow stationed in the center of the room.

"He's working in the other bathroom with the two cheerleaders," Jason answered before wiping sweat from his brow.

"How the hell did he pull that duty when we get this sperm-laden men's room?" Bronco growled.

"He's got delicate hands," Jason quipped in a feminine voice.

They laughed and talked shit about their quarterback before the conversation turned to the team and upcoming training camp. After a few more wheelbarrow trips to the outside dumpster, they decided on a break. Once Jason took all the lunch orders, he made Owen ride with him to pick up the food.

Pulling his hybrid Audi Q5 onto the road, Jason tossed out

what he felt was a fairly innocuous comment. "Listen, I don't know what's going on with Maude, but Brady isn't right for her."

Owen shot him a glance. "I don't think so, either, and have said so on numerous occasions, but then Mom got on my back about not being supportive. I think this move will be good for her. Maude's pretty pumped about it, too, so don't rain on her parade, Stafford."

For the rest of the drive, and while waiting for the food, they talked about the team, the Rec Center, and their food. But on the way back, an unidentified alien species took control of his mouth, and he blurted out, "Maude's been in the background of my mind for a while, now."

"Don't." Owen halted with his cup's straw near his mouth. "Just don't."

"I might." Jason shrugged but didn't turn to meet what he knew would be Owen's icy glare.

"I wouldn't."

"Why?"

"Seriously?" Owen cracked his knuckles.

"She's game."

"No. She isn't *game*. She is my sister, and that is all. Period."

Taking a deep breath, Jason opened his mouth to argue.

"No." Owen jabbed his dripping straw in Jason's face. "I know you. I've seen everything. Been there during all those parties and all those women. So, don't." Jaw clenched, he jammed his straw back in his cup and took a long draw. "Not to mention the fact your latest conquest is pregnant. Fucking pregnant." Owen shouted the last two words.

"I'm aware, and I can hear just fine." He made a show of wiggling his finger in his ear.

"You need to straighten your shit out, Jason. My sister is, and forever will be, in the no-go zone."

Jason considered Owen's stance. His friend was right, of course, but something about Maude had always created this happy buzz in his chest, and he was tired of holding back. Tired of feeling alone while surrounded by people. Maude knew him—deep down, knew him.

He took a draw from his own drink, and he shot a glance at his best bud. Owen not trusting him to be straight with Maude stung a bit. Hits on the field were nothing compared to knowing your best friend didn't believe you could change for the better. That shit hurt. "I think Maude's the only one who can handle me, because she's the only one who really knows me."

"I know you," Owen sputtered. "That's enough. So, no. Drop it."

"All right." Jason raised a hand between them and, for a brief moment, met Owen's gaze—the same chocolate brown as Maude's. He'd found comfort and friendship in that steady gaze from both siblings for over six years. Losing either of them would cut deep. "All right, Owen. No for now, but I can't, and won't, guarantee no forever. We're friends, always have been, always will be, but if you really know me, then you'll see that maybe I'm right about this."

"You're this close to stepping in a mine field, Stafford." Owen pinched his forefinger and thumb together. "Get your shit straight before I'm forced to explode on your face."

"That's seriously the dumbest threat I've ever heard." Jason puffed out his chest, puckered his lips, and mocked Owen's voice, "I'm gonna explode on your face."

Owen punched his shoulder. Hard.

And all was well again.

For now.

CHAPTER 9

Back at the Rec Center, Jason traipsed down to the toddler area. He'd already finished his lunch, but Maude hadn't joined them so, loaded with her order, he sought her out.

Jason gazed at Maude's back. She was staring out the only horizontal window in the room, surrounded by two separate piles of kids' stuff. Stuff he imagined he would become familiar with very soon. He bit back a growl. Ariel still hadn't called with any sort of doctor appointment plan. The woman was grinding against his last nerve. "What are you doing down here, Maude? Why didn't you come up for lunch?"

"Oh." Maude jumped and tucked her hand at her side. "I was just on the phone."

"Talking to who?" Concerned, he stepped farther into the room.

Her eyes filled with tears, and her lower lip wobbled. "Oh…um…j-just Brady." She flicked a hand in the air then swiped under her eyes with her index finger. "I was telling him about the apartments I looked at today."

"So, why are you crying?"

"Because…it's all so sad." Her voice cracked, and she covered her face with both hands before bursting into tears.

"Hey, stop this." He tossed her lunch bag onto a small, short table before grasping her shoulders. "What did he do?"

59

"Nothing, he's n-nothing." She eased closer, resting her forehead against his chest. "And t-that's the prob-problem."

"Okay." Wrapping his arms around her, he patted her hair— soft, red-brown hair, long, thick, and wavy. No hair product, just natural—like her.

"I'm sorry." Maude sniffled. "I'm getting your shirt all wet." She wiped at her eyes again. "Is that my lunch?" She pulled away and dug into the bag. After removing everything, she blew her nose with a napkin. "I'll just eat down here. Thanks. I'm okay now." She waved him away.

"I'm not leaving you here alone." No way, no how was she brushing him off.

She stared up at him with those familiar brown eyes. "So, is everyone keeping busy upstairs?" Grabbing her burger, she sank down onto the carpeted floor, her back against the wall. "This place really needed a lot of work, huh? Are you guys making any progress in the showers? It's nice of you to help today."

Sighing loudly, he settled beside her. "Eat your lunch, and quit making stupid small talk. This is me. Not some investor or the manager of this joint."

"Someone's growly today," she mumbled before unwrapping her sandwich and taking a hearty bite.

He refrained from arguing he wasn't grouchy, just irritated— by Owen, by her crying, by Ariel, by possible pregnancies, by stupid white facemasks blocking his breathing. Okay, so maybe a tad grouchy did describe his attitude. "So, Owen says you're moving out?"

"It's time." She wiped her mouth with a non-tearstained napkin. "I mean, I can't live on Owen's dime forever...and he and Ember need...I don't know, some privacy." She flicked her hand in the air before munching on a chip. "Mom has her own quarters, but me...I need to move on. I make good money, so I have no reason to stay."

Jason waited until she finished her burger before delving into his real reason for bringing up the subject. "Is Brady moving in, too?"

"No. I am starting fresh everywhere." She bit into a barbeque chip, the crunch seeming to emphasize her words.

"What does that mean?" Were she and "the bunch" finished? Over? Caput? Ah-ah-ah, something wicked this way comes and travelled right to his cock. He shifted. Super disgusting to lust after a woman mourning a relationship...and his best friend's sister...and his friend...and...he was sure he could think of more reasons—later.

Maude sipped from her unsweetened tea. "I'm starting fresh. My relationship with Brady was convenient and mostly easy, but not right, nor was he the great love of my life." She peered at him before blinking and clearing her throat.

She never wore much make-up, maybe a little mascara, but she was naturally pretty. He'd noticed before, but this close he actually saw a few small freckles on her nose. What else would he discover if he got closer? And closer? And deeper, until everything about her was no longer a mystery?

Unsure what the hell he was thinking, let alone thinking about doing, he glanced down the hallway, making sure they were alone.

Maude tugged on the heart necklace she'd received from her father on the birthday before he'd died. "I want more, and I intend to find it."

"You have a plan?" Normal, pleasant conversation was a nice direction to refocus his lustful thoughts, especially when she kept rubbing her hand up and down her thigh.

"Of course."

"Of course." He winked and squeezed her knee, leaving his hand to rest there. "Should have known."

"Not all of us are pretty playboys, flitting through life."

"Flitting. I don't flit." Jason scoffed and shoved at her knee. "And I do have a plan, I'll have you know. As a matter of fact, I just discussed it with your brother."

"He's a good listener." She nodded and picked through her bag, likely searching for the bent chips.

He usually saved his for her, since she liked those best, but he'd forgotten today in his starvation after working like a dog. He patted his jean pockets, searching for gum, as his mouth suddenly seemed dry. "Want to know what we discussed?"

"Football." Maude wadded up her wrappers and took another drink from her tea. "Blondes. More football. I don't know...what did you discuss?"

"Not blondes, but a red-tinted brunette." He fingered her hair. "You see, I've been itching for a fresh start, too."

"Ariel, right?" Maude eased back and set her cup to the side. "She's blonde, FYI."

With a finger, he traced a line down the side of her exposed throat. So soft. His arousal pressed against his jeans, making him shift slightly, though he didn't really care if she could see. "Ariel isn't my future."

Maude snorted out a half-laugh, half-scoff. "Ariel is carrying your baby."

"So she says."

"You think she's lying?" She turned and met his gaze.

Close, he was so close to her light pink lips. All he had to do was lean forward and take.

Then Maude tilted her head. "Jason? Do you think Ariel is lying?"

"Why wouldn't she?" He bent one knee and rested his wrist on top. "My interest was waning, so she likely played this card."

Maude's brow furrowed. "I hope she isn't lying. She seems nice."

"See, that's what I like about you, Maudy. You don't see how treacherous people can be."

"I'm not naïve." Maude shot him a glare. "Not some little girl who hasn't lived. I know a lot more than you think."

"Do you? And what is it you know?" Jason tilted her chin his way and met her troubled gaze before tracing his thumb over her plump bottom lip. "The tip of your nose and your eyes are all red. I'm tired of seeing you cry."

She heaved a sigh. "I am, too."

He clasped the back of her neck and slowly…so very slowly, drew her closer.

Heart thundering.

Barely breathing.

No coming back from this moment.

No way to later say he hadn't given her a chance to withdraw.

He wavered with his lips hovering directly over hers.

And she leapt.

Leapt and took and drove deep with her tongue and her mouth. Searching, driving, taking.

He let her lose control for a moment before he eased back and met her gaze. "It's okay. Take it easy."

She visibly swallowed and didn't blink, her breath coming in slight pants.

Then he dove back in, lightly kissing her once, twice. Softly, reverently.

She'd always been different.

A true friend.

A woman who could calm him, and yet, make him crazy at the same time. She'd always been there, always. Unlike anyone—ever. And because of that, she deserved a chance. He'd likely fuck up everything, but he wanted something real in his life. Someone who wanted him for him, and not the football status, or the money, or the fame. For far too long, the compass needle of his life had been spinning and shaking out of control, but with Maude in his arms, everything stilled and pointed in the right direction.

He couldn't get enough of her pillowy lips, so he nipped her bottom lip before soothing it with his tongue.

Eyes wide, Maude gasped before touching her lips. "Why did you do that?"

He wasn't sure, himself. Wasn't clear on, why now? Why, after all this time, he needed her, when he was all wrong for her—especially with the Ariel mess, the upcoming season, and just his normal non-commitment self. He needed to make this about something other than what it could never be. He rubbed his temple, since he may have hurt his brain with that thought. "Do you feel better?"

"I don't know. My stomach kind of hurts, and I know tonight, I'll replay this moment over and over and wonder…why?"

He pressed a finger against her lips. "I probably shouldn't have kissed you, but I've never done things I should."

"Why?"

"I have no idea." Jason huffed out a sigh.

"All right, then…" Maude slowly lifted her hands from his shoulders. "I think, maybe, we should consider this a moment of you comforting me and leave it at that."

"Yeah, leave it at that." He tucked a long reddish strand behind her ear. "I need to get my shit straight. You need to do your spring awakening, or whatever the hell it is…but the thing is…I need to know you're in my corner, Killion."

Maude scooted back and waved a shaky hand between them. "I *am* in your corner. Always have been."

"Just give me some time, then."

"For what?"

"I don't know, for me to kiss you again." *What are you doing, flirt-face? You were going to stop.* Maybe he would have, if she hadn't brushed off the kiss as comfort. His kisses were not comforting, they were pulse-pounding, clothes-ripping hot.

"I think all the dust has damaged your brain." She laughed.

Not a good laugh, but one verging on hysterical. "No, all the hits on the field took care of that a long time ago." Jason stood and brushed off the back of his faded jeans. "Probably should get back to work."

With kiss-roughened lips, Maude gazed up at him. "I feel like I've entered an alternate reality."

Jason nodded and his grin spread. "My kisses have that effect on women."

Eyes narrowed, she stood and slapped his arm. "Shut your face."

"Shut it for me." He grabbed her arm, skated his hand down to her fingers, and…heard the clicking of heels out in the hallway. He let go of her hand and stepped away, but not before dropping a bombshell sure to upset her further. "I know you've waited for me, Maude."

"What? You don't know anything, you conceited jerk." She shoved at his chest before glancing at the door. "If I *had* been waiting, I'd have stopped a long time ago. Now that I'm on my own, I'm heading into the man-free zone. I'm done with all of you, because you cause me nothing but stress." After her loud declaration and dramatic hand movements, she kicked a stuffed elephant.

Seeing her fury, he bit back a grin. She'd never let him get away with anything, and he kind of liked that thought. Still…he needed to lighten the mood. "Hey, hey, hey, don't take out your anger on poor little elephants." He picked up the injured party and rocked it in his arms.

Maude rolled her eyes. "Go away. And take that elephant with you."

She mumbled a few choice cuss words about him and elephants.

Since she rarely used such colorful language, she must be flustered. *Good.* The joys of teasing Maude ended when he glanced at the doorway and saw Ariel waiting. How much had she heard? The stoic look on her face didn't bode well.

Any woman who could pull off such a cold and emotionless

expression was likely some kind of psychopath, or sociopath. Although, he had no idea what the difference was between the two. Maybe he should hire Rachel to investigate Ariel. If he was having a child with this woman, he needed information. Real information, not the lies she'd likely feed him. She had said she was born in Virginia and hadn't had an overly-pleasant childhood, but they didn't generally spend their time together engaging in meaningful conversation.

"Jason, I've been looking for you." Stepping to his side, Ariel spoke in her schooled tone, her flowery spring dress and heels inappropriate attire around all this dust and dirt.

"You've found me." He raised his hands to his sides.

"Yes, I see." Ariel arched a perfectly sculpted blonde brow. "Maude, good to see you again. I came by to see if I could help. I imagine plenty of work remains, even though I seem to have caught you during a break."

"Right, we were just having a lunch. I mean, a lunch break." Clearing her throat, Maude leaned down, picked up her crumpled lunch bag, and tossed it onto one of the piles.

"Oh, and, honey, you have a smudge on your face." Ariel flicked a manicured finger toward Maude's left cheek.

"Thank you." Maude wiped at her face, and then grimaced at her dirty hand before grumbling something and taking off down the hallway.

Jason turned his attention back to the woman at his side. "You're not really dressed for work, Ariel."

"I brought other clothes." Ariel took his arm and steered him out of the room. "Actually, my primary purpose in attending today was to tell you I have a doctor's appointment in a few weeks."

He nodded and watched Maude's bopping ponytail and very fine ass as she slipped down the hall toward the ladies' room.

Listening to Ariel, he felt his emotional walls rise again. He didn't like the man he became around her—cold and unfeeling—but he hadn't liked much about who he'd become over the past couple of years. Jaded, lost, cavalier, but if he followed that curvy woman currently stalking away, he just knew she'd keep him straight.

CHAPTER 10

Ariel wrenched her gym bag out of her fifteen-year old BMW's trunk, using her breathing exercises to regain calm.

How dare that mangy brunette kiss Jason? No chubby, pasty-faced cunt would ruin her life. She'd caught them kissing, but had tiptoed back down the hall in order to school her features.

Now, she knew.

Jason had lied about his interest. "Just friends" didn't shove their tongues down one another's throats. Just friends weren't always sneaking off together. Maude Killion was no match for her physically, so truly Ariel had no worries, but still, the woman would pay. No one interfered with her plans and got away scot-free.

Stomping back into the building, she headed into a women's restroom to change. The entire facility was a filthy, grimy dump. Her child would never come to a place like this. Although, during her childhood, she'd passed many hours in a similar center. Ariel had sat in the corner, as far away from the other children as possible. Even then, she'd known she was different, that she deserved more. Only one good thing had come from her time in that place, she'd met Nicki there. A girl as grungy and jaded as herself. They'd formed an instant bond. She frowned. Memories of a place like this were unwelcome and only added to her irritation.

Making sure no one else entered, Ariel locked the main door before turning to stare into the mirror. Her face was flushed and a trickle of sweat formed at her hairline. "Calm down, Ariel." She met her own gaze in the mirror. "You deserve this. You didn't come all the way from a backwoods Virginia trailer park for nothing. Winners take what they want. Do whatever they have to in order to stay at the top."

Blonde highlights, straightened teeth, elocution training, etiquette lessons, bargain couture off Bluefly, Beyond the Rack, and Fashionesta. Her dog-eared copy of *How to Marry a Millionaire* sat on her nightstand, and she'd even added her own notes to a few chapters. Primed and ready, she had Jason right where she wanted him, and that mousy tubby Maude Killion wouldn't get in her way. What kind of stupid name was Maude, anyway? "Maude." Ariel over-enunciated the name, sticking out her tongue at the end. "It's like I'm puking as I say it."

One thing Ariel had learned from hours of watching reality TV and, if she was honest, from her group of friends, was how to be cruel without throwing a punch. Words hurt, and she could think of plenty of cruel things to say to Maude. Plus, wasn't she dating Brady Stephens? What would he think of her indiscretion?

She'd dig into everything Maude Killion. Plus, Jason *was* a flirt, and he'd fuck anything with legs. Ariel just needed to make sure he was in between hers…and he could be, tonight.

After her pep talk and quick change of clothes, she carried her dress and shoes out to her car.

An idea struck. She glanced around the parking lot then opened her passenger door, unlocked the glove box, popped down the fuse cover, and removed the fuel pump fuse so her car wouldn't start.

"Should've known you'd be up to your old tricks, *Dee Dee*."

Ariel froze. That voice. How the hell was that voice outside her car? Holy fuckety fuck. Chills coursed down her spine, while at the same time a fine sheet of sweat covered her upper lip. Nicki had found her. Nicki was out of jail. Nicki was standing just behind her.

The hair on the back of her neck went sky high. Ariel took a deep breath and turned. "Nicki, wanna tell me what you're doing here?"

Nicki smiled.

Still the same beauty as before. Dark, straight hair, green eyes, everything perfect. Gorgeously perfect. She'd thinned out a little, her skinny jeans highlighting twig-like legs, and her blue top fitting just right around her shapely chest. A chest that hadn't been bought and paid for. The bitch was all-natural. Always had been.

"Well, now, that was about the welcome I expected." Nicki leaned against the hood of her car, blowing a big pink bubble. She snapped the bubble back and chomped on her gum for a few seconds before spitting the wad at Ariel's feet.

"Nice. You learn to spit in prison?"

Nicki laughed. "I learned a lot in prison. A lot."

"So, what?" Ariel considered grabbing the gun she kept under her passenger seat. "You come back for revenge? Go ahead. Give it your best shot."

Nicki crossed both arms over her chest. "Now, why would I want revenge for going to prison? Did I blackmail a judge? No, I don't remember ever doing that. Must've been someone else. Someone who wanted me gone. Though for the life of me, I can't even imagine who would do such a thing to a poor, innocent girl like me."

"Innocent?" Ariel mocked. "You've never been innocent, Nicki."

"Ah, but I was, once, and only once, with one single person." Nicki strode forward and stood right before her, bending a little so they were close.

Her plump, thick lips just inches away. Ariel braced herself against the need to see if they were as soft as she remembered.

"I trusted her, loved her, gave her parts of myself I didn't even know I had to give, and you know what she did?"

Ariel remained quiet, not even daring to take a breath.

"She dumped everything we had in the trash, because she's a selfish, heartless woman."

With stiff arms, Ariel shoved her. "Stay away from me, Nicki."

"Oh no." Nicki shook her head. "Too late for that, now. Far too late." She mock-tipped an invisible hat then walked away, backwards, keeping her gaze the entire time before hopping in the passenger seat of an old Honda Civic and driving off with her co-conspirator.

Ariel couldn't tell if a man or woman was behind the wheel. "Shit." She kicked her car's wheel over and over. Just what she needed, a pissed-off blast from her past, hell-bent on revenge, smack dab in the middle of the most important scheme of her life. "I buried her before, and I can do it again." She sat in the passenger seat for a moment then bent over to retrieve her gun. "Nicki better behave, or this time, I won't be as nice. This time, I'll end her." She massaged the gun's barrel for a few moments, seeking calm from the cool, hard metal. In knowing she held real power in her hands.

She glanced at the open glove box. Her plan was in motion, and she'd stick to it. Nicki's reappearance could mean nothing. Years ago, they had moved to Ohio together, so likely Nicki was reconnecting with old contacts now that she was free. However, when Ariel found out who had been spilling her secrets, she would rip that bitch's eyes out. They'd learn to keep their stupid traps shut. She clenched her hands at her sides to keep them from shaking.

"One deep breath, two deep breaths." She inhaled and exhaled until her heart stopped pounding. She hadn't had much time to react before, but now her adrenaline was through the roof.

Focusing once again on her plan, she picked the fuse off the floorboard and stuffed it in her jeans pocket. *Oops.* Jason would have to take her home, now. He wouldn't want to leave the mother of his child in a cold parking lot on the wrong side of town, now would he?

Chin up, she headed back inside to find Jason. Her tight Marauders T-shirt highlighted her freshly-paid-off assets quite well. Plastic surgery aside, she worked hard to keep her body in shape, ate very little, worked out every morning, and used the best body products. Determined in her mission, she peeked into each room until she found Jason.

Yet, memories of Nicki rushed through her mind. From age fifteen until she skipped town, Ariel had worked at the grease-laden diner down the road from her mom's place. Her dad had taken off when she'd hit ten, and her mom blamed her for his departure, which made sense, since she'd stabbed him in the face the second time he'd come into her bedroom. Nicki had given her the knife and the courage.

"Ariel." Jason's voice jolted her out of unpleasant memories. "Should you be around all this dust in your condition?"

"Oh, I hadn't thought about that." She held a shaky hand over her mouth. "I suppose there will be a lot of things I can't do in the coming months." She slumped her shoulders and bit her bottom lip. "Do you have another mask?"

"No, I don't." Jason shook his head before lowering a junk-filled wheelbarrow. "Maybe you should ask Maude if there is something less messy and strenuous you can do."

"I don't mind hard work." And no way was she going up against Maude in her current mental state.

He furrowed his brow. "If you *are* carrying my child, you're not breathing in…whatever is in this air. Come on, we'll figure something out after I dump these tiles." He lifted the wheelbarrow and set off down the hall.

She followed him, enjoying the play of muscles in his back

and arms. "This is such a great cause. Did you ever come to a facility like this when you were a kid?"

Jason shook his head. "Nah, my sister and brother would walk me down to the park, and we'd shoot hoops."

"You have a sister?" Of course, she knew all about his sister. She'd investigated Jason Stafford quite thoroughly before sleeping with him.

"No."

"Did she die?"

"Yeah." He stopped before an outer door. "Can you get the door?"

"Sure." She held the door as he pushed the wheelbarrow toward a dumpster. Once he passed her, she fell into step beside him. "Losing a family member is hard. My father left when I was young."

"Where did you grow up, anyway? Virginia, right?"

Avoiding too many personal questions, especially with Nicki's reappearance, was crucial, so Ariel purposefully tripped over her own feet, causing her to stumble and fall, change the subject, and garner sympathy all at once.

"Ariel." Jason rushed to her side. "Are you all right?"

"I think I may have twisted my ankle. Can you help me up?" Sniffling a little, she wrapped her arms around his neck as he lifted her to her feet. "Thank you. Do you think you could take me home? This is starting to throb." She flicked a hand toward her ankle.

"Sure." He lifted her in his arms and carried her back inside.

"Can we get my bag? I left it in one of the rooms." She hadn't, but she wouldn't pass up the chance for Maude to see her in Jason's arms.

"What happened?" Maude popped her head out into the hall.

Some tiny brunette stood at her side—Rachel Harris, Bronco's girlfriend, was giving her the eye. She'd have to be extra careful around that one.

"Ariel tripped and fell," Jason answered.

Rachel rolled her eyes.

Ariel pretended not to see her reaction, only snuggled closer against Jason's body. "Jason is taking me home. I'm sorry to take him away before all the work is done."

"She said she has a bag." Jason glanced around the room.

Maude's brow furrowed before she glanced around. "Huh? I don't think she left anything in here. Is the bag in another room, maybe?"

"Oh, there are so many rooms, I can't remember." Ariel shrugged.

Jason settled her onto a metal chair and followed Maude, searching for a bag they'd never find.

"Well played, Ariel."

Ariel glanced at the petite, dark-headed troublemaker. "I'm sorry, I don't know what you mean, Rachel."

"Oh, you do." Rachel crossed both arms over her pitifully lacking chest. "You think I haven't run across your kind? That I don't investigate women like you weekly?"

"Maybe your preconceptions are getting in the way." She sniffed and bent to rub her ankle. "I truly care for Jason."

"Uh huh. Good luck with your…pregnancy." Rachel flicked a hand at Ariel's waist. "Oldest trick in the book."

"It's not a trick."

"No?" Rachel shifted closer and bent to look her in the eye. "Then how about we go down the street to the pharmacy, pull a pregnancy test off the shelf, and you can take it while I watch?"

Luckily, Jason hadn't asked that very thing. Yet. Ariel held her breath for a taut second. This woman could put thoughts in his head. Still, this was a game she meant to win. "Sure, let's go." Ariel didn't blink, didn't drop her gaze, didn't do any of those nervous tells she was sure Rachel Harris was schooled in recognizing. Jason and Maude chose that moment to save her from a trip she really didn't want to take and a conversation she'd rather not continue.

"We couldn't find your bag." Jason shrugged and then clapped his hands together.

"Oh, you know, now that I think about it, I may have taken it out to the car. I'm sorry."

"Okay." Jason drew out the word before glancing at Maude. "I'll see you guys at Owen's. He bought these major steaks so I'll be by after I drop off Ariel."

Rachel tugged on Jason's shirt. "Maude made those mozzarella, basil, and tomato bites you like. You don't want to miss out since they're your favorite." She glanced at Ariel. "I'm sure Ariel will be fine. In fact, if she's doing better, bring her by tonight. We don't really know her all that well, and if she's going to be part of our crew, we'll need to rectify that."

Maude gaped slack-jawed at Rachel before not-so-stealthily nudging her friend's foot.

Jason jiggled his keys and cleared his throat. "We should go."

True, they should. But Ariel couldn't let Rachel's comment go unanswered. "How very kind of you, Rachel. But, I doubt I'll make it. I have dinner plans." She glanced at Jason and licked her lips, making clear her plans included him. "I've worked up an appetite." She smiled at Rachel before winking at Maude.

Seduction was on the menu, especially since she needed to expel all the tumultuous feelings seeing Nicki had brought forth. A strong, hard fuck would clear her mind of everything but pleasure, and Jason Stafford could deliver over and over.

Once she got Jason in her apartment, she would need help getting ready for bed, and then she'd have him right where he belonged.

CHAPTER 11

"Jason kissed you?" With wide eyes, Ember stared at Maude. "And you're just now telling me this?" Ember scooted over as a guy in a business suit slid into a chair at the table beside her.

This soup and sandwich shop was always packed during the lunch hour as it sat surrounded by office buildings. The scent of a wood fire and smoked meat generally attracted a large lunch crowd.

"It just happened." Shrugging, Maude finished off the last of her vegetable soup. On the Wednesday after the Rec Center clean up, she had finally calmed enough to talk to someone else about the whole "comfort kiss" situation. She'd basically attacked Jason's face, taking her moment and rolling with it in quite an over-exuberant manner. He probably thought she was like one of those gross gray suckerfish she used to have in the bottom of her fish tank. She barely refrained from pounding her head against the table in embarrassment.

"But, what about Ariel? The one who's supposedly pregnant?"

"You know, you and Rachel could be wrong about Ariel." Maude fiddled with her spoon, wishing she'd gotten a big chocolate chip cookie. Cookies made everything better. She sighed and looked at Ember. "Maybe Ariel really is pregnant and wants to make things work with Jason. I'd hate to think she's lying, and I've told him that."

"He can't be kissing you and making things work with her." Ember picked a stray avocado chunk off her plate and popped it into her mouth. "I know you've always been interested in him, but considering the timing, and Jason being Jason." She made a "mehhh" sound out the side of her mouth. "Maybe not so great an idea."

"You're sounding more and more like Owen."

"I know. It's crazy, isn't it?" Ember grinned.

"You two are on some seriously weird frequency."

"I love him like a thousand nuclear bombs went off in my chest."

"You're not writing ad copy for your relationship. Silly, ad girl." Though she teased, Maude loved their love. They both deserved so much happiness, and they had found it. Together. The minute Maude had seen her brother around Ember, she'd known the redhead was the one.

"This wedding will be so epic." The goofy grin fell from Ember's face, and she bit her lower lip. "Have you checked Facebook lately?"

Based on Ember's tone and somber expression, this wouldn't end well. "No, why?" Her heart thumped a little harder, and her soup started swimming with creepy suckerfish.

"Okay, but don't freak out." Ember gripped her forearm.

"I'm already freaking out. I'm imagining fish floating in my belly."

"What?" Ember arched a brow.

"Nothing." Maude shook her head. "Just tell me."

Ember took a deep breath and blurted out, "Brady posted a risqué picture of you and captioned it, Love this woman."

Maude stared at her friend for a moment before Ember flipped around her phone to reveal the photo.

Her. In bed. Hair fluffed. A sheet resting precariously on the very edge of her breasts. But that wasn't the worst part. Her naked body lay covered just barely by a sheet that was nestled between her legs so the viewer had a clear vision of her thighs. Her naked thighs. "What the hell?" Maude scrolled down, hoping no more pictures were posted. "When did he take this?" She gripped Ember's phone tight in her hand and stared out the window. Barely seeing the people bustling by, not seeing the blinking Open sign, only seeing red. "I am going to kill him."

"Shhh, Maude, sit back down."

She hadn't realized she'd shot out of her chair, knocking it to the ground, and her words had likely come out like a shout. But how dare he! Clients would see this picture, co-workers, friends, everyone. "Oh my God." She fought to breathe past the rising embarrassment and feelings of utter betrayal. "He's lost his mind."

"Maybe just go to Brady and ask him to delete the photo." Ember righted her chair then re-settled Maude into her seat.

"This could ruin my career." With that thought, she considered her options. He had to delete the photo. Now. She picked up her phone and dialed his number. Hearing him answer, she tore right in. "Take down the picture now, Brady."

"What do you mean?"

"Don't play dumb. You posted a basically nude picture of me on Facebook no less than three hours ago. Take it down." Her fury level remained too high to care if others in the diner heard her. "If you don't, I'll report you to Facebook, and they'll block your page." She wiped at the tears streaming down her cheeks. Humiliation mixed with hurt, and that upset her even more, because she'd cried enough over this man. "How could you do that to me? What were you thinking?"

"I was thinking I miss you and that we had some beautiful moments together."

"*We* weren't together in that picture, Brady." Eager to return to the office and strangle her ex, or maim him in some manner,

Maude stood and tossed her trash in the bin.

"I'll take it down. Sorry, but I still don't see what the big deal is."

"You don't see?" Maude stepped outside into the cool spring air, unsure if Ember was following or where she'd gone. "You can't see how a *nude* picture isn't a big deal? Our clients are friends on your page, Brady. This could ruin my career, but maybe that's what you want."

"That's ridiculous." Brady sighed. "I'm hanging up."

"We *will* talk about this when I get back," Maude asserted, but he'd already ended the call. "Jerk." She stared up the sidewalk, wondering how many people had seen her glamour shot, until Ember touched her arm.

"Is he taking the photo down?"

"He said he would. Why would he do something like that?" Maude squinted against the sun, blinding her on this beautiful spring day. Too bad her ex-boyfriend had ruined any joy she might feel from the sun warming her face.

"I know, right? Especially when he says he wants you back. Pretty dumb move."

"Listen, sorry to cut our lunch short, but I have to get back for a meeting, anyway. Then I'm strangling Brady."

Ember glanced at her phone, moving a finger up and down the screen. "Photo's gone."

Maude hugged her friend and held on tight for a few long moments. "Thanks for telling me."

Ember hugged her back. "If you need to talk about Brady or the Jason kiss, let me know because I'm here."

Maude eased away but voiced her main concern. "What do you think my brother would say if he knew Jason kissed me?"

"He'd be angry, to put it lightly, but he can't stop you from being together. He knows how you feel about Jason."

"What?" Stopping in the middle of the sidewalk, Maude clasped both hands over her face.

"Everyone does."

"Oh, no!" Her cheeks had recovered from embarrassment over the nude photo, but now she was likely bright red again. Did her brother, of all people, know of her crush? "Is today Embarrass Maude Day?"

"Sorry." Ember sniffed and cleared her throat.

"Have I been that obvious?"

"No…well, maybe…I don't know, but I do know everything will work out." Ember squeezed her hand.

Maude wasn't as clear on her happily ever after. She sighed and shook her head. "I've got to go, but thanks for listening."

"Always." Ember waved before heading down the street to her office building.

Maude felt for Ember and all she'd gone through. But, she was a perfect match for Owen. Now she needed to find her own match, but first, she had to endure a meeting with Ariel Silvers.

# # #

Maude struggled to tune in to Kathy Weland's chitchat as she and her boss walked to meet with Jason's lawyer, Tom Taylor, and Ariel at a building a few blocks over. Too many worries over Brady's odd action and Jason's even odder kiss had her mind befuddled. She overanalyzed everything, always had, and likely always would. She tried to make sense of senseless things, got too caught up in the whys of life. Instead of concentrating on the upcoming meeting, she considered future conversations with both Jason and Brady in order to cease all the crisscrossing thoughts firing through her mind.

Upon entering the building, they took the elevator to the twelfth floor. The receptionist greeted them and led them into a conference room where Ariel waited.

Dressed in a stylish navy-blue suit, Ariel stood and offered them both a drink.

Maude attempted small talk and tried not to stare at Ariel's ankles, which looked fine in three-inch, blue-and-white striped heels.

Jason's lawyer arrived and they all settled into chairs at the round conference table.

"What can we do for you, Tom?" Her boss, ever the woman in charge, got straight to the point.

"Well, I'm concerned." Resting his folded hands on top of the table, he shot a pointed glance at Maude. "Ariel says she doesn't have all the files for the Rec Center project."

"Oh, I sent them over weeks ago." Maude frowned, mentally backtracking. Though she might be fuzzy on her personal life, her job's duties remained crystal clear.

"Plus she doesn't have copies of the schematics of the building or the builder's quote."

Maude glanced at Ariel, who merely offered an arched brow and a half-grin.

That slight grin was all it took before a light bulb exploded in Maude's mind. Ah, this was war—and Ariel had no problem shooting people in the back.

Her boss apologized profusely, yet still questioned the validity of the claim.

Ariel must have seen her and Jason kissing, because why else would she play this false game? Still, the accusations would linger. Jason's lawyer would doubt her abilities, no matter what she now said. So, she'd find the emails in her Sent folder and resend them. Easy.

"I'm very sorry." Maude straightened in her chair and kept her gaze on Mr. Taylor. "Since Ariel is having trouble retrieving the emailed information, perhaps I should send the files directly to you." She could throw punches, too, because nobody questioned her work. She'd studied hard in college, graduated with honors, and landed her dream job. If she made mistakes, she would own up to that fact, but the only mistake she'd made was believing

Ariel Silvers wasn't willing to do anything to keep her position in Jason's life.

"Ariel typically handles all the incoming mail. Makes my job easier." Mr. Taylor smiled at Ariel.

That smile was one of a smitten man. *Lovely.* "I understand," Maude agreed. "But, Ariel just started last fall, correct?"

Taylor nodded.

"She might not be up to date on everything. Perhaps it's best if we work direct, especially with such large donations. My apologies, Ariel." Maude finally turned to the blonde in question. "But, I know I've done my job, and I find it hard to comprehend how my e-mails got lost. Are you having similar issues with other clients? Maybe you should have your IT department look over your computer?"

"That's a wonderful suggestion, Maude." Ariel smiled, white teeth flashing. "I'm sorry to cause trouble. But, I just felt we should meet in person, in case issues were present on your end."

"I understand." Maude nodded, meeting Ariel's gaze so the woman would hopefully comprehend she did understand— completely. "But, there aren't any issues. I'll resend you *and* Mr. Taylor the files when I return to the office."

"Thank you." Ariel leaned forward in her chair. "And, if you find you haven't sent them prior, you'll feel better for having done so."

Maude ran a hand over her mouth before she ripped apart the smug woman with words she couldn't take back. Instead, she stood and offered her hand to Mr. Taylor. "Thanks for meeting with me today." Then she nodded at Ariel. "Ariel, glad to see your ankle is better. I doubt you'll be able to wear shoes like that much longer, though."

"What's wrong with her shoes?" Her boss, Kathy, glanced between them.

"Nothing." Ariel's face turned bright red. "I need to get back to my desk. Excuse me."

Huh, Ariel had shot out of there fast, almost as if she hadn't wanted Maude to reveal the reason behind her future shoe issues. Well, Maude would tuck that knowledge in her back pocket to pull out if necessary. These sorts of intrigues were Rachel's territory; all they did for her was make her stomach hurt. More than ready to leave this ridiculous meeting, Maude waited by the door as her boss wrapped up things with Taylor.

While exiting the building, Kathy didn't say a word until they hit the sidewalk. "Why do I feel like I just wasted an hour for a catfight?"

"Because, you did." Maude shrugged. "I'm so sorry."

"Care to explain?" Her boss slowed her pace.

"She's lying."

"Obviously." Kathy huffed out a sigh. "But, why?"

"She thinks I'm a threat."

"How?"

"It's personal stuff. A guy." Maude was lucky she and her boss were friends of a sort, but that didn't mean Kathy wouldn't fire her if it meant the company's reputation.

Kathy offered a simple, "hmmm" before walking on. At the door to their building, she placed her hand on Maude's arm. "Keep Ariel out of any future correspondence. Like you said, send everything straight to Taylor and cc me. I'm not letting some gold digger destroy our work."

And that label summed up Ariel completely. Maude had given her the benefit of the doubt, but after only one meeting with Ariel, her boss knew. Ember knew, Rachel knew, everyone but her had seen the woman clearly. However, after today, no uncertainty existed...Ariel had tried to destroy her professional reputation, all to warn her away from Jason.

"She really is a gold digger, isn't she?" Maude actually felt a small modicum of sympathy for Ariel, because Jason would never abandon the Killion family. Ariel's treachery would only push him farther away.

"Maude, that woman is textbook material girl." Kathy steered her inside toward the elevators. "Be careful. She's a clever one, and women like that can get vicious. Hence the little scene she just created out of nothing, but yet causes lots of damage. I won't have her harming your career. I have never doubted your abilities, and nothing about today has changed my mind."

Maude wrapped her arm around Kathy's shoulder and squeezed. "Thanks for believing me, boss."

Kathy chuckled before stepping onto the elevator, pulling Maude along at her side. "Do me a favor, kiddo. Steer clear of that woman and whatever man is making her desperate. You hear me?"

"I hear you." Too bad her heart never listened when it came to Jason Stafford.

CHAPTER 12

"Mom, you know I don't eat stuff like this anymore." Jason waved a hand at the spread on the table. "You've got carbs and more carbs."

"What?" His mom sniffed and sank into her dining room chair. "You've always liked my lasagna."

Playing for a pro-football team meant he focused on staying mentally and physically fit. Typically, he ate lean proteins, fruits, vegetables, but nothing else. Sometimes, he'd do pancakes with his teammates, and maybe a pizza, but generally he kept his diet clean. Plus, he didn't know that he'd ever said he liked his ma's lasagna. Growing up, they typically ate things like pasta because the ingredients were cheap.

His mom had gone through a lot of trouble to fix him something, so he kissed her cheek. "I do love your lasagna, Ma. Smells real good." He'd just sat down to dig into his salad when his brother, Patrick, banged open the kitchen door.

"You're late," his ma chastised.

"He's on Patrick-time," Jason quipped, rolling his eyes.

His brother literally had a few steps from his apartment above the garage to the kitchen door. Though neither brother ever spoke of it, they both knew Jason bought this house so Patrick could have a place to live.

His brother kissed the top of his mom's head. "I know. I have to head into work shortly, so I'm going to eat and run." He glanced at Jason then quickly looked away.

Oh, no. That look meant guilt and certainly trouble. What had his brother done now?

"Sit down and eat." His mom waved Patrick into a chair then passed him the garlic bread.

Eyes narrowed, Jason studied the interplay between the two. Something seemed off. He hated being suspicious of his brother. When they'd been kids, they were the best of friends. Patrick had taught him how to play football, and they'd plop down in front of the TV every Sunday night to watch their favorite teams.

After his injury pushed him out of the game, Patrick had interviewed for a sports announcer job, but people in the business had long memories. During his short football career, his brother had been even more of playboy than him, and that was saying a lot. He'd blown off interviews and hadn't shown up for press conferences after games—all of which hadn't endeared him to a job in broadcasting.

Sure, Jason partied, but he refrained from the darker side. No drugs and rarely, if ever, did he drink alcohol. He'd never understood how his brother could drink at all after growing up with their alcoholic father.

Yet, as careful as Jason was, he'd been snagged in Ariel's web. He hadn't been cautious enough, and now, he could be a father. She'd kept him at her place the other night, needing assistance due to her ankle injury. After he dropped her off, he asked for Owen's help in retrieving her car from the Rec Center's parking lot. He'd been pissed when Owen suggested she'd likely pulled the fuel fuse herself.

Still, he hadn't said a word after driving her car back to her place and then helping her into bed. He'd denied her advances. Huge bonus points for him, since a while had passed since his dick had seen any action, and Ariel was a tiger in the sack. But, he wouldn't touch her when all he could think about was Maude's sweet sighs as she'd kissed him, or the soft feel of her skin against his hands.

"You're being quiet." His mom stirred around some green beans on her plate before taking a bite of cottage cheese.

"Just a lot on my mind."

"When's practice start?" his brother asked.

The question was strange, because they rarely talked about football anymore. It'd become an unspoken agreement after his injury. The surrealness of the night continued as he and his brother talked football camp, recent trades, and thoughts for upping his game during the new season. While Jason appreciated the conversation, he held back any hope things would change between him and his brother. His heart ached for old times, for moments just like this, back when things were easier, but something about tonight wasn't real. He bit into a ranch dressing-covered cherry tomato, waiting for the other shoe to drop.

"I'm out, Ma." Patrick hugged their mom, which ratcheted up the weird factor. They weren't huggers, and Patrick sure as hell wasn't affectionate toward anyone. Ever.

What is going on?

"Thanks for dinner."

His brother even took his plate to the kitchen when he left. That sealed it. Something odd was happening in the Stafford house. "What was all that about?" Jason shoved aside his half-full plate.

"What?" His ma shrugged but didn't meet his gaze. "He's just being nice to his mother. You should try it sometime." She winked, but the cheeky effect was ruined when a tear fell from her eye.

"Are you crying?" He stood, unsure what to do. "Why are you crying? Is Patrick in trouble?"

"If you're finished asking questions, then sit back down,

because I need to tell you something."

"Ma, that's never good." He clutched the edge of the table. "So just spit it out."

She paused a second then placed her napkin on the table. "I've got the cancer."

"What?" He sank back into his chair, a little dazed the bad news was due to her this time and not his brother. His mind had trouble adjusting. And his heart…well, he didn't think it'd resumed beating since his brother dropped his dishes in the sink. "I'm sorry, what did you just say?"

"I've got the cancer."

"You've got cancer. It's not *the* cancer, Ma. It's just…" He heaved out a breath. Why was he quibbling over words?

"It's in my lungs. No surprise there." She sniffed then wiped her wet eyes.

Jason swallowed back a lump of fear. People beat cancer all the time. He'd pay. Get her treatment. Do whatever. Cancer wouldn't defeat his ma. She'd been through enough. Why burden her with this, too? Wasn't there a cap on human pain? Shouldn't there be a pass for moms who barreled through life like she did? Who loved as hard as she did? Who forgave?

"I'd like to go knowing you and your brother have worked out some kind of peace." She took a small sip from her water. "He's in a bind with this latest scuffle at the bar. Apparently, the kid's father is a big-shot lawyer. The situation has gotten very ugly."

None of that mattered. His brain and heart were still stuck on the cancer part. "How far along?"

"Patrick's spoken to a lawyer, but—"

"No, not Patrick." Jason interrupted, banging a fist on the table. "*You.* How far along is the cancer?"

"It's in my lungs."

"You already said that." Why was anger the one emotion shooting through his veins? But he was very, very angry. "How long have you known?"

"I've got this nagging cough, and every time I went to do something, I'd get short of breath."

"Why didn't you tell me?" He imagined her wheezing around the kitchen, fixing this big meal. "Should you be lying down?"

"I hate going to doctors, you know that. Plus, once this cough started, I figured I knew the reason. Been smoking my whole life, never once tried to quit." She tapped her two smoking fingers on the table. "A woman's got to have some vices."

"You may not like doctors, but you'll be visiting them a lot more, now." Jason considered his schedule over the next few months, and all the things he could clear.

She shrugged and started cleaning up the table.

"Don't shrug. Don't worry about cleaning up. And don't act like this diagnosis no big deal."

Patrick barreled back inside, glancing around. "Did I leave my phone in here?"

"How long have you known about this?" Jason stood and rounded the table.

"She told you?" Patrick studied him.

"Yeah, she told me."

"I just need a little to cover the cost of the lawyer. This is the last time, I pro—"

"What are you talking about?" Jason shoved against his brother's chest. "I don't care about your legal problems. Ma has cancer. How long have you known?"

"Back off, Jason. I took her to the doctor on Tuesday."

"And no one thought that maybe I'd like to go along?" He clenched his hands into fists at his sides.

"We didn't want to bother you." Patrick glanced around him at the table.

"Yet, you bring me over here to ask for money? Is that all I am to you?" Jason stood chest to chest with his brother. "You call only when you need a bank? Shouldn't I be a part of major shit like this going down in my family? When did I get left out?"

"I don't understand why you're bitching, Jason." Patrick bumped him with his shoulder. "She told you, didn't she?"

Jason stepped back before he threw his brother on the table and beat in his face. "Get out." He jabbed a finger at his brother. "You can work out your own legal problems. I'm done bailing you out." He grabbed the lasagna pan off the table, took it to the kitchen, and threw it in the fridge. The calendar posted on the fridge caught his eye. His mom had a doctor appointment in a few days. He shouted back into the dining room, "Ma, call me, and I'll take you to this doc appointment." Without waiting for a response, he headed out to his car and drove straight to Owen's garage.

Owen's dad had been a mechanic before he'd died of cancer. Maude would know about the disease. She'd guide him through this. Owen's mom, Nancy, and Owen would be helpful, too. But, at first, Jason needed a softer touch, an understanding ear. Hell, he might even cry, and that wasn't something he wanted his Marauders teammate to witness.

Luckily, Owen wasn't in the garage working on his latest project car. After parking off to the side, Jason grabbed a Gatorade out of the fridge and slumped into the Ranchero.

Why had life decided to kick him in the balls? His father was an abusive alcoholic who'd killed his sister when he'd driven drunk. His brother was a dick on his way to prison for assault. Girlfriend pregnant. Mom dying. And the one woman he wanted was his best friend's sister. "Fuck me." He swallowed the cold sports drink, considering how maybe a nice bottle of Kentucky whisky would be so much smoother and erase everything. But no, he wouldn't accept defeat, not yet. He needed answers, and one woman had them.

He grabbed his phone out of his front jeans pocket and texted Maude: *Where you at?*

He waited and waited, but she didn't respond. So, he texted

her again. *I'm out in the garage. Come out and play.*

He ignored a couple texts from Ariel and summoned a chuckle when he read a text from an ex-lover, which said she'd be his "cum cave." He and his football pals had heard it all. For a few weeks one season, they'd all written their most recent and best come-on lines from female fans on the white board in the practice room. Chewy had only beaten him once.

Ariel texted again, rambling on and on about her day, and asked to meet him for lunch sometime that week.

What kind of family was he offering his child? And would he even have any family left when the kid came around? Still, he knew the pain of being hurt by those who were supposed to love you most, so he'd try to establish a friendship with Ariel, for his kid's sake. Plus, tonight he didn't want to be alone.

He texted back: *I'll come by in a few.*

CHAPTER 13

"I'm sorry to bug you." Jason stood outside Ariel's door, hands stuffed in the front pockets of faded jeans and sporting a short-sleeved dark blue Henley that highlighted the lighter blue of his eyes. The man was handsome as sin. He knew it and used it, just like she did, which was part of what made them a perfect match.

"No problem. Come in." Ariel took his arm and led him to her couch. He seemed a little pale. "Is something wrong?"

"Yeah." He rested his head on the back of her couch and sighed. "I just have a messed-up family, you know, which makes me think of you, and the baby." Eyes closed, he shrugged. "Honestly, I don't know what I'm doing here. I shouldn't be."

"Like I said, it's no problem." Ariel smoothed her hair down. Luckily, she hadn't readied for bed yet and still wore her makeup.

Jason had turned to her, come during a time of need. This was her chance to show her compassionate side. "Would you like something to drink?"

"Yeah, sure, whatever." He waved a hand without opening his eyes.

"I just got in from a late work dinner." Her new boss had a sparkle in his eye toward her. While true, she had enticed him enough to get the job, she no longer flirted in any way, especially when Jason was his client. Still, the man almost hadn't taken no for an answer tonight, and she'd had to talk her way out of an awkward situation. Always leave them with a little hope, because she never knew when she might actually need to use the man. "I'll change and grab some drinks. Give me a minute."

Leaving her bedroom door open, she changed into a faded white T-shirt that highlighted her royal blue bra. Then she dug out a pair of short shorts and a comfy pair of socks. After fluffing her hair, she studied herself in the mirror. Should be enough to entice, comfy lounging look without too much seductress.

"Can I order you something to eat?" Stepping out of her bedroom, she headed for the kitchen and grabbed a bottle of white wine off the counter. Using her electric bottle opener, she pulled the cork free and poured one glass. Pregnant women couldn't drink, after all.

Her apartment was basically a living room, attached kitchen, one bedroom and one bath. She'd settled on these modest accommodations for now, spending her money on clothes and beauty products, instead. Besides, once men got here, all they cared about was a soft place to land.

"I'm not hungry," Jason mumbled, seemingly half asleep. He opened his eyes and looked at her, really looked at her. He shifted in his seat then leaned forward, bending his elbows on his knees. "Since I'm here, can I see the pregnancy test? The one with the two lines, or whatever?"

"I'm sorry." Ariel feigned surprise but the nervous laugh wasn't faked. "I threw that away. I didn't realize you'd want to see it."

He studied her for a moment. "This weekend, I'll bring one over and you can take it while I'm here."

She settled behind him on the couch and kneaded his shoulders. "What's wrong, Jason? You seem upset."

"Ariel, don't." Jason shot forward before twisting to face her, lifting his hands, palms up. "I didn't come here for that."

"Didn't you?" She arched a brow and reached for him again.

"No. Listen." He grabbed her wrist and held it at her side. "I'm not that guy anymore, the one seeking solace in sex. Coming here was a mistake. I thought we could be friends, but you're reading everything wrong. I'm trying to be a better man." Releasing her, he raked his fingers through his hair. "You deserve better. I deserve better. A few months ago, I would've taken all you're offering and thought nothing of it, but not today." He shook his head. "I'm sorry, Ariel, but I told you from the beginning, don't look to me for the wedding cake and white picket fence, all right? I came here because I needed to talk." He shifted forward, resting his elbows on his knees. "My Mom has cancer."

"Oh, I'm sorry to hear that." She scooted closer. Damn, he smelled so good, like a sugar cookie and she wanted to take a bite. "What kind of cancer?"

"Well, see that's the thing, I—" His phone buzzed on the coffee table.

Ariel glanced down and saw Maudy flash across the top.

"Excuse me a moment." He grabbed his phone and headed toward the kitchen.

That bitch. She and Jason were having an intimate moment. She'd been about to get fucked, legs-over-her-ears fucked, pounded-into-the-couch-cushions fucked, and that mousy bitch dared to interfere. Hadn't she laid down her warning the other day? Apparently, she'd have to up the stakes against her foe. Not a problem. She could mean-girl all day long.

She eavesdropped. His low tone and softly spoken words were audible in her small space. A space she'd decorated in soft blues and greens, creating a relaxing atmosphere. Some of her friends were more blatant in their apartment's color schemes, but she wasn't living with a red light flickering in her window, so her apartment shouldn't reflect that. She had a classy place, because she'd become a classy woman.

"I was at the garage earlier."

"I'm at Ariel's."

"Listen, can I call you back?"

"Okay. Hey, where were you earlier?"

Damn it! Possessiveness in his tone. Not good.

"I see. All right then, give me a bit and I'll call, unless it'll be too late."

"Thanks, Maudy."

Jason sauntered back into the room. His huge frame took up so much space. She'd been to his apartment. Large rooms. Large doorways. Large bed.

"Is everything all right?" She walked over to him, back straight, attributes on full display.

He rubbed the back of his neck. "I'm heading out. Thanks for letting me visit." He glanced at the door, stepped forward, and wrapped her in an awkward one-armed hug.

A fucking hug! *Oh, no.* She was more than primed and long overdue for sexual acrobats. Jason was one of the few men who saw to her needs first—and she had some serious needs right now.

"My head's not on straight. This thing with my mom...and with you...I need to find out more about what's going on."

"Do you know what type of cancer?" Gripping his elbow, she led him back to the couch.

She sat, he didn't.

"Lung cancer." He rocked back on his heels before glancing at the door again. "How are you feeling?"

"I get tired, and my chest hurts. I've been massaging myself, though." She flashed a wicked grin and lounged back on the couch. "You could help me." She lifted her shirt, nudged aside her bra, and massaged her breasts.

He shook his head and averted his gaze. "Not real subtle."

"Mmm..." She rubbed her thighs together. "It's all these hormones. A girl needs relief." She reached across and rubbed his cock through his jeans. "I think you need relief, too." She continued the caress, pressing harder when she heard him hiss.

"Let me take care of this for you. Just a friend doing a favor for a friend." Stretching, she pulled down his zipper.

"No." He jerked away. "I won't do this." He knelt and cupped her chin with his warm hand. "I told you, I'm not that guy anymore."

She leaned forward and touched his thigh. "I really think you should stay."

"Ariel, stop. No more." He shook his head then tugged her shirt over her breasts. "I won't use you for sex."

"Nothing wrong with two people enjoying one another, Jason."

"I agree. But at some point people want sex to mean something. I think I've reached that point, and if you and I are going to be friends, having sex is off the table." He sighed and straightened. "You deserve more."

"It's not about what *I* deserve." She tweaked her hardened nipples with her fingers. "Let me take all that sorrow out of your eyes."

"For a moment, yeah, you could, but the feeling wouldn't last." Jason leaned over and kissed her forehead.

Like she was a child who needed placating. Then he had the audacity to pat her shoulder.

This was all Maude's fault.

He'd been primed and ready to sink into her. Without that phone call, they'd be testing every surface of her apartment right now.

Maude had ruined everything, and she'd pay.

Ariel stood and wrapped her arms around Jason. "I can't help but think that phone call changed the pattern of this night. I won't deny I want you back in my bed, Jason. I get so hot thinking about you and me together. You know how to please a woman." She cupped his ass and rocked back-and-forth in his arms. Like a slow dance. "We were good together." She pressed a kiss to the bottom V of his shirt then stood on her tiptoes to kiss him.

He didn't kiss her back. "I can't, Ariel. I'm sorry." Jason eased away. "This visit tonight was between two friends. We may have a future together, we may not, so let's not complicate matters more than they already are." He dropped another light peck on her cheek. "I'll see myself out. Have a good night."

She watched him leave. Obviously, in a raging hurry to speak with that mousy little bitch. Overcome by fury, Ariel tossed his wine glass against the wall. It shattered and trickled white wine all over her beige carpet.

Biting back a scream, she crumpled to the floor. Two things became absolutely mandatory: she needed to research ways to pass a pregnancy test, and Maude Killion had to go.

CHAPTER 14

Saturday morning, bright and early at the Rec Center's second clean-up day, Maude stirred a can of light blue paint with a broken measuring stick. She got lost in the swirling motion as she recalled her two-hour conversation with Jason on Thursday night. He'd told her about his mom's cancer, about his pain over losing his friendship with his brother, and his worry they only included him when they needed money. She'd asked if he wanted to meet out in the garage, but he'd said spilling his problems over the phone was easier.

He'd asked about treatments and she'd explained that each cancer was different and he needed to know exactly what kind his mother had and how severe her stage. She'd even offered to send her mom over to talk to his mom. She'd talked about how she'd felt watching her dad suffer through the disease. Sharing her feelings with Jason brought about another level of healing. He would run through a similar gamut of emotions during the disease's progression, and after. Another important aspect of her healing was her work with kids who'd suffered through losing a parent to the disease. Maude led a support group each Monday night at the Cancer Treatment Center on the north side of Manchester.

Right before they'd hung up, Jason said he'd opened his

heart to her and that she needed to take care of it. What in the world had that meant? Opened his heart how? After all these years pining over him and wishing for this very thing, she had serious doubts his words were any real pathway to a long-term relationship.

Hope was a very dangerous emotion, especially when her heart hurt enough…over Brady's betrayal, Ariel's machinations, Jason's odd behavior, and change in general. She had no idea what to do or when to do it, or any actual idea what in the world had happened to her calm, ordered life.

Then, hearing Jason's voice in the hallway, she was drawn from her reverie. Egged on by her wayward heart, she leaned out into the hall to catch a glimpse. There he stood, just inside the front doors, talking to Owen, with Ariel draped on his arm.

The stick Maude hadn't realized she'd pulled from the bucket dripped paint all over her shoe, just like the drips coming from her bleeding heart. "Dramatic much, Killion?" she grumbled then scanned the room for a paper towel. After dropping the stir-stick back into the can, she wiped up her mess.

Ariel sported a cute pink sweat suit, likely the only grubby clothes in her closet. Maude's attire was due for the trashcan after today. Although, her paint-and-grease stained jeans and ripped T-shirt, were her usual weekend wear.

She hadn't mentioned Ariel's little work game to Jason. He had enough worries, and she could fight her own battles. That thought spurred her on. She'd waited a long time for Jason Stafford to finally see her, the real her. Ariel Silvers wouldn't stop her from obtaining the one man right for her. The one who'd always been right, and always would be right. She'd never been one for verbal or physical brawling, but she could try, she supposed. Sometimes, it didn't pay to be nice.

Determined, she held her head high and walked out to greet them. "Good morning." Maude smiled at Jason. "Ariel, glad you could come. We have all the paint supplies in the kitchen area.

Let's get you two set up." She maintained her professional facade as she handed over their supplies and led them to the room where Bronco and Owen already worked.

"You know, Ariel." Maude turned and met her gaze. "Now that I think about it, I don't know that paint fumes are good for the baby. Maybe you should sit this one out."

"Oh, is that true?" Ariel's perfectly-tipped nails rose to cover her mouth. "So many things I'll need to learn."

Maude just smiled, unsure if that were true, because neither she, nor anyone else, knew if the woman was really pregnant. Somebody needed to figure that out, and fast. That person being one, Jason Stafford. Why hadn't he demanded she take a test by now, anyway? What was he thinking?

"I came with Jason, so he'd have to take me home."

He'd already joined his pals, barely offering Maude more than a quick hello hug. What had she expected? Him to fall on his knees and kiss her feet?

Maude bit her lip and met Ariel's gaze again. "Actually, Jason doesn't need to take you home. Ember was headed out for more primer. She can take you when she goes." Score one for Maude's team. "I'll text her and see if she's leaving soon." Pulling her phone from her back pocket, Maude shot Ember a text asking if she'd take Ariel home.

"That's all right." Ariel waved her away and bent to pick up a paintbrush. "I don't even know if the fumes will bother me."

"The smell is pretty intense in here." Bronco piped up, halting in his rolling to glance over his shoulder. "I've already got a killer headache."

Maude just loved Bronco, sometimes. She winked at him.

He winked back.

Ember arrived, jiggling her keys. "I'm ready. Ariel, I'll take you home. I agree, paint fumes are bad for pregnant women."

"Jason brought me, so he should take me home."

Her voice slipped into a slight-Southern accent. *Interesting.*

"Oh, it's no problem." Ember smiled at Ariel, took her arm, and led her from the room. "We want you healthy, right?"

Ember's past was strewn with manipulative, evil people. Maybe she could discover a crack in Ariel's persona. "Thanks, Ember." Maude waved them away, inwardly grinning, but feeling a slight twinge of guilt. Although, if Ariel was pregnant, paint fumes were hazardous. Considering that, Maude opened a few windows to create an airflow.

Turning on her heel, Maude headed back to her own area, but she halted when Jason grabbed her arm.

"Come with me a minute."

Barely able to keep up with his long strides, she followed him down the corridor to an old gym. No overhead lights, along with the gray skies, kept the room dark.

Which might have been a good thing, because her mind blanked the moment Jason shoved her against the wall and kissed her.

In shock, she took a moment to catch up with his hungry lips before shoving against his chest. "What are you doing? What is this?"

He smiled his wicked playboy smile and drew her lower body against his own. "Gratitude."

"Gratitude for what?" Maude drew a deep breath, fighting past whatever blocked her throat and caused her heart to thunder.

He tucked her hair behind her ear. "For listening to me the other night."

"I didn't mind. I don't want gratitude from you. I want…I don't know, because I can't believe this is real. You kissing me isn't doing anything but confusing me." She stepped out of his arms. "Plus, you came with Ariel."

"I didn't leave with her."

"Oh, that's a great line, one I'm sure you've used often, but with me…no. Just no. I don't do lines, and I don't do grateful kisses." She needed to calm down. Her words echoed throughout the empty gym. God forbid, Owen should hear. Choosing a different tactic, one that might offer the answers she so desperately needed, she took his hand. "What are you doing? I'm not the kind of girl who just does this." She waved a hand between them. "I don't understand what you want from me. I left a relationship with Brady because I couldn't be who he needed me to be. I won't enter another because you need a friend. Please, don't use me this way."

"You're right." Jason raked his fingers through his hair before placing both hands on his hips. "I don't know what I'm doing. I just...I am so tired of being manipulated, but you make me..." Shaking his head, he sighed. "I don't have any idea why I do what I do. I never think things through, and I don't want to think about the whys of us, Maude. Why can't we just be?"

"Because, when you give someone your heart, they tend to want to return the favor. And what happens when I give you mine? Can I trust you with it?" His answer to this question meant everything, and a few years ago she'd never would have asked, just taken whatever he was willing to give. But, she was smarter now, and she wouldn't settle for anything less than a man who was all-in.

"Probably not." Jason wrapped his big hand around the back of her neck before lightly kissing her lips. "You're right. I shouldn't have dragged you down here, but I was excited to see you."

"Ah, Jason." Maude wrapped him in a hug, unable to remain unmoved when he said such honest and sweet things. "What are we going to do?"

"I know what I'd *like* to do." Bumping against her hips, he squeezed her bottom.

Maude placed her hand against his chest. "Keep that fertile stick away from me." Hearing his laughter, she shook her head and got serious. "Speaking of sticks, did Ariel show you the test?"

Jason glanced at the door before he scuffed the tip of his

grungy tennis shoe against the wood floor. "She said she threw it away."

"Jason…" Maude rubbed her forehead. Why would he believe such a thing?

"I know. I'll get the truth. Don't worry, Maudy." He cupped her cheek in his hand. "I'm not sleeping with her. I'm not dating her. I *will* figure things out. Okay?"

Maude nodded then leaned up and lightly kissed him, because why not? Might be the last kiss ever. Once he no longer needed a friend, he might abandon her. Go back to his party lifestyle, so she had to tread carefully.

"Your lips are like pillows, you know that?" After he whispered against her ear, he placed a hot kiss on her neck.

All thoughts of being careful flew out the door, as well as every legitimate reason not to rip off all her clothes and beg him to take her on this dusty floor…against the bleachers, maybe pressed against the door.

"Listen, you might be right about my reasons for being interested in you now, and you might not." Jason placed his hands on her shoulders. "You have always been this girl I couldn't touch, but now…I feel as if you're the only thing keeping me grounded. I need you—your friendship and your honesty. But, is that enough to take this further? I don't know." He cupped her face in his hand. "What I do know is I really needed you the other night, and you were there for me. I'm so tied down by the demands of my family, my friends, my team, my fans, but with you, I can just be me. That's a gift. Something very rare and I cherish it. I always have."

How many times could her heart break? Jason tended to joke and use sarcasm to hide his true feelings, but that man wasn't before her today. Still, she had no idea what this change meant for the future. "Stafford, you are very smooth."

"I've had lots of practice." He winked, and the cocky player was back.

"I'm aware."

"So? What of it? All my skills will pay off in the end."

"Will they?"

"Yes." He tweaked her nose with his index finger.

A familiar move between them. One she'd grown to hate as it was condescending, but today, she took the action as him being playful. Flirtatious. "I have a few tricks of my own." She licked her bottom lip then bit it.

"Oh, I like naughty Maudy." He tugged her lip from her teeth then hovered with his lips over hers. "She can come out to play, anytime."

"She can, but the question remains, will she?" After throwing down that gauntlet, she shoved away and opened the gym door.

He followed and nudged her shoulder. "Be careful, or you might get spanked by a paint brush."

"Whatever." She rolled her eyes then turned to go back to her paint can.

He gave her a mock salute and then slapped her butt. "See ya around, Killion."

CHAPTER 15

"I kind of get it." Leaning against the kitchen counter, Rachel plucked a big hunk of hard-boiled egg from Ember's potato salad and plopped it in her mouth.

They'd come back to Owen's after painting all day. Ember was putting the final touches on their meal, without much help from Rachel's sneaky fingers.

"Jason's carefree lifestyle suddenly gets disrupted," Rachel continued her musings after Maude had explained what happened in the gym. "He's faced with being a father. Unsure of what to do, he seeks shelter with someone he trusts. So, yeah, it could be a temporary thing, but I honestly can't say."

"Life would be much simpler if we could see the future, right?" Ember set out a tray of veggies then removed the lid and film from the top of the ranch dip container. "Have you heard much from Brady?" She set ketchup and mustard next to the plates and napkins.

Maude remained slumped in the kitchen chair, feeling guilty about not helping, but her arms were tired after painting all day. "I see Brady at work, but besides that he pretty much leaves me be. I asked for space and he's giving it, although a couple of times he's come by my desk to chat and he didn't used to do that. We're both too busy to take time out of our day to visit, so that's been kind of awkward."

"I've been meaning to ask you something." Rachel brushed

off her hands.

Maude groaned. "Is it about the Facebook post?"

"Yeah." Rachel tilted her head. "Kind of rude, Maude."

"What do you mean?" Her friend's tone seemed accusatory not consoling. "I didn't post it."

"Yeah, ya did." Rachel scoffed. "Not nice."

"I don't think you guys are talking about the same post." Ember glanced at them both before sipping her white wine.

Rachel frowned. "I don't like missing a puzzle piece, so what are you talking about?"

"Maude's talking about Brady's nudie pic, right?" Ember pointed at her.

"Yeah."

"And what are you talking about?" Ember turned to Rachel.

"Yesterday, I posted a picture of a new stripe on my jujitsu belt, and Maude made a comment like, I figured you'd be a black belt by now."

"What?" Maude slammed her beer bottle down on the table hard enough that foam poured out the top. "Why would I say that?"

"Yeah, why would you?" But Rachel wasn't really asking her, she just voiced the thought out loud, like her investigative mind was mulling the problem over, taking the matter and looking at it from a different perspective.

"Someone either hacked your account or knows your password. I'd change it. Right now." Rachel stomped over and held out her hand. "Give me your phone. Ember, you got a pen and some paper?"

Maude blinked, not quite following Rachel's thought process. "I didn't say anything about your belt. *I* didn't make that comment."

"I get that now." Rachel jabbed her shoulder. "It's all good."

"But you were mad at me?"

Rachel shrugged and pinched her forefinger and thumb close

together. "A little."

Maude gasped before wrapping her tiny friend in a big hug. "Oh my gosh, Rachel. I'm sorry. It really wasn't me."

"I know that, and I should have known that. You're squishing me."

"Then why didn't you say something before?" Maude eased back to look in her friend's brown eyes and saw something that looked a lot like hurt.

"I don't know what's wrong with me. This relationship crap with Bronco's got me mentally deranged. I figured I was being an oversensitive cow." Rachel pressed her small hand against Maude's chest. "You're squishing me between your huge boobs, woman. I don't roll that way, so back it off."

Maude laughed. Rachel tended to say anything at any time. "I really am sorry, Rachel."

"Gah, just give me your phone. We'll switch the password and add in a few other features so if someone tries to log in again, we can trace it back."

"Is that true?" Maude somehow doubted the ability to fire through the air on cell phone waves to catch a culprit, but then again, she didn't know anything about spy gadgets. "Don't put anything illegal on my phone."

Rachel chuckled. "As if I would."

"You so would." Ember and Maude said the same words at the exact same time, and then looked at each other and burst out laughing.

# # #

After their laugh fest, Maude and Ember had calmed their giggles and poked toothpicks through cherry tomatoes, mozzarella cheese, and basil leaves, constructing her little Caprese salad bites. Though she'd laughed along with her friends, Maude remained disturbed over someone making comments under her name. Were other comments out there? Who would do that? Her suspicions automatically turned to Brady, as he knew where she kept all her passwords. She jabbed a tomato extra hard while considering the hassle of updating everything.

Not to mention her absolute confusion over Jason's kisses. How had she stood so strong against him? Part of his attraction was his carefree way. She'd always believed that her calm, organized nature would mesh well with his jump-off-the-cliff boldness. Together, they'd find a middle ground. And now, more than ever, she wanted to soar with him, but she had to be sure of a soft place to land.

"Oh, no." Rachel's eyes went wide.

Mid-stream in her pour of Italian herb-flavored olive oil, Maude halted and stared at her plate. "What's wrong? Do you think I'm using too much?"

"No," Rachel whispered out the side of her mouth. "Don't turn around."

"Why?" Arching a brow, Maude slapped Rachel's hand away from the cheese cubes. "Because now I'm curious, and all I want to do is turn around." She shook a bottle of balsamic vinegar before drizzling it across her appetizer, and then sprinkled a Mediterranean herb mix over the top.

"Here, use this." Ember placed a sprig of basil in the center. "There, all finished and so pretty."

"No, it's ugly."

"Rachel, that's not nice." Maude frowned at her friend.

"No, no, not that." Rachel placed her Dixie cup in front of her mouth as if she were imparting national secrets and didn't want anyone reading her lips.

"Your boy just showed up with the blonde."

"They're friends." Maude shrugged, though her heart was anything but nonchalant over the news.

Ember and Rachel stared wide-eyed.

Their looks indicating they both wanted to say something but would refrain. At least, Ember did. Rachel, not so much.

"She sabotaged your job. She's fake pregnant. She's psycho-clingy." Rachel emphasized each point with a jab of her index finger against the countertop. "Say the word, and I'll investigate her. I'm dying to find out if those roots are real." Eyes narrowed, she sipped from her cup. "Might dig, anyway, because something is definitely there."

Maude wouldn't tell her friend no, because honestly she was curious, herself. Plus, she didn't want Jason hurt.

Rachel tapped her cup against the counter. "Mark my words, if this thing with you and Jason continues, then she'll strike again. Everybody always thinks, oh it's no big deal, I can handle it, but let me tell you something. Things get out of hand real fast. People do horrific things to one another over the stupidest, most minor of offenses. She's already struck once." Rachel stuck a toothpick in her mouth and met her gaze. "The very last thing I want is you hurt, or dead, because Ariel lost her mind over Jason."

Maude couldn't discount her words. Though she'd told Jason she wasn't naïve, in many ways, she was. Be kind. Be fair. Those were the qualities her mother had taught her, but she'd recently discovered sometimes she had to look at life with a more cynical eye. Sad lesson, really. "Maybe, Ariel and I could have a reasonable conversation about Jason and me, but I'm not even sure if there *is* a Jason and me, or if he's just confused, or I'm confused." She huffed out a breath. "I have no idea."

"You've lost your damn mind, girl." Rachel tossed a toothpick at her head.

Ember patted her shoulder. "I think Jason is completely out of his element with this girl. Time will tell, but I'm a little worried. I hate to say this, Maude." Ember winced. "But Ariel is a fighter, and you…well…"

"I'm pampered, never had a rough day in my life. I know all this, and honestly, I don't want any more trouble, because you're right, I'm not a fighter."

"You might not have a choice." Ember squeezed her shoulder.

"Then I'll draw my strength from you and Rachel." Maude offered a soft smile to her friends. "You've both been through so much. I can only hope to be as strong as you two, one day."

"Group hug." Rachel wrapped her slim arms around them both.

"Thanks, guys." Maude leaned her head against Ember's shoulder. "I hope Ariel doesn't try to poison me. I'll sniff my food before I eat it today."

"Jerk, that's not funny." Rachel shoved free.

"You're just hoping for more fodder for those suspense books you write," Maude shot back.

"True." Rachel tilted her head and flashed a smug smile. "And not to throw storm clouds over your rainbow, but Jason is Jason. He's not really…known for…ya know…consistency with women."

Maude pretended she didn't see Ember's flinch at Rachel's words. They didn't know Jason the way she did, hadn't been there when he'd poured out his heart. Sure, he had that devil-may-care side, but he had many others, too. Maybe she was fooling herself, but this fear inside felt more like her own insecurities over not being enough for him versus the truth.

Because, up until now, having Jason Stafford was only a dream, the reality scared her to death. But, hadn't she just promised to be strong? These women before her didn't back down from anyone and had overcome horrific struggles, so to make them and herself proud, she would defeat her self-doubt. Believe in herself. "I've been waiting for Jason my whole life, but now that I have this chance, I'm almost afraid to take it. But then I see him, and I say, jump." Maude glanced at her friends, who both nodded their agreement.

"I say go for it." Rachel's brown eyes met her own.

She always had a little shimmer in them, like she really was a tiny pixie just as her small frame suggested.

"Here they come," Rachel mumbled, keeping her gaze locked on the approachers.

Maude shoved down all her worries as she prepared to be a gracious hostess. Taking a deep breath, she turned and smiled. "Hello, Ariel, how are you feeling?"

After working at the Rec Center all morning, Maude had come home and scrubbed the paint from her face and arms. Dressed in her best pair of jeans and a purple top that hugged her body well, she'd also thrown on some mascara and a little lip gloss, knowing she'd see Jason. Was this her life now, trying to out-pretty a woman who made personal grooming her life's mission? No way could she keep up unless she borrowed millions of dollars from her brother and visited some spa deep in the Swedish mountains. *Maude Killion, stop feeling sorry for yourself.* The words shot through her mind in her mother's chastising tone, making her question her sanity. Hearing voices, considering she had a chance with Jason...yeah, she'd lost her mind.

"I'm well, thanks." Ariel smiled up at Jason as if he were the reason her spirits were so high.

"What kind of trouble's brewing over here?" Jason leaned against the kitchen's center island, plopping one of her tomatoes in his mouth. "I love these." He shot Maude a wink before devouring a couple more.

On the verge of slapping his hand so he wouldn't eat them all, she went from saying, "Stop that" to a yelp when he grabbed her hand and tugged.

"Do you have a second? My lawyer called earlier and had some questions about the paperwork for the Rec Center."

Ariel snapped around, gaze darting back and forth between her and Jason. "Tom didn't say anything to me."

"Nothing to be concerned about." Jason waved Ariel off and then nudged Maude away from the group, toward the stairs. "Will you ladies excuse us for a minute?"

Ariel frowned, but luckily Ember acted fast by offering her a drink and drawing her toward the back patio.

Jason led Maude up to her room, which was currently filled with boxes and in complete disarray as she prepared to move. He shoved her through the door and then shut and locked it.

"What are you doing? You can't keep dragging me off to secret rooms."

He'd gone home to change, too, and his faded jeans and old college tee looked mighty fine on his burly body. His hair was still damp, and he hadn't gotten all the paint off his arm.

"What's all this?" He glanced around. "Oh, that's right, you're moving." He frowned at the boxes then met her gaze. "I brought you up here to explain."

"Explain what?"

"Ariel called and said I'd left a few items at her house." He cleared his throat then shoved one hand in his front pocket, gesturing with the other. "From before…" He waved his hand.

A gesture he probably thought would explain the entirety of his relationship with Ariel. It didn't.

"When I was there, she asked if I'd like to stay for dinner. I told her I had plans to come here, and she says, "Oh, that's sounds fun, I'll get ready." As if I invited her." He shook his head. "I'm sorry, but I'm just trying to keep the peace with Ariel until I find out if she's truly pregnant. Tyrone is worried about negative press and…"

"It's fine." Ariel being in her home wasn't really fine, but Maude was touched he'd felt it necessary to explain. Another side her friends didn't see. True, he could have brushed Ariel off, but he'd never be purposefully cruel. He'd lost his sister, so he tended to be overprotective of women. Maybe that blinded him, sometimes. "Thanks for explaining. I don't know how to feel about Ariel, and maybe you don't, either. I feel like we're all in some kind of holding pattern."

"No." Jason shook his head and closed the distance between

them.

Maude swallowed past the lump in her throat. "No?"

"No." He wrapped an arm around her waist and pulled her against his body. "I should be in a holding pattern, and I should hold off, but I—"

A sharp knock came on the door, followed by Bronco's deep voice. "Yo, Stafford. Red alert. Owen's looking for you." His chuckle practically rumbled through the door. "I'd say you got three minutes. So, hustle."

"Shit." Jason raked his fingers through his hair. "Maude, you really have to stop pawing me all the time. Owen wouldn't like you molesting his best friend." He released a dramatic sigh and shook his head. "I know it's hard to resist all this"—he waved a hand down his body—"but please, try."

Maude chuckled. "You are so full of it." She scraped at the paint on his arm, avoiding his gaze. "You know, if you really want to be with me, you'll have to tell Owen sometime."

"I'd prefer to wait until pre-season, when I'm wearing a lot more padding."

"Good idea." Was that really why? Or did Jason know he would be back to his carefree lifestyle by then? *Insecurity much, Killion?*

"Hey, will you stop digging your nails into me for a second and listen?" He smacked her hand away from his arm. "Look at me." He lifted her chin with an index finger. "I already said something to him. I told you that."

"You did?" Maude scanned her memories, but nothing popped up.

"Yes, the other day, remember?"

"Um, no."

"Yeah, that's pretty much what Owen said." Dropping his hand from her face, Jason sighed then rubbed the back of his neck.

"What he said to what? I'm confused."

"I told him I was interested in you, and he said no."

"He doesn't get to say no." Frowning, Maude crossed both arms over her chest, her mind firing with choice words for her brother. "Owen has no right to—"

Jason placed a finger over her lips. "Yeah…yeah, he does. He's my best friend. He knows me, and he loves you. He has every right." He opened the door and quickly ducked out before stepping from her room. "All clear." He gripped her shoulder. "Listen, let me handle your brother. He and I will discuss any issues when the time comes."

"That's what I'm afraid of. I know how Owen handles his anger."

"Oh, he won't be angry, he'll be homicidal."

# # #

"You understand why this is necessary, right?" Jason leaned against Ariel's bathroom doorway. "In my profession, we see a lot of this. A friend of mine recently got burned, I'm sure you heard all the stories in the news. I'm sorry, but I don't really know you, and I need actual proof of this pregnancy."

"It's all right, Jason." Ariel flicked open the bright pink box and unwrapped the test.

He averted his gaze for a minute while she got situated. He'd left Owen's early and driven Ariel home. Normally, he stayed and crashed in the spare bedroom. Overall, the group had a nice time talking football and eating burgers by Owen's pool. Ember and Maude had tried to engage Ariel in conversation, but Ariel had spent the majority of the evening talking and flirting with Chewy.

Tired from painting at the Rec Center all day, Jason had planned on dropping her off and then heading home. Instead, she mentioned she'd bought a couple pregnancy tests and was willing to take one tonight in order to "expel his doubt" as she'd phrased it. Now that he was here, faced with the consequences of his indiscretions, he almost wished Maude was at his side, holding his hand, but that was the weirdest, not to mention rudest, thought he'd ever had. *Man up, Stafford.* Still, thinking about Maude's gentle smile and soft brown eyes did bring a level of comfort. He'd get through this with Ariel and then slowly, but surely, figure out what he and Maude were meant to be.

At this point, he wished he hadn't eaten so much because he was on the verge of tossing everything. He closed his eyes and took a couple deep breaths. This moment could change everything. Would hearing she was a grandmother make his ma fight harder to beat her cancer? She'd told him she was in Stage three. After researching what that meant, he'd shut off his phone and hit the punching bag for a couple hours. He had a sinking sensation he'd be doing the same thing tonight.

"Oh, shoot." Ariel's jeans pooled by her feet as she sat on the toilet.

"What?" Jason shifted his gaze to her face.

She held up an empty paper roll. "I have more in the closet. Can you grab me some?"

"Sure." He turned and opened the hall closet's door. Wow, he'd never seen so many beauty products in his life…but no toilet paper. "Um…I don't—"

"It's on the bottom."

"I see." He tugged free a roll and handed it over.

She did her business and tidied up. "And now, we wait." She drummed her nails along her copper bowl sink. "Would you like a drink?"

"I'm good. I just want to get this done and get home." He didn't think he'd blinked or breathed since she set the test on the back of the toilet.

"This test is supposed to be faster." She glanced down at the stick and nodded. "Oh, it's ready." She held the box and the test right at his eye line. "See? I wasn't lying."

Two stripes.

Pregnant.

He sucked in a breath and bent over. He'd been hit on the field. A lot. But damned if this wasn't a game-winning gut punch. "You weren't lying," he managed to whisper, mostly to himself.

"No." Smiling, she tapped the stick against her palm before laying it on the counter.

The two bright pink lines were like a beacon, blinding him with an absolute truth, signaling an earth-shattering change.

Two pink lines that made the fact clear he was responsible for another life.

A father.

He simply nodded before turning and walking out of the apartment with absolutely no destination in mind, because nothing could erase those two pink lines burned forever into his corneas. Nothing.

CHAPTER 16

Maude tossed her phone on her desk. This Wednesday was the perfect definition of a hump day, from the gray skies outside her office to the worry in her heart. She hadn't heard from Jason since Owen's cookout on Saturday. She'd even asked Ember if Owen had seen him, as they generally worked out together in the mornings.

Ember said he hadn't been around all week.

Had he changed his mind about the direction of their relationship? Or had he slept with Ariel the night he left? She hated to even consider such a thing. Why couldn't she have more faith? What really worried her was, due to Jason's mother's illness and his stress over possibly becoming a father, perhaps the anniversary of his sister's death was hitting him harder this year.

When Maude was nineteen, she'd accidentally walked in on Jason talking to Owen about his father's release on bail and relocation to a retirement home. Jason raged and then broke, sobbing against Owen's shoulder while her brother kept him wrapped in his burly arms. The moment hadn't lasted long, but Jason sounded like he released a lifetime of torment. He'd even stayed with them for a few months before moving back to his place.

Unsure on what to do now, she sat and stared at her laptop's screen. The numbers on the Excel sheet had her eyes crossing. Her stomach growled, and she realized she'd worked through lunch. She stood and stretched, wondering if she could make it to Jason's apartment and back in an hour.

"Been working too hard, again?" Brady walked up to her area, wearing black slacks and a teal button-down shirt. He'd rolled up the sleeves, revealing his lion tattoo.

Maude held back a giggle. The whole king of the jungle thing really was over the top.

"I came down to see if maybe we could do lunch." Brady stuffed his hands in his front pockets and rocked back on his heels. "You haven't eaten yet, have you?"

"All right." They hadn't really had a chance to discuss the Facebook photo incident. Nor had she secretly interrogated him on whether or not he had played games with her account. She'd changed all her social media and email passwords. As far as she knew, no further incidents of someone using her identity had occurred. "Actually, I am a little hungry." Maude shut off her computer, not as if she'd been an overly productive employee today, anyway. "Let me straighten up my area a little."

Making peace with Brady might keep him out of mischief and make their work relationship less awkward. They could be friends, because they truly did have a lot in common. Same college, same major, same company. Clearing things between them would hopefully ease others' discomfiture when they both attended social engagements with their mutual friends and coworkers.

"Should we hit our Thai place?"

Maude's internal warning system clamored, as that restaurant was where they'd started their relationship. The place had a quiet, intimate setting. Not the type of place two friends would dine. Perhaps transitioning into friendship so soon wasn't the grandest idea she'd ever had. "I was hoping for something a little quicker. Plus, I don't think eating at that particular place is…well, I would rather not eat there. I'm sorry. I just feel that restaurant wouldn't be...appropriate."

"Maude." Brady clasped her arm. "You asked for time. I've given it to you, but nothing is settled between us. I'm in limbo here and...not knowing hurts." He placed a hand against his breastbone. "All I'm asking is for a few minutes of your time. I'd like to work things out."

A thousand conflicting thoughts rushed through her mind. Did she really want to be with him when he'd been so odd the last time they were together? Yet, didn't she owe him a final decision? Wouldn't tearing off the Band-Aid today be kinder? Although, she'd already stated her intentions, perhaps he really did need further clarification. "All right, we'll go." Maude squeezed his hand. "I'm sorry if I wasn't clear before, but we'll go to lunch and discuss a few things."

His claim that he was hurting surprised her. Though, she couldn't pinpoint why. Maybe because she'd always felt he was using her as a pathway to the Marauders' public relations office. Were her own insecurities clouding her real value in Brady's eyes? Perhaps. None of that mattered now, because though they had a lot in common on the surface, Brady was too competitive, too domineering. He wanted those around him to bow to his greatness, to see him as something special. At first, Maude had been drawn to his shine, but that wore off quickly, burned too bright, especially once she understood he never intended to share the spotlight.

Brady pressed a hand against the small of her back and directed her toward the elevators. They took his car across town and were promptly seated as the main lunch rush had tapered off. Over her objections to their dining choice, she still sat across from him at their favorite Thai restaurant. A trendy place on a street where a person wouldn't think such a nice establishment existed. Within the restaurant, booths lined the outside walls and tables for two filled the middle. The color scheme was black and maroon, with local artists' paintings for sale on the walls.

After the waiter took their orders, Brady reached across the table and held her hand. "Thanks for coming today. I've thought a lot about my behavior and how some of my actions and words may have seemed unsupportive or callous. I apologize if I've ever made you feel as if I were using you for the advancement of my career and for my less-than-flattering reaction to your acquiring the Rec Center account." He shifted forward in his seat. "The thing is, we make a good team, and maybe in the future we could work together on projects. We get along well, have for months now, and I'm not ready to give that up."

"Thank you for that." Maude stalled a moment, unsure how to continue. His words seemed so sincere, but deep down she worried he'd resume his overbearing behavior. Plus, she'd already moved on emotionally—with Jason. With that thought in mind, she eased her hand from Brady's grip and rested it in her lap. "I *have* always felt you were disappointed because I couldn't get you a job with my brother's team. And I do feel you are overly competitive at work."

"Maude, look at me." Brady shook his head, his lips pursed. "How can I reassure you if you don't tell me how you feel? I can't defend myself if I don't know why I'm on trial, and that isn't fair." He dropped his gaze to the table, running a finger along the edge of the black tablecloth. "I believed you and I would be together long-term. We're perfect for each other on so many levels. I love you, Maude." He lifted his gaze. "I thought you loved me, too?"

Maude took a deep breath, exhaled slowly, and leaned back in her seat, as if his words had struck and were, bit-by-bit, weighing her down.

The waiter delivered their food, giving her a few more moments to think.

Could she and Brady work things out? Was she out of her mind to believe she could go from a relationship with Brady to Jason Stafford? Was Jason even capable of an adult relationship?

Sure, he'd kissed her, but how did that make her any different from his stable of women? With Brady, she'd never experienced this endless churning in her stomach as worries tumbled like nuts and bolts on a never-ending spin cycle.

No. She clenched her hands together in her lap. *Remember your fresh start, Killion.* False hope and Brady's smooth words wouldn't, and shouldn't, keep her in a relationship. She met Brady's gaze. No sparkle. No flash. No passion.

"Brady, you *are* right." Maude swirled the Thai noodles around with her fork. "We are well-matched in a lot of ways. We could surround ourselves with a white-picket fence. Have two kids and settle into a perfect home. Everything would be good." She took a deep breath and met his hopeful gaze. "But I want more than good. I want spark and intensity and chaos." She noted his furrowed brow and that he'd stopped eating. "I did love you, and still do, but not in a long-term way. I'm sorry."

Brady straightened his silverware on the table before taking a sip of his chai tea. "What more do you want? I'm willing to give you everything. As a matter of fact, I already have." He pounded a fist against his chest, right above his heart. "I'm not willing to let you go. I will fight for us, Maude, even if you won't."

Uh, oh, this is new. Perhaps he really didn't see the faults in their relationship. Or, maybe she'd never given Brady a true chance, because she'd been blinded by her forever crush on Jason Stafford.

And right now, she was so close to that dream.

Still, her heart faltered a little, because Brady seemed so earnest. She needed to be clear they were over. He'd never been overly effusive about his feelings, so his words today were a tad shocking, to say the least. A side of Brady she'd never seen. But, still...a case of too little, too late.

"Please, Brady." She met his gaze and kept her tone calm. "Please, listen this time. I don't mean to wound you, but continuing this relationship is unhealthy both emotionally and…well, even sometimes physically. You have a domineering side I don't like. I am not the right woman for you." She patted his hand. "I would like us to remain professional at work and perhaps, after a time, we could become friends."

"I absolutely disagree." He clenched both hands on the table. "I won't give up."

Was this display part of his competitive nature? Did he feel he had to win her back? "Brady, you asked for my decision, and I've given it. Now, while we're here, we should discuss the photo you posted the other day." She folded her hands together on the table, breathing steadily, because a confrontation was coming. She'd have to channel her inner Rachel.

Brady simply shrugged and flicked a hand at the waiter.

Maude narrowed her eyes. "I listened to you, now I'd appreciate the same courtesy in return."

The waiter arrived and Brady asked for a box. Since he didn't ask for two, she asked herself.

When the waiter left, she nudged his arm to garner his attention. "Posting that partially nude picture was completely uncalled for. First of all, I have no idea when you took that photo. Second, private moments between us should remain exactly that. Private." She eyed him as she continued, "Not only that, I've had a few odd incidents occur recently: my business credit card is missing, and someone posted a comment on Rachel's Facebook account pretending to be me. I don't have to be her to figure out the culprit is someone with easy access to me. So, if you're the one committing these pranks for whatever reason—professional jealousy or anger over our relationship ending—I'll ask you to stop, please."

"Are you out of your mind?" He practically shouted before throwing his napkin on the table. "How dare you accuse me of such things? Perhaps you missed out on what I said earlier." He glared at the waiter when he dropped off their check and to-go boxes. "I just said I love you, and I want our relationship to continue, and you have the audacity to accuse me of such treachery? Who do you think I am?"

"I'm sorry, Brady. I just couldn't think of how else it could happen." Maude bit the inside of her lower lip. She'd hating believing him capable of such petty offenses, too, but someone was responsible. If not him, then who?

"So you accuse me?" Brady huffed.

"I-I just want everything between us to stop for a while, and I don't want any trouble. Okay?" She met his gaze again. "I didn't mean to upset you, but you *are* the only person with ready access to my personal things."

"You're being very rude, Maude." Squaring his shoulders, he sniffed. "You should know me better than that."

And this condescension was why she had to break away from Brady Stephens. He could twist anything around so it was her fault. Not anymore. She shoved her noodles into the to-go container and stood. "Thanks for lunch. I'll walk back."

"Maude, sit down. Now." Brady jabbed a finger at her seat. "We're not finished."

"I asked you nicely to just stop." Maude shook her head. "We are finished, and I am leaving. I'm sorry, Brady." She offered a small smile then walked out the door.

Though she felt his blue-eyed gaze boring into her back, she would carry through on walking to the office. At this point, she could only hope he didn't make her work environment intolerable, somehow. She hated to believe he'd stoop to childish games, but he *had* posted that picture. What else had he done, and what more would he do? Rachel always said, emotions made people do crazy things.

As Maude trudged along her five-block walk to the office, she stopped a moment and glanced up at the bright yellow sun. The day had started out gray and cloudy, but now everything became clear as the sun's rays warmed her face and lifted her spirits. She'd made her direction clear to Brady, and by speaking the words, she'd finally illuminated her own path. A weight had actually been lifted. She no longer owed Brady anything. And not for another moment would she despair over who was right for her heart, when she knew who owned her soul.

CHAPTER 17

After a productive afternoon at work, Maude entered Owen's kitchen and downed a cup of peppermint tea. Her stomach remained a little unsettled after her lunch with Brady. She'd planned on packing her winter clothes, books, and other items for her new place, but a hot bath followed by bed seemed a sure cure for her woes. Hopefully, her mom, Owen, and Ember weren't looking to chat, because they'd see everything she was feeling on her face, especially her mother.

Luckily, her housemates were nowhere in sight, so she bounded up the stairs to her room, changed into comfy sweats and a faded pink T-shirt, and plopped face down on her bed. Drawing a bath seemed like too much work.

Jason still hadn't texted. Maybe he had decided to continue a relationship with Ariel and was afraid to tell her? Or maybe he'd just been flirting as a distraction from his life? "You've lost your mind, Maude. No one said he had to talk to you every day. He's probably with his mom. Have a little faith."

After checking her social media notifications to ensure no more shenanigans were occurring on her account, she read a little from Rachel's latest book before drifting off.

The sound of Jason's ringtone floated through her dreams. A few moments passed before Maude acknowledged the sound was real. Groping for her phone, she swiped across the screen and noted the time. 2:30 a.m. Didn't he know she had to work the next day?

Blinking awake, she winced as the light from her screen blasted against her eyes. Squinting, she read his text.

Come out to garage.

Was this the type of relationship he intended? Sneaking around? Sex in the back seat of one of Owen's cars? She groaned, because that actually sounded kind of hot.

Sexual fantasies aside, the fact Jason was out in Owen's garage again struck her as a little odd. Why did he keep sitting out there in the middle of the night? Would she ever understand the man? Did she really want to? No one would ever tame him, but maybe she could join him on the wild side. Hadn't she always dreamed of moments like this? So, why was she stalling?

She threw off her blankets then shoved on a sweatshirt and considered brushing her teeth. Maybe combing her hair. "Nah." A man came calling in the middle of the night, he'd have to take her as she was.

Tiptoeing down the stairs, she turned off the house alarm, hoping the chime didn't wake Owen and cause him to come out guns blazing. Maybe Ember could distract him if he woke up. Hopefully, he'd become immune to the sound since this wasn't the first time she was messing with the system late at night.

But, her mom...she would likely investigate. She had specialized "kid radar" which seemed capable of distinguishing between true trouble and her kids needing a quick check up.

Sure enough, her mom rounded the corner and shuffled into the kitchen.

"What's wrong? Do you need some peppermint tea?" Her mom's short red hair was all mussed, and she was having the same issues with the light blaring in her not-quite-awake eyes.

"No, I just need some fresh air." Maude headed for the door, keeping to the shadows, because she hadn't fooled the woman in twenty-two years.

"Maude Killion, it's the middle of the night."

"I know."

Her mom studied her for a moment before nodding. "Tell Jason I said hello." Then she turned on her worn, blue slippers and headed back to her room.

What? Frozen in place, Maude stopped breathing for about sixty seconds. Of course, she knew. The woman had probably pierced her mind and saw everything inside. Or Ember had spilled the beans. Either way, her mother hadn't lectured her on the dangers of dating Jason Stafford, so maybe she was in the clear. Her mom had a soft spot for Jason, growing wheatgrass for his smoothies, and even helping him start his own patio garden, because the man was very conscientious about the food that went into his body.

Stepping outside, Maude wasn't overly chilled as she made her way to the garage. She'd teased Owen that, after his football career was over, he could always do one of those TV car shows since he had the garage space and all the tools, not to mention the know-how, learned from their mechanic father. When she opened the door, all was quiet, except for a busy cricket.

A minute passed before she found Jason in the expansive space.

The Ranchero, again.

Jason lay slumped in the driver's seat, a half-empty bottle of Jameson Irish whiskey in his lap. "Hey, Maude. Come on in." His words were slightly slurred as he waved her on.

"I'll come in if I can have a swig of your bottle." She'd take a drink, but she didn't plan to give it back. The situation must be very, very bad as he rarely, if ever, drank. Not after his sister had died, anyway. Her heart ached at whatever had brought him to this state. And she took a deep breath, preparing to hear the worst. She already knew she'd forgive him. Whether or not she'd want a deeper relationship, though, remained to be seen. She slid into the passenger seat, ready for what came next.

He handed her the bottle. "Only a small sip, Maudy. Stuff's bad for you."

"That's very true, which makes me wonder why you're drinking it." She took a fake drink and then placed the bottle by her feet. "Drinking, Stafford? Would you like to tell me why?"

He frowned as he traced the blue Ford logo in the steering wheel's center. "You're not the only one who can make changes."

She nodded and tucked her suddenly chilled hands into her sweatshirt's front pocket. "You'll regret drinking this." She kept her gaze trained on the view outside the windshield, though not really focusing on Owen's tools and car parts. Her world seemed hazy, hinging on what Jason said next. "Whatever happened, we can get through it, together. Haven't we always? Don't drink. You know that never solves anything."

"You're wrong." He shook a finger in her face, accidently flicking her nose. "I'm following my father's path in every other way. So might as well become a drunk, too."

"I don't believe that."

"I didn't either, until I saw it with my own eyes."

Her breath hitched. "Saw what?" Even after asking the question, she knew.

"She's pregnant." Jason stretched out both arms and gripped the steering wheel, his knuckles turning white. "I'm gonna be a father, Maudy. What the hell do I know about that?"

Maude took a moment to catch up and mentally repeated over and over: *This isn't about you. Focus.* She glanced at Jason and swallowed hard before speaking. "Ariel took the test in front of you?"

"Yeah." He nodded.

"Then you'll do what you have to do." Likely the hardest words she'd ever spoken, as she held back screaming, no, just no! Her heart seared with pain, caused by the jealousy poisoning her veins. *She* wanted to be the one carrying his child. Wanted a guaranteed place in his life. But Maude was with him now, and whatever that meant or wherever they went from here, she would always be his friend. She wouldn't lose that. So, she would act the part, ignoring her own agony and focus on getting him back on track. "I know what today is, Jason, maybe that's part of why you're taking the news so hard."

He sighed and was quiet for a long moment before clearing his throat and speaking in a low tone. "My sister used to come to my room with this Dr. Seuss book, *Yertle the Turtle*. I loved that story. Jessica always smelled like bubble gum. Mom always bought a big tub of it at Wal-Mart, because Dad liked it." Jason shook his head. "Anyway, Jess would come into my room, popping that gum, scooch me over in the bed, and read until I fell asleep. Just me and her. That's what I miss the most. That turtle and the smell of bubble gum. I haven't chewed that brand since. Can't even look at the tubs around Ma's house. She has like three or four of 'em stuffed with other crap, and they annoy the shit out of me." He laughed and rubbed the back of his neck. "I'm just slightly insane." He glanced at her then at the seat. "Hey, where'd my bottle go?"

"You aren't insane," she responded, ignoring his question. "Losing your sister and your issues with your dad are all reasons you live like you do. I understand that, Jason."

He rolled his head back and forth on the headrest.

Lord, he was drunk. A lightweight, especially since he never imbibed.

"I need you, Maude." After slurring those words, he met her gaze, his blue eyes a little wet along the lower rims.

"Do you?" Hope was a glorious and scary thing. Still, she scooted across the bench seat until their thighs were touching.

"Always." He cupped her face with his hand.

"I've been calling you for days."

He sighed and leaned back, rubbing his hands up and down his thighs. "After I left Ariel's, I just drove around and ended up over by a Wal-Mart. So I went in and headed for the book section. They have books on baby shit, so I grabbed a few, and I've been reading 'em." Again, he gripped the steering wheel. "With Jess…and the baby thing, I just needed time to think everything through."

"And, what did you decide?"

"To get drunk."

"And after that?" She couldn't suppress an eye roll toward his ridiculous solution to a very serious issue.

He leaned his back against the driver's side door and pulled both of her hands into his lap. "After that is up to you."

"Oh, no." Maude narrowed her eyes and shook her head. "Your future is *not* up to me. Do not put that responsibility on my shoulders. I won't make the decisions in your life."

"Okay." He brought her hand to his lips and kissed her fingers. "I'm going to be a dad. I'm playing football. I'm telling Owen I want his sister, and if I don't get murdered, I'll convince her to move in with me and we'll go from there."

Maude struggled to pull her jaw from the floorboard. "Whoa." She held up a hand. "That's a lot to process, let alone believe." She closed her eyes for a moment, but when she got lost in thoughts of lounging day-after-day in Jason's bed, she blinked twice and refocused. "First, let's talk about the baby. Your whole life will change. Maybe you and I should take things a little more slowly. Stay friends until things with Ariel straighten out."

"You're scared." He jabbed her shoulder with his index finger.

"Am not."

"Never thought you'd puss out, Killion."

Maude smacked his finger. "You think I'm just supposed to fall at your feet and say, "Okay, let's go"?"

"Why not? I'm what you've always wanted." He ran a hand down his body. "All this."

"All that." She jabbed his upper thigh. "Got you in trouble.

So…quit thinking you're all that."

"I love it when you get all flustered, baby." Jason drew her closer and lightly kissed her lips.

Stiffening, she shoved away. "Baby being the operative word, so keep your roving hands to yourself."

"I don't understand women." Jason huffed out a sigh. "Plus, you never gave me back my bottle." His lower lip jutted out. "If I can't have you, at least let me drown my sorrows."

Maude suppressed a smile over his indignation.

"I don't want to be like my father."

And that was the root of his troubles, the reason he was out here, the reason he'd sought solace in a bottle. "You'll never be like that man."

"My brother is…sometimes."

"You're not Patrick, either."

Jason barked out a laugh. "Patrick'll love this. He'll rib me for the rest of my life."

"Yeah, he likely will."

"Mom's dying. So, the kid won't have any grandparents on my side. I may despise my dad, but I did like my grandpa. Poppa was larger than life, carried me around on his shoulders. I get my size from him." Jason tapped a finger against the steering wheel. "You wanna know why I come out here, Maude?"

"Yeah, I do," she whispered, caught up in the quiet moment, afraid to break the spell.

"Because of what you, Owen, and your mom represent." Jason sniffed, not turning to meet her gaze. "You're a real family unit. I come out here, and I think of all the everyday stuff going on just a few steps away in that house, and picturing it soothes me. I know if I wanted, I could go inside, and I'd be greeted, fed, and loved by you three. But instead of reaching out, I just sit here. I don't know why I can't go inside. Something keeps me out here. Keeps me separate." He pulled her legs across his lap. "I don't want to be separate, anymore."

"You've never been separate. We love you, always have." She placed her hands on both sides of his face. "You're always welcome. You should know that by now."

"I'm so fucked up." He pulled away her hands, but he held onto one and played with her fingers.

"No." Maude nudged his chin so he'd meet her gaze. "You're just like the rest of us. We're searching for comfort, for love, for security. A place free from fear. A home base. We can be that for you. I can be that for you." She refrained from adding, *even if you break my heart.* A real possibility, but after tonight, she wouldn't hold back. Hadn't ever truly resisted him anyway. Why bother trying now, even though a rough road lay ahead.

"All along, it's been you." He huffed out a half-laugh. "Lord knows, I've fought this connection I feel toward you, but...I won't deny us anymore."

"I can't be the only strong one." Maude met his gaze, her heart in her throat. "I'm too scared to believe any of this is true."

"Does this scare you?" He wrapped a hand around the back of her neck and kissed her deeply. "Are you feeling terrified?" A cocky smile lit his face before he nipped at her lower lip. Delving into her mouth, he kissed her until she couldn't breathe, skillfully using his tongue to entice her into a dance of pull and retreat. "What about now, Maudy? Still afraid?"

Just when she thought she'd caught her breath, she gasped as he kissed her once more, holding her in place, yet with each strong caress, each plunge of his tongue, she remained frightened of spilling everything she'd ever felt for him, of being over-eager. He was so skilled and had her fantasizing about lying back on the seat and engaging in car sex, right here, right now.

So she tugged him down.

He followed, his warm hand finding its way under her layers and skimming along the side of her body, making its way across her breast.

She shivered as his field-roughened hand slid across her skin.

Maude broke from the kiss, fighting for air. "Jason, I…"

He pulled his hand free but kissed her again, a soft kiss, reassuring, as if he knew he'd pushed her far enough tonight.

"We can't keep doing this." She glanced around the car's cab.

"Um…yeah, we can and will." He bent and kissed her neck.

"I mean, not here…or, I don't think…this garage is not right." She huffed out a sigh over her brain's inability to send words to her mouth. "I have no idea what I'm saying."

"Then stop talking. I can think of other ways to pass the time." He ran a hand down the side of her neck before tilting her head and kissing a path to her ear. "We could throw a couple blankets in the back and check the shocks." He nipped her earlobe. "Whadya' think, Maude?"

She drew his face to hers and kissed him. She'd show him what it meant to tease. Plus, she loved kissing. Loved the playful dance.

He tried to amp up the moment, but she kept everything smooth. That was her role, after all, keeping him calm. Grounded. When she eased back, she combed her fingers through his soft blond hair. "Jason, I'm tired, and you're a little drunk. Let's go up to the house, and we'll sleep on it. Then, in the morning, Mom can make us some breakfast, and we'll talk everything out. Okay?"

He shook his head. "I'll stay out here."

"No." She tugged on his hand. "Come inside, please."

"Can I sleep with you?"

He flashed that gorgeous, panty-dropping grin. "No." She wrinkled her nose, envisioning Owen pounding down her door, and then pounding on Jason. "Not yet."

"Then I'm staying out here." He adjusted himself through the top of his jeans. "Although, I'm hard as fucking stone right now, thanks for that, by the way."

Maude shrugged. "You started it."

"I could end it." He waggled his brows.

"I certainly hope so."

He took her hand and squeezed. "Stop, Maude. No more words like hope. It's all good. I told you, where we go from here is up to you. Two pink lines have decided my fate, and even though I'm scared, I'm okay with a kid. I really am."

"I've waited for you my whole life, so if I cling to hope a little bit longer, let me, all right?" She squeezed his forearm. "And as far as your role as a father, you have a big heart you don't let anyone see, but it's there. I see it."

"You're just blinded by my awesomeness."

"Oh, absolutely." She rolled her eyes again and feigned a fainting spell. "Oh, Jason. You super studly O-Liner, I need you so badly."

He grabbed her and put her in a headlock.

"Stop it, you oh-so-sexy jerk." She bit his arm.

"Ow! You little vamp." He released her then kissed her forehead. "Go to bed, Maudy. I'll still be here in the morning."

Alternate thoughts crashed through her mind. She could stay and steam up the windows, but she wanted their first time to occur without any outside drama. Wanted a bed with warm sheets. Wanted him thinking only of her. So, though her libido was screaming to stay, she grabbed the bottle, scooted across the seat and out of the car. "I'm taking this with me. I need it more than you do."

"Bring that back, brat." Jason leaned across the seat, hand outstretched.

"No." She stomped off, sure the smile on her face was pure goofy.

"That's okay, I've got another." Jason's voice carried across the garage.

"If you vomit in Owen's car, don't expect help from me."

"You'll help."

"Will not." She wasn't sure if she got the last word since she shut the door and tromped back to the house. And, did it really matter? She'd finally gotten her wish.

Good thing the bottle wasn't empty, she really needed a shot...or three.

CHAPTER 18

The whirring of an opening garage door woke Jason, but the piercing pain shooting through his temples kept him from opening his eyes. Why had he downed all that whiskey? Why did he always go from zero to one hundred?

Next, he heard Owen, Bronco, and Chewy talking about him like he wasn't there. They were likely standing right beside the Ranchero's door, because their loud voices pounded through his ears and rattled his pained head.

"Going to charge him rent?" Chewy asked Owen.

Jason popped open one eye and quickly regretted the action.

"Stafford, you better not have drooled on that leather," Owen growled.

Bronco slid into the passenger seat and handed him a Gatorade. "Ready for some breakfast?"

"Let's see if I can keep this down, first." Jason unscrewed the top and downed a big swallow. "How'd you know I was out here?" He arched a brow at Bronco.

"Maude told us. Plus your car's parked alongside the building."

Jason glanced at Owen and Chewy. Owen was showing Chewy some new tool, some kind of blaster, which only made sense to Jason if it was featured in a sci-fi movie. He appreciated

Owen's skills in the garage, but he had no idea what his friend was talking about half the time. After finishing his drink, he tapped the empty bottle against his palm. "Maude say anything else?"

"Like what?" Bronco waggled his brows.

Jason sniffed. Fucker thought he was some sly private eye, now that he was dating one. "Since you think you know what's going on, tell me. You think I should?"

Bronco shrugged. "Doesn't matter what I think."

"Yeah. It does."

"Bro, after everything that happened with my family and Rachel, I see things differently. Life is full of lies, deceit, and pain, so take happiness when and where you can." His gaze shot to Owen. "Thing is, that big boy out there won't take too kindly if you take happiness...or anything, from his sister."

"This thing." Jason circled a hand around by his chest. "This Maude thing...has been there for a while."

"On her side, maybe." Bronco took the plastic bottle from his hand and donked him on the head. "You sure you want to go there? Owen's gonna be pissed, and with the season starting..."

"Go on." Jason rolled his hand in a "please continue" motion, curious as to what his friend had to say.

"And you party. A lot. Not to mention you got this Ariel thing."

"A baby is not a thing, and yeah, the baby is a fact."

"Fuck, dude."

"Yeah."

They were both quiet for a minute, until Bronco made a ticking noise out the side of his mouth. "Well." He slapped his thigh. "You ready for breakfast?"

Jason rubbed his stomach. "I need a cleansing shake. Stupid to drink all that whiskey."

"True." Bronco nodded. "Although, the way you look right now, I'd say you need a plate of greasy bacon and eggs, maybe some sourdough toast or pancakes to soak up all that alcohol." He opened the passenger door but glanced back over his shoulder. "We'll get you through...today...the baby...other stuff..." he whispered the last, but they both knew he meant Jessica. "We got you."

Bronco's words were way too lovey-dovey when dealing with a hangover...or really ever. Jason had spilled enough of his guts to Maude last night. His friends were there for him each year since his sister's death, same thing over and over. They never discussed it. Never said why they searched him out and hung around him all day, but he knew. And he loved the big bastards for it. Hell if he'd admit it, though.

"Fuck off, and go get me some breakfast." He tossed his wallet and hit Bronco's leg.

"That's what I thought." Bronco started pulling out all of Jason's credit cards and pocketing them. "Get your ass out of the driver's seat, crybaby, so I can go."

"Get the keys from Owen."

"He ain't gonna let you drive."

"While you're at it, get me some pain meds. About ten." Jason closed his eyes and leaned against the headrest. Today was the anniversary of his sister's, death. Eight years ago, the news had changed him forever. His drunken father had picked up Jessica when her car broke down just outside of her job. They'd crashed, and she'd died instantly, but his father had only lost the use of his legs. Never in his life had Jason experienced such rage. To be honest, he was still furious and hadn't accepted Jessica was gone. The one constant in his life, his older sister and best friend, taken forever by his jackass drunk father.

Was that why Maude had caught his eye? Was he searching for a replacement? In a way, Maude reminded him of Jess, strong and sure, yet in a quieter way. He barreled his way through life loud and wild, banging and clanging into everything, but not Maude or Jess. They swam through life in a gentle, rolling stream.

Maude, like Jess, had always been able to read him. Could see beneath all his bullshit. Jess had held him after one of his father's beatings, and she'd even taken a few in his stead. He missed her every day. Bubble gum and turtles, man. And the only one capable of soothing his soul was the one girl he should probably leave alone…but he wouldn't. Jess couldn't live, so he had to live harder and love stronger—for her and himself.

He heaved a sigh, got out of the car, and headed for the cabinet where Owen kept his medical supplies to find an old bottle of Advil.

"Bottle's old, but the medicine's new." Owen handed him a water.

"Bronc', you getting some food?" Chewy hollered at Bronco, who was checking his phone.

"Nah, let's hit that breakfast buffet."

"That's like an hour away," Chewy groused.

"You got somewhere else to be?" Bronco finally looked up from his phone and arched a brow.

"Fine." Chewy flicked him off. "I'm driving. You drive like an old lady."

They all avoided the elephant in the room. Why they were there. Never once was Jessica's name mentioned. Jason was cool with that. All he needed was their presence. They didn't need to discuss and dissect the whole thing like chicks did. They all clambered into Chewy's ride and hit the breakfast buffet, talking football the whole way there and back.

And, in honor of his sister's death, he ate enough bacon for two people, because everyone knows fried pig heals all wounds.

# # #

After a day out in the garage and an impromptu football game, Bronco and Chewy took off, and Jason and Owen headed for the basement man-cave. Owen had a wide couch, huge TV, and small bar area. The perfect set-up.

"Haven't you seen this movie like five thousand times?" Jason glanced up from his phone at *Rudy* playing on the big screen. He'd taken, and then posted, a bunch of photos at breakfast and during the game. Now, he was responding to comments. Had to keep up with his fans or there wouldn't be any. He ignored all the haters and focused on his true people. Marauders' fans were the best in the world.

"Yeah." Owen rocked his leg back and forth on top of the coffee table. "You've probably watched it with me all five thousand, so what's your problem? You're not watching it, anyway. You got your nose in your phone."

Jason started to answer but thought better of it. Last thing he wanted was to start an argument. He needed Owen calm before he brought up Maude.

His mouth seemed oddly dry, so he headed for the kitchen and grabbed a water bottle, ready to talk, especially now that he was out of Owen's immediate reach.

A robot took over his brain and he spat out, "Maude and me are dating, and Ariel is pregnant."

Owen didn't look at him, didn't speak for a few minutes. "Why?"

"Why? Out of all the things you could say, you chose why? I have no idea how to answer that. If you're asking why Ariel's pregnant, just dumb luck. As for Maude, I don't..." Jason scoffed and then rubbed his forehead. He had to answer this carefully, but then again, nothing he said would matter. Words meant nothing. Wasn't Owen always harping on that prior to a game? Actions mattered. "Maude and I...she is...I'm not explaining that kind of shit to you. We just are, and now I've told you, so do what you gotta do."

Owen met his gaze.

Jason braced for whatever was next. "You really want to hear why I find your sister attractive?"

"No, I don't." Owen switched his gaze back to the TV, jaw

tight. "Ember already told me what was brewing after I mentioned our discussion at the Rec Center. I've thought about it a lot." Owen took a swig from his beer bottle. "I count you as my brother in all but blood. You get what that means, right?"

Jason nodded, a little choked up, because yeah, he'd known, but sometimes hearing the words did matter.

"Every person plays a certain role in my life. I don't like when things change." Owen shook his head. "Don't like when I'm not the one in control."

"Ever since we met on that field, we've been tight. I know that." Jason pounded the side of his fist against his chest. "I'd never jeopardize that bond."

"The life you lead, Stafford..." Owen sighed before pulling his legs off the table and straightening. "That isn't Maude's scene."

"I'm tired of that scene."

"Are you?"

"That question is about trust, and you either trust me to be straight, or you don't. It's that simple. I said I'm done, and I am."

"Maude is my sister, my blood, and if she starts hurting, if you make her heart bleed..." Owen pounded a fist against his heart this time. "Then we're done." He finally dropped his gaze and placed one sock-covered foot on the coffee table. "Maude is my responsibility. She doesn't want to hear that, and neither do you, but my role in her life is very real. Sitting beside his deathbed, I made my dad a promise to look after the two most important women in his life, and I won't fail in that." He sniffed then glanced down at his foot, rocking back and forth on the table. "This thing with you and Maude affects us all. Everything we've built together could fall apart, and I don't like that kind of uncertainty." He stood, walked over, and then knocked his knuckles against the bar's top. "You go ahead and do what you got to do, but do it right. You feel me?"

"That's it?" Jason half-laughed.

"You and my sister isn't something to joke about, Stafford."

"Would you like to hit me?" Jason spread his arms wide. "I'll let you get one good shot. Make it count."

Owen shook his head before grabbing another beer. He opened it, took a long draw before heading for the stairs.

Jason couldn't be sure, but he thought he heard Owen mumble something about castrating him. "Are you after my big dick again, Killion?"

Owen stopped with one foot on the first step and glanced over his shoulder. "Let's just say you shouldn't be on the other side of the practice line for a long, long while."

"Gotcha, Big-O. Can do."

And that was that.

CHAPTER 19

A slight breeze rustled through Jason's hair as he gazed down at his sister's headstone. Jessica Stafford. Beloved daughter.

He set a dozen yellow roses upon the grassy mound covering her body and noted the colorful bouquet his mom had left yesterday and the single yellow rose, likely from his brother.

Each year, Jason came out the day after Jessica's actual death, because he didn't want to run into anyone else. This year was no different, as he had a lot to say, and he didn't want an audience.

He sank against the side of her headstone, uncaring if his track pants got damp. "Have you seen what I've been up to, Jess? I'm going to be a father. Not sure how that'll shake out, but I'll do my best to make you proud." He swallowed a hard lump of emotion and blinked back tears. "Ariel isn't so bad. I don't know." He rubbed the back of his neck. Was that even true? He didn't really know the woman carrying his baby. "Anyway..." He plucked a dandelion out of the grass then tossed it aside. "I'm sure you already know this, but Ma is sick. She's got *the* cancer. That's what she calls it, *the* cancer." He tossed up air quotes with his fingers. "All those years smoking, and now..." Jason sighed but couldn't continue, because what else could he say? He'd told his ma to quit smoking so many times over the years, but she wouldn't stop.

Closing his eyes, he rested his head against the cold headstone. "I finally went straight with Maude. I know she'll be my rock through...the baby...and Mom's cancer. Maude's a beautiful woman, both in looks and in her heart. I can be a better man for her, Jess. At least, that's the plan. Help me out, won't ya?" Chuckling, he shook his head. "You see me acting up, feel free to trip me, or something." He opened his eyes and stared up into the big blue sky. "I miss you...so much. Every single day. I may have Maude, but I need you, too."

After a few more moments, he stood and brushed a hand across the top of the headstone then tapped it with his knuckles. "I'm off to Mom's. I need more information on her cancer diagnosis. Plus, I should probably tell her she'll soon be a grandmother." He huffed out a laugh. "Patrick's going to kill me, or I'll kill him when he starts lecturing me on getting some chick pregnant. If you were here, you'd smooth everything over, just like always. But, since you're not...I'll *try* with Patrick, because deep down, I miss him, too. We were all so close once, and now everything is broken...and I'm tired of living like that. I'm changing, and this family has to change, too." Jason glanced at the time on his phone. "Better head out. I'll come again soon."

After slogging through the freshly mowed grass, Jason slid into his Audi and headed to his mom's place. Flying across town, Jason pulled into his mom's driveway, right on time. Patrick's car was there, as well as another car Jason didn't recognize.

He tapped on the back door before walking into the kitchen. Rosemary and baked chicken filled his senses and roused his hunger. "Smells good."

His mom was tossing a salad on the countertop. "See?" She dumped cherry tomatoes from a strainer into the bowl. "I listened when you said you wanted healthy."

"Thanks, Ma." He leaned down and kissed her cheek before sitting at the kitchen table. "I'm taking you Friday, remember?" He glanced at the calendar on the fridge, which marked her appointment time.

"Yeah." His mom cleared her throat. "They want me to talk to an oncologist, although doc said I'm in the advanced stages already. Don't know what that means." Shrugging, she sank into the kitchen chair beside him and rubbed her eyes. "I'm afraid I'm pretty far along, Jason." She gripped his hand then squeezed. "You didn't get any prep time with your sister, so it's good you'll have some, now."

"Mom, they have treatments. Chemo, and all that stuff." Jason tapped the saltshaker against the table. "And just because I know your death is coming doesn't mean it'll be any easier." He stared out the window. The smell of stale smoke filled the air—always had, always would. "I'm not preparing for your death until a doctor tells me I should."

"Did you go see Jessica today?"

"Yeah."

His mom nodded and slumped against her seat.

She looked so tired. When had she gone and got old on him?

The timer on the oven went off. She glanced at the stove and sighed.

"Just sit. I'll take care of it." And he would, he'd take care of the cancer, hire someone to take care of his mom full-time, and go to as many doctor appointments as he could. They were family. She wouldn't face this disease alone.

He stood and tugged both golden brown chickens out of the oven, grabbed a bowl for the roasted vegetables, and then burned the shit out of his fingers cutting the meat from the bones.

"Your brother's bringing someone. They're over at his place now, doing whatever. She came home with him last night."

Jason simply nodded. "Great." He had no illusions this girl would be different from any other woman in his brother's life. Stafford men weren't much on commitment.

Just as Jason finished setting the table, he glanced over as his brother barreled through the back door, towing a tall brunette behind him. She wore skinny jeans, a tight purple V-neck shirt, and a pair of black wedge sandals.

"Mom, Jason, this is Katie." Patrick waved a hand around before dropping into a chair. "I'm starving."

"Hey." Jason nodded at the gal, trying to recall where he'd seen her before. Likely at the clubs. He placed the last salad dressing bottle on the table. "Let's eat."

His mom nudged his arm. "When are *you* going to bring a girl around?

Unwilling to mention Maude, he shrugged. She was his alone, and he didn't want to share her yet. He mumbled that he was involved with Ariel and hoped the questions would end. Not a lie, because he was involved. Way involved.

"Ariel Silvers?" Katie piped up. "I've partied with Ariel."

Jason chewed a mouthful of salad. *This could get interesting.*

"She said she was after a football player, but I thought she meant your quarterback. The Chewy guy. She set her sights on him." Katie smiled. "She got you instead, huh? Lucky girl."

"Who is she talking about?" Eyes narrowed, Patrick placed his fork to the side of his plate. "And what does she mean, 'after a football player'?"

Jason inwardly groaned. *Could this day get any worse?*

"I heard she's pregnant." Katie dropped that bomb and then just reached across the table to grab the ranch dressing.

Jason cursed and rubbed his forehead, which likely ached from his mom's and brother's piercing stares. Like laser beams digging into his brain, trying to extract all his secrets.

An uncomfortable silence continued, and Jason fidgeted in his chair, his concentration on counting the number of carrots on his plate. Seven, he had seven.

"Pregnant? You got some girl pregnant?" Patrick shot back in his chair. "You dumb son of a bitch. How many times did I tell you to wrap that shit?"

"Patrick, sit down and stop yelling at the table." His mom

coughed, a racking cough that continued for a few minutes.

Jason met Patrick's gaze. "Should we make her some tea, or something?"

"Yeah, I'll do it." Patrick stood and tossed his napkin in his chair.

Once his mom finally caught her breath and drank several sips of the tea Patrick made, she turned to Jason. "Is this true? Am I going to be a grandmother?"

"Yes, I planned on telling you tonight." Jason shoved away his plate, no longer hungry. "I'm having a child. It's not something I can change."

"Please, don't tell me you're planning on marrying her." Patrick glared across the table.

"No." Is that all his brother could say? His whole life was about to change, and he needed his family. Needed his brother. What he didn't need was the guy acting like he was some little kid who should be punished or lectured.

"You sure Ariel ain't lying?" Katie asked, cutting into her chicken. "There was this girl who knew a girl who was already pregnant and she had that girl pee on the stick, see? So, then, when her guy came over, she did a test but switched sticks to the pregnant one." Shaking her head, she shrugged. "Easy to do. Then he got her pregnant…for real. No big thing."

A cold sweat covered Jason's skin. *Faked pregnancy tests?*

"That's horrible." His mom dropped her teacup onto the table with a clang.

"Oh, Mrs. Stafford," Katie continued, flicking her hand in the air. "I stopped hanging out with those girls about a year ago. Ariel and her friends were mad at my friend, Sara, because she snagged this rich investor-type guy whose wife had just died. Ariel and her friends make it their mission to know all the rich guys in the area, and then hunt them down." Katie rambled on, waving her fork in the air. "Sara was like, so beautiful, but then Ariel and her friends pinned her in this club bathroom and beat her up. Put her in the hospital. She still has a scar." Katie ran a finger down the right side of her chin. "It's really long."

In his stomach, Jason's salad rumbled and tumbled as he recalled when Ariel had him grab the toilet paper. Was that a distraction technique? This malicious girl Katie described wasn't the Ariel he knew. Could she wear a mask to make herself more appealing? As much as she'd changed her body, she'd likely also masked her true self. Had she tricked him about the pregnancy?

"Then, one time, Ariel and her friends were mad at this girl for scoring this basketball player, so they basically cyber-bullied her and posted ugly lies about her all over. Ariel isn't someone I'd ever cross." Her eyes widened, and her hand rose to cover her mouth. "Oh...please don't tell her I said all this stuff. I probably shouldn't have." She glanced at Patrick. "I don't want her and her bitchy friends coming after me."

"Language, babe."

Katie's gaze shot to his mom. "I'm sorry, Mrs. Stafford."

"No problem." His mom cleared her throat. "Sounds like they *are* bitches."

Katie chuckled then lifted her fist and bumped it against his mom's. "True story, Mrs. Stafford."

Jason stared at Katie. His brain had hit overload. Questions fired across all his synapses. Thank God, this woman had come to dinner. Because now he knew for sure a different side of Ariel existed. What he didn't know for sure was if she was truly pregnant? He really, really didn't want to go through that worry again.

No answers existed except one. He needed more information. Time to bring Rachel Harris and her partner, Clayton Kincaid, into the picture. He wasn't about to get railroaded by Ariel Silvers. He'd have investigators delve into the woman's secrets. And, if she'd somehow faked the pregnancy test...well, he wasn't sure what he'd do.

But right now, worrying about Ariel and her possible

schemes wasn't as important as just being with his ma. So he sat through dinner, learned a little more about Katie and her friends, actually, a lot more. Maybe the girl was nervous, or maybe she always talked a lot. His brother basically frowned throughout the whole meal, but Katie kept their mom entertained.

After his brother and Katie left, Jason cleaned up then settled his mom in her bed so she could watch her shows. He sat beside her and, using his phone, looked into businesses who offered home care for the sick. When she finally fell asleep, he turned off the TV, but just sat in the chair for a few more hours, rocking back and forth and thinking of everything they had been through together. In silence, he wiped away a tear rolling down his cheek.

CHAPTER 20

Heaving a deep sigh, Maude eased onto the highway ramp that led across town to the Rec Center for another clean-up day. One of many scheduled throughout the spring before the construction crews were scheduled to finish during the summer

"Why the big sigh?" In the passenger seat beside her, Ember glanced up from her phone. She'd been snickering and her cheeks were a slight pink, which meant she was likely naughty-texting with Owen.

"Brady," Maude answered, as if that one word should explain everything.

"Yeah, the kitchen's turned into a flower shop." Ember shrugged. "Smells good."

"He's lost his mind," Maude growled, thinking of the roses and the plethora of bouquets Brady had delivered to her desk this week. "Bombarding me with flowers won't change my mind." She huffed, feeling tension invade her shoulders. "Not only that, I look like the bad guy at work, because everyone is oohing and aahing over how romantic he is. Again, he's trying to manipulate the situation." She eased off the gas pedal as she realized, in her fury, she'd almost hit eighty miles per hour.

"Be careful." Ember glanced out the front window. "Those personality types can turn ugly, and sometimes violent."

Maude shot a side-glance at Ember. Discussing controlling men was a sensitive subject for her friend, especially since one had almost killed her...then there was Ember's mother, which was another nightmare all together. "Sorry, Ember. I don't have to talk about Brady if doing so brings back bad memories."

"I'm fine. I have Owen, but I also know I'm strong on my own. I guess...I'm just more careful, now."

"Good, that's good." Maude smiled at her friend then flicked on her turn signal to ease over to the next exit. "Brady's gestures are sweet, but he's gone way over the top. He's bringing me lunch, chocolate, snacks. I'm starting to feel really bad, because even though I'm not encouraging him, I can't get him to stop." Maude tightened her grip on the steering wheel. "My boss called me in her office the other day and asked what was going on."

"Yikes." Ember winced.

"Yeah, she reiterated that Aceso Pharmaceuticals was a place of business, and Brady and I needed to be professionals." Maude sighed. "I told her I couldn't get him to quit, so she would have to talk to him." She stopped at the light and used a tissue from her travel pack to scratch her itchy nose. Allergy season had officially begun. "This "Woo Maude" campaign Brady's waging is very distracting to everyone in the office, but especially for me. The more distant I become, the harder he tries. Maybe I should take vacation time to get away from him for a while." Once the light turned green, she drove two more blocks to the center.

"Maybe you should. Just don't tell anyone where you're going, or he'll track you down." Ember laughed but then suddenly quieted and glanced at her sideways with a widened gaze. "Actually, that's not funny, now that I think about it."

"I don't think Brady would go that far."

"You never know." A tiny frown formed between her brows as Ember stared out the window. "Sometimes, people lose their minds."

Maude turned into a parking space, noting Jason's Audi

already in the lot.

After Maude turned off the car, she remained in her seat, since Ember hadn't made a move to exit.

Her friend turned and took her hand. "I really do think time away from your office would be beneficial…if you can swing a vacation. However, and I know you may think I'm overreacting, but, please, listen. Brady seems overly desperate, and desperate people do desperate things. He likes to win and sees you as his prize. I'd be careful." Ember squeezed her hand. "I didn't see the signs before all of my…trouble, so let's make sure we're being diligent in your case, okay?"

"Okay, I'll be careful." Maude leaned over and hugged her friend.

Brady had seemed a tad jittery lately, as if he had an excess of energy. She'd considered perhaps he was nervous speaking with her, or that he'd had too many energy drinks. But what if something else were going on? What if he'd upped his recreational drug use? He had a problem abusing his ADHD prescription, Adderall, in high school and his early college years. While they were dating, he'd sometimes do a few lines of coke when they were out with friends.

Whatever was causing Brady's odd behavior, he needed to cease and desist right away. If he progressed to coming to her home or posting more pictures, then she'd get her brother involved. Have him talk to Brady. If Brady was so interested in getting a job with the Marauders public relations department, he wouldn't want to be known as a calculating, manipulative schemer. Owen could get rather scary, and so could their friend, Clayton Kincaid. Plus, Kincaid was a cop before he quit to work for Rachel. Between the two of them, maybe they could force Brady to quit…at least, she hoped so, because this situation had quickly become untenable.

# # #

Jason had texted Maude last night and asked her to find him when she arrived.

After her somewhat unnerving conversation with Ember, she was more than happy to seek him out. His large presence always made her feel safe, plus he knew how to tackle people.

Walking toward the gym, she heard his voice, directing and then laughing. A booming laugh, which had her smiling in return. Following the sounds of his joy, she ended just inside the gym's open double door.

There he was running up and down the basketball court, followed by boys and girls of various sizes and ages.

She couldn't tell which ones were on defense and which were on offense as they all just surrounded him. Since she'd grown up with bigger men, she sometimes forgot how enormous Jason and his teammates were until she saw them next to kids.

Jason passed off the ball to one boy, smiling the whole time as he hefted another kid up by the basketball hoop's rim. "Toss it up to him," Jason directed.

Cheers erupted as the small boy slammed the ball through the hoop.

Maude dusted off her hands and headed over. She'd been playing with boys her whole life, and she wanted in on this game. Besides, the other team needed a bigger player.

"Hey, sorry, these guys drew me in." Flashing a wide grin, Jason wiped the sweat from his brow.

"No problem." Maude shrugged before slapping the ball from his hand. "I thought football was your game?"

"I got all kinds of game." Jason smirked.

Maude kept her expression very serious. "I was lead forward on my high school basketball team, so we'll see who's got game."

Jason arched a brow.

"Are you going to play, miss?" A little boy tugged on her sleeve.

"Yes, I'm on the team opposite Stafford here." Maude glanced around at the little people surrounding them. "Who wants to be on my team?"

When no hands shot up, she tried not to take their lack of enthusiasm personally. She couldn't blame them. She'd been Team Jason for a long time, too. Still, she may have pouted a little.

Jason winked and locked an arm around her neck. "Don't feel so bad, Killion. I'll let you on to my team anytime."

The boy tugged her arm again. "I'll play on your team. My mom says you should try to be nice to people and…and, so I'll be on your team and then…and then you won't be sad."

His big brown eyes in his light brown face were so sweet. His shirt was one size too big, but his shorts fit just right. She just wanted to hug him, but she wasn't sure how appropriate that would be. So, she just squeezed his shoulder, instead. "Why, thank you, kind sir." She handed him the ball. "How about you dribble it down the court?"

After that, it was game on. While the exercise felt good, she simply enjoyed watching the group of kids play together. Their laughs and smiles reminded her of the importance of this facility. Her heart pumped from her exertions, but also from watching Jason move. The man was a natural athlete, and even though he could easily smoosh ten kids at a time, he was careful not to stomp on any little toes.

He acted like an adolescent half the time, anyway, so this side of him—playful, fun-loving, and carefree was a joy to watch. These were the moments she dreamed of, when a little bit of him rubbed off on her and made her forget her worries for a time and just live in the now.

Dribbling the ball down the court, she set up to shoot.

Jason elbowed her.

She made the shot anyway. "Total foul." Grabbing the rebound, she dribbled the ball right beside him, sticking out her tongue.

"Got to get my hands on you, somehow," he whispered and quickly kissed her.

The children erupted in a chorus of "ewws" and "gross."

"Behave." Laughing, Maude shoved him away but then turned and caught a flash of someone standing by the door.

Ariel stood with her arms wrapped around her body.

Jason called an end to the game, stating Maude as the reason they had to quit because she was the boss.

Frowning, she rolled her eyes.

The kids all grumbled and moaned.

Jason promised they'd play again next time he visited. He even managed to make a game out of them saying how they were going home. Then he lined them up and gave them each a high-five. Watching as they ran from the gym, he hollered, "Hugs, not drugs."

Maude shook her head.

"What?" He twirled the basketball on his index finger and met her gaze with a look that was all innocence.

"Sometimes, you surprise me." She refrained from saying how sweet the whole situation was. He had to know those kids had a touch of hero-worship. Lord knew she did. She bit back a sigh.

"They're good kids." Jason placed his sweaty arm around her shoulders, using his other arm to tuck the basketball against his side. He drew her across the room before stopping in front of Ariel. "What do you need?"

His tone seemed a little harsh, as if he was angry. *Huh?* What had Ariel done to upset him? She'd never sensed any animosity from Jason before. *Interesting.*

With an arched brow, Ariel gave a measured stare to Jason's arm around Maude's shoulders before answering, "Dropping off paperwork."

Maude thought about remaining quiet and non-combative. Her kindness to others frequently made her a doormat, but no way was Ariel stepping on her with those five-inch heels. Not happening, especially when the paperwork comment was a lie. She no longer dealt with Ariel, and all the paperwork was handled weeks ago. "What paperwork?"

"For the Center."

"Hmm…I didn't send you anything. Who is it for?"

"I just dropped it off."

Not really an answer, but just as Maude was about to dig deeper, she felt Jason squeeze her shoulder.

He left her side and dropped the basketball into a wire bin. "Maude and I were just heading out. Did you need something?"

"No." Ariel winced then cradled her stomach.

"How are you feeling?" Maude asked, knowing any future with Jason involved this woman, too, so she would try to be considerate.

"Well." Ariel dropped her gaze. "I fainted at work today."

Jason took Ariel's hand. "Are you okay?"

"Apparently, I need to eat a bigger breakfast, but I have a hard time keeping food down."

Unsure of what to say, Maude bit her lip. She disliked the thoughts flashing through her mind, which screamed Ariel was lying in order to gain sympathy. *Real nice, Killion.* Jason had seen the positive test, so she supposed she had to truly accept the matter…at some point.

Jason frowned then glanced back at Maude for a moment before turning to Ariel. "I'll send over a couple smoothie recipes with high protein content. You need to eat, Ariel. You're supposed to gain weight when you're pregnant, so don't hold back due to vanity. Plus, I read you're supposed to take vitamins. Are you doing that?"

"Yes." Ariel brushed her hair over her shoulder. "But about the smoothies, I don't have a blender."

"I'll get you one." Jason took Maude's hand and tugged her past Ariel, but then stopped two steps into the hallway and turned back. "By the way, I met a friend of yours the other day."

"Oh, who was it?" Ariel tilted her head.

"Don't recall her name, but she had some enlightening stories about you."

"Is that so?" Ariel narrowed her eyes.

Maude glanced back and forth between them. Based on the tension in the air and Jason's less-than-welcoming demeanor earlier, she felt as if she were sitting on the edge of her seat watching a drama unfold. *Darn!* Now she craved popcorn.

Jason continued, "I kinda had to wonder, though, if she and I were discussing the same person, because the woman she described was a devious bitch."

Stilling, Maude gasped then glanced at Ariel. *Oh, no!* What had he learned? And from whom?

Ariel was quiet for a moment before responding, "As you say, she likely meant someone else."

"Right, right." He lifted his free hand and rubbed his chin. "Lots of girls named Ariel frequenting the clubs, prowling for rich men, I'm sure." Raising his thumb above his fist and pointing an index finger, he mimicked a handgun before making clicking sound out the side of his mouth. "My mistake." Dismissing her, Jason turned and towed Maude down the hall.

Though sure she wouldn't like what she'd see, Maude glanced over her shoulder.

Ariel gazed at her with cold, emotionless eyes.

A shiver ran over her body.

Now two unstable, and likely malicious people had her smack dab in the center of their bulls-eyes. *Great.*

Maude Killion, the human dartboard. What a lovely visual.

CHAPTER 21

Ariel stood in line outside Plunder, the bar where Patrick worked as a bouncer. Using her cell phone's camera, she touched up her deep mauve lipstick. She didn't do cherry red, because that screamed I'll-drop-to-my-knees-for-a-bottle-of-Cristal. Though cherry red would match the fury raging deep within after her words with Jason today. Someone was telling tales again. If things with Jason didn't work out, she might have to skip town, start over someplace new, with a different name and identity. Hell no, to all of it. She was sticking to Manchester.

A light spring breeze kept her from overheating at the thought of Maude Killion winning her man. Jaw clenched, Ariel counted the number of people in line before her. Seven. Waiting, waiting, waiting, seemed that's all she ever did.

The glow of cell phones illuminated the partygoers both in front and behind her. A pink-haired chick, standing before her, obnoxiously blathered on her phone and kept snapping her gum. Clenching her fist, Ariel seriously considered knocking the wad from her mouth.

Wearing a violet sequined dress, Ariel stood out like a newly born butterfly amongst the general insects. Designer dress. Designer shoes. These ornaments, gave her a sense of power. She could do anything. Be with anyone. And tonight, she would. Time was running out, and she needed a sperm donor—aka Patrick. Both brothers were known players. She'd waited until this time in her monthly cycle to make her play. He'd have to do, since his brother had his dick stuck up some pasty bitch's ass.

She'd seen them kiss today. Right in front of those kids. Pervy fuckers.

Still, she'd played it off quite well. Ariel Silvers, the actress. Once she had Patrick Stafford on his back, she wouldn't have to play a part anymore. She'd be pregnant for real and pass any stupid DNA tests Jason forced her to take.

Not that sleeping with Patrick would be much of a chore. He was just as gorgeous as his brother. Hopefully, he didn't know her. If so, she had some drugs in her purse that would make the evening's events a bit fuzzier.

Using drugs as a persuasion tactic seemed an unnecessary option as Ariel had studied Patrick for the past couple weeks, watching which women caught his eye. She'd adjusted her look accordingly. Classy, with a dash of sleaze, seemed his type. Usually brunettes and big-breasted, so she qualified for one preference.

A few losers walked by and whistled. Ariel merely rolled her eyes and glanced at her friend, Bethany. "This line is taking forever tonight. We should do like Gina and just pay the bouncers a monthly fee for guaranteed placement on the VIP list."

"Gina has a sugar daddy and can afford to pay those fees." Bethany brushed her multi-colored hair over her shoulder. "We do not."

"I will soon." Ariel sniffed. Her friend's foray into striping her hair with various colors, like the bright purple tonight, made her look like a skanky skunk. With hair like, that she'd have to reconsider their friendship.

"You better hope this plan works." Bethany waved a hand toward the bar's entrance.

Her friend was aware of her plans to seduce Patrick, though why she'd given the woman ammunition to use against her was beyond her.

"It will." Ariel stuffed her lipstick back into her metallic silver handbag.

"So, Jason has another woman." Bethany smirked. "The great Ariel Silvers has competition, whatever will she do?"

Ariel shrugged. "*Ariel* doesn't worry about such petty matters. She'll fade, but *I* have a connection to Jason. He'll come back, eventually. Family is important to him, and I'm giving him that." She caressed her stomach.

"Based on what you've told me, I think you may have to take more drastic measures." Bethany nudged her forward as the line moved.

"Why don't you spend more time worrying about your stupid fucking clown hair? I don't need you to tell me what to do."

"Whatever." Bethany smiled, apparently glad she'd gotten under Ariel's skin. "When you're desperate for help, you can apologize for your bitchy tongue and call me. Gina used these people who are good with computer stuff to get her current guy. She had them manipulate these photos to make it look like the guy's wife was cheating and then sent him the altered pictures. Problem solved."

"I have it handled." Ariel had already spoken to Gina, but Bethany didn't need to know that. In this business of bagging a rich guy, all single women were competition. She'd cut any bitch to win. Bethany was beautiful, naturally so, which seriously annoyed Ariel every time they went out. Why did some girls have it so easy and others had to drop thousands on plastic surgery?

"Oh my God," Bethany exclaimed, tapping Ariel's upper arm over and over. "It's Erik Pavel. I heard he left town. I wonder why he's back." She released a dramatic sigh. "He's so dark and gritty. He just oozes sex."

Refraining from rolling her eyes, Ariel followed Bethany's gaze to a man standing beside a black Bentley with tinted windows. His gray suit fit perfectly, no tie, black hair and slim, tall build. He opened the back passenger side door. A woman's long legs were followed by a manicured hand reaching toward Pavel.

Ariel gasped as Erik Pavel pulled Nicki from the back seat of the car.

Damn her.

Her green dress molded to her body perfectly, the color matching those cat-like eyes. Her dark hair fell softly around her shoulders in a gentle wave. Well, well, someone had certainly been busy since leaving prison. If Bethany thought Pavel was gritty, she'd lose her mind if she ever knew everything Nicki had done. Was still doing, by the looks of things.

Nicki smiled at Pavel and took his arm before glancing over at the line of people waiting to get in. Her searching gaze stopped when it hit Ariel's. Her grin went Cheshire cat wide, and she whispered something to Pavel.

He nodded then led her over, but stopped a few feet away.

"Good evening, Ariel." Nicki arched a brow before meeting her gaze with those piercing green eyes. "So interesting that I'd run into you here. I had no idea you frequented such places, especially in your condition." She glanced at Ariel's stomach.

"Careful." Ariel smirked. "I don't know what kind of game you're playing, but I have plenty of ammunition. I've used it before, and I'll use it again." She gave Nicki a blatant once-over. "I think orange suits you much better."

Nicki threw back her head and laughed. "Oh, you're certainly right about that. Orange *is* my favorite color. I used to like sunny yellow." She glanced at Ariel's hair. "But not anymore."

Ariel glanced at Pavel. "Does he know of your...shall we say, appreciation of women?"

"Oh, I've had my fill of women." Nicki flicked her hand in the air. "As you say, orange did flatter me." She glanced back at Pavel. "Go ahead and play your games with that man, Ariel. But before you do, I'd ask your current boy toy, Jason Stafford, to fill you in on just how lethal Erik Pavel can be."

"I heard he's got ties to the mafia," Bethany piped up after obviously eavesdropping into their whole exchange.

Nicki glanced at her like she was a piece of shit she'd found on her shoe. "As Ariel has alluded, I do prefer women…she should know, but I just hadn't found the right man. Until now." She flashed her white teeth. "Excuse me, will you? I've kept him waiting long enough."

Ariel seethed as she watched Nicki disappear inside with Pavel. She'd never really paid much attention to the man once she'd heard he was more criminal than sin.

"I never knew you were bi," Bethany spoke up beside her.

"Not now," Ariel answered between clenched teeth. She'd controlled her rages for a few years now, but Bethany was pressing on her last nerve. Just what was Nicki up to?

"If I knew you were into women, then you and I could have—"

"Shut your mouth, before I shut it for you."

Bethany narrowed her eyes but kept quiet until they got closer to the entrance.

Ariel kept her gaze on the line of people before her, breathing in and out in small increments. She had one goal tonight. Worries over Nicki would not distract her. Whatever her old friend's plan, she'd meet her head on. Hadn't she already defeated her once? Thing was, she'd had more connections with powerful men at the time. Lately, she'd narrowed her focus too much, and that could cost her. Yet, she wouldn't return to the escort business. No way in hell. This seduce-Patrick-and-pass-off-the-baby-as-Jason's plan would work. She bit her thumbnail. Maybe she should do her own research on DNA tests instead of trusting people like Bethany, who said they knew doctors who would fake the results for a fee.

Closer to the door, she caught a glimpse of Patrick talking to the doorman. She shook her head, clearing her thoughts, and then narrowed her focus on the evening's prize. She gave his burly body a quick once-over before meeting his gaze and winking.

He arched a brow then turned and spoke to a brunette before heading back inside the bar. He wore faded jeans and a bright yellow T-shirt with Plunder Security in black letters on the back.

Once she was finally inside, Ariel danced and drank, keeping an eye on Patrick, making sure he knew she was interested. She did not see Nicki, but the conniving bitch was likely in the upstairs VIP section, sucking down expensive liquor...as well as other things. She may dress nice, but Ariel knew exactly who Nicki was deep down, because they were cut from the same cloth.

Her evening started to look promising when the next round of drinks came from Patrick. Hook, line, and sinker.

After hitting the bathroom and touching up her lipstick, she sauntered over to thank him.

Patrick shrugged off her gratitude. "You seemed a little thirsty." He tore his gaze from the crowd and eyed her. His hair was a little darker than his brother's, but they had the same blue eyes. "What's your name?"

"Amanda." Using her real name might set off alarms if Jason had mentioned her. "And, as you say, I am very, very *thirsty*." She placed a hand on his shoulder, making sure she pressed her chest against his arm.

"That so?" He looked her up and down. "What're you thirsty for tonight, sugar?"

"Whatever you have back at your place." She smiled, because why not be blunt? The man was a notorious womanizer. Still, she might have appeared a tad overeager, because he sat back, eyes wide.

"I've seen you in here a lot, lately." Patrick glanced at her then shifted his gaze back over to the crowd.

She mentally rolled her eyes. Nice to know she'd caught his attention, but he was technically working. However, the night was winding down. Since most fights occurred at the end of the night, maybe he was just being diligent by keeping an eye on the overly drunk patrons. "Maybe I come here so often…because I like what I see." She ran her fingers along the back of his neck.

He shivered before glancing back toward the bar.

At the brunette.

The one who'd been with him by the front door.

Ariel had partied with that girl before. No competition there.

"So, what else do you like, *Amanda?*"

Why was he emphasizing her name like that? Did he know who she was? Had the stupid brunette—what was her name? Carrie? Katie?—told him her name? "I like the finer things. Doesn't everyone?"

"Finer things, is it?" Patrick trailed a finger down the side of her neck to her breasts. "You plan on following up on that invitation in your eyes?"

"I find myself in need of a man."

Since he sat on a bar stool, he was in perfect alignment for her to slip in between his thick thighs. "I've been watching you for weeks. My last man cheated, and I'm feeling like a little revenge sex is in order."

"Revenge sex. No strings. Just fucking." Patrick tilted up her chin with his forefinger. "And you aren't looking for strings, isn't that right, Amanda?"

"I've heard about you from my friends. They say you know how to treat a woman right. So, no, I don't want strings, but I do want a night where you treat me real good…or real bad." She wet her lower lip with the tip of her tongue. "Doesn't matter to me."

Patrick crooked an eyebrow. "Got a reputation, do I?"

"I know exactly who you are, Patrick Stafford."

"Hmm…" Patrick met her gaze for a moment. "You really want to do this?"

"Yes." Very much, yes. She inwardly smirked as she raked her nails along the inside of his thighs.

He hissed before pulling out his phone and sending off a

quick text. "All right, then." With a quick nod, he pointed toward the back door. "Let's go."

CHAPTER 22

Maude leaned against her open apartment door, shooing away an exhausted Ember and Owen, who reminded her to lock the door three times before he was tugged away. Rachel and Bronco had left about an hour earlier after agreeing to drop off Maude's mom.

Taking her friend's advice, Maude had taken the day off work to move into her new apartment. She'd done as much as she could with three huge males bumping around in her small place.

Jason placed a hand on her shoulder, drew her inside, and then shut the door. He nudged her into the living room and handed her a cold beer.

"Why do I feel like crying?" Maude shuffled over to her couch and plopped down, wiping her eyes with the sleeve of her grubby shirt. "I'm being a big baby."

"It's a natural feeling." He plopped down beside her. "You're saying goodbye to your mom and your brother after living with them for so long. Change can be hard, sometimes."

"I'll miss them, but I need my space." Maude took a long draw from her beer bottle. "I feel bad about that, but it was time."

Jason nodded and then glanced around the room. "Looks good. Smart to move everything at once. Those delivery guys cracked me up when Chewy wandered in this afternoon. His fandom never ceases to amaze me."

"You have your own fans."

Jason rolled his eyes. "Yeah, but Chewy's a good guy and deserves the accolades because he trains hard."

"Um, I don't know." Maude arched a brow. "I'm on your social media pages. You share way too much."

"Nothing personal."

"What?" Maude eased back and her eyes widened. "You posted a picture of yourself in nothing but boxer briefs the other day. How is that not personal?"

Shrugging, he chuckled. "What's the matter, Maude? Want a private showing?"

She did, actually, but not when she was covered in moving dust. Plus, all of a sudden she felt shy. They were alone. On a couch with a ready-to-use bed in the other room. Was she ready for this step? Her lower anatomy stood up and shouted, "Heck yes, we're ready!"

"I need a shower then bed." Maude rested her head back against the couch and closed her eyes.

"I can help with that."

Outwardly, Maude showed no signs of nervousness, but inwardly, her heart was doing jumping jacks. Instead of answering, she decided to let her actions speak, because she probably wouldn't have said anything that made sense, anyway. Jason Stafford was willing to help her shower. One fantasy down, which left about five million to go.

Be brave. Be the change. Taking a deep breath, she opened her eyes and stood before lifting her shirt over her head and heading to the bathroom. On the way, she downed the rest of her beer. Liquid courage.

She left the door open, turned on the water, and then headed to the sink to brush her teeth.

Jason leaned against the bathroom's doorway. "My dick is completely on board with this, but my mind is throwing up some roadblocks. I never question sex, I just dive in, but I can't do that with you. I can't shut off my heart."

"I don't want you to." Maude finished rinsing out her mouth then turned and met his gaze.

"Maybe we should slow things down. We were going to wait, weren't we? Did I say that?"

"Sure, let's wait." With a shrug, Maude unsnapped her bra and tugged it off.

"Geez, Maude. I'm trying...I think I should do the right thing here and take our next phase kind of slow." He took another step into the steam-filled room.

Some siren must have taken over her body, because slow left her agenda. Slow was crushing on Jason Stafford since she was sixteen. Slow in no way described the racing of her heart. "I've already done slow. I am thinking I might like fast better." She shimmied out of her jeans.

He swallowed then opened his mouth to say something, but he just shook his head instead.

"Here's the thing, I know you're in a difficult situation with everything going on with Ariel, the accusations you heard from Katie, your mom, the season coming up, and then me." She met his gaze, but she didn't quite know what to do with her arms, because she stood basically naked. In front of Jason. Her body hadn't been nipped or tucked, so she hoped he liked what he saw. Too late now. Sighing, she gripped his hand in hers. "Listen, we can't know if we want to continue if we don't try the...um...physical side of our relationship. I could touch your"—she waved a trembling hand toward his crotch—"and you aren't turned on. There's only one way to find out. I, for one, am ready. Ready to put aside everything else and just test who we can be together. I want this." She squeezed his hand. "I have for a very long time, so join me, if you want."

Holy smokes! Did I really just say all that? The gauntlet had been thrown. Now she'd see if he'd pick it up. Not that she knew what a gauntlet was. Maybe she'd Google it. And why was she thinking of stuff like that when she stood in nothing but her underwear in front of her dream crush?

She released a shaky breath. "Don't know how long the water stays hot in this building, so I'm not wasting it." Maude shimmied out of her undies then situated a couple towels on the shower hook attached to the wall. "I'm going in, Jason, both literally and figuratively. Stay or go. The next move is yours."

Opening the glass door, she offered a silent prayer to the love gods and tried evening her breathing. Part of the reason she'd liked these apartments was because the showers had the wide rainfall showerheads. Soaping up, she let the spray coat her body.

A few moments later, Jason joined her.

A breath that had been lodged in her throat released. *Thank you, love gods.*

Biting back a grin over her ridiculous thoughts, she ran her hands through her wet hair and squeezed out the excess water. Her shower stall wasn't overly small, but as big as he was, she rubbed against him quite well. No need to worry about chemistry on her end. Her libido shot through the red zone and went ultra-violet. She'd seen his body. As she'd said, he posted half-dressed selfies all the time. But live and in person with his dick jutting out from a groomed patch of light brown hair, she practically melted. "That is…" She pointed at his cock. "It's on a massive scale."

He chuckled and took the soap from her limp hand.

Her eyes were hypnotized by his erection. She blinked. Not quite sure what she was seeing was real. "So…well…my eyes are bugging out of their sockets. I knew you were a big guy, but…" Wildly waving her hands at his dick, she contemplated everything she wanted to do with it. Tonight. Now. Later. On the floor.

She finally tore away her gaze and looked at his face, which seemed to be a shade pink. "Am I embarrassing you?"

"No, I get hot watching you, watching my cock."

His cock seemed to nod in agreement, bobbing up and down

against her stomach, leaking at the tip.

"*I've* aced the physical attraction portion of this test. But I'm not so sure about you. I'll have to check."

Jason's words sent an electric sizzle to all the pleasure points in her body. But all of a sudden, her mind urged caution. Something it should have done minutes ago. "So we're doing this, Jason? We'll both try? I-I mean, you're willing to be true…to just me?" She placed a hand against his cheek. "Can you promise?"

"We're done talking about whether we will or we won't. I'm here. That's the promise I'll give you." He wrapped one big hand around her waist and cupped one ass cheek with the other, drawing her against his slightly bent knee. "Now, we were in the middle of a test, so quiet in the classroom." He flashed a wicked grin and spanked her. "Don't make me break out the ruler." After running his hands up her body, he cupped her face. "I'll start with your mouth and test you farther from there."

His driving kiss erased any doubt that he wanted her as much as she wanted him. How that happened, she'd worry about later, right now she met his plunging kisses with equal fervor. Finally, glorying in the fact she could touch his body as she wished, freely roaming her hands through his groomed chest hair before reaching down and caressing his hard, thick cock.

He gasped, then spun her around and kissed her neck. "You've passed the kissing portion, so what's next? Shall we test how you respond to my touch?" He dumped a handful of liquid body soap, she generally only used to shave her legs, into his hands.

Every fantasy, every dream she'd ever had of this man was nothing compared to the real thing. The lather he worked all along the front of her body created a silky glide. A sense of surrealness floated through her mind, as if she were watching another couple, but no, she'd waited, hoped, and now, she would take her rightful place in this man's life. No longer would she wait patiently on the sidelines. She would take. As she watched his hands slide through the bubbles, she realized this moment was very real.

Her inner thoughts shut down as he thumbed her hardened nipples before journeying his skilled fingers to her core. Lost in sensation, she rested her head against his shoulder and arched up on her toes as he skillfully massaged her. "Yes, I want more. Test me farther."

Jason bit her neck.

Pulse racing, she glanced over her shoulder. "Don't stop."

He eased away, turned her, and then met her gaze with a hint of hesitation in his blue eyes. "I feel like I should stop, like this should be wrong, but I can't...my heart and body are drawn to you. What I feel can't be wrong, can it?" He wrapped her in his arms, water trickling over their skin. "Wanting you is selfish, but I've always needed you." Easing back, he cupped her chin and lightly kissed her. "Please, don't ever doubt that, Maude. Besides, I kind of like the whole friends-to-lovers story, don't you?"

"Yes, this is even better than my dreams."

He smiled. "Mine, too."

When she tried to look away, she was pulled back to meet his seeking lips. Being part of his dreams, maybe even his fantasies, stirred the fire building inside her even higher.

Then, with expert fingers, he delved into her core, gliding two fingers deep inside. His mouth roamed over her mouth, her neck, before he bent and rasped his tongue across her nipple and sucked. Sensations raced down her spine and pooled before shooting across her lower body. She pulsed against his hand, tightened, and then she exploded into pleasure with a moan against his lips.

Hot kisses continued, and he rocked his lower body against hers.

After taking a moment to catch her breath, Maude dropped to her knees. "Your turn." Not giving him a chance to say no, she held his cock by the root and tugged him closer to her mouth. His tip leaked, so she licked him clean. Though not a particular favorite sexual activity in the past, with Jason, she wanted to devour him. Make his knees buckle. Make him beg.

Set on her course, she licked the mushroomed tip then widened her mouth and swallowed him down before coming back up and releasing his hard cock with a pop. She gazed up at him. "Tell me what you like."

He brushed her wet hair from her face. "Take me deep."

Not such an easy command to follow, but she took as much as she could, ignoring her gag reflex.

"Now, tug on my balls."

She cradled both in one hand and pulled.

His entire body jerked. "Maude, I'm gonna…so pull back, unless you want a mouthful."

"I want it." Her words were mumbled out around his thick cock before she began working him again with both hands and her mouth. Her bedroom skills weren't quite as honed as his, but she figured her enthusiasm made up for anything she might be lacking.

A few seconds later, he came. Hot streams pumped into her mouth and down her throat. Though she'd never enjoyed swallowing before, she relished every drop of his pleasure upon hearing Jason's mumbled curses and breathy whispers.

With his hands circling her arms, he drew her to her feet and kissed her, his tongue dueling with hers.

Fighting for air after their heated exchange, she pulled away. "Let's finish this in the bedroom. The water's getting cold."

"No, Maudy." Jason rested his forehead against hers. "I need some time. I never knew sex could feel like this. I thought an orgasm was the same no matter who I fucked, but with you…I'm…to be honest…I'm a little worried." After chuckling, he eased back. "Imagine that, big ol' football player scared of a girl." He turned off the water, and then wrapped her in his arms. "What we just did, I felt this wave of pleasure from my cock to my heart. Don't laugh." He pinched her butt, because she had giggled. "We need to do this right. *I* need to do this right. I won't just fuck you."

"I understand." She kissed his chest and smoothed her hand over his hard bicep. "But I don't need to be coddled."

He laughed. "Yeah, maybe you don't, but I do."

Though her body was revved and ready again, she understood how he felt. Their connection was real, something neither had much knowledge about, so moving forward would be a learning experience. Another test. Love could be very confusing, and yeah, as he'd said, scary. Maude leaned back to meet his gaze. "So, you're having a hard time, because you actually enjoyed sex with your heart and not just your...uh...dick?"

"I think that's it, yeah." Chuckling, he shook his head. "I'm sorry, Maudy. I'm a mess."

"True." She smiled. "But, just to be clear, I really would be okay with getting fucked."

"Ah, hell, Maude." He kissed her then drew her close until nothing existed between them. His kisses went from demanding to soft and languid. Once, twice, he lightly kissed her lips before easing away. "Be careful what you wish for."

"Everything I've wished for is right here." Unwilling to let him see the tears in her eyes, she practically jumped him, wrapping her limbs tight around his body. Everything in the outside world would intrude soon enough. Right now, she had him in her arms. Right now, all her wishes were coming true, so why not make one more? Forever. Closing her eyes, she wished for forever.

He slapped her bottom. "Come on, Killion. You're shivering."

Before she could frown or retaliate, she was yanked from the shower, dried off then drug half-wet to the bedroom.

With a cocky smile, Jason lifted her under the arms then tossed her onto the bed.

She landed with a bounce.

Hands on his hips, he stood at the side of the bed. "Woman,

you scare the shit out of me. I can't promise our relationship will be easy, but I can promise I'll always come home to you." Jason tapped a finger against his lower lip. "Actually, now that I think about it, I always have."

"Then come home to me now." Maude lifted her arms and beckoned him. "Let's get some rest."

He settled beside her, his knees on each side of her hips before leaning down and bracing her head between his hands. He kissed her long and sweet, never moving his hands from her face.

Finally, when she squirmed beneath him, he eased back and plopped down at her side. "Goodnight, Maudy."

She turned on her side to study his handsome, dear face, knowing her wide grin gave away everything she felt inside, but she couldn't bring herself to care. He already knew. Had always known. And now, so did she. "Goodnight Jason."

CHAPTER 23

On cloud nine after a weekend of canoodling with Jason, Maude was knocked back to reality when her receptionist texted and told her she had a visitor.

Ariel waited in the lobby.

Whatever the woman had to say wouldn't matter. Saturday, during a lunch break in their Rec Center clean-up, Jason had informed them all about Katie's revelations. He'd even hired Rachel to dig into Ariel's past and uncover the truth about her current allegations.

Maude was proud to see Jason take control over that aspect of his life. He needed answers instead of remaining in limbo about what was true. Another issue in his life was his mother. They'd visited her yesterday afternoon. Jason had temporarily asked the cleaning lady to stay with his mom until he could hire a more skilled nurse.

Maude's heart ached because even though Sharon was dying of a lung disease, she'd still smoked two cigarettes during their three-hour visit.

Jason begged her to stop, but she merely shook her head. His somber mood remained as they headed back to her apartment to unpack more boxes. He'd left soon after, claiming he needed to spend time with the punching bag.

Releasing a heavy sigh, because she had no doubt she'd soon feel the same, Maude glanced at the clock. High noon. "Great. Where's a cowboy when you need him?" she mumbled then rolled her eyes. Not one for confrontations, she took a deep breath before straightening her spine. She could do this, even though fighting over a man seemed silly.

Ariel took her pursuit of Jason a little too seriously, popping up here and there. One never knew when she'd arrive. Maybe Rachel had begun her surveillance already and would ride in and drag Ariel back to her car. "Not nice, Killion."

Frowning, she turned to step out of her cubicle and bumped into Brady. "Oh, Brady, you startled me." She leaned over to pick up her cell phone since she'd dropped it. He must not have any client meetings today because he was dressed down, wearing black Dockers and a light blue polo.

"Why are you talking to yourself? And why is Ariel Silvers here?"

"I don't know." After checking her phone for cracks, Maude shrugged. "She's Jason and Chewy's lawyer, and she's been involved with the Rec Center account." How did Brady know who Ariel was? And what was he doing down in the lobby? She narrowed her eyes. "Do you know Ariel?"

"I've met her at the clubs." Brady leaned against her desk, arms crossed over his chest. "I heard she was pregnant...with Jason Stafford's kid."

"Where did you hear that?" Maude snapped around and met his gaze.

"We're Facebook friends, and she posted a photo a few weeks ago. Everybody guessed who the father was, and she said in the comments that it was Jason."

Maude nodded, while inwardly storing that information so Jason would be prepared for any oncoming media storm. "Jason *is* the father, but...Brady, I feel I should tell you..." She bit her lip, unsure if she should mention this now, but why not? The timing was right. She could drop the bomb and then escape to speak to Ariel. "Brady, Jason and I are seeing each other."

Brady laughed and shook his head. "Good one."

"I'm not joking." Would this be everyone's response? Utter disbelief? "I spent the weekend with him."

Brady leaned forward and grabbed her forearm. "Are you insane? Jason Stafford, the player of all players? Not only that, the man has a child coming. What are you thinking, Maude?" He gave her a little shake. "I can't believe you'd fall for that bastard's charms. You wouldn't believe some of the stories I've heard about him. He's wild and discards women like old pennies."

Maude yanked away her arm. "I know who he is, and he's more than the rumors. I am trying to be kind by telling you I've moved on to another man. Now, will you please stop sending all the flowers and gifts? I'm sorry, Brady, but I *am* with Jason now." Her phone buzzed again with a text from the front desk. "I need to go." She started to walk away, but she turned back. "Brady, I am really sorry, and I just felt I should be honest."

"You might be honest with me, but you're not honest with yourself if you think Jason Stafford is the right man for you." With that, he shoved away from her desk and stalked off.

# # #

Stomping down to the lobby, Maude yanked the hair tie from around her wrist and whipped her hair into a ponytail. Her hair was getting in her face. Brady was getting in her face, and now Ariel thought she could do the same. One confrontation per day should be enough. Although, if she really thought about it, she was grateful for the opportunity to mention Jason to Brady. Perhaps now he'd stop the barrage of gifts and let her go. His credit card had to be on fire with all the money he'd been spending on his "Woo Maude" campaign. "Enough is enough, though, geesh."

After rounding the corner and catching sight of Ariel, Maude practically groaned.

Blonde perfection personified. Designer suit. Killer shoes. All black. If Maude didn't know any better, she'd say Ariel came ready for a funeral. Nope, Maude wouldn't go down so easy. Not after finally having Jason in her arms and in her bed. "Ariel." Maude stopped before the woman, fingers clasped together at her waist so her enemy wouldn't detect her shaky hands. "I don't have much time. What can I do for you?"

"I thought we'd go to lunch." Ariel tucked her cell phone into her small black purse, which had some sort of gold logo on the front.

"I'm sorry. I don't have time today." Maude glanced outside at all the people bustling by her downtown office. What if she ran out the door and escaped into the crowd? Much better plan than enduring whatever Ariel had to say. "If you want to go to lunch with me, you should make an appointment."

"Won't you sit?" Ariel waved a hand toward the lobby's couch. "I'm sure those clunky shoes you're wearing can't be comfortable."

Maude huffed out a laugh. "My sandals feel just fine, Ariel." Mentally rolling her eyes, she turned on said shoes and headed toward an empty conference room. "Let's talk in here." Based on Ariel's mean-girl volley, their conversation wouldn't be pleasant. Yet, Maude refused to be bullied. Rachel and Ember would never forgive her if she let Ariel get the better of her. Should pregnant women be engaging in stressful verbal battles? Was she even pregnant? How much of what Katie told Jason was true? Likely all of it, something she was sure would become crystal clear momentarily.

Ariel stepped inside the empty room, but she stopped just inside the door.

Maude remembered her manners, okay, more like engaged in a stall tactic. "Would you like something to drink?"

"I offered to go to lunch, but since you said no, I'll decline, as well."

"Suit yourself." Maude crossed the room to the mini fridge and took out a water bottle. She needed to calm down. She twisted the lid and took a long, cool drink.

Ariel remained by the door.

"Why don't you sit down?" Maude moved closer to the frigid woman, pulled out a chair, and then waved a hand toward the seat. She took another drink from the water bottle and leaned her hip against the table, feigning a nonchalance she certainly did not feel.

Ariel did not sit, but kept her ice-blue glare hard and focused.

Nerves whirling, Maude sighed. "What can I do for you, Ariel? I'm sure your purpose isn't just to stand there and glower."

The corner of Ariel's mouth quirked, and she shifted her weight before coming to stand directly in front of Maude. "I thought I'd come by and offer a warning."

Maude stiffened. Then she glanced around to be sure she was still in a boardroom, not a high school locker room, because really...

"Before I became...involved with Jason, I researched him. Studied him." She tapped a pink-tipped nail against her lower lip. "I know you are not a fool, nor ignorant of my obsession. I freely admit I want a better life and a man who can give it to me. Why should I settle for anything less?" Ariel arched a brow. "The same is true for you, Maude. We deserve more than a nine-to-five life, more than working every day with nothing to show for our troubles." She sniffed. "But you see, dear, I've already laid claim to Jason. I understand the kind of man he is, and none of his partying ways or...indiscretions with other women will bother me. Can you say the same?" Ariel patted Maude's hand where it rested on the table. "Jason doesn't spend time with just one woman. He moves on and on and on." Her smile softened, but her gaze remained cold and direct. "He'll do the same to you."

Maude shook her head. Score one to Ariel. Playing on her deepest fears, on everything she knew to be true about Jason was a great move. But wasn't there more to him? Hadn't she always seen him for who he really was? A scared, lost boy who partied and lived like he was dying because he'd seen how quickly life could end? Had Ariel studied that? Had she dug beneath the surface? Why would she, when only the surface of a person mattered to her? "I know who Jason is, Ariel. I appreciate the warning, but…if that's all you came here to say, you can leave. I need to get back to work."

"I'm not finished." Ariel narrowed her eyes. "What do you think will happen when Jason travels again? He'll revert to his old ways and leave you brokenhearted. Me, I accept who he is. And I'll wait, patient, and content, because he'll always come back." She grinned like the cat who had stolen all the cream.

Maude clenched her hands at her sides, hoping against all hope she wouldn't strike a pregnant woman.

"I have something you don't. A piece of him. His child."

Maude took a deep breath then shoved away from the table and from Ariel. Although, she may or may not have purposefully bumped into the blond woman's shoulder. "Every word you've said has some grain of truth. However, I've done some studying of my own. I'm good with who he is, and I trust that his future is with me."

Ariel opened her mouth, but Maude lifted her hand, palm up. "No. Will Jason Stafford break my heart? Yes, he likely will. He's already done so many times before. However, I have faith that he'll remain true. I believe that yes, if in fact you are pregnant, you will have a platonic relationship with him, and due to that, I believe we should at least try to get along instead of placing Jason in the middle. That isn't fair to him or your child. This can work if you just step back and let it."

Eyes blazing, Ariel charged forward and jabbed a finger against her chest. "I do not step back. Not for you or anyone."

Maude sidestepped, wary of that poking finger. "Ariel, I'm trying to be reasonable, but none of that includes dealing with your blade of a finger. Stop. Okay?"

"You listen to me, you mousy bitch." Ariel raised a finger again but didn't poke this time. "Just try interfering with my plans. I guarantee you'll regret it."

"Are you threatening me?" She'd watched enough shows on the Investigation Discovery channel to know that some women actually followed through with their threats in deadly ways. "I'd prefer you didn't show up at my house with a hatchet." Maude tried to laugh it off.

Ariel's gaze remained steely. "I'm glad you think this is all a joke. Gives me a slight advantage."

"I've tried to be kind today, Ariel. I brought you in here for privacy. Listened to everything you had to say." Maude pinched the bridge of her nose and sighed. "And yes, I'll take your words seriously."

"I hope you do, because I'll do whatever I have to in order to keep Jason Stafford." Ariel headed for the door. "Don't test me, Maude."

"I'm not finished." Maude grabbed Ariel's shoulder and spun her around, because screw that. She wouldn't bow down to threats, and Ariel wouldn't get the last word. Time for nice Maude to take a lunch break and assertive Maude to take her place.

Jason Stafford did that for her. He made her stronger, and whatever their future held, this gift of confidence in herself was enough, for now. "It's your turn to listen to *me*, Ariel." Standing tall, she did her own finger pointing. "For years, I was happy to stay in the background and take Jason's crumbs of attention. But now, all that patience has paid off. So, I *will* test you, and I *will* remain at Jason's side, as I always have, and as I always will. Play your games. Concoct your schemes. I am not afraid, but let me give you a bit of advice." Maude leaned in like she was giving away top-secret information. "You won't win."

"I will," Ariel answered through tight lips.

"Will you?" Maude crossed her arms over her chest. "This is the second time you've interfered with my job. You don't see me knocking down your door, so I'd maybe re-evaluate who is scared and who isn't in this childish scenario you're creating."

Ariel glowered. "Watch your back. And by that, I mean your backside. Women like you get fatter with age." She gave Maude a quick once-over. "And let me give *you* some advice. The women who set their sights on Jason aren't pasty, fat, freckled cunts like you. If I don't seduce him, someone else will, and where will that leave you? Never pictured Jason as a chubby-chaser."

"Oh, so original." Rolling her eyes, Maude shook her head. "Yeah, yeah, I'm not super-skinny. Great observation, now here's another." Maude jabbed her finger toward the exit. "There's the door. Use it."

With a final glare, Ariel stomped off.

"Well, that was just awful," Maude mumbled to herself before leaning against the conference room wall. Then her knees gave out. She slid down and covered her face with her hands. Tears poured down her cheeks. Why did they have to fight like that? And why was Ariel so mean? Were there vicious bitch classes Maude knew nothing about?

Angry she'd become so disturbed, Maude wiped her cheeks and took a couple of deep breaths. She wasn't a chubby cunt. She wasn't. *Don't let her hateful words cut so deep, Killion. You're stronger than that.*

Right now, she needed Ember and a whole lot of Rachel. She needed tough and cocky and no nonsense. Rachel would have known exactly what to say to someone like Ariel. "I said some good stuff, too. I did good." Maude sniffed.

Still, Ariel's words hurt, because they cut straight to the heart of her deepest fears. But what about trust? And love? Didn't Jason deserve those things from her?

Maude heaved a sigh, dug her cell from her pocket, and

called Rachel.

Ariel's warnings were real, and she'd handle them. Ariel Silvers would strike again. And Maude refused to become the next victim featured on the imaginary TV show, *Psycho Blonde Murderers*.

CHAPTER 24

Since Jason hadn't been to his mother's house since Sunday, he figured he'd stop by Tuesday afternoon and tell her about the nurse he'd hired. Spring training was set to begin soon, so he needed to spend as much time with her as he could before his schedule got crazy. He'd told his agent to scale down the endorsement deals. Commercial shoots took too much time, and he had enough money for two lifetimes. He pulled into the driveway just as his brother rushed out, holding their mother in his arms.

"What the in the world?" Jason threw the vehicle in Park, opened his door, and got yanked back into place by the seat belt. "Damn it." He quickly unfastened and bolted out the door.

Sirens wailed in the background.

"What the hell?" He approached his brother and studied his mother's limp, unconscious state. "What happened?"

"I came over for breakfast, and she was passed out on the floor." Patrick cupped their mother's cheek in his beefy hand. "Sausage was burning on the stove. The room was full of smoke, and the smell w-was so…was so b-bad, and I-I just…she was…" His brother paused and took a deep breath. "She could have died."

Shaking, stuttering, his eyes red-rimmed—all signs his

brother was on the edge of losing it. "Okay, okay, calm down." Heart racing, Jason squeezed his brother's shoulder. Where to start? *Were those sirens heading here?* "Patrick, look at me. Did you turn off the burner?"

Patrick just stared, glassy-eyed.

Mumbling every curse word he knew, Jason headed toward the back door, but after taking two steps, he turned around. "Did you call 911?"

"I don't know." Patrick readjusted his mom in his arms.

"You don't know?" Exasperated, Jason huffed and then rubbed the back of his neck. "Don't know *what?*" Jason spared a glance at his mother. She remained unresponsive. He blinked then focused back on the house. If he didn't look at his mom, didn't see what was happening, then maybe the moment wasn't real. Couldn't be real. They were fighting this cancer thing, not losing the battle before it even started. No. Not happening. Yet, fear crept through his veins, from his heart to his mind, bringing a whole lot of doubt and unanswered questions. When had she become so fragile? Would she die today? Was the kitchen on fire?

"Patrick, did you call 911?" Jason repeated.

"I don't remember if I turned off the burner, but yes, I called 911." Patrick glanced down at their mother. "Fuck, Jason. She's dying."

Jason bit his bottom lip. "No. No, she isn't. Give me a minute. I'll be right back." Jason ran into the house, waved away the smoke and stench of burnt meat. He glanced at the stove. "Okay, good, the burner's turned off." Breathing out his mouth, he kept one hand over his nose and with the other grabbed the pan of shriveled sausages and tossed the entire mess into the sink. After turning on the faucet for a few seconds, he raced back outside.

An ambulance and fire truck were stationed at the curb.

His brother was settling their mom onto a gurney.

Jason hustled to his side. "Is she breathing?"

"Barely."

Jason ran a hand over his dry mouth and swallowed heavily, choking down the fear ripping through his chest and threatening to come out as a scream.

The EMTs lifted his mom into the back of the ambulance then explained they were taking her to Manchester General.

Jason grabbed his brother's arm. "Come on. I'll drive."

Quiet filled the cab of Jason's Audi SUV, but right before they pulled into the ER's parking lot, his brother finally broke the silence.

"This just doesn't seem right." Patrick stared out the front windshield. "She's been through enough, already. It isn't fair she has to fight this disease, too. I'm not ready for this." His jaw went tight, and he sniffed.

Emotion? From his selfish brother? A lot of harsh and hurtful comebacks poured through Jason's mind like, *Don't worry. I'll still pay for the house*, and *Oh, you're upset because your cook and laundry service is dying.* But Jason couldn't say those words. The sincerity and worry pouring from his brother was very real. This moment could define how they continued. Could change things between them.

As kids, his brother had frequently drawn their father's wrath away from him and Jessica. Only after Patrick left the NFL did their relationship suffer. Should he try again? Put forth the effort and reopen his heart? Stop seeing his brother as an asshole and a burden?

Jason had tried when Jessica died, but his brother had pushed him away. Maybe he should push back. Fight and dig deep to find his old friend again.

They were all that was left of the Stafford clan, except for his father, who didn't count. They should face this issue with their mother as brothers, not enemies. Jason bit back his own tears. This sappy, miss-my-brother shit got old. But, the loss was a constant burr in his heart.

Jason found a spot deep within the Emergency Room parking lot and decided to take a chance. After taking a deep breath, he looked at his brother. When was the last time he'd done that? Really looked at his brother and all he'd become. Jason wasn't blameless in the state of their relationship. So, he'd try. One more time. "Patrick, I'm only saying this once. I'm laying out all this pansy-ass shit, and you can take it or leave it, but I need you to listen to me. Really listen."

His brother turned and met his gaze. "What?"

"I miss you. I miss who we were together. I worshiped you, man, but then you just became…this, I don't know…a raging dick. I need you to get through this thing with Mom. So, quit with the my-life-sucks bullshit. I'm sorry your life didn't pan out how you wanted. I'm sorry I'm playing, and you ain't."

Jaw tight, Patrick turned away.

"I can't change what happened. But we *can* change who we are together."

"I'm supposed to be the big brother." Patrick huffed out a laugh. "During times of trouble, I'm supposed to spout life lessons and all that shit."

"Yeah, so do it."

"What can I say to you?" Patrick shook his head. "You've got it all."

"I don't have it all." Jason bit down hard on the inside of his cheek to keep all the stupid emotions at bay, because his next words ripped open an empty place inside. "I don't have my brother."

"All right. I hear you." Patrick nodded. "I hear you."

Jason closed his eyes for a moment, wishing Maude were here to tell him what to do, how to feel. More than ever before, he realized how much he needed her calm, steady presence.

"I'm trying, Jay Jay." Patrick lightly punched his shoulder. "Come on. Right now is about Ma."

Jason raked his fingers though his hair and opened his eyes.

Patrick was right, they needed to get inside. He'd said his piece, and now they either fell in line or fell apart.

CHAPTER 25

After Jason's phone call, Maude raced around her office, finalizing everything so she could get to the hospital. On the schedule was a huge meeting later that afternoon with a potential Rec Center donor, which she had to leave in her boss's hands. Jason had asked her to come, his voice sounding a little stuffy, so there'd been no other choice. Plus, after Ariel's visit yesterday, she really needed to see him, too.

"What's wrong?" Brady stopped by her cubicle. "You're running around like a chicken with its head chopped off."

"Gross visual." Maude frowned.

Brady tapped her shoulder. "Hey, I'm sorry about earlier. Regardless of what happens, I hope we remain friends." He wrapped her in a hug. "Let's not lose each other, Maude."

Holding herself stiffly, she gently patted his back, feeling a bit awkward in his arms. "Thank you."

He squeezed her tight before easing away. "So, what's up?"

She wasn't sure how much of Jason's troubles she wanted to share with Brady. Things were difficult enough between them without talking about her new boyfriend. "I have to head to the hospital. Jason's mom was admitted earlier."

"Will you be driving yourself?" Brady clasped her arm.

"I'll be fine." Maude placed her laptop in her purse, which

was actually more of a briefcase, then lugged the strap over her shoulder. "I need to go. I'm sorry, Brady." She shrugged and met his gaze. "Just sorry about everything, you know?" Why was she apologizing all the time? Maybe with all the emotional trauma, she'd become a bit nostalgic. Brady wasn't a bad guy, just not the right guy. Everyone made mistakes.

"Let me walk you out."

Having argued enough for the week, she simply nodded and headed for the parking garage.

Upon reaching the car, he braced an arm against the driver's side door, blocking her from getting in. "I'm sorry, but I just can't...this thing with Stafford." He gripped her shoulders. "I'm worried about you. I've seen him at the clubs. He takes home a different woman every night. I don't want that for you."

"I know who he is." Maude stepped out of his hold. "I appreciate your concern, but I really need to go." She jiggled her keys. "This bag is really heavy."

Brady took her keys and unlocked her door before setting her bag in the back seat. "You're sure Jason is who you really want?"

"Yes." Taking back her keys, she settled into the driver's seat, trying to buckle her seatbelt, but her hands were so shaky she gave up trying.

"Fine, Maude. Do what you want, but don't come crying to me when he breaks your heart." He slammed shut her door, but he remained standing there.

He had this switch that could go from normal, sweet guy to scary, rage guy in a moment's notice. These occurrences were rare, but they had startled her in the past. Today, his glare sent a shiver down her spine.

Worried she'd run over his toes, she rolled down the window. "Um, Brady. I need to go, and I don't want to hit you." She always backed into her spot. Most of her co-workers did. Doing so made leaving easier.

"Fine." He pounded a fist against her hood but turned after taking two steps toward the elevators. "But remember, I warned you."

"Yes, yes," she murmured. "Everybody's issuing warnings about Jason. Jeez. I get it." She started her car and followed the bright yellow arrows to the exit. On the first curve, she pressed the brakes, trying to slow down since another car was coming up the spiraled ramp, but her foot shot straight to the floor.

No resistance.

"What the heck?" Owen had just serviced her car, so she shouldn't have any issues. But her brakes were gone.

No brakes.

No stopping.

"Oh, my God. Ariel, if you cut my brake line..."

Heart pounding, Maude steered her car, but as she descended, the momentum grew and the car just travelled faster and faster. "I will not crash. I will not crash. Think, damn it."

What had Owen said about stopping on ice? Was this the same thing?

Stop the car, Maude.

Should she throw the car in Park?

That was right, wasn't it?

Traveling fast and barely in control, she steered as best she could to avoid bumping into parked vehicles and prayed no other car came up the ramp. At the bottom, she threw the car in Park.

Too late.

Her car crashed into the concrete embankment between the entrance and exit. The dangers of not wearing a seat belt flashed through Maude's mind as she flew forward and banged her face against her steering wheel.

Someone honked.

She may have screamed.

Blinking open her eyes, she spat as a copper taste filled her mouth. Her entire face stung and with that thought, a surge of pain raced from the tip of her nose through her body, stopping by her heart, making the organ thump faster and faster.

The ticket guy, Derek, opened her door. "Maude, are you all right?"

She glanced in the lopsided rear view mirror and saw blood dripping from her nose and her split upper lip. With this move, the opponents were now in full battle mode, because brake lines didn't cut themselves. Maude winced against the pain. *Time to mount up, Killion.*

First blood had been drawn.

CHAPTER 26

Fresh from a much-needed shower, Jason opened the bathroom door and then tossed his towel in the laundry basket by his closet. He had a lady who washed everything for him, and she cleaned his house. Maybe lazy, but he could afford the luxury, so why not?

Clean from her own shower, Maude shifted on his king-size bed. She'd been restless since he'd laid her down and ordered her to sleep.

He hadn't thought his day could get any worse until Owen texted him from the emergency room. He'd gone down, saw Maude's blood-covered face, and pretty much lost it. Raging with the need to take out his aggression on anything and anyone, he'd started a fight with Owen. Bronco had broken them up before hospital security became involved.

Not that he was mad at Owen. Owen knew that, and so did Bronco. The day had just sucked all around, and he'd needed to hit something. Owen's jaw worked well enough.

Jerk had got him good in the ribs, though. Guess his friend needed to release a little steam, too.

After Jason had calmed down and the police came to take Maude's statement, he'd called Clayton Kincaid.

He wanted answers, and he wanted Kincaid to get them.

He'd barked orders into the phone at the poor guy, but Jason didn't care. All that mattered was that Maude's face was all banged up because someone cut her brake line. At least, that was Owen's theory, which was likely true, because the man took great pride in servicing his family's vehicles.

Maude told the police she had no idea who'd do such a thing, but she'd been lying.

Owen had caught on, too, but Bronco had kept them from badgering her and shoved them out of the curtained cubicle. Jason had taken exception to that, but Bronco, being Bronco, diffused him. Owen generally instigated, but Bronco…that mammoth man always hit Jason with words and common sense.

He could use his friend's words right about now, because he had none.

Mom dying of cancer. Maude banged up. Ariel maybe pregnant. If he knew a blues song about women troubles, he'd sing it with every piece of his soul. His rendition would probably hit the top of the charts.

"What are you thinking about so hard over there?" Maude murmured with an arm over her eyes. Her nose had a split at the center that'd required stitches and so had her upper lip.

"Get some rest, babe."

"I did. So come here and tell me about your mom." She rubbed her hand over his comforter.

"I need to get back up there."

"I understand. You can go." She flicked a couple fingers. "I told you to let Mom take me home."

"Have you seen your face?" He stood beside the bed with his hands on his hips, afraid to touch her, because he didn't want to apply any pressure to areas that might hurt.

"Actually, yes," she mumbled.

His heart hurt at the thought of how bad her injuries could have been. Jason groaned and gently settled on the bed beside her, careful not to bump her.

"Jason." Maude took his hand. "I'm okay. The drugs have all but alleviated the pain. Talk to me."

"Mom's moved past Stage 3, the doctors said." He raked his fingers through his hair. "I sort of zoned out after that, because he was speaking in doctor language. Basically, because of the cancer, her heart's dying. Fluid has gathered around her lungs and her heart and it's squishing her organs, making them work harder. I don't know. I just know her condition is real bad." He bit his lip, focusing pain on somewhere other than his heart. "I thought I'd have time to research the disease and find specialists, come up with a cure." He scoffed. "Yeah right, there is no cure."

Maude took his hand and kissed his knuckles. "I'm so sorry."

"I just never thought…" He cleared his throat. "Her heart, Maude. Her heart's been through so much, why burden it with more? I've watched her break so many times. With my dad, my sister, hell, even sometimes me. She's always been so resilient, you know? Her heart so strong." He bit his lip harder, but a few tears escaped, anyway. "Damn it. I don't want the problem to be her heart. I need it. You know? I need her. She's my ma."

Maude had no trouble letting the tears fall down her cheeks.

He wiped them away. "Don't cry." He kissed her lips, lightly, so as not to hurt her. "I thought of you, Maude. How much I needed you in that moment, and then look what happens, you get in a wreck."

"Wasn't your fault, Jason." She cupped his face in her hand.

"I got Clayton on it."

Her eyes widened. "It?"

"The accident." He frowned. "Someone hurt my woman. That ain't happening twice. I had two of the most important people in my life in the hospital today. Someone's going down for that. Clayton said he'd sit in when the detectives reviewed the video surveillance from the parking garage."

"Oh, good idea." She met his gaze, her lips pursed. "You shouldn't have provoked Owen."

"He didn't mind."

Maude sighed then ran a hand down his shoulder. "You're naked."

He waggled his brows. "Yeah, so?"

She shifted onto her back. "I know you need to get back to the hospital, but let's take a few moments."

"To do what?" He kissed along her jawline from the tip of her chin to her ear.

"To live. To forget. To just feel."

"Maude, in case you forgot, your face is all smashed up. You look like you went twelve rounds with some bruiser heavyweight."

"My lower anatomy is just fine." Her gaze skittered to the side. "Unless, I gross you out."

He laughed. "I could just put a pillow over your head."

"Shut up." She smacked his arm.

"Hey, come here." He kissed to the side of the stitches on her lip. "I love your face, even if it is a little gross."

She poked him in the ribs.

"Just kidding." He braced himself above her. "You really want to take this next step when you're full of pain killers?"

"Absolutely."

"Just like your brother, a glutton for punishment."

"Your dick is hard against my stomach. Could we please not talk about Owen?"

"Good idea." He nodded. They were doing this. He needed this. Needed to lose himself in her heat, in her sighs of pleasure. "Let's get you out of my T-shirt."

Once he pulled the shirt free, careful to avoid her face, he bent and sucked hard on her nipple. Her breasts drove him crazy. She had one of those hourglass-shaped bodies. As a bigger man, he liked a more substantial woman beneath him. Not that she was overweight, but perfect. And they lined up perfect. He'd always known they would. And now he would test that theory for real.

He teased and licked her hard pink nipples, rolling them

across his tongue until she yanked on his hair.

After lifting his head to kiss her, he eased back. "I can't kiss you. It'll hurt."

"No." Maude arched up. "Please, just a little one."

Unwilling to deny her plea, he did as she asked, but when he heard her hiss, he pulled back. "No kissing."

She started to argue, but he pressed a finger on her lower lip.

"I can kiss you someplace else." He flashed a wicked grin, and then shifted to his knees. With his fingers, he teased her mound, pressing hard with two fingers in just the right place. "How about I kiss you here?" Not waiting for a response, Jason tugged down her panties. Bending his head, he worked his tongue across her folds before driving two fingers into her wet heat.

She moaned and arched into his repeated plunge, rocking her hips. Knowing she was close, he reached up and tweaked a nipple as he continued his ministrations with his other hand and mouth.

Hearing her groan his name, he shifted to her other nipple and smiled when her entire body shuddered. He rubbed his thumb on the outside of her body, while still massaging the inside, and she stiffened and called out his name as she came. Uninhibited, her gasps matched the twitching of her body. After she finished shaking, she jerked a little when he pulled his fingers free.

"How was that for kissing?"

"Amazing." She rolled her thoroughly rumpled head back and forth on his pillow. "My face may still sting a little, but other than that, I'm floating."

He grunted before hopping off the bed and grabbing a condom out of his side drawer. "Amazing is yet to come. Even though I'm not real sure about doing this."

Eyes closed, she mumbled something incomprehensible.

"Maude," he kissed her cheek, "you still ready for this?"

"Muh, huh," she mumbled, but she opened her eyes and smiled.

After he slid on the condom, he entered her in one smooth

thrust.

She shrieked in surprise then sighed as he bent and drew her nipple into his mouth. "Jason, I need you to move." She ran her nails down his sides. "Please. I really am okay."

"I've been waiting for this for so long, I thought I'd make it last." Plus, she felt good. Damn good. Tight.

"No, please, no laster, just faster." Arching against him, she gripped his hips and started rocking against him from the bottom.

"Laster?" He chuckled and stared down into her sweet, bruised face. "Now I know you're out of it."

"No, I only ache down there." She reached up and cupped his face. "Please, make love to me."

"I will, sweet girl." After kissing her forehead, he shifted back on his knees so he wouldn't put any pressure on her chest, plus her flushed body offered one hell of a sexy view.

Maude beneath him. His Maudy. His home.

He needed to mark her in some way. Make sure she never forgot she was the one for him. "Tell me when I hit the right spot, Maudy." Rolling his hips, he moved against her.

"Right there." Her body tensed, and she groaned, "Don't stop. You've got it."

"Fuck, you're so tight. Tell me how I feel inside you."

"I'm tingling all over. I just need...just need a little more."

"Will this help?" He pushed his thumb against her clit.

"Yes, oh, please, yes." She lifted her arms above her head and gripped a pillow.

"Tell me when you're coming. I want to hear you."

Gasping, she opened her eyes and met his gaze. "Faster. Touch me harder." She stiffened then cried out. "I'm coming for you." After her words, her breath went ragged, her mouth went wide, and her body arched against him.

Maude's tight heat gripped him over and over. "That's my girl. Squeeze me..." Pleasure shot down his spine, lit up his balls, and fired out his cock. "Oh, fuck, Maude..." With a shout, he erupted inside the snug condom. After his body stopped shaking, he collapsed onto the bed. "Fuck me, Maude. Do you do kegel exercises or something?"

"No," she mumbled, half-asleep.

"That was different."

"Jason..."

"No, I didn't mean the tight, squeezing thing, but damn, you must have come hard, because I felt all of it."

She slapped him, but her effort was more of her arm falling against his side.

"What I meant was, the sex...was different. Just like the last time we were together."

She lifted one lid and stared at him. "It's because you love me."

"I *have* loved you, but I am getting there in a different way, I think." And, after that sexual experience, he was thinking that was all right with him. Maude sex blew all other sex out of the water, and that was with an injury. When she was at her full capacity, she'd probably blow his mind.

"Well, I..." She cleared her throat, and her cheeks and chest flushed even redder. "That's a nice thing to say, Jason."

"I've never had sex feel so right. I'm melting or something. That's pure sappy, but I don't know how else to explain what I'm feeling." He shook his head. "I must be on some kind of emotional overload with all this Mom shit, I even went all therapy-time with my brother."

"Thash nish." She closed her eyes and sighed.

Studying her banged-up face, he found a bit of peace in understanding he already loved her in that different way. No one else in the world was like Maude Killion. She'd been put on this earth for him and him alone. God, help her.

After a moment, he eased off the bed, tied off the condom, and tossed it in the garbage can by the bed. "Maude, are you asleep? Are you sure you're okay?"

"Wha, huh?" She blinked then licked her lips.

"Hey, wake up for a second." He patted her shoulder. "What happened in that parking lot today? Do you think Brady tried to hurt you? Some kind of revenge?"

She humphed, turned away, but then mumbled, "Ariel came by…threatened me."

Jason straightened and braced both hands on his hips. "What the hell are you talking about?"

"No yelling." Maude winced. "She said stay away, but I have a brother."

She wasn't making any sense. He ran a hand over his stubbled chin. "I don't know what that means other than Owen would know what happened to your car."

Maude mumbled a response that sounded something like battle ready before she drifted off to sleep.

Jason sighed and rubbed his eyes. If Ariel was responsible, she'd get caught. Clayton and Rachel were very good at their jobs. Ariel's sly tricks had him feeling like a fly caught in a black widow's web. Just what kind of game was Ariel playing, and how far would she go to win?

CHAPTER 27

An incessant blaring echoed through Jason's bedroom. Groaning, he opened one eye and felt for the stupid iPhone that wouldn't shut up. Two hours of sleep was enough, because he needed to return to the hospital and give Patrick a break. Poor guy was probably snoozing in a metal chair.

"Turn that thing off," Maude grumbled at his side.

"Not a morning person, Maudy?" He groped her, patting his hand up and down, hitting all the soft spots.

"What are you doing?"

"Searching for my phone?"

"My breast is not your phone."

"You sure?" He chuckled as he once again squeezed.

She shoved away his hand with a faint giggle. "I'm sure."

Relenting, he finally grabbed his phone and turned off the alarm. He kissed her bare shoulder. "Seven in the morning, Killion. I should get back to the hospital. You're not going to work today, right? I don't want you around Brady until we know more."

"Jason." Maude huffed. "Brady didn't do anything to my car. The man knows nothing about vehicles. He was always asking Owen stuff."

"He could've found YouTube videos demonstrating how to cut a brake line." He nudged her blanket-covered butt then dragged himself upright, setting his feet down on the side of the bed. He considered taking another shower. This time with Maude in attendance.

His bones creaked and cracked as he stood and glanced back at Maude. She remained a fully hidden lump. He quietly slipped to the side of the bed where she lounged with one of his throw pillows over her face. Whipping the covers off her body, he laughed when she bolted upright.

"What's happening?" Maude blinked at him, wide-eyed, arms covering her breasts.

His answer was to pick her up, one arm under her knees and the other under her arms, and carry her to his bathroom.

She shrieked, "Put me down. I'm too heavy and too tired for any morning shenanigans."

"A shower will wake you up."

"You're blinding me." Now on her own two feet, she leaned against the wall and raised a hand to cover both eyes. "I need tea and my medicine."

Jason pressed start on the shower panel. The high-tech gadget kept his preferred temperature, but Maude would likely prefer it hotter. He could do hotter. With that thought, he grinned. "Where's your medicine?"

Eyes squinting, she moved her hand to cover her mouth. "In my purse."

"I'll be right back."

As he stepped out, he heard her grumble about toothpaste then the sink turned on.

While searching for her purse, he heard his apartment door slam shut. He literally froze, naked in the middle of his bedroom, because only one person had access to his apartment.

Oh, shit.

Owen barreled into his room, followed by Bronco.

Stark naked wasn't such a big deal in the locker room, but when Owen's sister was stark naked in his bathroom, problems were on the horizon.

Big problems.

O-Line problems.

Jason rubbed his neck and tried herding Owen and Bronco in the other direction by walking toward his door. "I know you guys can't resist seeing me naked, but get out of here." He flicked his fingers toward the outer hallway.

Bronco frowned, blocking his exit. "We came by with breakfast. Rachel stayed up with your mom while Patrick went home to change." He cracked his knuckles. "We got that smoothie you like."

Rudeness when his friends were obviously worried about him and offering comfort in their own way created a wiggle of guilt down his spine. Any other day, he'd give them both shit to cover how much their actions meant, but today...not so much. Still, breakfast was in the kitchen. Perfect escape.

"I was just about to shower, but I'll come out to the kitchen and grab my drink." He'd almost escaped when Owen stepped right in front of him, his brow furrowed, and not in a good way.

Feeling way too exposed, Jason grabbed a damp towel from his overflowing laundry basket.

Owen pointed to something in the corner of his room. "Is that Maude's purse?"

Jason slowly tightened the towel around his waist, worried any quick movements might provoke the beast. Getting caught with Maude was bound to happen at some point, especially since they were always in each other's business.

Before he could answer, his worst nightmare occurred right before his eyes.

Maude burst from the bathroom. Naked. Bare as the day she was born. Assets on full display.

He groaned and rubbed his temple.

"Jason, what's taking so long?" Maude mumbled around the toothbrush hanging from her mouth. Then she caught sight of

Owen and stilled.

A raspy inhalation sounded then Owen cursed.

Jason knew the hit was coming, stood still while waiting for it to happen, but one punch was all he'd take. After that, game on.

Owen's right cross struck his chin.

Jason went down from the force of the blow. He stayed down, because being out of Owen's reach was the smartest move right now.

Bronco yelled at Owen and stood right in front of Jason, his beefy, jean-covered legs blocking the view.

Owen hollered back.

Maude charged over—still naked—shouting at them all.

Jason rested his back against the wall, waiting for the drama to end.

"Maude, what the hell are you doing? Put on some goddamn clothes." Owen ordered, shuffling out of his T-shirt and handing it to her. "And Bronco." He shoved Bronc's shoulder. "Get the hell out of here."

"I will get dressed when you leave, Owen." She ignored his clothing offer, instead standing with both hands on her hips.

Her quite lusciously shaped hips. Still, this was a little odd. Naked Maude. Fuming Owen. Frozen Bronco. Definitely odd. "Maude, put on your brother's shirt. This is way beyond normal, even for me."

"What do you think you're doing storming in here and hitting Jason?" She yanked her brother's T-shirt over her body then poked Owen in the chest. "We *told* you."

"I don't care what you said," Owen shouted back. "I don't want to see it."

"Then leave."

He growled, stood there for a moment longer before grabbing Bronco, and storming out the door.

"Jason, I—"

"Go take a shower, Maude. I'll talk to him." Jason sighed,

rubbing his sore jaw.

"I'll go with you."

"No." His response was sharp and definitive, but being caught red-handed did that to a man. "I'm sorry." He shuffled to his feet and took her by the shoulders. "Please. Just let me handle this."

She glared then headed back to the bathroom, pulling off Owen's T-shirt and tossing it on the floor.

"The whole stomping away thing is ruined by your sweet ass, Maudy." He chuckled. Her ruffled anger was absolutely the cutest thing he'd ever seen.

Her middle finger appeared in the door's crack before she slammed it shut.

Shower sex was definitely off the table.

# # #

Ready to meet his doom, Jason tugged on some workout shorts, grabbed Owen's shirt, and padded into the kitchen.

At the counter, Bronco had two bagels split open, spreading cream cheese on each piece. "You want a bagel?"

"Maybe." Jason shrugged then grabbed a big smoothie off the counter. "This mine?"

"Yep."

Owen sat at the kitchen table, sipping his takeout coffee.

Jason jerked his head toward their pal and asked Bronco. "He sitting in the corner?"

"Pretty much."

Giving Owen a contemplative stare, he decided they needed to work this out. He'd taken his hit, now they had to move on. Jason couldn't lose his mom and his best friend all in the same week. After a long sip from his smoothie, he sauntered over to the table, handed over the shirt, and sat across from his friend. "I'm not apologizing." He tapped a finger against the table. "I told you we were together."

"Doesn't matter." Owen pulled the shirt over his head then ran a hand through his ruffled hair. "I walk in, see naked guy, see naked sister, and I see red." Eyes narrowed, he met Jason's gaze. "With you, it's fucking titanic red because...well, it's you."

"What the hell is titanic red?"

"It sank, Jason. You got that? The Titanic sank." Owen shot back as if any fool could follow his reasoning.

"Why are we talking about the Titanic?" Seeking clarity, he glanced at Bronco, who merely shrugged and took a big bite of his bagel.

Owen rubbed his eyes with his fists.

Perhaps he thought if he dug them out, he could erase all the visions of nakedness and ships that had sunk back in the early 1900's.

"I thought I could handle this thing with you and Maude, but I hadn't seen it yet. Now I've seen too much, and I don't know if I can handle it," Owen rambled before setting his elbows on the table and roughly scrubbing his fingers through his hair. "What are you doing with her when you've got some other woman pregnant?" He raised his head and sank back against his seat.

"Fuck off, Killion." Jason shot out of his chair and paced beside the table. His friend didn't want to believe in him? Fine. Owen chose to throw his mistakes in his face? Whatever. The dickhead could kiss his ass.

"It's a legitimate question, Jason," Bronco piped up from his spot at the counter, ever the peacemaker.

"Doubt? That's what I get after all this time?" Jason glared at them both. "You guys act like you don't know me at all."

"We do know you," Bronco mumbled around his bagel. "That's the problem."

"Have I ever hurt anyone? Ever lied to a woman about what I want? I'm straightforward. No one ever got anything from me I didn't want them to have." He paused to catch his breath because their distrust had clogged up his throat. "No one ever got me, except Maude. And she just took." He sighed, because that was more truth than he'd even admitted to himself. "That woman slays me, man. Sure, this whole thing"—he waved a hand toward his bedroom door—"crept up on me, but it's here." He slammed a fist against his chest. "So, you two can just blow me if you don't believe me, all right? I won't let you ruin what's between us."

Owen drew an invisible circle on the table. "She's been in love with you forever." He met Jason's gaze. "And Maude, she's...she's not hard, bro. She's kind and has this huge heart. I've had to be her father and her brother, you get that?" He glanced away. "Then I come here and see her naked in your bedroom, and I-I...I don't know what to think."

Bronco pointed his bagel at Jason. "You sure you know what you're doing? What it'll mean if you and Maude go south?" He tipped the bagel toward Owen.

Apparently, strawberry cream cheese was serving as a pointer in class today. Jason refrained from rolling his eyes. "I've thought about a lot of things." He yanked on the straw in his drink. "Like, how I thought we"—he waved a hand at Owen and then Bronco—"were family."

"We are family," Maude's sure tone and honest words quieted the room.

She'd snuck in, her hair still wet, her face one big reddish bruise. Poor little thing. Pure male pride shot through him as he noted she wore his oversized T-shirt.

"Owen, please leave Jason be." Maude folded her hands together at her waist.

"You stand there with your face all banged up and tell me to leave things be." Owen shook his head. "I'm sorry, but no."

"I didn't say leave *things* be, I said leave Jason be."

"I don't care what you said or what you mean. None of that matters, because I have to sit here and look at my sister's jacked-up face." Jaw clenched, Owen huffed. "I'm not having it." He pounded a fist against the table. "You need to get dressed and go home. You're not safe."

"Owen—"

"No." He waved her off. "Do *not* use that placating tone with me. I'm taking you home. End of story."

"Enough, you two." Jason glanced at Maude, but she had turned her back and was opening and slamming shut cabinet doors in search of something. "I'm in enough trouble without you guys fighting because of me."

Owen had received a shock, and so, quite frankly, had he. Everyone needed to calm down, forget all the nudity, and they'd be good. Besides, nothing would stop Owen when he was in I-am-the-captain-of-the-Titanic mode. Jason glanced at Bronco.

"He's right." Bronco nodded. "Let's all take a breather."

"Come on, Maude." Jason tossed his half-empty drink in the sink. "I'll help you get your things."

"But, Jason"—she pressed a hand against his chest—"he can't come in here and boss me around. I'm not—"

"Maude." Jason squeezed her hand. "Not now."

"Fine." Tears welled in her eyes as she shoved away his hand. "I don't need your help getting my things. I don't need any of you big, stupid bullies telling me what to do. I've had it with everyone." With her fiery gaze and her beat-up face, she looked like she could go gangster on their asses. "I'm going home, but to *my* apartment, not the house. So…so…you all can just kiss m-my…butt." With that, she marched back to his bedroom.

"Well, I *had* planned to kiss her ass, until you two assholes showed up."

"Stuff it, Stafford." Owen glared.

Smiling, Bronco shoved Owen's shoulder. "All this talk of asses and stuffing is making me a little uncomfortable."

Jason laughed, and even Owen cracked a slight smile, which was really more of a scowl. But with that light moment, he had a faint hope their friendship would be just fine.

CHAPTER 28

That afternoon, Maude hefted an insulated grocery bag onto her kitchen counter with a little more "umph" than necessary, causing two apples to tumble free. "Stupid apples."

Her nose and lip ached. Pain exacerbated by arguing with three knuckle-dragging men.

Why did her brother think he could snap his fingers and she'd simply agree? Sure, she appreciated the fact he'd just seen his sister naked—with his best friend. That alone would cause any brother to have a fit. Still, the fact Owen, Bronco, and Jason— now fully dubbed "the traitor"—thought she should just head back home because of whatever Neanderthal reason brought forth every I-am-every-woman feeling she'd ever had. "Stupid men."

Though preferring to kick her apples against the cabinets, she refrained and gently settled their freshly-bruised bodies in a bowl at the counter. "Stupid bruises. Stupid psychos messing with my car. Everyone is just stupid." Realizing she stood in her kitchen talking to herself, she laughed then headed for her door. Two bags were left in the car she'd borrowed from Ember.

"Darn it." Having no idea where she'd left Ember's keys, she wedged a flip-flop in the door so it wouldn't shut all the way. Maybe they were under her shopping bag. Who knew?

On her way out to the car, she glanced at her phone to see if

Jason had texted again. While grocery shopping, he'd sent a message, asking if she'd come by the hospital after lunch. She'd agreed, but included an emoticon with its tongue sticking out. He'd replied that she could use her tongue on him anytime, which she'd ignored, but actually had her smiling like a loon in the middle of picking out avocados.

Shaking her head at the crazy man, Maude lugged her bags back up to her apartment.

Even though she hadn't responded after his blatant remark, she continued to get messages from him. Each one full of wise and all-knowing thoughts about letting Owen cool off, and on and on. Though she might agree, she hadn't responded. Those three oafs continued to believe she was just a little girl who needed constant protection. Nothing irritated her more than when all three went big brother on her…especially Jason.

After shoving open her door with her foot, she headed to the kitchen. Placing her bags on the counter, she stiffened after hearing a sound, like the rustle of a jacket swishing.

"Just the bags." She laughed, though her heart raced, because what if…what if someone was in her apartment? The same person who cut her brake line. She quieted her breathing, almost to a full stop, so she could hear any foreign sounds.

A creak sounded behind her. The hairs on the back of her neck stood on end, and she glanced around the kitchen for her phone.

"Whoever is in here, you should leave. My brother is on his way." Perhaps she was just imagining things, frightened over someone meaning her harm. She wiped her clammy hands on her pants, took a deep breath, and turned toward the kitchen entryway.

Something black caught her eye. "Oh my God." She grabbed the counter as leverage to propel her around the island, but her wobbly legs wouldn't move.

The black speck became a tall man in a black nylon hoodie

and cotton mask. He rounded her kitchen entryway and lifted, of all things, a jumbo red wiffle ball bat.

"Wait, wait, wait, please d-don't. Wha-whatever you're thinking, p-please don't." Maude backed up a few steps and raised her hands, palms up and out.

The man slammed the bat against her counter and rushed her.

She screamed and made a half lap around her island before he tackled her and knocked her down.

Landing on her bottom with a jolt, she winced when her head banged against a wooden chair leg. She gasped and coughed, fighting for air—the wind knocked out of her.

With his hand, he shoved against her face as he rose to his feet, pressing on her already battered nose.

She blinked back tears from the stinging pain.

But that slight sting was nothing compared to the hard blows he rained down on her thighs and arms with the bat. She crunched into a ball and covered her head with her arms.

Was this how she'd end? No. She would fight.

With a bellow, she grabbed for the bat and tried wrenching it from his hands. Pure adrenaline rushed through her. Ignoring the pain, she fought for survival. She kicked out as hard as she could against his left knee. Pivot points, she could practically hear Rachel directing her on self-protection.

He hollered and dropped, hands cupping his knee.

"Help me!" Maude screamed. "Help, someone. Please."

The intruder vaulted on top of her body, using his gloved hand to cover her mouth.

A waved of pain engulfed her face. She wiggled and tried to shove free, but he was too heavy, too strong.

He pinned her arms above her head and lowered his face so his nose touched hers. Then he kissed her hard, pressing against her stitched lip. Though his face was covered in black fabric, she still felt the shape of his lips. The sharp stench of sweat and body odor mixed with a slight trace of bubble gum.

A wash of copper coated her tongue, and she gagged. "Get off me." Yanking her face to the side, she rose on her elbows and attempted to squirm free.

Chuckling, he breathed against her neck, expelling hot, moist air through the mask, dropping more kisses along her jawline. "He shouldn't get you, too."

Hot breath. Damp cotton. Her skin crawled. She fought to steady her breathing, prepared to fight against whatever was next.

Tears trickled down her cheeks, and she cursed their presence. *No.* He would not see any weakness. She bit her upper lip, seeking the pain to jar her mind into fighter mode.

He stopped his sick kisses right by her ear and whispered, "Stay away from my b-bro...from Jason."

Her eyes went wide, and she froze. "What? Did you just say—"

He jarred his elbow under her chin, knocking her head against the tile floor.

Gripping his bicep, she fought to breathe. Fought to break free. She kicked and cursed. Spat in his face.

He reared back and slapped her, his blue eyes glaring from beneath the black slits. "Bitch."

Dazed, Maude again tried kicking his knee, but her eyes were full of tears, and her body was at a threshold of pain that not even adrenaline could surpass.

"No. I won't let you hurt me anymore." Using reserves she didn't realize she possessed, she rose to her knees before rearing back her fist and trying to punch him but he blocked her.

Too weak.

Her arms were like noodles slapping against a pan of boiling water. They couldn't escape, and neither could she.

She yanked her fist from his grip. Ignoring all the red welts on her arm, she pointed at the door. "Get out! I've been b-bullied enough, and I will fight." Gasping for breath, she licked her lips and tasted the blood trickling from the open stitches.

Sweat and tears meshed together and poured down the side of her face. Her chest heaved with the weight of her beating heart.

Please, legs, carry me. In two seconds, she was making a break for the knives on the counter. In two seconds, she was going lethal on his ass.

The smug bastard stood before her, his crotch right in line with her face.

She fought back a shiver.

Her phone rang with Jason's ringtone.

The intruder stepped back and shoved the end of the bat against her nose. "End it."

Maude planted one foot on the ground, ready to make her move.

But he reared back with the bat and knocked her face straight out of the ballpark.

# # #

Maude awoke with a scream.

A big blond man crouched beside her, repeating her name over and over.

"No. Stop." She shoved away, blinking, glancing around to get her bearings. She sat on the floor, propped up on both elbows.

"Maude." Clayton raised his hands, palms up at his sides. "It's me, Clayton. What happened here? Were you attacked?"

Once she heard the word attack, all the pain hit at once, and she crumpled. Between the sobs, she tried to explain. "He...h-he...he said..."

"Shhh....it's okay." Clayton drew her close. "Calm down."

"What the hell is going on in here?" Jason thundered into her kitchen.

Too many men. Too much pain. She couldn't take it so she just curled closer to Clayton.

"I-I made a mistake…I-I shouldn't…I left…he just came in, and apples were all over." She managed between her racking sobs.

Her face had hurt before, but after taking a beating from a bat, well, now she knew how a wiffle ball felt. Not to mention the stinging ache, like a white hot heat pulsing and throbbing with an unending fire, burning her arms, legs, and sides. Even her tears stung.

Clayton's grip hurt so she eased away.

Jason gently cradled her face in his hand. "Oh baby, what happened? Your poor face."

"H-he said to stay away. And he said…he said…I'm sorry, Jason." Fear still raced through her system, but she'd heard the intruder's slip-up. Clearly. Yet, her next words would break Jason's heart. But Patrick had done this to her, made her one big welt of pain, so she had to tell the truth. "I think…I-I think it was your brother."

CHAPTER 29

"Where *is* your brother, Jason?" Clayton leaned against the kitchen archway, arms locked across his chest. "Let's get this story straight before my buddies from the Manchester police station arrive."

"Last I knew, Patrick had gone home and was on his way back to the hospital." Jason rubbed the back of his neck. "I texted him but haven't heard back."

After calming Maude and getting the horrifying story of a guy being in her apartment—after she'd left the door unlocked, a fact he'd focus on once she was better—he'd called Rachel and asked her to come by. Rachel arrived with a firefighter friend who was also an EMT, and together, they got Maude cleaned up, drugged, and settled in bed.

"Why would Patrick do this?" Clayton rhythmically tapped his fingers against his arm.

"He didn't."

"Maude says the perp slipped up, almost called you his brother, and the description fits."

Jason headed for the fridge, opened it then closed it again. "No. Wasn't him."

"You guys don't necessarily get along. And this Ariel chick...she sounds like she knows how to stir up trouble."

"Patrick doesn't even know her."

Clayton shifted, scratching his back side-to-side against the wall. The guy swam all the time, resulting in a lean build. He was one of those dudes who could pull off a tuxedo, no problem. Jason always felt like an overgrown orangutan in dress clothes.

"Thought you said you met Ariel at a club."

"I did."

"Which one?"

Jason growled out a sigh. "Plunder."

"Exactly." Clayton nodded like some prosecutor who'd just tricked the witness into revealing their darkest secret. "So the possibility *does* exist that Ariel and Patrick know each other."

Jason shook his head, unwilling to believe Patrick's guilt in this matter. "Clayton, the same person who cut her brakes is the same person who did this...Brady Stephens. The dude is obsessed. If he can't have her, no one can." Jason paced in Maude's tiny kitchen, feeling too tight, edgy, caged. This whole place annoyed him now, especially after he'd used Clorox wipes to clean Maude's blood from the floor. Scowling, he jabbed a finger at Clayton. "Look into Brady."

"I have been."

"*He* goes to clubs, too."

"All right." Clayton nodded.

His friend didn't sound convinced. Jason clenched his fists at his sides. After coming here and finding Maude once again banged up, he needed to hit something. Hard. Maybe Owen and Bronco would help him slam against the training sled for a couple hours. And speaking of Owen...the dude would freak when he found out. Jason was not looking forward to that call. Maybe pretty-boy Kincaid would talk to him. Maude's mom would be a mess, too.

His own mom was a mess. His entire life was a complete disaster. A storm cloud had formed over his head, and the stupid thing wouldn't go away.

"This whole situation is out of control, Clayton." Maybe the hospital had a rec center with a boxing bag. Something had to relieve his pent-up aggression…and soon.

One thing would for sure ease his mind—Maude removing herself immediately from this location.

He tapped his lower lip and considered Maude living in his secure apartment building and found no true objections. Actually, quite a genius idea, because why not? However, at this point, he needed to get through the next minute. "Look, Kincaid, my mom is dying from lung cancer. Maude's all banged up. Ariel's pregnant, or whatever. My life is anything but rainbows and sunshine right now. I need answers." Jason pounded a fist against his palm. "Find them."

"Rachel's looking into Ariel." Clayton opened a cabinet, found a glass, and then filled it with water from the faucet. He leaned back against the sink and took a sip before tilting the glass toward Jason. "You know, faking a pregnancy test is easy. Hell, all you have to do is go online. Lots of articles there."

"Yeah?" Jason halted in his pacing. "Like what?"

"Diet Dr. Pepper."

"Really?"

"Yup, I've tested it myself. It works, and Lord knows, I'm not capable of getting pregnant."

Jason scrubbed a hand over his bristly face. "I don't have time for all these games. If Ariel is behind all that." He pointed toward the bedroom. "Then she'll pay."

"Leave it to me. We'll check this Brady angle and—"

"Why are you checking into Brady?" Maude stood in the doorway, Rachel at her side wearing a big frown on her pixie face. "I *told* you my attacker was Patrick."

"What the hell, Rach'?" Jason plastered his hands on his hips and glared at the woman who was supposed to keep Maude in bed.

"She had to pee, then she heard you two out here discussing her life like you know what you're talking about." Rachel shrugged. "Sorry, but people gotta pee."

Clayton visibly winced as he glanced at Maude. "Sugar, you need to go back to bed."

Maude glanced around the room then froze as she stared at a broken chair. "Let's talk in another room."

"Yeah, your bedroom." Jason trudged over to her side and wrapped his arm around her waist.

She hissed and eased to the side.

"Damn it, Maude. You should go to the hospital."

"I'm just bruised." She wobbled into her room, holding her arms stiff against her body.

"The man beat you with a wiffle ball bat." Jason practically shouted then immediately regretted his tone as Maude flinched. *Double damn it!*

After his mini-rampage, when he'd first arrived, which had him shouting and almost ripping Clayton's head off, he'd calmed and tried to remember soothing Maude was his priority. Since that moment, he'd focused on the fear she must have experienced, of what more could have happened, on the fact that all of her pain was basically his fault.

Maybe they *should* cool things down, as the intruder requested.

A good man would walk away. A great man would realize Maude deserved someone better. Was this his penance? To finally find the right woman only to have her driven away? And didn't he deserve this, after his cavalier treatment of women? Hell, he should just leave. But he couldn't. Just couldn't. "I'm sorry, Maude. I'm trying very hard to stay calm in your presence. This man has likely hurt you twice now, and I'm—"

"Not "*the* man" or "*this* man," Jason." She turned and met his gaze. Bruises and Band-Aids covered her sweet face. "Patrick. *He* was my attacker."

"No, Maude." Jason softened his voice. "He wouldn't do that to you…or to me."

"He's in cahoots with Ariel," she shrieked then moaned and clutched her head. "Patrick did this." She pointed at her face before slowly bracing herself on her bed then lowering onto her side.

"I won't argue about this now." Jason shook his head, at a loss over what to do and what to say.

Clayton cleared his throat.

He and Rachel had followed them into the room. Rachel bit her lower lip, and Clayton took a sudden interest in his tennis shoes.

Tears trickled down Maude's cheeks. "Why don't you believe me? You should be arresting him right now. Clayton, can't you go do that, please?"

"I don't arrest people anymore, Maude. Sorry." Clayton glanced around the room then grabbed Rachel's arm. "We'll wait in the living room. My buddy just texted, he's down the block."

Jason nodded then sat on the bed beside Maude. "Those two will figure this out."

Maude sniffled and curled up into a ball. "You should go."

"Maude, come on." Jason brushed her hair from her face. "I'm sorry this happened."

"Not sorry enough to believe me."

"It's not that I don't believe…" He sighed, unwilling to delve into the argument again. "Please, just get some rest."

"He really scared me, Jason." Her voice was barely above a whisper. "Why would Patrick do this to me?"

"I don't think he did." He reached for her face.

"I was there." Stiffening, Maude shoved away his hand. "Go. Just go."

Jason heaved another heavy sigh then stood. Not wanting to leave, but he acknowledged he could do nothing. No way was he one hundred percent certain his brother wasn't involved, except for the niggling notion in his head that said absolutely not.

But then, why had the man almost said brother? Did Patrick

hate him that much? Hadn't they passed a crossroads while caring for their mother? His frank car talk had done some good, and Patrick just wasn't capable of a betrayal at this level. His brother didn't have it in him to be truly violent to a woman, especially not after how they'd grown up. All those hits he'd taken for Jessica. No, Patrick wouldn't.

Besides, the big lug would never buy a stupid, pussy-ass wiffle ball bat to beat someone. Jason grimaced. That *someone* was the woman he loved. Loved? Hell, he had the woman moving in with him, his stomach hurt, his head hurt, and he was scared to death. Yep, love.

But, was that same emotion blinding him with his brother? Maybe his brother was still up to his ears in gambling debts? Hadn't the debt collectors beaten him bloody once before? Too many questions and not enough answers. Except for one. These attacks against Maude would stop. He'd use his vast financial resources to hire bodyguards. Damn woman would likely fight it, but all her friends and family would be firmly entrenched on his side…especially after they saw her face and her beaten body. What he wouldn't give for five minutes alone with the man who'd used a bat against his woman.

The doorbell rang. Manchester's finest had likely arrived. Jason could hear deep voices speaking in low tones. Was Maude up for telling her story again? Rachel had explained the detectives needed to ask their questions right away, while Maude's memory was still fresh. While here, Rachel said, they'd likely review any security or surveillance cameras in the area.

Jaw clenched, Jason stopped at the door of her bedroom and stared back at the slight mound on the bed. "All right, Maude. I'll leave you be. I think the cops are here, anyway. Probably best if the brother of the prime suspect isn't in the room."

He sighed when he didn't hear a response, only sniffling. He'd get Rachel to stay with Maude while he dealt with Owen. "Great," he mumbled at the thought as he headed down the hallway to the living room. "He's gonna use more than a wiffle ball bat on me. More likely, a tire iron. Yeah, a tire iron."

Rubbing his eyes, Jason pulled up Owen's name in his contacts. After this unpleasant conversation, he'd speak to Clayton about hiring a bodyguard. Another person protecting his woman didn't sit well, but something had to be done to protect Maude from Brady Stephens. That psycho was behind these attacks. Jason just knew it.

But, one question remained—just how did Ariel Silvers figure into the equation?

CHAPTER 30

The next day Maude lounged on Owen's living room couch, letting her family fuss. After a laborious discussion with a couple of detectives and a lot of embarrassing photos of her battered body, she'd taken four Advil PM to help her sleep. She'd woken up at her apartment to find Jason gone and Owen in his place. With barely a word between them, he'd gathered her things and put her in the car. She hadn't argued because the look of genuine horror on her brother's face broke her heart. He loved her, wanted her safe, and she wanted that, too. What else was there to say, really?

Ember had left her in the living room with the TV set at low volume on a nameless romantic comedy. A light movie with no violence. Grateful for her friend's care, Maude nestled under the soft, hunter green throw blanket.

Just like Owen's kitchen, a rustic feel permeated this room, with a large moose statue on the mantle and an eagle painting on the wall. Dark green couch and maroon chairs. Why couldn't this cabin-like room be located deep in a forest? Away from everything? But, wouldn't that add more points to Ariel's scoreboard? Her fear. Her pain. Ariel would not continue to beat her. If she could move without everything stinging, she'd find the woman and tell her so. Enough was enough! Hopefully, the detectives could tie Ariel to Patrick somehow, at least then a reason for his actions might be discovered.

Maude wiped away her stupid anger-tears.

The cup of peppermint tea currently warming her icy hand was intended to soothe her senses. *Not hardly.*

She'd been attacked.

In her home.

By Patrick.

Why wouldn't Jason believe her?

No one had chastised her for leaving her door unlocked— yet. Actually, no one was saying a whole lot, except lie down and get some rest. She'd avoided the mirror when Rachel had cleaned her up. No use rubbing her nose in what she knew was an ugly situation.

Her whole face ached like a minuscule alien ship hovered around her head, continually firing mini-blasters that stung and burned.

Maude hadn't believed Ariel would strike so soon and so viciously. Her own mind didn't think like an evil witch, so understanding the woman's motives remained difficult. Still, who threatened a person one day then attacked right away? Not very stealthy.

Rachel planned to spend today alongside a Manchester detective as he questioned Ariel. Clayton and Rachel would solve the puzzle. They excelled in aligning pieces, seeing the world as others didn't, and questioning everything.

Sitting here alone had her questioning a few things of her own. What would become of her and Jason if, in fact, Patrick was responsible? She sighed then lightly tapped her nose, since she couldn't scratch her stitches, which was slowly driving her mad. Maybe a good book would distract her?

Her mom scuttled into the room, a tray in her arms filled with a sandwich, chips, and a fresh cup of hot tea. Then she halted, spilling the tea over the rim of the cup. "Oh. Do you need Sprite? I can go get you some."

Maude shook her head, and then winced, from the pain *and* because she wasn't hungry. Her poor mom had gone to the trouble, and she couldn't eat. Her stomach remained in knots, her body still tense as if waiting for the next blow. No way could her stomach unravel enough to digest anything. She rubbed at the Neosporin Ember had put on her upper lip. How would she eat without getting icky cream on her sandwich, anyway?

"Thanks, Mom." Her voice cracked, still raw from either screaming or the verging-on-mentally-unstable crying fit she'd suffered through after Jason left. Luckily, Owen's maid kept each room stocked with tissues, because Maude's tears were still flowing, adding to the crusty mess of her face. She sighed. All this water loss couldn't be good for her system.

"Honey, can you sit up and eat a little?"

Maude glanced at her mom, with her short bob of red hair, her Cracker Barrel shirt and Capri pants—she was home, always would be. Her mom's red-rimmed eyes didn't bode well and churned her stomach a little more. "I'm okay, Mom."

"No, you're not." Her mom sniffed then settled at her feet on the wide couch. "Eat your lunch."

"I'm not sure I can."

"You need to keep up your strength."

"No...um...I can't open my mouth very wide. My upper lip sort of hurts still from the wreck."

"Oh." Her mom straightened then stared at the tray before covering her face with both hands and bursting into tears. "I-I can't take it. Seeing you so banged up. I want...I want you to come home for good. Then I go and make you a lunch you c-can't even eat."

Now Maude had no chance of stemming her tears. "I made a big m-mistake. I'll be smarter. I promise." Bracing against the pain, she rose from her slouch and hugged her mom with one-arm. "Don't cry, please. I'm okay."

"Someone has hurt you twice." Her mom clenched her hand on her knee, her wedding ring glittering in the light. "I want you back home until we figure this out."

Maude heaved in a breath, ready to expel all the reasons she needed to stay at her own place, even when she really didn't want to. "Mom, I'll stay for a few—"

The doorbell rang. And suddenly, all her reasons flew from her mind as fear kick-started her heartbeat into fifth gear. Surely, she'd have a heart attack at this rate.

Her mom had flinched, too.

Was this to be her future? Jumping at unexpected noises? Her heart in her throat anytime she saw a strange man? Fear coursing down her spine at the unknown? Dear God, she hoped not.

"Who could that be?" Her mom rose and grabbed a tissue from the box on Maude's lap. "I'll go see."

"Mom, don't go alone." Panic rose in a huge swell, and her heart rallied straight past sixth gear. "Where's Owen? Make him answer the door." She barely breathed as her mom headed for the foyer.

"Maude, the alarm panel is right by the door, and I can see out the side windows. If it's someone I don't recognize, I'll trigger the alarm…and something else."

Something else? Was her mom carrying? Owen *did* have a gun collection. The vision of Nancy Killion walking around with a gun strapped to her hip did bring a momentary smile to Maude's face. Mamma bear was packing. Oh, her life had truly skidded straight into Insanity-ville.

Although stress eating was never good, Maude picked a small chip off the plate, placed it on her tongue, and let the barbeques smoky goodness melt in her mouth. Even if she couldn't crunch, she could swallow them soggy. Some people craved chocolate, but her poison was salt.

"I don't know if she's up for visitors." Her mom shuffled back into the room, followed by Brady.

Maude groaned, not in the mood for social calls, especially not from her clingy ex. As she watched Brady stroll in, his gait a bit stiff, she couldn't help but think of Jason's accusations. Was he behind her attacks? No. The man in her apartment had slipped and almost said brother. She was sure of it. But the voice…something about the voice seemed…fake, purposefully rough. Recalling that terrifying moment wasn't on her to-do list right now—or ever. "Hi Brady."

Her mom hovered near the side of the couch, wringing her hands. "I think I'll go see if Owen wants some lunch."

Mom code for, I better warn my son his sister has a male visitor. And for once, Maude didn't mind.

Brady sat on the coffee table before her, nudging away her used tissues and the decorative nature books.

He wore a pair of khaki Dockers and a white polo shirt. A long, red scratch ripped through his lion tattoo. A fresh scratch. A possibly during a struggle on the kitchen floor scratch.

Maude's heart thundered once more as she gazed into his eyes. Where had that injury come from? Her? She straightened and swallowed past her fear. Why had everyone left her alone with this guy? Hopefully, her mom would return soon with Owen.

"Maude." Brady took her hand. "I came as soon as I could. I thought I should let you know Kathy is handling your work at the office. I figured you might be concerned about your accounts."

"No…I mean, I hadn't really considered…" Easing away her hand, she rubbed her temple. "I trust everyone to handle things for a few days."

Brady frowned. "Shouldn't you be in a hospital?"

The doorbell rang. That remote cabin in the woods became even more appealing. Right now, she did actually want to rest.

Again, the doorbell toned, as if the person outside were mega-impatient.

Just great. Maude considered whether or not she could hobble to the door then heard her mom holler, "I'll get it."

"It's like Grand Central Station around here." Maude shook her head. "Thanks for your concern, Brady, but I'm fine."

"I'm sorry to say this, but you don't look fine." He grazed a finger along her jaw. "Whoever did this, really got you good. Do they know who's responsible?"

"Please don't touch me. It hurts." Maude couldn't stop her gaze from wandering to Brady's scratch. Odd and very suspicious. But, if he were guilty, why wouldn't he cover up the evidence? "Rachel and Clayton are working on the case."

"Yes, they *are*." Clayton stormed into the room. "Brady, nice of you to stop by. Saves me a trip." With a glare at Brady, Clayton stopped right by the couch, arms folded across his chest. "I'd like a word, if you wouldn't mind."

"With me?" Wide-eyed, Brady placed a hand against his breastbone.

"Yeah. With you." Clayton nodded. "We can do it here or down at my offices."

Maude stifled a giggle at Clayton's I-still-think-I'm-a-cop tactics.

"Why can't you speak in front of Maude?" Brady never knew when to back down. He was all about winning and showing he held the upper hand.

"Maude needs rest. She doesn't need anything else upsetting her."

If only they knew, when her eyes closed, she visualized the attack that much clearer, much better to stay alert. Too bad her eyes weren't getting that message and were drifting closed that very moment. She blinked.

"I came here to visit her. We can speak after she and I are finished." Brady shifted around the coffee table, rudely showing Clayton his back.

"No, we'll speak now." Clayton placed a hand on Brady's

shoulder.

Brady's nostrils flared, and he opened his mouth to speak.

"Brady, I *am* tired," Maude interrupted, before things got violent. "I need to take more medicine now that I've eaten. Plus, I really don't want anyone seeing me like this." She flicked a hand toward her face. "I haven't processed everything, and I-I…I just need some alone time. I'm sorry. Your visit was very…thoughtful."

He nodded and patted her hand. "Let me know if you need anything."

Clayton remained immobile by the couch.

Testosterone replaced the scent of peppermint tea as Brady stood right in Clayton's space. "I have nothing to say to you, Kincaid."

Clayton's jaw ticked.

For a second, Maude wondered if a brawl would start, officiated by her and the moose on the mantel.

"Do you need anything for that scratch on your arm?" Maude didn't know what possessed her to ask Brady that. Maybe fear was making her suspicious of everyone? Or, more likely, she hoped the question would distract Clayton from laying Brady out on the floor.

Brady glanced at his arm, his cheeks turning a slight pink. "I'm watching the neighbor's cat." He sniffed. "Remember Smoky, the cat from across the hall? The gray one with the flat face. Apparently, he doesn't like being picked up and moved off my bed."

"Oh." Maude nodded, keeping her gaze on her index finger's hangnail that hurt almost as much as her face.

Clayton grunted and turned on his heel, leaving Brady to follow.

"What does that man wish to speak to me about?" Brady huffed. "I'm not a suspect. How utterly ridiculous."

Maude swallowed hard. "I really don't feel well, Brady. I'm

sorry, but I think you should go and speak to Clayton now."

"I understand." He nodded before bending and kissing the top of her head. "Take care."

What did he understand? Because, she didn't understand anything.

Especially how a cat who'd been declawed could dig a scratch that deep into someone's arm.

CHAPTER 31

She's asking a lot of questions.

Drinking a cup of coffee in her office break room, Ariel sighed when she read the text. Who cared, really? Rachel, her sexy ex-cop sidekick, and Manchester's finest couldn't prove anything. Her accomplice had worn gloves both times, and if they found a blond hair or fiber, well, they were covered there, too, because the man did spend time around Maude.

Ariel texted back. *She who? I told you to meet with me if you wished to talk directly.*

Then let's meet.

I'm sure I'm unavailable. And they were being watched. Being seen together was not a wise move.

I held up my end, now I want my payment.

Good God. Did the man not understand these messages could be misconstrued and used against them? Rachel probably had some high-tech gadget monitoring her phone even now. Distraction was the key here, which would serve to mislead anyone watching them. After quickly glancing around the room, she lifted up her shirt, tugged down her pink bra, and snapped a shot of her breasts.

With a couple of finger taps, the photo was sent. *There. Satisfied? You've been paid.* She flipped back through their messages.

Her quick thinking should save them—this time. How many more times would she have to cover for this idiot?

Hardly enough. He texted in response. *Plus, I'm having to wear this stupid knee brace and it hurts like a bitch.*

Greedy, greedy. She never should have approached him about helping her, but she sensed something in the man. A dark pain similar to her own, but perhaps she'd read him wrong.

I want more.

So, the man got off on the power, did he? After he'd swung a home run with Maude, he'd come to her office, dragged her to the nearest bathroom, and shoved her to her knees.

Steaming hot. But then, her tastes had always run toward the wicked.

However, Ariel Silvers used men, they didn't use her. Next thing, he'd be asking to use the bat on her. Not happening.

Patience. She texted a picture of herself pinching her nipple. "That should hold him over for a time."

Keep them on their leash and yank back when they stray. Sex, and the promise of it, was the proper way to handle men. *I'll see you soon.* She sent a final text, ignoring her phone when his text ringtone sounded again.

They had met at Plunder. If he wished to see her or speak to her, they could do so there, surrounded by others, looking as if they were just enjoying the evening.

The first part of her plan had been quite successful. Smiling, she ran her fingers through her hair, but she winced when a slight chip in her nail caught and yanked out a few strands.

Sighing, she shot back in the metal chair and dumped her cold coffee down the drain. Not only did she have to work at this stupid job, now she had to schedule a manicure between planning Maude's downfall and convincing Jason she had nothing to do with the poor woman's misfortunes.

She'd texted Jason with the time and date of her doctor's appointment. Too bad, she'd have an unfortunate tumble before then.

Her progress so far had weakened Maude. The woman was likely rethinking her attachment to Jason. But still, she had a final play in mind—burning Maude's hopes and dreams to ash. Quite literally.

# # #

In Owen's living room, Jason settled on the coffee table and took Maude's hand. "You should be sleeping." After a few hours at the team's gym, hitting the heavy bag with Bronco, he'd decided to stop by before he headed to the hospital.

Maude shook her head, her soft curls swishing against the throw pillow.

"How are you feeling?" Jason observed the used tissues, the cups of half empty tea, the redness of his woman's eyes and sighed. He'd take all her pain in a minute.

"I don't want to answer that question ever again," Maude croaked out, her voice raspy. "Tell me about your mom."

Jason dropped to his knees beside the couch and then rested his head by her stomach. "She's dying, Maudy, and I can't take it. You're here, and she's there. I'm scared to death. Sad. Angry. I have no control over anything, and I hate it."

She combed her fingers through his hair. "I'm sorry."

"You're both in so much pain." He pounded a fist against the floor. "And, selfish me, I need you, Maude. I can't get through losing my mom without you. But how can I ask that when you're lying here wrecked because of me?"

"You never have to ask for anything." She continued to draw her fingers through his hair. "None of this is your fault."

Jason barked out a laugh. "Yeah, baby, it is. I was irresponsible. Got mixed up with the wrong woman, and now look what's happened."

"Rachel wasn't happy when she came back today, but she

wouldn't tell me what Ariel said."

Jason straightened a little and met her gaze. "She basically got really haughty and told them to prove it."

"Ah...Rachel doesn't like being challenged."

"Something Ariel will find out at her peril." He shook his head. "No more. I don't want to talk about her. I came here to see you."

"I'm good with that." Maude hummed out a sigh. "When do you have to go back to the hospital?"

"Soon." He took her hand and pressed it against his chin. "I'm afraid." He choked back his emotion. "I need to be there when Mom goes. I want her to know I was with her at the end."

"She'll know." Maude cupped his face.

"Yeah, so maybe it's me who needs to know then?"

"Nothing wrong with that." She smiled.

"Except, I can't be here with you."

"You've been texting me." She wiggled her phone back and forth.

"And you haven't been answering."

Maude tensed then looked away. "I just wanted silence for a while."

Jason nodded and leaned closer. "Can I kiss you?"

Maude's eyes widened but then she expelled a long breath. "Softly, yes."

He placed his hands on both sides of her face before pressing his lips against hers. The stitches on her upper lip scratched a bit. Before easing back, he carefully kissed her nose. "Is there any part of you that isn't bruised?"

She pointed to a spot on her forehead so he kissed it. Then she pointed to her a spot on her neck so he kissed that, too.

"I thought I was in pain before, but not being able to feel your skin against mine is excruciating."

"Maude, you naughty, naughty thing."

"I'd love to get naughty, right now. Last time really took my mind off the pain."

"But, not this time." Jason shook his head.

"No. Not this time." She sighed. "Not when there's a big elephant in the room named Patrick."

Jason sank back, scooting the coffee table aside. "Maude, the only elephant in the room is my enormous di—"

She giggled and placed a finger over his lips. "Not appropriate. Okay?"

"Fine." Jason waggled his brows. "But I could show you? Even let you pet *my* elephant?"

Her lips pursed as if she were fighting back a smile.

"All right, since you must be so serious." He winked and heaved a put-upon sigh. "Clayton spoke to Patrick earlier today while Owen and I were both there. When you were being attacked, he was down in the cafeteria then returned to stay with Ma. He's pretty torn up about everything and rarely leaves her side. He only went downstairs to get a coffee."

"Coffee, huh?" Still not sure what to believe, Maude closed her eyes for a moment then opened them. "I'm terrified of what the answers will bring. What if the truth tears us apart?"

"It won't."

"I can't be around your brother for a while. I'm sorry." She used a ragged tissue to blot her nose. "I just can't."

"Don't worry about my brother. Worry about healing. How about a kale smoothie?" He nuzzled her neck, dropping kisses along her smooth, lavender-scented skin.

Her face scrunched. "Gross. No."

"Kale is good for you."

"Brady came by."

"What?" He stilled then shot to his feet. "Who let that fucker in?"

Maude glanced away. "Mom."

"Damn it, Maude. I don't want that freak show Brady-bunch anywhere near you."

"I didn't ask him to come." Her lower lip wobbled.

"Okay." He settled back beside her. "Okay, I'm sorry I yelled…just…why was he here?" And why hadn't anyone told him?

She shrugged and sniffed. "Checking on me."

"That is not his job anymore," Jason growled.

"Clayton arrived and took him away."

"Good." His phone buzzed in his pocket. He glanced at the text from his brother.

Doctor just came by. News wasn't good. Tell you when get here.

Jason sighed and rubbed the back of his neck.

"What's wrong?"

He stared into Maude's big brown eyes. Eyes that usually calmed him. But not today. Nothing was right about today. "I need to go, and I don't want to."

"Your mom?"

"Yeah."

"I wish I could come with you." She opened her arms. "Come hug me."

Jason hovered above her, unsure how to go about this without hurting her.

She yanked him down. "I love you, Jason Stafford. Always have. And I hope…" her tone dropped to almost a whisper. "I hope that someday you'll want to hold me just like this and never let go."

"I'm already there, Maudy. Already there." He tightened his hold, drawing on a strength only she could provide. Maybe, if he stayed in her arms, she'd take away all the pain.

No, she had suffered enough.

And life didn't work that way, not for Stafford men, anyway.

So, he'd take her love and hold it close, because his next few days would surely be hell, and in his red mist of pain, only this woman was heaven.

CHAPTER 32

Jason left Maude with a thousand questions running through his mind. His phone pinged with a text. Not one to text and drive, he pulled into a McDonald's drive-thru for a large coffee. He'd need the caffeine to stay up with his mom, anyway.

After reading the text, he practically threw his phone against the windshield. Ariel questioned why he wasn't returning her calls or texts. The woman had some nerve. She'd verbally threatened Maude, was likely the mastermind behind her injuries, and then figures, I'll contact Jason and tell him about my doctor appointment. Mental. The woman was mental. Cunning and without remorse. He was no longer fooled. Whoever Ariel was, she wasn't real.

Although, the thought of being a father had snapped him to attention long enough to realize Maude was his future, the rest of Ariel's machinations he could do without.

The woman was completely unhinged and willing to do anything to find a man to support her.

Ariel wanted a man? Then fine. He'd pay her a visit, even though he was already halfway to the hospital. He texted Patrick and said he'd be running a few minutes late.

He handed a five to the drive-thru gal, grabbed his coffee, and then took off to Ariel's apartment. Not big on drinking lots of caffeine, but with everything going on, he could barely keep his eyes open.

Using the hands-free device in his vehicle, he called his agent, Tyrone. "Good evening, buddy."

"Stafford."

"Hey, sorry to be calling after hours, but I felt I should tell you I'm confronting Ariel tonight."

"Jason—"

"No, she's lying. I know she is, and I've got a couple private investigators working on the truth even now. At this point, I don't care what Ariel does to me publically."

"You really don't think she's pregnant?"

"No, but I do think she's dangerous. Things are a little hairy right now with my mom and some other…things." Jason didn't want to share his relationship with Maude with the public yet, so he kept quiet on that note. "Once Ma…when she goes, I'll need some time. Start working up a statement now, because I won't want to talk when the time comes. No cameras in my face. No interviews. Nothing."

"All right, Jason. I understand, and I'll be on the lookout for any blips about this Ariel situation. I'll do what I can to cut off the hype before it starts."

"Or work your spin magic."

"You know it." Tyrone chuckled.

"Thanks, man." Jason nodded. "Catch ya later."

"No problem."

Jason disconnected. He wouldn't say he and Tyrone were best pals, but the guy did a great job. He barreled down the Interstate then slowed as he took the exit leading to Ariel's apartment. After he arrived, he parked in a visitor's spot and texted her.

I'm here. You want to talk then let me in.

A few moments passed before she responded.

Wonderful.

Arriving just outside her apartment door, he felt a small niggle of fear. Maybe this was a mistake. The woman was crazy enough to shoot him or hold him hostage. A 6' 5" dude, weighing over 290, and he was worried about a small blonde taking him down. *Stupid.*

Still, he shot off a quick text to Clayton, alerting him to his whereabouts. Then set his phone to silent so he didn't have to hear the numerous, "Are you insane" texts from his PI pal.

Lifting his hand, he readied to knock on the door.

But Ariel opened it.

He barreled past her. "Leave the door open. I'll make this quick."

She slammed shut the door, anyway. "I like quick."

He turned and watched as she stretched her arms above her body, shoving out her chest. "Are you insane? You think I'd have sex with you after all you've done?"

"What do you mean?" She arched a brow.

"You were just…with the…whatever," he grumbled and threw up his hands. Because he, of all people, knew when a woman was casting a lure. But he had no desire to bite. The thought actually churned his stomach and increased his desire to get done, and get out. "Listen, I know you're responsible for all these things happening to Maude." He paced just inside the doorway, hands tucked in his front pockets because he'd likely choke her, otherwise.

"Oh, Jason, if only…" Ariel shook her head before covering her face with her hands and bursting into tears. "Y-you don't understand…there is this…I've had this…I knew you would think I was responsible. This has happened before."

Unmoved by her performance, Jason cocked a brow. "You lie, Ariel. I don't believe you're pregnant. And you pointed the finger at yourself when you threatened Maude. Did you really think I wouldn't find out about your little office visit?"

"Those were just words." She wiped her face. "I didn't tell

this to the police when they visited earlier, because I knew they wouldn't believe me, but…please, Jason…just for a minute, would you listen?"

"What are you talking about?" Witnessing her tears, he felt a small portion of his steam deflate, but with this woman, he could never be sure what was real and what was faked.

"Can we sit for a moment?" She waved a hand toward her living room.

"You can." He moved farther into the room and leaned against the wall by a curtained window before checking the time on his phone. "I've only got a few minutes, so make it quick."

Ariel settled on the light-blue-and-cream-colored couch, tucking her legs under her body.

Her faded pink sweats and light yellow top were the shabbiest clothes he'd ever seen her wear.

"You don't know me, not really. And…and yes, I do keep my past private." She sighed and combed her fingers through her hair. "When I first moved to Ohio, I came with a friend. We were both desperate to leave…and start over, but she became clingy, jealous of my boyfriends, because she was…in love with me. Things between us got really ugly. She started using drugs, and then she got in debt and…and she had to work to pay it off."

"Work? As in prostitution?" Jason blinked. He'd seen documentaries on girl's who'd been trafficked. The entire scene was a blight no one seemed to talk about. He sighed and straightened against the wall.

"Yes…unfortunately…though she did work for an escort service, so she wasn't working on a street corner or anything." Ariel sniffed and plucked at her couch cushion. "I'd kicked her out of our apartment, but she kept coming back. I cared for her very deeply, because we survived our childhood together."

"I see." Jason nodded. "I don't know what this has to do with Maude though, so can you get to the point?" Though his words were harsh, he understood why a woman with a rough childhood would strive for more. Hadn't he done the same? Not that he wanted to sit around drinking tea and discussing the various perils of their lives, but maybe this was where Ariel's need to fight came in to play. She didn't know any other way to resolve her problems.

"My friend, Nicki, was recently released from prison." Ariel shivered and then covered herself with the throw blanket resting on the back of the couch. "Now that she's out, Nicki keeps popping up in places, following me. She blames me, you see, for her incarceration, and I think...I think she's the one hurting Maude and making it look like it's me. She wants revenge."

"So, you think this Nicki is scheming against Maude to get back at you?" Arching a brow, Jason scratched his stubbled chin. "How would she even know about Maude and I?"

"She's smart. Nicki was...a lot tougher, harder even. Back in Virginia, her home life was worse than mine because, you see, my father left, but her mom's boyfriends, they hung around." Ariel met his gaze. "She and I took off, and we never looked back."

"How long has this Nicki person been out?"

"She came to visit me once outside the Rec Center." Ariel ran her hands up and down her arms. "I've seen her a couple times since then and each time...she threatens me. You see, I'm the reason she went to jail. She'd been blackmailing a very powerful man and got caught."

Jason rubbed his eyes. Should he swallow this tale? "If all of this is true, then finding this Nicki should be easy. I'm giving Rachel and Clayton this info as soon as I leave. If, in fact, this woman is behind the attacks on Maude due to some convoluted plan to frame you, then we need to know that now. You should have told the police this information when they came by." Jabbing a finger in her direction, he shook his head. "What's this Nicki's last name?"

"Nobles." With slumped shoulders, Ariel released a ragged breath and whispered, "I'm sorry."

"I don't know how to respond to that." Jason huffed. "If you knew some woman had ill-intent against you and that others were in danger, then you should have spoken up. I had a rough childhood too, Ariel. I understand how that can cloud your judgment sometimes, but you will tell the truth now. Look at me." He pinned her with his gaze. "As far as this pregnancy is concerned, are you really going to continue with that lie? Because I don't believe you."

"I'm not lying!" Ariel shot off the couch and charged forward. "I showed you the test."

"Yeah you did, but you see, so many inconsistencies exist with you…and I stopped being naïve a long time ago." He crossed both arms over his chest. "I know you want me for my money, that's just fact. And I know pregnancy tests can be faked."

"Oh, right." Ariel wildly waved her arms. "I just fake peed on a stick right in fucking front of you."

"Ariel, you make the story fit as it suits you. So, I guess the answer is we'll see." Jason eased away from the wall, pissed because he'd come here for answers and now only had more questions. "We'll see if you're pregnant, and we'll see if this Nicki Nobles has anything to do with attacking Maude."

"You're damn right we'll see. When this is all over, you and everyone else will owe me one hell of an apology." She sneered and tossed a magazine at his feet. "You'll owe me."

"Calm down." He waved a hand, palm up. "The way I see it, Maude never would have been hurt had you come forward with your suspicions. So no, I don't owe you anything." Fighting to remain calm, he picked up the magazine and set it back on the coffee table. "I'm done with you, Ariel. I don't want to see you anywhere near me, my brother, or Maude. You understand? If you need to contact me, you can do so through Tom."

"I will not let you falter on your responsibilities." She crumpled onto the couch. "I let you take my body. I let you in. How is that fair? You used my body, yet now that I'm carrying your child, you think to leave me?" She clutched the throw blanket to her chest. "I've done nothing wrong, just tried to live a good life, tried to overcome my past, but I can't escape," she whispered. "I can't."

Puffing out a breath, Jason raked his fingers through his hair. "Ariel...I'm sorry, all right, but if in fact you are carrying my child, then you'll get your dream. We'll work with Tom and get things arranged, but if not...if this whole "poor me" act is nothing but that, an act, then God help you." His stomach churned from the nasty coffee plus a whole heaping of guilt, because Ariel was right about one thing—he had used her for sex. "Ariel, maybe you should see someone. Get some medication. Traumatic childhoods are hard to overcome. I get it, I've been there." He sighed and glanced at the clock on the wall. "I have to go. I'll let you know what Rachel and Clayton find. Until then, if you need anything call Tom, and if you see this Nicki person, tell her she's wanted for questioning."

"She won't care." Ariel shook her head, an odd smile on her lips. "She knows what she wants, and she'll win in the end."

Jason took two steps toward the door, but he turned back. "I've played a few games of my own, Ariel, and I don't lose."

"Ah, yes, you do play games." Ariel stood, walked toward him, and then opened her door. "I guess, as you say, we'll see."

Jason tipped his chin. "Yeah, we'll see."

CHAPTER 33

Three days after her big "I love you" bomb with Jason, Maude lounged in her old bedroom, more than ready to get back to work, but everyone still coddled her and said she wasn't ready. Even her I-don't-take-vacations-boss, Kathy, urged her to stay home.

Maude's face remained a scary mix of yellow, purple, and brown. Her welts from that bat were down to light pink blotches. Her stitches itched and her general attitude was one level below grouchy.

She couldn't go to work

Couldn't go to the hospital.

Couldn't go to her apartment.

Hadn't visited with her cancer counseling kids in weeks.

Mr. Attacker had built a prison around her, and she was dying to break free.

But, could she be alone without experiencing fear? She could and would, if only she could escape for just an hour.

Now that she'd semi-recuperated, she'd endured lectures from everyone about the dangers of living alone and her irresponsibility at leaving the door unlocked. She spent a lot of time gritting her teeth when she really should be appreciative they cared. However, as she'd explained to the detectives, she truly believed the man was already in her apartment, somehow. Or maybe she had a stalker. Wasn't that a lovely thought?

The detectives hadn't seen anything suspicious on the security camera footage taken at her apartment building. Whenever Maude asked Rachel about her case, she received no direct response, plus her friend seemed crankier than usual.

Maude growled and rolled her eyes before punching a throw pillow. "How am I supposed to feel safe if no one tells me what's going on?"

Had Jason spoken to Ariel lately? Was she still claiming to be pregnant? Was all this craziness Ariel's attempt to secure Jason? Surely, the woman had to understand none of that was possible now. However, Maude had a complete understanding on how a woman could become obsessed with Jason Stafford. His charm, charisma, and that sexy smile melted her every time. But still, she wouldn't create some elaborate ruse and then injure her competition in order to obtain him. That sort of psychotic behavior only happened in horror films, didn't it?

"No, Maude, obviously you're living a horror film right now. Buck up and think. Ariel's crazy, and she wants you gone. Too bad she's using Jason's brother to do it. And now, I'm crazy, too, because I'm sitting in my bed talking to myself." Maude chuckled then picked up her phone and checked her social media feed. Maybe something on there would distract her. Nope. Nothing but quotes and a video of a kitten playing with a turtle. Finished flipping through her page, she wondered where Jason was right now.

He texted when he could, but his mother had been moved to hospice yesterday, so every moment counted. Maude understood Jason's need to remain at his mother's side. She'd experienced the same when her father was dying.

Still, Maude couldn't help but believe Jason needed her. She sure needed him, and he shouldn't have to face his mother's death alone. Not that he was alone, but he should have someone who understood the loss of a parent at his side. She'd counseled many kids through the stages of grief, and she would do the same for Jason. But not from her bedroom. And not from this house. But with her hand in his, as he said goodbye.

"That's it." Maude shoved aside her blankets. "I've always been there for him, and I will do so now." Maude clenched her hands into fists and pounded the bed.

Owen had a ton of cars. With her car totaled, she'd hijack one of his vehicles and make a break for the hospital.

Decision made, she scurried into yoga pants and a long-sleeved coral top, brushed her teeth, and slipped on her warmest socks. Hospitals were always freezing, for some reason. Glancing down the hallway from a crack in her bedroom door, she tiptoed to the kitchen.

Her phone rang. She shrieked, practically jumping out of her skin. "Jeez." Cover likely blown, she answered the phone since the ringtone was Jason's. "Hello."

"Maude."

Oh, no. Not Jason, but Patrick. *Why is he calling me?*

Panic froze her in place and she fought to breathe evenly.

"Listen, I know I'm the last person you want to hear from, but…so Jason's all messed up, and he needs you right now. This thing with me and you, it's created this rift between us…and I-I…we were doing good, ya know?"

"Mmm hmm," Maude forced out a sound of agreement. Was this a trick? Was Jason really distancing himself from Patrick?

"I know you've not been…well, but could we maybe…like, talk or something? I don't really want him to know, because he'd stop us. I won't hurt you, Maude. That guy in your apartment wasn't me. And, from what Jason says, they're following some new leads."

"New leads?" Her heart pounded. "No one said anything about new leads."

"Oh…" He cleared his throat. "I'm sorry. I really don't know much."

Maude huffed, because yes, he did, and she would find out what he knew about these "leads."

"Um, so...your dad died of cancer, and maybe, could we talk? I just need to talk to someone who's been through this. I'm sorry."

Maude leaned against the kitchen counter. "I'm not sure." Her desire for information warred with memories of a jumbo red bat.

"I get that." He sighed. "There's a Starbucks across the street from this building. Would you meet me there? After we talk, we could show Jason we're a united front. It'd give him one less thing to worry about. Plus, I think he'd like you here."

Maude melted a little at his words. Jason needed her? Hadn't she just convinced herself of the same? Maybe a line on how he was really doing would be helpful before she actually talked to him. Having that info would help her prepare emotionally, because now that she thought about it, watching another person die from cancer might be hard on her, too. A sad truth, but a truth all the same. Plus, the whole "new leads" thing remained like a green-means-go sign in her mind. "Why do you have Jason's phone?"

"He's sleeping. First time in a while, so I thought now would be a good time to call. And I knew you'd answer."

Maude bit her bottom lip. Could she trust him? Starbucks was a public place but... "Sort of sneaky, calling like this."

"Yeah, it is, but I can't go through Mom dying without him. And right now, he's not fully on my side. I can't handle that."

"I'm afraid of you, Patrick." There. The blunt truth.

"I know, and I'm very sorry for that. I was at the hospital the whole time, I promise. Your family has been good to my brother, I wouldn't hurt that."

"I'm still not feeling well." Maybe she could avoid this meeting and just go straight to Jason, but her soft heart had a hard time saying no to a person who asked for help. Especially someone who was losing their mother to cancer.

"I understand." Patrick sniffed. "I've not given those around me much reason to believe in me lately."

"I don't want to believe you were responsible."

"Good, 'cause I'm not."

He sounded so sure, so positive. No hesitation. Nothing. But, could she take this chance?

"All right, but I'm asking Rachel to meet us at Starbucks. I won't go without her. Plus, if you weren't responsible, someone else was, and I'm sort of freaked out about all that. I've been watching too much Investigation Discovery, and now I think I've got stalkers hunting me down."

"The Starbucks is literally across the street. And I am fine with you asking Rachel along, that's fair. Thank you, Maude. You coming means a lot."

"I'll be there in an hour." That should give her enough time to escape and maybe even talk herself out of this stupid plan. But, he'd called *for* Jason. Reached out to mend the breach she'd caused between them. Maybe she'd heard wrong during the struggle. Or maybe someone was purposely misleading her. Who knew?

Maybe she'd even ask to see his knee. She'd nailed her attacker there, which meant he'd be bruised. She sighed. "Why hadn't I thought of that before?" She smacked herself on the forehead. "Oh, right, Maude, you're a regular doctor slash private detective." Chuckling, she shook her head. "I'm doing this. I will look Patrick in the eye and ask if he was responsible. I'm stronger than my fear." Maude tapped her phone against her open palm. "Yeah, but the question now is, am I strong enough to convince Rachel? Yes, yes I am. Besides, she owes me an explanation for this whole new lead thing. People are keeping secrets, and I don't like it." Eyes narrowed, she glanced out the window at the sunny spring day and made her decision. "I'm spending way too much time talking to myself. I'm going crazy locked up in this house, and while heading out when crazy people are after me may be insane, I won't live my life in fear."

She hummed "Eye of the Tiger" by Survivor then headed out the door toward the garage, wondering which vehicle best captured her rising to the challenge mojo.

# # #

"Woo hoo, finally free!" Maude rolled down the Ranchero's window, cranked up the radio, and flew down the interstate on her way to meet Patrick. She had an affinity for the vehicle, since she and Jason had spent so much time in it together. Though, she'd always thought the vehicle bulky and ugly before, it'd kind of grown on her, like those little pug dogs who snarfed and snuffed all over but were really chubby barrels of cuteness.

When she'd called Rachel, she'd endured about two minutes of cussing and threats to chain her in the basement, but Maude persisted, and her friend finally conceded. Bopping her head to an old country song about a "Grundy county auction," she powered down the exit.

This meeting with Patrick was for Jason. And, in a way, for her. She would either face her true attacker and prove she wouldn't be cowed, or crumple into a ball of fear. Not that she could read people…but Rachel could. The woman knew how to detect body language cues. So Patrick was either screwed, or he'd be cleared.

And if he were cleared, then who attacked her? Ariel was clearly involved, but who else? Brady's scratch sure seemed sketchy. Then there was this new lead thing, which Maude had asked Rachel about on the phone, and had ultimately turned the tide in her friend's attitude.

Maude tapped her fingers against the steering wheel. *Remember, you're doing this for Jason. Think of Jason.*

After taking the exit to the Starbucks, she glanced at the clock, realized she was a bit early and that Owen's beast didn't have much gas. So, she pulled into a gas station and, after turning off the engine, scouted the coffee shop's parking lot. Rachel's jeep wasn't there, and no way was she going in without backup. Pumping gas into Owen's Ranchero, she ignored the intense stare of the person at the other pump, very aware her face remained a bruised, multi-colored mess.

If she had to endure the stares of nosy people, along with a freakish face, she at least deserved a snack. Something salty, like a Payday candy bar. A sweet treat after the trauma she'd been through. Today was about freedom, and calories didn't count. Heck, she might even grab a big bag of Reese's Pieces. Finishing at the pump, she went inside the station and meandered through the candy aisle. After making multiple choices, she paid and went back outside.

Rachel's jeep still wasn't parked at Starbucks, so she pulled the Ranchero into a spot along the side of the gas station, backing in so she had a clear view across the street.

Munching on her candy bar, she yelped then choked on a peanut as a man in a black hoodie opened her passenger door.

Clutching her throat, she tried to cough but couldn't expel the nut.

Rough hands grabbed her around the waist.

Eyes watering, she gasped for breath. Wheezing, she fought through her panic and groped for the door handle.

The man shoved her down onto his upper thighs and struck her between her shoulder blades.

Once. Twice.

The peanut flew from her mouth.

Maude gasped for air, drawing sweet breath into her lungs over and over.

His arms tightened.

"Let me go," she croaked out, struggling to break free from

the man's tight grip. Heart racing, she surged upward. Primal desperation overcame everything as she battled against his hold.

"Stop fighting," the man growled before pinching the stitches on the bridge of her nose.

"Ah." Wincing at the sharp sting, she shook her head back and forth. "P-please, you're hurting me."

A cold, sharp point stabbed against her neck.

A hot prick followed.

"N-no!" Screaming, Maude tried to jerk free, stretching for the passenger door handle.

He pressed what seemed like a mile-long needle deeper into her neck.

Trying to slap him away only earned her a hard cuff against her ear. She moaned as her ear rang. Her entire face and neck were on fire and pulsing with pain.

"Jason." She blinked, suddenly very dizzy, the candy bar churning in her stomach. A tunnel appeared before her eyes. Jason was there, waiting at the other end. "I'm coming." She felt the words pour from her mouth, but they were nothing but a slurred mess. "Jason."

"You wish." Her attacker covered her mouth with his hand. "You're all mine, now."

That voice wasn't Patrick's? Was it? Everything around her began floating on waves. Waves and swaying. She swallowed hard, on the verge of vomiting. Licking her lips, she blinked again, squinting to focus.

Dancing boxing gloves raced down the tunnel, making a beeline for her face. Red and black. Red and black. They swayed back and forth, laughing. Closer and closer. And then they struck, biting into her neck with sharp teeth.

Maude flailed, batting them away. But they just ripped out her throat, taking her breath with them.

Slumping forward, Maude floated to her corner. Defeated. "I-I thhing I'm knocked ooowtt."

CHAPTER 34

Jason sat beside his mother's bed, watching her chest rise and fall. That motion kept him going. Patrick had just left, saying he needed some fresh air and might head over to the Starbucks. Made sense, he might do the same once his brother returned.

He closed his eyes for a moment. So tired, so confused about everything happening in his life. Rachel and Clayton hadn't run down Nicki Nobles yet, but they were still looking. They had discovered Ariel was telling the truth in regards to her general story. Which had him thinking about the pregnancy in a different light. He'd already talked to his lawyer about everything involved with setting up a woman and his child, and how the whole process would work. He sighed and rubbed his temples. His head either ached from no sleep or from thinking too hard. He wished Maude could be here to give him a neck and shoulder massage. He just wanted her hands on him, period. An escape into her body sounded pretty fantastic right about now.

When he heard a man clear his throat, he jerked open his eyes. A well-dressed guy stood in the doorway, next to a striking brunette with vivid green eyes. A memory stirred. "Pavel?" Jason sat straighter in his seat. What was Erik Pavel, Rachel's gangster brother, doing in the doorway of his mother's room? "Erick Pavel right? Are you supposed to even be here? I thought you'd left town…or something." He'd helped Rachel and Bronco through their troubles months ago, but Jason hadn't heard anything regarding the man since. News stories covering Bronco's family traumas hadn't said a whole lot about the man either, even though he played a major part. *Interesting.*

"I understand you're looking for Nicki." Erik waved a hand at the woman by his side.

Jason nodded. "The police are, yeah." He glanced at his mom, considering how to remove the possibly dangerous man from the room. "My mom's sleeping. Let's have this discussion out in the hallway." He palmed his phone in his hand and texted Clayton.

Nicki's here

Clayton texted back immediately.

On my way

He'd better be. Interrogating people was not Jason's forte.

Once outside the room, Jason noted the couple stood close to each other, Pavel with his arm around Nicki's waist. "Rachel know you're back in town?"

"No, and though I would have preferred to keep it that way, Nicki asked that I come along today."

"Clayton's on his way. Rachel is likely right behind him."

Erik chuckled. "Yes, my sister is tenacious." He shrugged. "A family trait."

Jason studied the woman at his side. "Why not go to the cops?"

Erik lifted a shoulder. "Meh…the authorities and I…let's say it's best if I remain in the shadows. I'm here with Nicki, but I'd prefer that information was kept between us."

"I suppose that will depend on what she has to say."

The woman smiled. A real beauty, yet a sadness existed in her eyes. Something he detected since he'd become so familiar with the emotion lately.

"Jason, I understand you've become involved with Ariel

Silvers."

"I have." Jason wouldn't give her any more info. She'd have to tell her version of the story without any leading comments from him.

"She's very clever, even beat me at my own game, but I...I guess you could say I was blinded."

Erik leaned against the wall, bracing both hands across his chest.

Jason led Nicki to a metal chair set up outside his mom's room. "Blinded by what?"

"She and I spent our childhood together—she was my sister, my lover, my friend. Everything. We are both very dark people, Mr. Stafford. I won't deny who I am. Ariel, however, longed to be someone else. She changed her name, her appearance, and turned her back on me." She pursed her lips, her green-eyed gaze meeting his own. "Erik discovered the police wished to question me. I have only one answer—Ariel lies."

Jason's stomach sank. How much more twisting of this tale could he take? How had this woman even met Pavel? "She says you're the liar and that you want revenge."

Nicki smiled. "What I want is complicated." She glanced at Pavel.

The silent man met her gaze then looked away.

"Well, what I want, Nicki, isn't complicated at all. I want whoever is conspiring against me to stop. I want whoever is hurting Maude to stop. Whether it's you or it's Ariel, or whoever, just stop."

"She is not responsible." Erik took a step toward him.

"Listen guy, I don't give two shits if you're some bad-ass gangster, don't step toward me. I'm not in the mood, but if you want, we'll go outside. Your call."

Dipping his chin, Erik stepped back.

"Jason." Nicki grabbed his tight fist. "I want everything to stop, too. That is why I'm here. I want to tell you about—"

"Jason!" Rachel barreled down the hall, eyes wide. "Oh, I'm so glad you're here. Is Maude here? Is she in the room?" She skidded to a stop right beside him, and her jaw practically hit the floor. "Erik? Wh-what? Why?" Frowning, she glanced up and down the hall. "What are you doing here? Are you insane?"

Nicki stood and held out her hand. "You must be Rachel. I'm Nicki Nobles."

Rachel stared at the woman and then blinked. "No. Nope." She held up a finger, bent over at the waist, and took a couple deep breaths. "Okay. First, I need to find Maude. Second, I will deal with you." She pointed at her brother before turning back toward Nicki. "Third, you're like amazingly beautiful and I say that with no intent to jump you or anything, but, lady, I'm not sure how you know my name." She tore her gaze from Nicki and glanced at Jason. "Stafford, is Maude here?"

"No, why?"

"Just great." Rachel stomped her foot and spun in a small circle. "I told her not to go. I said the whole thing was stupid."

A trickle of sweat traveled down Jason's spine. "Rachel, calm down. What are you talking about?"

She glared at her brother. "You should go. We'll be calling the cops, and you shouldn't be here."

"This is how you greet me?" Erik cocked a smile. "Good to know you care."

"People, can we have the family reunion later?" Jason grumbled. "Rachel, where is Maude?"

Patrick came running up the hallway, favoring his left leg a little. "Rachel, is Maude with you?"

"Why would Maude be with Rachel?" Jason practically shouted. "What the hell is going on? And is your knee acting up?"

"What? Yeah, a little. Listen, about Maude...I called her." Patrick lifted his shoulders and shook his head. "I just wanted to talk about you and Mom and the whole misunderstanding with the bat."

"The bat?" Pavel piped up, eyebrow raised.

"And, so? You called her and what?" Jason clenched his hands at his sides.

"We planned to meet across the street, but she…she isn't there." Patrick ran a shaky hand over his mouth.

Jason stared at his brother for a moment, breathing deeply past the panic building in his chest. "Maude isn't there. She isn't there. Okay then." Fury barreled straight past confusion. Didn't pass Go. Didn't collect two-hundred dollars. Eyes narrowed, he stepped toward Patrick. "You called Maude and asked her to leave the safety of her home, and now she isn't there!" He shoved his brother's chest. "What the hell is wrong with you?"

Rachel jumped in between them.

"Rachel. Move," he growled.

"Stafford, I wouldn't touch her." Pavel came to Jason's side and placed a hand on Rachel's shoulder. "Sis, I see you're still putting yourself in the middle of trouble."

Jason glared at Pavel then at his brother. "So, where *is* Maude? Maybe she just hasn't arrived yet."

Patrick rubbed the back of his neck. "Owen's Ranchero is across the street."

"Across the street from where?"

"The Starbucks. The car caught my eye when I was out in the parking lot searching for her."

Jason dialed Maude's number but received no answer. "Are you sure she was coming?"

Rachel nodded. "Yeah, she wanted to be here for you." She glanced at the doorway to his mom's room and winced. "I'm sorry, but she was determined to get here, and she was upset I hadn't told her about Nicki." She gasped then shoved Jason aside. "Nicki. Of course, you are *that* Nicki."

Jason dropped his head in his hands. "You've got to be kidding me."

"Jason, it's okay." Rachel clutched his arm. "I put a tracker on Maude's phone."

# # #

"Maude! Maude!"

Her entire body shook, and she could swear Jason was yelling her name. Maude frowned and lifted her tongue up and down in her mouth, nausea rising.

"I need to puke. I'm gonna…" Maude blinked awake, clutching her throat. "Why is it so hot in here?" She blinked again and waved a hand in front of her face. "Where am I, and why is it so smoky?"

From somewhere in the fog, or was it smoke, she heard a voice call for her. *Jason?*

"Why are we in a cloud?" Rolling to the side, she realized she was on the floor. The carpet fibers were rough against her cheek, and stinky, smelling a little like baby vomit. Her stomach rebelled at the stench.

Feet appeared in her line of vision. Big feet in expensive tennis shoes that were covered in black soot.

"Jason?" Maude coughed and then winced. "My throat hurts."

"Maude, can you walk? We need to get out of here." His voice was coarse, as if he'd just woken from a deep sleep.

"What?" She squinted, trying to take in her surroundings. Tiny desks and chairs surrounded her. Flickering yellows. Roiling grays. And heat. Her arms glistened with sweat. "Jason, what's happening?" Lifting her head, she glanced at him. His eyes were red-rimmed, and he was crying. "Why are you crying?"

"I'm not." He crouched down beside her. "The Rec Center's on fire."

"Oh, no. Call the fire people, those people who do fires." Her eyes watered, and she coughed against the smoke burning through her nose. "What's wrong with your voice? Are you sick?"

"Maude." Jason tugged on her arm. "Stand up. We need to go."

She lifted her arms, but they felt like Jell-O, so she wiggled them. "I'm so happy to see you."

"I'm happy to see you, too." He drew her to her feet, and with his arm around her waist, he helped her stand.

"Wait a minute." She blinked as the smoke irritated her eyes. "Why am I at the Rec Center?" Maude cleared her throat and breathed deep, fighting for air. "Why is it so hot?"

"The building's on fire." Jason tugged her down the hall.

And that's when she saw the flames all around them, dancing, frolicking in yellows and oranges. Eyes wide, she gripped Jason's shirt. "All that work...I don't understand...I'm going to vomit." She stopped and clutched her stomach.

"No." He gripped her hand. "Come on, Maude, don't give out on me now."

"Right, right, be strong for Jason." She smiled as he ducked under a burning wooden beam. Jason was saving her. Her head remained woozy, just like the smoke swirling through the room. The air so murky she couldn't tell which way he was taking her. "Jason, get on the ground." Eyes watering, she coughed as the smoke entered her lungs. "Crawl or roll, right?" She swallowed again, not sure where this severe nausea was coming from. The peanut. A masked man. A pinch against her neck. She gasped. "Jason, I was—"

"Shh...someone's shouting." He halted and raised a finger to his lips.

She listened, too.

A man in a yellow suit with a light blasting from the helmet on his head shoved through a double door and waved them over.

"Come on." Jason lifted her shirt over her mouth, and then did the same with his own.

The firefighter grabbed her arm and led her and Jason out of the building.

Once outside, sweet, clean air swept through her lungs, and she bent at the waist, coughing and wheezing, fighting for breath. "Jason, oh my gosh." She crumpled to her knees and rested in the grass.

"I'm right here." He rolled through the grass to her side, his face grimy with tears leaking from the corners of his eyes.

"How did I get here, and how did you find me?" She wiped her eyes with the back of her hand. The nausea hadn't subsided, and she shivered, which was at odds from the heat surrounding them.

"Rachel has you tagged."

Maude shrieked when Owen raced up and dropped down beside them.

He wrapped her in his arms. "Maude, what the hell?"

"She needs medical attention, buddy." With his fist, Jason bumped Owen on the shoulder. "Let's get her over to that ambulance." He pointed and waved at the EMTs.

Once the EMTs had her set up with an oxygen mask, she breathed freely once more but had tons of questions. She tugged on Jason's arm where he stood whispering with Owen. "I remember Patrick stabbing me with a needle," she croaked out. "I was supposed to meet him, but I choked on a peanut then almost died, and he came in and tried to kill me by fire. Why not just let me choke?" She growled, "Idiot."

"Not possible." Jason crouched before her and tucked her hair behind her ear. "Patrick was the one who told me you were missing. He wasn't gone long enough to move you here."

"No." She frowned, still certain Patrick meant her harm. Though her behavior was petulant and childish, she wanted the problem to be solved so she wouldn't be scared anymore. As it was, she'd likely never leave the house again.

Tears trickled down her cheeks as she watched flames pour from the building. She stood and buried her face against Jason's chest, wetting his T-shirt. "It's ruined. All that work. Those poor kids, their place of escape is gone because someone is insane, and has needles, and bats, and I don't even know what else." Her throat hurt, her body hurt, and now her heart hurt.

Jason's phone rang. All he said was "okay" before hanging up. He eased out of her arms. Shoulders slumped, he staggered two paces away and bent over at the waist, hands resting on his knees.

Maude glanced at Owen.

Eyes hooded, he shook his head.

Sucking in a breath, Maude stilled, her stomach clenching. "Oh my God, Jason. I'm so sorry."

With glassy eyes, he turned and met her gaze. "Yeah, my mom, she's dead."

And he hadn't been there.

Because of her.

CHAPTER 35

Hands still shaking even though many days had passed since the fire, Maude wrapped up the deviled eggs then stuffed them in the fridge, balancing the glass dish on top of a covered tin filled with sliced ham. After washing her hands, she glanced around Owen's kitchen for Jason.

Focus, Maude. Focus on everyday things. Normal things. Concentrate on something other than fear. Impossible, because her throat still hurt from the smoke inhalation, and no matter how hard she tried, she couldn't get warm. Not only that, she'd taken to lying. To everyone. "I'm fine" had become the only words out of her mouth. Yet, deep inside, she'd reached a point of no return. Of never wanting to be alone. Of living in constant fear of the next attack.

Rachel informed her the gas station's cameras had video of a person in a hoodie, but the image didn't include the face. Arson investigators were still digging through the Rec Center's charred remains.

Owen's car was found at the Rec Center, but nothing was left except a metal carcass. Her attacker had set his Ranchero ablaze. Guilt weighed heavy in her heart over that. She'd run away and now...and now...the Rec Center, and her brother's car, and her calm, ordered world were nothing but ash.

Splintered. Broken. Her heart singed. She needed someone to hold her together. She'd made it through the funeral, but now…now her façade was slipping, and she needed Jason's warm arms wrapped tight around her body. Real death. Real fear. Raw emotions and her pain kept her too focused on herself. She desired an escape from reality, and Jason could make her feel something else. Anything else. Pleasure. Love. Something.

But he'd disappeared.

His mom's funeral this morning had likely sent him to his comfort zone. Although, he'd have to choose another vehicle. Maude sighed and leaned against the kitchen counter, rubbing her forehead.

Four days after Jason's mother died, they'd laid her to rest beside her daughter. During the proceedings, she'd tried not to flinch around his brother and had even hugged him when he'd seemed on the edge of losing it. She had to admit, he'd stuck by Jason all day. Plus, her fears were unfounded, since Patrick couldn't be responsible for her attack at the gas station or her almost-death by fire.

After the funeral, Owen hosted a catered brunch. The mood somber. Guests had barely even touched the food, and now Owen's fridge was packed with catered meats and various salads.

The ceremony today was quite lovely with only one hitch. Patrick arranged for their father to be there, but Jason hadn't acknowledged his presence. A scene had almost occurred when his father called out to him, but Owen and Bronco quickly intervened.

Rachel took her arm.

Maude fought not to flinch.

"We're leaving now. Let us know if you need anything." She gave Maude a quick once-over. "You're looking better on the outside, at least."

"My stitches came out a few days ago. As for the bruises, they're fading."

"So will everything else." Rachel squeezed her hand. "Have you been back to your apartment?"

Maude shook her head.

"You'll get there." Rachel offered a lop-sided smile. "I have some information about Ariel and Nicki. You were upset before when I left you out, so I'm trying to make amends."

"Oh, Rachel." Maude hugged her petite friend. "It's all right. I can come by your offices when I head back to work the day after next."

"Sounds like a plan." Rachel nodded. "I can't believe Ariel had the audacity to show up at the funeral."

"I know. Hurt my stomach and I thought Jason would lose it. Good thing Patrick took her aside."

"She's oblivious. She threatens you, has likely followed through with that threat then she shows up dressed in black, and expects us not to kick her conniving ass out?"

"I know. I think she's unstable. She stared at Jason the whole time." Maude nodded at Bronco as he joined them.

"Like I said, I've got some things to tell you. We're getting closer to the truth, Maude." Rachel squeezed her hand and smiled. "Stay strong."

"Ready to go?" Bronco locked his arm around Rachel's waist, practically engulfing her.

Rachel nodded.

"I'm off to find Jason, anyway."

"He's probably out in the garage." Bronco waved his hand toward the garage.

"So, you know Jason goes out there?"

"Owen got suspicious once, set up a video camera, and that was that."

Maude bit her bottom lip. "Are there still cameras out there?"

Bronco laughed. "Nope…you're free and clear to…comfort Jason however you think best." Then the big lug wrapped both her and Rachel in a hug.

And for a moment, as Maude blinked away a tear, she felt warm again.

# # #

Sitting in Owen's refurbished Mustang, Jason didn't bother turning toward the garage's side door when he heard it open. He'd known Maude would join him after everyone had left. All the people had been too much. His mother gone, his father and Ariel causing a scene, his brother doing a complete 180 and actually taking charge for once. Everything compounded in his head, and nothing resulted in any calm—only a pounding headache. Yet, seeing Maude eased him a little.

She and her mom had guided him and his brother through the funeral arrangement process. He'd been at a complete loss. How would he fit everything his mom had meant to him into a tiny wooden box? Nothing had been soft enough or fine enough for his mother. Everything was so dull and mundane when she'd been full of energy. How could he close everything she was inside a wooden box forever?

He'd already decided to donate more funds to cancer research, especially now that the Rec Center was no longer accepting contributions.

Maude opened the passenger door and made herself at home. She didn't say anything, just sat there, comfortable in silence.

No mundane small talk to fill the void. Not his Maude.

But today, the silence was deafening. Today, he wanted to crawl out of his skin so he no longer felt any pain.

"I made a decision today." She spoke the words quietly.

"Oh?"

"I'm going back to my apartment."

Though she'd healed over the past few days, she still bore

several bruises. He finally glanced her way. "You sure?"

"I am if you'll come with me."

"No."

"Oh." Eyes rounded, she sucked in a breath. "All right."

He wrapped his arm around her waist and tugged her across the bench seat. "I said no, because you're moving in with me."

She froze. Not the reaction he'd hoped for.

"My building is much more secure, and I need to know that you're safe. Plus, just knowing you're waiting at home, well, that thought does something to my heart I've never felt before. I'm not going into all the emotional shit. I'm not in the mood to charm or offer romantic words." Jason trailed his hand up and down her arm. "I want you in my apartment, and I don't want to discuss it. I just want it to happen like, today."

Her response was welcome, though unexpected again. She undid the belt around his black dress pants, unfastened the button, and drew down the zipper before pulling out his apparently-not-sad-if-bj's-were-involved cock. Next thing he knew, he hissed as she drew him deep into her warm, wet mouth.

He gathered her hair in a fist and held it aside so he could watch her cheeks suck in and out. "Is that a yes, baby?"

She hummed around his cock.

Closing his eyes, he dropped back against the headrest. "This is what I want, Maudy. Every day coming home to you, knowing you're mine for the taking whenever, however, I want."

She gripped the base of his cock and worked her hand in tandem with her slick mouth.

Quickly, his balls drew up tight. He groaned as she nipped his rigid head and then tongued his leaking slit.

She opened wide and raked her teeth up and down. Once. Twice before sucking him down to the root.

Moans and deep sighs escaped his mouth. "Maude...yes...this is what I need, take away the pain, baby...that's it."

She used her free hand to tug on his balls.

More than willing to accommodate, he spread his legs wider. "That's right. You're in charge."

Her mouth's intense suction had him gripping her head and likely tugging too hard on her hair.

"I'm coming, Maudy...pull off."

She mumbled her no, then picked up the pace, hand tugging, the other smoothly working him up and down, her mouth guiding him to an exquisite finish.

He blocked out everything but her beautiful mouth and rocked up against her.

She hollowed her cheeks as she sucked hard on the down stroke.

That sight pushed him over the edge, and he cursed as his cock jerked and pulsed his seed deep into her mouth.

She never once pulled back, just licked every drop.

Every drop.

Everything.

Nothing was his alone, anymore.

They were sealed.

They were one.

His Maudy knew what he needed and then gave and gave. And so he asked for more. He pulled her against his chest and sobbed.

Sobbed for everything he'd lost that day, buried his face in his woman's thick, soft hair and opened his heart. All the pain. All the loss. This woman in his arms would always be the strong one. Always stay at his side. Always love him. Always take...and give everything.

CHAPTER 36

As light from the morning dared to shine through her bedroom's window, Maude gazed at the man lying beside her. His blond hair thoroughly ruffled. He'd been through so much this week and needed rest.

Last night, they'd come back to her apartment. His plan was to help her pack and then move her things to his place. Likely moving a little fast, but she didn't care. She'd dreamed of this, hoped for this, and now here he was.

Jason blinked then stretched his muscle-thickened body. "Good morning, Maude." He grinned and drew her against his chest.

She smiled and let him hold her for a while before she spoke. "I had the biggest crush on you, you know? A crushing crush. So very painful and embarrassing. I hated it."

He chuckled and then combed his fingers through her hair. "Here's a secret," he whispered into her ear. "I figured it out."

"Wasn't very smooth, was I?" Maude shook her head.

"It was cute."

She pinched his nipple.

"Ow." He slapped away her hand. "What was that for?"

"I am *not* cute."

In retaliation, he pinched her butt. "Yeah, you are, always

have been."

She squirmed but let him get away with his pinch. "Remember that brunette model you brought by Owen's?"

"How could I forget? You put horseradish sauce in her ranch dressing."

"Maybe." Maude shrugged. "People shouldn't come to BBQs and only eat a salad. It's rude."

"And what about the time you dropped a June bug in that redhead's hair?"

"Hmm." Maude tapped her bottom lip. "I don't know what you mean."

"Bugs are gross."

Maude rolled her eyes. "You and my brother are both scared of wee little spiders, like that time a few months ago in Owen's basement. Mom and I thought a zombie apocalypse broke out down there, but no, just a spider and two big scaredy cats."

"That spider had fangs."

"As if you got close enough to see it." Shaking her head, Maude rolled her eyes.

Jason shot on top of her, locking her arms above her head. "You questioning my manhood, woman?"

She nudged him with her hips. "Absolutely."

He kissed his way down her jaw before trailing more across her chest. "How about now?" Using the tip of his tongue, he flicked her nipple.

Liquid heat flared through her body and ended at her core. "Okay, okay." Practically breathless, she writhed beneath him. "*Maybe* you are a big strong man, not afraid of anything. What else you got?"

He lightly kissed her lips but didn't delve too deep.

Luckily, because morning breath and all. Her throat was still a bit raw from breathing in all the smoke. Plus, her nose was stuffy, which forced her to breathe through her mouth.

Arms locked beside her head, he raised a brow then

straightened. "You know, one time this woman asked me—"

"Get off me." Maude shoved at his arms.

"Why?"

"Why are *you* talking about someone else?"

"I wasn't."

"You were."

"Stop interrupting me, or I'll gag you."

"I don't think so." She crossed her arms over her chest. "Continue."

He cocked a sideways grin and bent to kiss her again, before resting back on his knees. "Anyway, she asked me what I thought about during sex."

Maude arched a brow. Not sure where he was going but willing to listen.

"I said I come up with these fantasies, like kinky stuff we could do, things like that."

"Kinky?" She stilled, thoughts flashing to Brady and their horrid experience. "So then, would you do them?"

"No, never really felt comfortable opening up that much."

"Oh." Maude frowned. She hadn't, either. Brady had wanted to play a lot of dominance games, but that wasn't what she wanted. Still, she wasn't opposed to trying some new things. Especially with Jason.

"But, with you"—he trailed a finger between her breasts—"I don't need to think of any fantasies, and I don't hold back on how good you make me feel."

"Really?" Her cheeks heated, likely due to a raging blush. "I don't know what to say to that other than your words make me happy."

"Don't give me too much credit." He winked. "Because, when I'm not with you, I think of all the kinky shit I want to do to you. For you. In you."

Maude lowered her gaze and ran her finger along his inner thigh. "So, do it."

He braced himself above her again. "I think I will."

A few delicious moments later, just when he'd found a particularly sensitive spot on her stomach, she heard the doorbell.

Jason's head popped up. "Who the hell is that?"

"Don't know." Breathing raggedly, Maude shrugged. "Don't care."

Again, the doorbell rang, followed by a hard knock on her door.

"Who knows you're here?"

"Well, I texted Mom when we left Owen's garage last night."

Jason grunted then got off the bed.

"I'm yanking that doorbell off the wall," Maude grumbled while watching Jason throw on his dress slacks.

"My building has about twenty layers of security before you can even get to the door, and no doorbells." Jason knocked his fist against her bedroom doorframe before disappearing into the hallway.

"Just great." Maude huffed out a sigh. Realizing their morning interlude was over, she hustled out of bed and was headed for her dresser when she heard the first shout.

She threw on some pants and grabbed Jason's black T-shirt from the floor, shoving it over her head as she bustled to the front door.

In her doorway, Jason stood nose-to-nose with Brady.

"Hey, hey, no. Stop it." She raced over and, with a shaky hand, clutched Jason's arm. No more violence. Dizziness crashed through her, and she swayed a little. Enough fighting, enough pain, she couldn't take any more.

"Get out of here right now." Jason jabbed a finger at Brady.

"Maude deserves better than some playboy like you."

"I know that, but she's made her choice. Don't let me see you around here again."

"Jason, come on." Struggling to even out her breathing, Maude tugged on his arm.

"Why the hell are you here, anyway? You following Maude around? Just like you did at the gas station? And to this apartment?" With both hands, Jason shoved Brady. Hard.

Brady tumbled into the hallway.

"I know you're responsible for hurting Maude, and I'll prove it. Attempted murder, arson, all that shit should put your ass in prison for a long time."

Brady got to his feet and brushed off the back of his pants. "You're deluded, Stafford."

Jason grabbed him by the throat and shoved him against the opposite wall. "You've yet to see deluded."

Wide-eyed, Brady clutched at Jason's hands, his face turning red.

"Jason! Stop this!" Maude yanked on his forearm, but he was too strong, too determined. "Let him go."

Based on the look in Jason's eye, he'd shifted beyond reason. For a moment, she considered calling her brother. Or back up of some sort, because Jason remained lost in a rage. She'd never seen him so angry. The pulling she did on his arm had no impact. Her happy-go-lucky guy had turned into the Hulk.

"I know you and Ariel are playing games together. When we get proof, I'm coming for you. You tell that bitch, she keeps this up, I'll take my baby, and she'll rot in prison right next to you." Jason leaned forward. "You wanna hurt someone, Stephens? How about you hurt me?"

"Hey!" Owen shouted from down the hall.

After a very loud pounding of feet, Maude was eased aside by Bronco. "Come on, Maude." Bronco nudged her arm. "Let's go back inside."

"They'll hurt each other." She kept her gaze on Jason.

Bronco glanced back at the shouting men.

Jason's arms were flying all over the place, and he practically snarled in Brady's face.

Owen stood beside Jason, his glare dark and directed at

Brady.

"Owen won't let Jason kill Brady...I think, anyway." Bronco winced before meeting her gaze. "I'll handle it. I always do. Now, please go inside. If fists start flying, I don't want you anywhere close by."

Maude nodded but, at her doorway, she turned back.

Bronco had separated Brady and Jason and was speaking in a low, calm tone. Jason's entire body heaved, as if he couldn't catch his breath.

She glanced at Brady and caught him staring—a direct stare, almost menacing.

Then he smiled.

The kind she was sure serial killers used before they turned on the power saw or sharpened their knives.

"He shouldn't get you, too."

A shiver ripped down her spine. With that recollection, she feared every accusation Jason had leveled against Brady was correct. Maude tried smiling back. Why, she couldn't say? Nerves? Hope her fears were unfounded?

He maintained that cold, I'll-murder-you-in-your-sleep stare.

With Brady's icy look lasered into her vision, she escaped into her apartment, shut the door, and then slid down the wall. She closed her eyes, but all she could envision were those same blue eyes staring through the narrow slits of a black mask.

CHAPTER 37

Ariel shoved the gun's barrel against Brady's forehead. "Why would you go to her apartment? What were you thinking? I told you to stay away." She fought down her concern over this man's ineptness. How dare he go rogue? She'd half a mind to pull the trigger and be done with the fool. The metal warmed in her hand, and she let her finger rest on the trigger. Such power in something so small. A quick end. And easy, so easy. But, a tad too messy...and loud, especially when they were sandwiched inside a family bathroom located on the lower level of Manchester's downtown shopping center.

"You told me to create chaos, and I did." The blond shoved the gun away from his face. "Don't question me, Ariel."

The fool looked a mess, his hair askew, his pants and shirt wrinkled, sweating through his pits like a disgusting pig. If someone was following her today, she'd likely lost them. She'd slowly worked her way through each store. No private eye would bother tracking her through lingerie and body wash for hours on end. Plus, she hadn't noted anyone staring or reappearing over and over.

"Listen to me, Stephens. I will question you, because *I* am the one in charge." Ariel tapped the gun barrel against her chin. "I'd almost believe you *were* lovesick over the whiny little bitch."

"You don't know anything about Maude so shut your mouth."

"Oh, but I know plenty about you." She ran a finger down his nose.

"Drop the pretense, Ariel."

"We need to finish her off."

"Too dangerous."

"I have an out. A woman named Nicki Nobles. She was my dealer and a high-society escort." Ariel met Brady's gaze. "She got greedy, tried blackmailing one of her clients. He found out, and she went to jail for trafficking in both sex and drugs. She's been out a few months now, slithering around in her high heels, drinking cocktails with her new lover. She's a threat, so I'm sending her back to prison where she belongs." Ariel paced in the small confines. "I won't be trapped. I've set up each domino, now we'll just watch them fall."

"You said Maude would be mine again." Brady leaned against the white porcelain sink. "That hasn't happened, so forgive me if I don't have much faith in your plans." Sweat beaded on his upper lip, and he waved his hands. "Not only that, Jason knows it's you and me doing everything. Everyone knows. They just need time to prove it."

Ariel shook her head, a slow smile building across her face as she purred, "Everyone will owe me a huge apology when they find out they were wrong. I gave them Nicki, gave them the rope. Just sit back and enjoy the ride as I finish this off and hang her with it. You'll have Maude back, and I'll have Jason. This will be my greatest victory yet." Ariel smoothed her hand up and down the gun barrel over and over again.

"Um, Ariel…what are you doing?"

"What?" She snapped to attention and glared at Brady before tugging her shopping bags off the bathroom door's hook. "Around the same time Nicki goes to jail, I'll conveniently have a miscarriage. I know a doctor who will say anything if you pay him enough." Or blow him enough. Either way, she'd pay the bastard. She patted Brady's shoulder. "Stop worrying. I have everything covered. Now, come with me, we have work to do."

"I'm done with this, Ariel." Brady spun her around and shoved her against the wall, placing his hand around her throat. "You've gone too far."

"Hands off." She grabbed his wrist, yanked, and then shoved the gun against his crotch. "Maybe I won't tell them about Nicki, maybe I'll pin the whole thing on you. Is that what you want?"

He jutted out his chin and jabbed a finger against her chest. "You'll go down with me."

She narrowed her eyes, unwilling to be cowed by this fool. "No one is going down. I told you, I've got the police angle covered. Now, I'll go first, and you can follow after. We'll both go back to work for a few hours then I'll text you with my plan. Be ready." Pushing him aside, she stuffed her gun in her purse, and left the filthy bathroom—and filthy male, behind.

On her way back to her car, she vowed once again she would not lose. Her friends would never let her live it down if they found out that freak show, Maude Killion, won the prize, and she didn't.

Her entire reputation was on the line. All her friends fought to get to the top. Each one searching for the best sugar daddy, but Ariel was different. Always had been. She'd have more. Not only a rich man, but a famous one, too. Plus, Jason was drop-dead gorgeous, not a wrinkly old bastard sucking on a cigar while you sucked his limp dick.

She belonged on a pedestal. A queen. Those bitches would never snub her, ignore her, or snicker behind her back again.

Ariel Silvers was a winner. She would become the leader of them all, and then they'd follow her advice on fashion, decorating, food, makeup…everything. Only one thing stood in her way, but not for long. Maude had to go, regardless of any promise she'd made to Brady. That man was worthless and had certainly outlasted his usefulness. Perhaps, she'd pin the entire scheme on him. A consideration. If Brady took the fall, then she'd not only have Jason's forgiveness but Nicki's, too. Ariel could have her old friend back, gain her trust again. Maybe Jason would even be willing to share her with Nicki, or they could all just live together.

Yes, definitely a consideration. Her head began to pound, a side effect of Brady's doubts and unwillingness to play along, but no matter. Once Brady and every other obstacle was knocked aside, everyone would see the exact picture she'd been painting since she left that rural Virginia town years ago. Dee Dee Davis, small town nobody, was now Ariel Silvers, a priceless work of art.

After hearing Rachel's update on Ariel and Nicki and her brother, Erik, being back in town, Maude realized she had a lot to consider as she made her way to the parking garage elevators beside her friend.

Two women told the same tale, but one was lying. Erik vouched for Nicki, so Rachel leaned more toward Ariel. However, Ariel was a woman, not the man who had attacked Maude twice. So either Ariel was working with someone or a man out there hated her. Brady was the likely culprit, since no one else fit. Plus, he had said he knew Ariel, which meant they were likely in this together. But why? They had to comprehend they'd be caught eventually, unless they were both insane, which at this point neither she nor Rachel counted out.

Rachel jiggled her keys. "It's all right, Maude."

"What?" Maude glanced at her friend.

"You are breathing a little heavily. Being scared is normal, but I'm with you, okay?"

Maude nodded. "Sorry."

"Don't be sorry." Rachel punched her shoulder. "Be tough."

Forcing a grin, she flexed her biceps. "With these guns, I got it covered."

Rachel chuckled then pulled her onto the elevator.

Now that their meeting was over, Maude wanted nothing more than to wrap her puny biceps around Jason, but he was officially back on a practice schedule. He'd said the physical exertion would help. He'd argued against her meeting with Rachel at her downtown offices, but Maude had explained that just because she had taken some time off work didn't mean Rachel had. Plus, her friend had agreed to pick her up from his place and take her home.

Maude sent him a quick text.

Heading back to your place. See you soon.

Her new friend, fear, trickled up and down her spine as Maude stepped out of the elevator and into the dimly-lit parking garage. Darkness had fallen while she and Rachel caught up, not only with her case, but their lives in general. Few cars remained.

Maude didn't blink once while making her way to Rachel's jeep. Eagle eyes had nothing on her. After everything she'd gone through, she had become hyper-aware of her surroundings. Smells, sounds, approaching people—all had her full attention.

"My heart is about to explode." Maude slid into Rachel's Jeep. Not really her vehicle of choice in evading psychos, but it'd have to do. "I was sure we'd get attacked by Brady or Ariel like some old horror movie. They come out swinging axes, chopping us to bits."

Rachel laughed. "I know. I was nervous, too." She turned on the Jeep, backed out, and then followed the arrows down.

Halfway down, Rachel's windshield exploded.

Screaming and batting away glass, Maude shrank into her seat. "What was that?"

Rachel slammed on the brakes. "Stay down! I'm barreling through." She kicked out the shattered windshield, and then straightened. But didn't hit the gas, she only stared straight ahead. "Does she really think I won't run over her ass?"

"Who? What do you mean?" Maude followed her gaze.

Ariel stood right in front of them, holding a handgun.

Rachel revved the engine then hit the gas pedal.

Ariel smirked and fired two more times, never moving from her stance in the middle of the parking garage.

The Jeep's front driver's side tire blew, causing the vehicle to skid to the left.

Maude covered her face with both arms. "Don't stop."

Rachel cursed. "I'm trying to keep 'er straight."

Another gunshot echoed through the garage.

The sound so loud someone would likely hear. Someone would call the police. With that hope in her heart, Maude could only scrunch up her body as the Jeep swerved and crashed into a parked pickup truck.

Maude's head snapped back as the air bag exploded. Face stinging from the blow, she slumped in her seat and prayed she wouldn't die on the cold, dirty concrete with a bullet lodged between her eyes. Her heart practically jumped out of her chest when someone hopped onto the Jeep's hood. A knife slashed in front of her face and stabbed the inflated air bag.

Brady winked then smiled. "Hello, Maude. And here *you* thought you were through with *me*. Seems you were wrong. Now, get out." He flicked the knife toward her door.

"B-brady," Maude sputtered. "I-I knew it, but…wh-what…how could you?" Maude stared at the man she had once loved, stomach sinking at the reality of this moment. Her ex-boyfriend really *was* insane. She blew out a slow breath and glanced at Rachel. Her friend hadn't moved, her entire face remained buried in the half-deflated airbag.

Maude pulled her free so she wouldn't suffocate.

"Get out!" Brady commanded. "Or Ariel will shoot Rachel."

Fury over this man's treachery. Fury over his threats and all the pain he had caused shot a rush of bravery down her spine. Maude shoved open the passenger door, jumped onto the asphalt, and took off at a sprint. Unsure of where she was within the garage, or if bullets would fly at any moment, she started shouting, "Call the police! She has a gun!"

Footsteps pounded behind her.

Sirens sounded in the distance.

The sound of her rasping breathing echoed through her ears.

"Help me," she screamed, rounding the garage to the next level. "Call 911!"

Another gunshot echoed through the parking garage. Final and deadly.

Maude jolted to a stop, chest heaving.

Eyes closed, she slowly turned. If they'd killed Rachel…Oh, my God, if Rachel were dead because she'd run, she'd never forgive herself.

Her pursuer's footsteps came to a halt beside her, and yet, she still refused to open her eyes. Would there be a pool of blood? A body? Was she next?

Her head was wrenched back, and then Brady's voice growled into her ear, "Going somewhere?"

"D-did you kill her?" Maude opened her eyes and glared. Then she shoved him hard again and again until he slapped her, but Maude felt nothing. "Brady, don't do this."

"Too late." He leveled a knife against her throat. "Too late for me and for you. Ariel just screwed me over. She said we'd be quiet." Hand trembling, he wiped his sweaty brow. "Said, we'd just surprise you…but no…" His gaze went wide, and he stared right through her. "She goes and stands in the middle of the garage and fires her stupid gun." After a slight shake of his head, he met Maude's gaze before caressing her cheek with the knife. "It's over for me. So, we'll go out together."

"Brady." Maude clutched his arm. "I'll help you through this, but right now, I need to know…" Heart pounding with dread, she sucked in a breath. "Did you kill Rachel? Did you?"

He smiled and shook his head. "*I* didn't."

CHAPTER 38

"Jason...there's something I should probably tell you. I completely spaced it until now." Patrick glanced over at Clayton before he sank into one of their mother's kitchen chairs.

Tired from practice, Jason wanted nothing more than to go home to Maude. Plus, he was distressed over having to pack up his mother's things. Most items would go to Goodwill, others he and Patrick would keep. He'd already started a pile on the dining room table.

"What do you need to tell me?" Jason glanced at his brother before he opened the fridge and grabbed a water bottle.

"It's about Ariel." Patrick rubbed the back of his neck.

Body tight, Jason spun on his heel and glared at his brother.

Clayton stiffened and halted in the middle of taping a box of kitchen items. "What about her?"

Good thing his pal asked, because Jason was on the verge of lunging for his brother's throat.

"She came on to me one night at the bar. At Plunder."

"Yeah, and..." Clayton waved his hand in a keep-talking motion.

Patrick sniffed then looked away. "I took her up on her offer."

"What?" Jason charged, but Clayton shoved him back.

"I didn't have sex with her. I swear." Patrick raked his fingers through his hair. "Katie pointed out Ariel a few nights before. Explained who she was." He cleared his throat and kept his gaze on Jason's. "I got Ariel out in my car and asked her what she wanted. She told me in explicit detail, and I told her to get lost. That I didn't bang skanks."

"Did she say anything? Did you explain you knew who she was?" Clayton dropped questions like they were in an interrogation room. "Did she say anything about Jason?"

Patrick shot Clayton a wide-eyed look. "See, that night I had my suspicions, but now that everything is coming together, and with Ma…now that Ma…" He glanced away and took a deep breath. "Anyway, I've had time to consider what was off about the whole thing. Ariel says she's pregnant by my kid bro, but then shows up at my bar, trying to get me to fuck her…I may not be the sharpest tack in the bunch, but even *I* know what she was up to."

"Get pregnant by you, so she could pass off the baby as Jason's." Clayton shook his head. "Doesn't work. Both of you would take the paternity test, but only one would have all fifteen markers the services generally check. It's simple science."

"What he said," his brother jerked his head toward Clayton.

"So, she's not pregnant." Jason tossed out that statement even though he'd known. Deep down he'd always known.

"I'd say no, or why else would she basically drop her drawers for me?"

Jason glared at Patrick. "And you didn't?"

"I said I didn't." Patrick glared back and shot to his feet. "I won't take your sloppy seconds."

"Not funny, dick." Jason kicked his brother's shin. "Why the hell didn't you tell me this weeks ago?"

"It happened right before Ma…I don't know, Jason." Patrick huffed out a breath, bouncing the back of his foot against the lower kitchen cabinet. "Maybe I was more concerned about Mom for a while, all right?"

"I guess." Jason nodded as he heaved out a breath. His brother had been all about caring for his mother in those final days. And so much more had happened. This slip-up made sense.

"This is good." Clayton rubbed his chin. "This means we're on the right track. Unfortunately, this info also means Ariel is very desperate, and desperate women do lethal things." He paced back and forth in the kitchen. "Ariel, also known as Dee Dee Davis, thinks she's so much smarter than the rest of us."

Clayton's phone pinged. He stepped into the dining room to take the call.

"I don't believe anything that comes out of that conniving woman's mouth." Jason took a long sip from his water bottle. "Clayton's right, she is clever. Ariel always tells just enough of a truth to make the story seem real."

"Where's Maude now?" Patrick straightened and cracked the knuckles on both hands. "Is she someplace safe?"

"She's meeting with Rachel. She texted a bit ago to say she was on her way home." An uneasy tingle slithered down Jason's spine. Pieces were aligning, and Jason didn't like the picture they created. Ariel's story about Nicki seemed unlikely now. Not only that, she'd slipped by making a move on Patrick.

Clayton came back in, heaving a heavy sigh before meeting Jason's gaze. "My buddy at the police station says after responding to a 911 call claiming shots fired, they found Rachel's Jeep in a downtown parking garage."

Jason's heartbeat pounded in his ears. "And Maude? Was Maude there?"

"No, they're both gone."

"Gone." Jason couldn't swallow, couldn't breathe. He grabbed for the counter. Maude was gone. Dead.

Patrick raced to his side. "No, not gone-gone. Right, Clayton? You didn't mean dead."

Clayton tapped his phone against his palm. "I won't lie.

Blood was found at the scene, bullet casings, and Rachel's Jeep was banged up and full of bullet holes. The windshield gone, front tire flat."

Jason breathed air in through his nose and out his mouth over and over for a minute, until that choking sensation left his throat. "Okay, okay…let's think about this. What else did he say?"

"Surveillance cameras got a bead on a blond male dragging off a brunette female, but the image doesn't continue on the next level. They did, however, catch a shot of a BMW, Ariel's, leaving the garage seconds later. A blond male was in the passenger seat, but nothing in the backseat, as far as they could see."

"If I learn those fuckers stuffed Maude in the truck, I'll kill 'em."

Patrick braced an arm around Jason's shoulders and looked at Clayton. "How do we find them? You found Maude before, right? At the fire? You can find her again, can't you? Do that thing with the phone? Track 'em."

"Right, sure." Clayton pointed a finger at Patrick. "You got a computer. I'll log into Rachel's account and go in the back way to locate Maude's phone."

"Can you do that?" Patrick asked.

"Of course." Clayton glanced at his cell. "Let me try Rachel. See if she'll pick up. Knowing her, she might've left the scene and followed the bastards."

Patrick went to his room to grab his laptop while Jason remained unmoving, seething, so full of fury he saw only red.

Clayton put the phone on speaker but only got Rachel's voice mail message.

"All along, we knew they were responsible." Jason clenched his hands at his sides and paced in the kitchen. "They kept slipping through, but we've got them now. She'll pay, and Brady…he and I have a date with a bat. Not a pussy ass wiffle ball bat, either."

"Stafford, I get you're pissed, but—"

"Oh, I'm far beyond pissed, Kincaid." Jason spoke between clenched teeth. "So far beyond." Not to mention what Bronco would do if someone had hurt Rachel. *Shit!*

"Jason, I hate to bring this up, but Brady was leading *a* brunette away from the scene. Do you get what that means? One lady. Until I see the footage, I can't know if Maude or Rachel is in Ariel's car, which means…"

Jason gripped his hair in both fists as his heart sank even deeper in his chest. "One of them is someplace else."

CHAPTER 39

The acrid smell of smoke and ash burned her lungs as Ariel marched back and forth through the remains of the burned-out Rec Center. "Did you know that women in some countries who displease their husbands can have acid thrown on their faces and the men suffer no consequences?"

Ariel had chosen this place because the location seemed poetic. Maude and Jason's relationship began here and would end here. They were in a portion of the Center that still remained standing. Brick and steel beams were visible, but she and her prey were basically closed in. The entire back wall had been saved by firefighters but was scheduled for demolition tomorrow morning. Perfect.

Maude had only just resurfaced from her drug-induced delirium. Brady had knocked her out using a dose of ketamine.

Ariel smiled at Maude then dug a vial out of her bag. "Oh, what do we have here?" She wiggled the vial back-and-forth between her fingers. "Should I just throw it on your face? Or would it be better if I poured it on your head?" The vial only held water, God forbid it actually contained real acid and somehow splintered open and injured her. Still, the fright factor was high. She knew a friend who'd used this scare tactic before. "Think Jason will like you then? With a scarred face?"

Maude struggled in her bindings. "Where is Rachel? Did you shoot her? That parking garage has cameras all over the place. You'll never get away with this."

Brady nudged Maude's shoulder. "Be quiet."

"Listen to her whine and moan, Brady." Ariel smiled at the man standing behind Maude.

"Jason will never believe you." Maude shook her head and wet her lips. Her left eye twitched, likely an after-effect of the ketamine. "Give up now, Ariel. He knows you're lying about the pregnancy. That you've lied about everything."

"Of course." Ariel tapped Maude's nose with a finger. "Making a false positive on a pregnancy test is easy, and I plan on pulling off a believable miscarriage, too. I know all the tricks." She smiled as she imagined telling her friends how she'd won Jason. They'd be in awe of her daring. Bow down in fear, even. She'd show them all she was a force to be reckoned with. "Now." Ariel popped the vial's cork, right before Maude's eyes. "Are you ready to give up Jason? Or do I have to remove you myself?"

"He'll never be with you. No one is stupid enough to believe you are innocent. Go ahead, and do your worst."

Ariel laughed. "Well, well, Brady, this one has a lot of spunk. No wonder you're so obsessed." How dare this bit of nothing challenge her? Her plan would work. Hadn't she gotten this far? Nothing would stop her now, and maybe...maybe maiming wasn't enough. Maybe she should actually kill the girl. Then no one would ever deny her again. Her .45 warmed in her hand, glowing, calling on her to use it. Just pull the trigger, and together they'd feel the power. "Maybe I'll just kill you."

An overwhelming sense of supremacy rushed through her. Why shouldn't she? From now on, she'd destroy everyone who got in her way. Her breathing quickened and her entire body flushed. The power of life and death simmered under her skin, calling on her to prove her authority.

After she put a bullet in Maude's head, she'd shove Brady to the ground, stick the gun in his hand, and pull the trigger. Murder-suicide. Easy. "I never knew before, but your death was meant to be. I have the power, not you." Ariel lifted the gun and aimed at Maude's forehead.

Maude breathed out slowly. "You may have a gun, Ariel, but you have no power over Jason's heart. Even if you kill me, you'll be the one left out in the cold. Remember my words when you're locked away in a dark, lonely cell."

"Do not speak to me." Ariel threw the vial of water in Maude's face. "See what you get, you stupid bitch? Maybe that will shut you up."

Maude screamed and then sputtered. Eyes wide with fear, she shook her head.

Do it now. An inner voice crooned. *Pull the trigger. End her. She's weak. Don't let her beat you.* Ariel laughed. "I am in control. In taking your life, everyone will glory in mine." Hadn't she sacrificed? Changed everything about herself, and to let this mousy bitch stop her? No. She was Ariel Silvers.

"Ariel, just finish this," Brady growled. "Then finish me, too. I'm not spending the rest of my life on the run."

Her gaze shot to his. "Oh, how sweet. A murder-suicide. They'll write love songs in your name." Laughing, she flicked the gun in his direction. "I'm not running either, so I appreciate your willingness to take the fall."

# # #

Jason thought fighting through a roaring fire was bad, but walking through the Rec Center's ash burned his eyes and his throat. None of that discomfort mattered, though. His woman was trapped here. Raw fury had him shaking with rage. And now that he saw Rachel's nose, which was swollen and a mass of dried blood, he worried he might bust a blood vessel.

Patrick stood beside him. His brother had done that a lot

lately, and he could only be grateful. Except when the son of a bitch waited until Clayton had detected Maude's phone at the Rec Center before tricking him into the basement and locking the door. Wide-eyed, Jason had simply followed his brother out to his SUV and went along with his plan to extract revenge and obtain Maude without any police interference. Sounded like a good idea at the time, but now that he considered the real danger Maude faced, and the fact neither he nor Patrick had a weapon, he wasn't as keen on their rescue plan.

Luckily, they'd found one of their missing women, but this one was not happy to see them.

"Damn it." Scowling, Rachel hissed, "What are you two doing here?"

Jason merely shook his head before wrapping the tiny woman in his arms. A modicum of relief came from seeing her alive and spitting fire, as usual.

Patrick peeked around the charred brick wall before glancing over his shoulder and answering Rachel's question. "Jason needed to be here. It's payback time."

He could hear Ariel speaking but couldn't make out what she was saying. Then, Jason heard the low murmurs of Maude's voice and had to stop himself from charging past the crumbling wall to save her. Jason peered down at Rachel. "Patrick's lost his mind, but that's okay, because when Clayton gets here he's dead, anyway." He kept his tone low. "Is Maude all right? Did she get injured in the accident?"

"No, she's good. Those fools"—she waved her hand, which held a huge gun, toward the wall—"they just got here. I'm waiting for backup," Rachel whispered, which came across as a low growl, "You and Patrick need to—" she eased back and jabbed a finger at him, but lost her balance.

Jason caught her before she landed with a thump and blew their cover. "What's wrong?"

"Bitch shot me in the leg." Rachel lifted her jean-clad right leg. The bottom portion was stiff with dried blood. She'd tied a black bra around her leg to stem the bleeding.

"Flesh wound, but it stings a bit." Rachel closed her eyes and took a deep breath. "Listen, I know you're out for revenge, but Ariel has a gun. You go charging in there, and crazy shit happens. Chaos. Gunfire. So, we'll wait for the cops."

At her words, sirens sounded in the distance.

He edged closer to Patrick and whispered, "Bro, I'm going in. The cops have probably spooked Ariel."

"No, wait." Patrick drew him into a one-armed hug before speaking in a deep rumble by his ear. "I'll go around and come in from the other side. Distract them while you grab Maude."

Jason glanced at Rachel, who was peeping around the wall. He nodded at his brother. "Go."

For such a big guy, his brother moved like a wraith around the outside of the crumbling structure. Hopefully, a way inside existed on the other side of what was left of the building.

Rachel shot him a glare. "Where the hell did Patrick go?"

"He's distracting them."

Her lips pursed. "He's going to get shot. You two are idiots."

"Oh, really? What will Bronco say when he learns you got shot but went hell bent for leather after these two idiots instead of heading to the hospital?"

"He will be a tad disturbed." She winced, lifted her gun, and darted a glance around the bricks again.

Jason heard his brother yell, "Hey, Ariel."

A shot was fired.

A loud bellow echoed.

Rachel took off.

Jason gasped as an icy wave of dread shot down his spine. Dear God, if his stupid brother was shot. Or dead. That thought propelled Jason around the wall.

Another shot fired.

Jason sprinted around the wall in time to watch Ariel

crumple to her knees.

Rachel kicked her in the face and grabbed her gun.

"Jason!" Maude screamed.

His gaze shot to where she sat in a metal chair. One side of her face bright red. Her hair slightly wet. Her arms bound behind her back.

"Oh, my God, Maude." He rushed to her side. "Maude." After drawing her against him, he brushed her hair from her face. "Were you shot? Are you hurt?" He ran a hand all over her body, checking for injuries.

"S-she threw acid in-in my-my f-face."

"No, your face is fine. It's fine." Her teeth were chattering so loud he could barely understand her. He gripped her tighter. "Never again are we doing this. Never. My heart can't take it. I love you too much. I can't...I just love you so damn much." He buried his face in her soft curls. She smelled of smoke. They'd both need a deep cleansing, from this place, and from their terror.

Clayton arrived, like a superhero bounding out of the shadows and chased a retreating Brady across the space. He lunged and tackled the idiot. They fell right beside his brother.

His motionless brother.

Jason gasped. "Oh, shit...Patrick."

A flurry of police officers barreled into the room, weapons raised, shouting for everyone to lift their hands.

Crouched beside Patrick, Clayton ordered an ambulance.

"My brother." Arms raised, Jason glanced at the mound still lying on the floor. His gut clenched. His big brother better not be dead. Not now. Not after losing his mom. Not when he needed to be strong for Maude. He leaned back and met her gaze. "I need to check on Patrick."

"Patrick is here? Is he hurt? Oh, no." She peeked around his arm. "W-where is Ariel? Did they get her gun...and the acid? She has acid."

"Shh-shh-shh...it's okay. Don't worry about her." Jason

smoothed a hand over Maude's hair. Her entire body shook, likely coming down from her adrenaline high. *Why did she think Ariel had acid?*

A gray-haired cop, likely in his late-fifties, meandered over to their side. "What happened here?"

Maude gasped and stared at the cop. "He didn't do anything."

"I'll answer your questions, but can you free her arms first?" Jason eased away from Maude, patting her face. "Honey, I have to let you go for a minute so he cut those bindings."

Her eyes widened as the officer pulled a knife off his belt. "Jason…"

"Maude, look at me." He gently lifted her chin. "I need to check on my brother."

She nodded and softly whispered, "Okay."

Jason glanced at the cop.

The man nodded. "Go ahead."

Releasing a heavy breath, Jason turned and started toward his brother.

Had Ariel killed Patrick? He heard her spitting more lies. Caught red-handed, she still thought she'd charm her way free. Two cops stood on each side of her, speaking with Rachel. Ariel's mass of blonde hair covered one side of her face. Jason felt no sympathy as tears streaked a line through the gray soot on her cheek. Gray was certainly all she'd see for the next ten to twenty. Gray bars. Gray walls.

Suddenly, his brother snorted, almost like laughter.

"What's so damn funny?" Heart pounding, Jason stomped to his side.

His brother opened his eyes. "I just asked Clayton if the reporters were coming."

"And why is that funny?" He glared at Clayton and then Patrick. Grateful his brother was alive, but he was pissed the asshole was laughing when he'd been on the verge of falling off an emotional ledge.

"Chicks dig heroes."

"I told you not to get shot. Damn it, Patrick. I thought I'd come over here and find your ass dead, but instead, you're over here joking with Clayton." He glanced at Clayton. "And why aren't you kicking his ass for locking you in the basement?"

"I'll wait." Clayton straightened. "I'm sure he's in enough pain…for now."

Jason crouched down and patted his brother's shoulder. "Where'd she get you?"

Patrick pointed to his side where a mass of blood had turned his shirt black. "Flesh wound. Stings like a bitch, though."

"Oh, Patrick." Maude ran over and dropped to her knees, awkwardly wrapped her arms around his neck, and promptly burst into tears.

Jason almost did the same. Almost.

"Just think, little brother, you can brag about injuries on the football field, but taking a bullet to save a pretty lady will trump that forever."

Jason shook his head. "I love you, you big stupid bastard."

Patrick smiled and patted Maude's head. "Hey, Clayton. I'm pretty good at this undercover stuff. You looking for another partner?"

Clayton met Jason's gaze, and they both groaned.

CHAPTER 40

After hours at the police station, Maude remained in a fog as Owen drove her and Jason home. As her mom and Ember cried on her shoulder. As they received Bronco's reports on Patrick's and Rachel's conditions.

Brady and Ariel were responsible for everything. Ariel, she understood. Brady...that truth would take a while to digest. He'd committed horrible acts against her, and for what? The more she dissected their actions, the thicker the haze became until she just couldn't...just couldn't. In the middle of the family discussion of everything that had happened, Maude stood and headed for her room, searching for the quiet and the dark.

How was she supposed to feel now? Hateful? Angry? Shocked? Could a single person feel every emotion all at once? Was that why her head hurt so much? No one had followed her to her bedroom, so she slipped out of her smoky, dirty clothes, turned on the shower, and sat on the floor of the tub, wrapping both arms around her legs. No tears. Nothing but a small sigh as the hot water poured over her body and cleansed her in more ways than one. She had survived, would survive, and would use this story to help others just as she'd used her experience with cancer. Sure, she'd likely need to speak to a therapist, or maybe Ember, who'd gone through a similar trauma, but not for a while…not yet.

"Don't stay still, Maude. Move on. Get out of this shower. Get some rest and tomorrow"—she breathed deep to block the tears—"tomorrow, we'll start stronger."

She suited words to actions, exiting the bathroom and slipping beneath her bed's cool sheets. Not waking until light poured through the sides of her curtained windows.

Stretching her arms above her head, Maude tried wetting her dry mouth. She headed into the bathroom and shrieked at seeing a note written in what looked like eyeliner on her mirror.

Come out to garage.

After her morning ablutions, she grabbed her phone and texted Jason, sure he had left the cryptic note.

I'm up now. Still want me in the garage?

He immediately texted back.

Yes.

She smiled.

Her phone pinged again.

If you're up to it.

Was she? Yes, she was up for it. It being Jason. It being his arms around her, and whatever else she could take. Hadn't Jason always lived like he was dying? Well, yesterday, she had almost died, so that would be her mantra, too.

Once downstairs, Maude couldn't escape the kitchen until she once again assured her mother, Ember, and Owen that she would be fine. Her mother still held her tight, and her brother even hugged her for a long time. His show of emotion brought a few tears to her eyes. Already on the brink, she had to step back and pass off her sniffling relatives to Ember with the request she take care of them. Standing in front of the mudroom door, she gave herself a mental pep talk and stepped outside.

A perfect spring day greeted her. Sunshine. Birds chirping. A chipmunk scrabbling to hide under Owen's deck. Life was precious. Fleeting, so she'd revel and glory in the fact she would live another day. She'd bury those thoughts of crashes, and bats, and guns…and acid, and just be. Just be.

Opening the garage's side door, she glanced around. And there he was. Her first love. Her only love. Her crush.

She raced to him and jumped into his arms, laying a big kiss on his lips.

"Whoa, hey…" Jason chuckled. "You okay?"

In response, she just kissed him again, sucking his tongue into her mouth, rocking against him with her lower body. "You're here. I'm here. So, yes, I'm okay." She smiled then kissed his shocked face once more before shimmying down his body and landing on her feet.

He smiled back but scratched his chin. "Woman, you never cease to surprise me."

"I'm kind of surprised by me today, too." Maude winked.

Rocking back on his heels, he stuffed his hands in his pockets. "I've never taken you out on a date, have I?"

"No." She shrugged.

He brushed her hair off her shoulder. "Well then, I'm about to remedy that oversight."

Maude merely arched a brow and followed as he led her farther into the garage.

"Oh." Maude placed her hand in front her mouth. "You made breakfast. Is it cold? Did I sleep too late?"

"No." He pressed against the small of her back, leading her into a metal folding chair. "I just finished everything about an hour ago. Food's been in the oven's warmer until we heard you moving around upstairs." He poured her a cup of tea. Then he lifted the lid off her plate. Underneath was a steaming omelet and a side of fruit.

"Oh, this all looks nice, Jason." She'd attempt to eat for him, even if her mind was digging the "it's all good vibe," her stomach hadn't quite caught up. "You know, Jason, everyone keeps asking me if I'm okay, but how about you? Yesterday was traumatic for you, too."

Jason shook his head as he took his seat across from her and lifted the lid on his food. "I wasn't the one terrorized." With his fork, he moved a strawberry around on his plate. "You're sitting beside me and my brother's heading home today, so I'm better than I could have been."

"Yeah, definitely better than we could have been," Maude agreed, because who wanted to die when they'd finally found love? No one. Ever.

"How are you feeling today?" Jason cleared his throat and then sipped his water. "Do you want to talk about what happened?"

Maude bit into a red grape and chewed to stall for a moment. "I'm not saying I want to forget what happened or never discuss it again, but today, can we just move past it all and focus on what's next? I'll talk to Ember soon, since she understands. And you, Jason." She met his gaze and smiled. "But honestly, I just feel happy to be alive. I'm sure I'll have issues, but right now, you made me breakfast, and I want to focus on just being in the now."

He blinked. "Sure. My emotions are too raw now, anyway. I'm still so angry." He clenched his fork in his hand, knuckles turning white. "I'm so sorry, Maude, for everything. I should've waited to get involved with you until everything had been cleared with Ariel. I didn't realize her mind was so bent."

"Her and Brady, both."

"Fucking Brady-bunch. He squealed and ran like a bitch once he knew he was caught."

"Okay, okay." Maude raised a hand, palm out. "Let's just enjoy our meals. Please?"

"Fine, but he pisses me off, so don't say his name if you want me calm."

"I promise." She bit back a smile as she crossed her fingers over her heart.

Jason finally quit playing with his food and dug in. "Training camp started last week. I've missed more practice than I should, so I need to get back at it."

Maude bit into her omelet, yummy cheese and mushrooms meshed perfectly. "Is that all you need to get back to?" Because why not ask his intentions? Had they changed? She'd stared down the barrel of a gun yesterday, so today she could certainly ask the hard questions.

"Not necessarily." Jason sat back in his chair and wiped his mouth with the cloth napkins he'd set under their forks. "However, know this, I'll prove my sincerity, my loyalty by my actions. I can say I love you, but I also have to show you. If I lie, if I cheat then I'm less of a man, and I won't be that to you." He met her gaze. "I will *not* promise that, on occasion, I won't party or hit the town with my friends. But I can promise I'll have you with me either literally or figuratively. We're young, hell, you're only twenty-two, and you need to have more fun."

"I think your fun levels are a little higher than mine." She lifted her hands up and down as if balancing the differences.

"So we'll meet in the middle."

"In the middle." A wide smile split her face. Her heart thumped like a happy basset hound's tail in her chest. Jason Stafford, her crush, her long-time love, was making her promises. He loved her. Suddenly, all the recent traumas didn't seem so bad, because she'd won in the end. She'd found love. The still-kissing-and-holding-hands-when-we're-fifty kind. The-we'll-have-kids-and-grandkids kind. The right kind. The forever kind.

In order to keep from crying tears of happiness, Maude glanced across the table, and let herself get lost in Jason's blue eyes. "Basically what you're saying is that we'll have lots of fun together, and you'll consider any issues in our relationship in football terms?"

"Football terms?" His brow furrowed.

"We'll meet in the middle. That's what you said, right?" She tilted her head, loving teasing him. "Like on the offensive line, is that what you mean? Or is it the defensive one?"

He reached across the table and took her hand. "Any line you want, Maude."

"What if an imaginary line existed in this garage?" She waggled her brows. "What then?"

Jason paused, his lips forming a slight moue before he folded his hands across his stomach. "You propositioning me, Maudy?"

"How quickly can you drive me home?"

He gave a slow shake of his head. "Oh, now, honey, the only place you're going is against the side of that wall."

She clasped her thighs together and released a panted breath. "I don't know, that work bench looks pretty sturdy."

With a growl, he shot out of his seat and yanked her to her feet, locking his lips to hers, delving deep with his tongue. "I'm anything but sturdy, Maude. I need you so much. Need to feel you all around me."

Beckoning with her finger, she walked backwards until her back hit the side of the garage.

He followed, shucking his shirt and unbuttoning his pants. Wrapping his hand around the back of her neck, he bent and kissed her. Soft sighs. Deep moans. The smell of citrus and brown sugar soaked through her senses, making her drunk. Blissed. Lost to his heated kisses, she gasped as she heard the pounding of her heart. Literally.

Thump. Thump.

"What the fuck?" Jason rasped against her neck. "They have to know better than to come out here."

A throat was cleared. Loudly.

Jason kissed her nose and sighed, dropping his forehead to her neck. "Owen, you said you didn't want to see this shit, so I suggest you leave." He shifted and buttoned up his pants. "Your brother, the cock-blocker."

Maude giggled and kissed his temple.

"Believe me, I wouldn't have interrupted, but..."

Maude glanced around Jason. Her brother stood beside Erik Pavel, who had his arm wrapped around a strikingly beautiful brunette. Wasn't Erik supposed to be in witness protection? After the events involving her brother last fall, Rachel had sworn them all to secrecy. So, why was the man standing in Owen's garage? And why was her brother just waving and heading back outside?

"I'm so sorry to interrupt." A sideways grin appeared on the woman's face. "Very sorry, Maude." She laughed. "I'm Nicki. An old friend of Ariel's."

Maude stiffened, unable to prevent the reaction to the horrible woman's name, and that irritated her. "Yes?" Why would she want to speak to any friend of Ariel's?

Jason squeezed her. "It's okay."

Nicki moved closer, her hands locked together at her waist. "I heard what happened on the morning news. I'm so sorry. I should have watched her closer." She sighed and brushed her long, straight hair away from her neck. "Of all people, *I* knew what Ariel was capable of."

Stepping to her side, Pavel patted her shoulder. "Nicki wanted to come by and apologize. But, as I can see, you two are busy appreciating life, so we'll excuse ourselves."

Maude stepped over the intervening space and took Nicki's hand. "Please, don't blame yourself."

Nicki just smiled and shook her head.

Searching for a way to take the burden from the woman's green eyes, Maude expressed a hope she'd considered. "Maybe Ariel will get help in prison. Perhaps she needs medication."

Nicki laughed. "Oh, she'll get help all right, but none of it will be good. Believe me, I know."

Nothing the woman's dry and brittle laugh, Maude frowned. *What did that mean?*

Jason placed an arm around Maude's waist. "I'll explain later."

"Please, know this." Nicki squeezed her hand. "Ariel will

never hurt you again. I give my word. I created her, loved her, and I let my heart cloud the truth, but I won't make the same mistake twice." Her gaze was direct and intense as she nodded then clasped Pavel's hand and left.

"I created her? Loved her? What does that mean?" After a whole-body shiver, Maude stared at Jason. "She's like one of those mysterious women who arrives at a high-end gala and dances with a man before she poisons his vodka."

"If she's spending her time with Pavel, then yeah, I'd say she knows a thing or two about poisons and knives and a lot of other lethal shit."

"I think you know a thing or two about poisons."

"How do you figure?" Arching a brow, Jason braced an arm around Maude's shoulder and led her outside toward his SUV.

"I figure you poisoned me with something a long time ago and caused my fevered crush. It's a very serious disease."

"Is that right?" He spun her against the passenger door and dropped his hands on her shoulders.

"Yes, I had shortness of breath, crying fits, stomachaches. Crushes are very poisonous."

"Is that what I really am, Maudy? Poison?"

He seemed so sincere in his question, as if still worried she blamed him for everything that had happened. "Yep, pure poison, and I'm dead to anyone but you."

"Don't like hearing the dead part," he growled, his brows wrinkling into a frown.

"Then, as you say, we'll live together somewhere in the middle and do what we can to avoid all the crushes and poisons and little irritants that get in our way."

"Nothing little here." He bumped his hips against her and kissed her.

Crushed against the vehicle, Maude inwardly laughed at his ability to make any comment an innuendo, but she wouldn't take him any other way.

And, as he held her under the bright sun of a perfect spring day, she decided that sometimes…just sometimes, being the victim of a crush wasn't so bad, after all.

EPILOGUE

Jason patted Owen's butt. "Okay, Big-O, what's the play?"

Owen crouched beside their teammates, a rugged group of bandits all dressed in various shades of black.

The other team huddled across the field wearing yellows and greens.

"Um, Mr. Football Guy, do you think I can get a drink now?"

Jason smiled at the mini-baller. His tiny face had more black paint on his cheeks than under his eyes.

"Yeah, buddy, after this play, we'll call a time-out, okay?"

Jason glanced at Owen, who simply smirked.

A light fall breeze gently shook the tree's brightly colored leaves. The sharp scent of freshly-cut grass filled the air. The cool afternoon was the perfect temperature for a charity football game. The Marauders had come together as a team and raised funds to rebuild the Rec Center, which included, a track, baseball field, and, of course, a football field.

Surprisingly, his brother had asked if he could be in charge of the project. Patrick had done a fantastic job from start to finish, and he more than earned the title of Director of Recreation.

Jason couldn't be more proud, except when his brother was playing on the other team…and his team was down by seven.

Still, they were here for fun, so after the next play, Owen called a time-out. The kids rushed to the bench like they'd been lost in a desert for days. Once they hit the field again, most of them groaned, their bellies being too full of water. A few kids got sick, so the team captains, Patrick and Owen, called an end to the game.

Patrick's team won, and Jason owed the ass fifty bucks, but hey, they were having fun.

On his way over to a shady area where Maude and the ladies had set up a picnic, he heard his phone blowing up with text notifications. Saturday night. Parties. Friends. Old hook-ups. All wondering at his destination for the evening.

Easy. A brunette with big brown eyes. Here, with these kids and a handful of Marauders players was the only action he wanted tonight...until later, with Maude.

He halted to take in the scene, thought for a moment and realized, nope, contentment existed right here. Giving back to the community created the same feeling as when he completed a pancake during a game. Not one he ate, but when he flattened a defensive lineman.

That feeling continued, until he saw Clayton bend a bit too close to his woman, wearing a charming smile.

After grabbing a water bottle out of a cooler, Jason headed over. "What's up, Clayton?" He lifted his closed fist for a fist bump before wrapping Maude in his arms. "We won. Pay up."

"You didn't win, but I'll still pay." Maude smiled then stretched up on her toes and kissed him.

Four months had passed since Ariel and Brady almost destroyed his future. He and Maude had actually come together quite seamlessly. She returned to work. He played the game. They visited a therapist together for a few months, and Maude continued on her own a while longer. But overall, a smooth transition.

They'd been over all the whys, whats, and hows with Clayton

and Rachel. Brady knew Maude's passwords, took her credit card, and engaged in cyber-harassment. He'd met Ariel at Plunder, and they worked toward the same goal—hurting Maude. Brady admitted to breaking into her home and kidnapping her from the gas station. His reasoning being, she'd be scared and run to him for comfort.

Ariel lied about the pregnancy. But, she actually was from a small town in southern Virginia. The trial was coming up the next week, and he and Maude had decided not to attend.

"So, where you been all morning, Kincaid? Working hard or hardly working?" Jason leaned against the picnic table, keeping one eye on Maude in her nicely-fitting jeans. Maybe they could find an empty room in the Rec Center. Nah, too many kids. He'd wait until they were home before bending that fine ass over something. To his utter amazement, he actually wanted her more, not less. Just his morning, that seemingly-innocent woman had taken him on a very intense ride through a blissfully pleasurable storm. Damn woman must've taken seduction classes at some point. All that time, he'd never guessed his sweet little Maudy was a siren in the sack.

"Jason?"

He jerked. "What?"

"Quit leering at Maude's ass for five seconds, will ya? Kids are around."

"Can't help it, man." Jason sniffed. "Working any new cases?"

Clayton shrugged. "I took on something. Don't know if it's a case, though."

"Ah." Jason hid his smile behind his water bottle.

"What's that supposed to mean?" The private investigator crossed both arms over his chest.

"Only one thing can put that look on a man's face."

"Shove it, Stafford."

"What's this?" Maude nudged Clayton's shoulder. "Am I to

understand a woman has sparked your interest?"

Clayton merely grunted. "You have no idea."

Maude caught Jason's eye and winked, a warm smile lighting her face.

They'd been through their journey. Both a little battle-weary but their love remained strong and true. And in the end, when Jason took stock and looked back on his life, he knew he'd always believe Maude was his greatest score.

Thank you for reading *Maude's Score*. I hope you enjoyed Maude and Jason's story. If you did, please leave a review at your purchase site. Reviews are appreciated by the author.

Coming Soon from Jillian Jacobs

Book #4 in The O-Line Series, *Clayton's Star* available Fall/Winter 2016.

Erik's story, I'm thinking...thinking...

Available Now

Contemporary suspense and mystery
Book #1 in The O-Line Series, *Ember's Center*
Book #2 in The O-Line Series, *Rachel's Guard*

Paranormal romance
Book #1 in The Elementals Series, *Water's Threshold.*
Book #2 in The Elementals Series, *Fire's Field.*
Book #3 in The Elementals Series, *Air's Vision*

Please enjoy the following excerpt from *Water's Threshold*, **Book #1 in The Elementals Series.**

Since arriving in Wyoming only a few months ago, Maya had experienced a strange energy pattern that interrupted her sense of peace. A consciousness never felt before, as if something attempted to anchor her in place—a pull unlike anything she had experienced since starting this new life nearly one hundred and fifteen years ago.

This internal strife was because of him—Terran Forrester. Mother had warned this would come. He was part of her purpose in being in this place at this time. Her orders were to guide him, because their destinies were entwined. Having Mother Nature set her up on a "fate date" left her feeling like a contestant on a game show. During her human life, Maya strove to control her own destiny, never handing over power. As an Elemental, she remained determined to give her all to their cause, but it chafed when Mother asked for more—to open her heart. Why now? Why was this burden of love thrust upon her with a mate she had not chosen?

Mate. What a ridiculous word.

Maya blew out a breath, causing a bevy of bubbles to dance their way to the surface. She couldn't have children so Mother using that specific word made the whole idea more ludicrous. Yet, Mother's wishes had come to fruition and that fact rankled. When spying on Terran, Maya experienced emotions surfacing she'd thought buried in a deep well long ago.

Her duties included watching him as he went about his daily human life. She enjoyed observing his frequent visits to the banks of the Snake River where he filled little glass vials. A soft hum raced through her body each time she spied him doing ordinary things, like working up a sweat at the gym or grabbing a cup of coffee at the local café. Since her last sexual adventure occurred in the free-love laced 70's, she was more than overdue for male attention. Terran would, no doubt, approach sex with the same care he did his experiments—meticulously and thoroughly.

That trickle of lust thrummed especially strong tonight at the gas station, when he'd touched her shoulder, all concerned citizen, seeking to offer assistance to an unfamiliar woman. Her waterlogged heart had pumped like a steam engine traveling uphill.

About the Author

In the spring of 2013, Jillian Jacobs changed her career path and became a romance writer. After reading for years, she figured writing a romance would be quick and easy. Nope! With the guidance of the Indiana Romance Writers of America chapter, she's learned there are many "rules" to writing a proper romance. Being re-schooled has been an interesting journey, and she hopes the best trails are yet to be traveled.

Water's Threshold, the first in Jillian's Elementals series, was a finalist in Chicago-North's 2014 Fire and Ice contest in the Women's Fiction category.

Jillian is a: Tea Guzzler, Polish Pottery Hoarder, and lover of all things Moose.

The genres she writes under are: Paranormal and Contemporary romance with suspenseful elements.

Connect with Jillian Jacobs online

Website: www.jillianjacobs.com

Twitter: https://twitter.com/GreenMooseProd

Facebook: https://www.facebook.com/pages/Jillian-Jacobs/737689872920933

Goodreads: https://www.goodreads.com/JillianJacobs

tsu: http://www.tsu.co/JillianJacobsAuthor